THE PLAGIARIST

THE PLAGIARIST

A NOVEL BY

BENJAMIN CHEEVER

ATHENEUM   NEW YORK   1992

Maxwell Macmillan Canada
Toronto

Maxwell Macmillan International
New York   Oxford   Singapore   Sydney

Chee

✓

This is a work of fiction. Names, characters, places, and incidents either are the product of the author's imagination or are used fictiously. Any resemblance to events or persons, living or dead, is entirely coincidental.

Atheneum
Macmillan Publishing Company
866 Third Avenue
New York, NY 10022

Maxwell Macmillan Canada, Inc.
1200 Eglinton Avenue East
Suite 200
Don Mills, Ontario M3C 3N1

Macmillan Publishing Company is part of the Maxwell Communication Group of Companies.

Library of Congress Cataloging-in-Publication Data
Cheever, Benjamin, 1948–
    The plagiarist : a novel / by Benjamin Cheever.
      p. cm.
    ISBN 0-689-12153-9
    I. Title.
    PS3553.H34865P58 1992
    813'.54—dc20   92-11503
                       CIP

10 9 8 7 6 5 4 3 2 1

Printed in the United States of America

To William Maxwell

"Let's start a magazine

to hell with literature
we want something redblooded . . ."
              e.e.cummings, NO THANKS

THE PLAGIARIST

ONE

There is a giant oak in front of World Headquarters with a sign on it. The sign says that the tree was a mature specimen when the First Continental Congress met in 1774. The sign does not say that the tree was in Connecticut until 1939. That was the year they dug it up. The roots were wrapped in damp burlap, the leaves coated with paraffin, so that it would not dry out on the truck. The behemoth survives to this day, although it has to be fed regularly with chemical fertilizer. Most of its larger branches are held up by cables.

"In this part of New York it's hard to tell a World Headquarters from a Bloomingdale's," Mongoose had told Arthur when they talked on the phone. "If you see the tree you're in the right place.

"Get off at exit twenty-nine," he said. "That's the one right after Paradise. The main building is a brick wedding cake with white trim."

"I think I've seen it from the parkway," said Arthur. "Doesn't it look like one of the colleges I decided against?"

"That's right," said Mongoose. "People like to say the grounds look like the world would look if God had had money."

"I thought God did have money."

"Sometimes he has money, sometimes he doesn't. But that's theology, you and I were talking business. Come at noon. The bells will be ringing. I'll wait outside. You might have trouble recognizing me."

"Oh, I should be able to pick you out," said Arthur, who knew the older man only casually. "You'll be the one with the beard."

"That's right, although you know me in mufti. You're looking for someone about my size and shape but more solemn, responsible and in a suit."

There had been a slight drizzle when Arthur stepped out of his house that morning. By the time he reached the offices of *The American Reader* the June sky was as blue as the sky ever gets any more within fifty miles of Manhattan. The change was so dramatic that he could not help wondering if it might not still be raining at home.

A slate path led from the visitors' parking lot to the front door. Arthur found the setting hauntingly familiar. He thought of it as early robber baron. He also thought of it as home. Arthur had grown up in a rented studio on the estate of an American tycoon. The paths there had been slate as well, the rhododendrons enormous, the gardeners and statuary Italian. The mantelpieces in the mansion on the hill had been torn from European palaces to please a prince of finance who had started out as a lathe operator. Like the big oak, many of the landmarks in Arthur's childhood had been gorgeous, traditional and false. Just how false was something he was only beginning to suspect.

2

The man everybody called Mongoose already had a job as an editor at *The American Reader*. It was because of his association with Arthur's parents that he had volunteered to spend his lunch hour giving the tour.

The two met on the broad front stairway. The bells in the building's vast ivory cupola started to chime over their heads as they shook hands, forcing Arthur and his guide to stand awkwardly and wait for the noise to cease before they could talk.

"I recognize that hymn," said Arthur.

" 'Once to every man and nation,' " hummed Mongoose, " 'comes the moment to decide.' "

"That's right," said Arthur. " 'In the strife of Truth with Falsehood/for the good or evil side.' " Then he laughed. "Not exactly subtle," he said, following Mongoose inside.

The main foyer had two brilliant Van Goghs, but Arthur's host drew his attention to a dour man in a blue uniform who was standing beside a large marble foot, which was on a low pedestal and in a Lucite cube. "That's Doc," said Mongoose, his voice dropping to a whisper. "We believe he's the world's richest security guard. He earns more than the director of advertising."

The man in question had a shock of prematurely white hair and a scowl. Since they couldn't possibly have been overheard, Arthur assumed that the look must be a reaction to his own long hair, which contrasted sharply with the brush cut and neatly trimmed beard of his guide. This was the spring of 1974, and police of any sort took haircuts seriously. Arthur had intended respectability. He was wearing a dark suit, his one suit, his weddings-and-funerals suit. He was wearing his best shoes. Unfortunately, his best shoes were a pair of somewhat battered desert boots. Mongoose was also wearing a dark suit, but his shoes matched his suit and it was a much better suit.

Behind the guard there was a painting of a woman with an enormous neck. "That's Modigliani's mistress," said Mongoose. "The marble foot is from an early version of Michelangelo's David."

3

"I didn't know there was an earlier version."

"Yes, there were several, although there's some question whether this is one of them. It's been carbon dated. If it's a fraud, it's a very old one." At this point Mongoose shot his right hand into the breast pocket of his shirt, as if looking for a cigarette. Arthur watched eagerly. When the hand came out it held nothing.

"Fallow has always been attracted to biblical images," Mongoose said, putting an arm around Arthur's shoulder and leading him out of the foyer and up the central hallway. "The Bible is the best-read book in the world, and we are the world's most widely read magazine. Cummings called us the world's best seller. They asked him to write for us. We were much smaller then."

"Exactly how big are you?"

"The circulation department probably inflates its figures, but they say that readership worldwide is more than one hundred million. In this country we go into one out of every four households."

"Extraordinary," said Arthur with forced enthusiasm. He had read in *Psychology Today* that people who were lying, or being lied to, often put their hands in front of their mouths as if to stop the source of falsehood. "What an accomplishment," he said, as his right hand floated involuntarily upward.

"That's the library," said Mongoose, pointing into the big room at the end of the center hallway. "The paneling is walnut."

Arthur nodded and looked in. He saw a long wooden table of conspicuous antiquity. Beyond this there was a cluster of overstuffed armchairs upholstered in pink-and-white-striped silk. Beyond the armchairs there were French doors with lace curtains. One of the chairs held a woman with jet-black hair. She had a volume of the *Encyclopaedia Britannica* spread open on her lap. Her head was back in the pillows. Arthur couldn't be certain, but it looked as if she were sound asleep.

"That's an executive editor," Mongoose said in a whisper.

"She looks like a girl," said Arthur.

Mongoose smiled. "That's where they put the casket when Mrs. Fallow's brother died," he said, gesturing to the long table. "We all had to come by and take a look."

At this point a middle-aged woman wearing a silver lorgnette appeared from behind a stack of books and asked if she could be of assistance.

"No," said Mongoose, waving and smiling to indicate that words weren't necessary. He ducked back out of the library and led Arthur down the hallway to the right. This brought them into a room lined with glass display cases. The exhibit on one wall had a copy of every one of the twenty-seven foreign editions of *The American Reader*. Another display held a pair of old glasses, one leather glove and some war medals.

"The story is probably apocryphal," said Mongoose, pointing through the glass case, "but I've been told that was Mrs. Fallow's glove, before she was Mrs. Fallow. She's supposed to have dropped it, and young George kept it until they got back together. Carried it under his tunic at Verdun."

"Did it stop bullets?"

"No. Shrapnel is what got him. I don't think he was hit in the glove."

There was an antique globe in the middle of the floor. Right beside this stood a low table with a wooden jigsaw puzzle of the world. Mongoose tapped the table with his index finger. "Every section is from a tree that grows in the country represented," he said. "Most of these pieces of wood are gifts from heads of state."

"You aren't in every country in the world?" Arthur asked.

"No," said Mongoose, and he scratched thoughtfully at his right ear. "There's very little penetration behind the Iron Curtain."

"No," said Arthur, scratching his own ear. "There wouldn't be."

"Domestic trends are also somewhat troubling," said the older man. "As our flock grows larger, it also grows older and poorer. We lose thirty thousand readers a month to failed eyesight. There are still a lot of people who read The Magazine. But I bet that nobody you know reads The Magazine."

Arthur shrugged. "*The American Reader* isn't exactly, I don't know, it isn't, well, it isn't exactly hot," he said lamely.

"That's right," said Mongoose easily. He had stopped to examine the Braille issue of the Korean edition, which was exhibited on a small antique pedestal. "But no one could accuse us of uncertainty. We're definitely on the side of truth. Mr. Fallow believes in the perfectibility of man, and he intends to have his company help in this work. Optimism is an article of faith around here. We're sort of stuck in the Enlightenment. It's unusual for the twentieth century, but if you're going to get lodged some place in history, the Enlightenment is clearly the place to be."

The nerve center for all this right thinking was in the Georgian style and had been modeled after the Governor's Palace in Colonial Williamsburg. The hallways had dark wainscoting, ivory walls and vaulted ceilings. The central building had a courtyard in which white cast-iron benches were arranged around a small fountain.

The two men walked quietly through the halls. It was lunchtime and most of the offices were empty. When they talked, they whispered. "Mrs. Fallow selected the art herself," said Mongoose. "She is supposed to have said that a painting is like a man. The only ones worth having are the ones you can't live without."

Arthur nodded. "I'd heard she bought a lot of the great impressionists."

"Yes," said Mongoose. "Although there's a whole section of the basement full of somewhat less distinguished work."

"Is it good?" asked Arthur.

"It's all right," said Mongoose. "Or most of it's all right. Actually some of it's quite bad," he said and smiled. "There's a lot of Norman Rockwell. There is also a portrait of The Founder on a palomino. Fallow doesn't like horses. They painted him at his desk, and then they painted in the horse.

Mrs. Fallow presented it to the old man for his sixtieth birth-day. He hated it. That's in the basement."

Of the works that were on display, Arthur was particularly taken by an oil of a stretch of shoreline. It looked like something out of the art section of the five-and-dime, only it was a little more plausible.

"Who painted that?" he asked.

"It's not by anybody," said Mongoose. "Or at least it's not by anybody you've ever heard of. It's Monterey, California, done sometime in the 1840s, when Monterey was still the state capital. Mrs. Fallow liked the joy in it."

"So do I," said Arthur. "The sand looks like somebody just poured it out of the sugar bowl."

After the tour, they went to Mongoose's office. This was on the second story.

"It's a corner office," said Mongoose, "but it's not *the* corner office."

The visitor's armchair was crimson. The desk was of gray metal. There were five representations of snakes on the walls—three paintings, an etching and one photograph. The desk had a brass cobra, erect with hood flared. Arthur hoped this might be an ashtray.

Mongoose gestured to the armchair, and Arthur sat.

"Your father knows you're here?" asked Mongoose, settling behind his desk.

Arthur nodded.

"He approves?"

Arthur nodded again, wondering as he did so if a nod could count as a lie.

"I value that friendship," Mongoose continued.

"So does he," said Arthur, crossing the line between a sin of omission and one of commission. Mongoose had once been described by Arthur's father as "living proof that a man can learn a great deal and know almost nothing."

Arthur almost always had this sort of observation in mind when he spoke with one of his father's acquaintances. This put him in the awkward position of having to fight an impulse

to condescend to people who were clearly his elders and betters. Since to repeat any of his father's observations would
have been extremely rude, as well as a violation of confidence,
Arthur never did. He respected Mongoose, liked him. But as
always, his father's barbed words were clearly remembered.
This left him both armed and helpless, like an infant with a
pistol.

"What does he think of The Magazine?" Mongoose
continued.

Arthur shrugged. "It's a magazine, he's a writer."

"He admires it?" asked Mongoose.

"I suppose," said Arthur. "Actually, I don't know." This
at least was almost the truth. Arthur had never heard his father
speak on the subject of *The American Reader*, although he had
once been in his presence when somebody else was attacking
The Magazine as reactionary. "Like shooting at the broad side
of a barn" was all Icarus had had to say afterward.

Arthur sat back in the crimson armchair and looked at his
hands.

Mongoose reached into his breast pocket. Again there was
no cigarette.

The New York Times was folded on the table to Arthur's
right. The front page had a picture of Patty Hearst with a
rifle.

"What about her?" Arthur asked.

Mongoose shrugged. "I think the wig is quite becoming."

"What about the gun?"

"I like that too."

"I know, but was it loaded?"

"I can't tell," said Mongoose. He took a paper clip out of
the center drawer of his desk and began to straighten it. "Are
you interested in a job here?" he asked. "Your wife didn't
sound enthusiastic."

"Oh, you'd be surprised about Faith," said Arthur. "She's
enthusiastic now. She's done a one-eighty."

"Good," said Mongoose. "I enjoyed talking with her at the
Hammersmith party. I'd heard she was a beauty, but I didn't

know she had such a lively mind, such a critical intelligence. Does she work?"

"No."

Mongoose grinned. "Barefoot and pregnant."

"No," said Arthur awkwardly. "I mean she has many more pairs of shoes than I do."

Mongoose opened the center drawer of his desk and put away the ruined paper clip. "You couldn't write," he said.

Arthur nodded.

"You'd write titles and blurbs, but you might go a year without getting a word of your own into The Magazine."

"I don't know whether you'd want to call what I do now writing," said Arthur, putting a hand over his mouth. "Whatever it is, I can't afford it."

"I hope you won't consider this indelicate," said Mongoose, "but if you came here, that particular problem might be solved. Mr. Fallow has a reputation for being whimsical, but he's also extremely generous."

"I gather," said Arthur, "although I still don't understand about Doc. How can a security guard earn more than the director of advertising?"

"It's a special case," said Mongoose. "He was once rude to Fallow."

"But Fallow still owns the place," said Arthur.

Mongoose picked up the brass cobra. "I think it was twenty years ago," he said. "Many people had been leaving their cars right in front of the building, under the oak. So they had 'No Parking' signs installed. One bright morning Fallow himself parked there. Fallow drives a Ford Fairlane, so that was no tip-off.

"Doc had only been on the job a week, and he didn't know what The Founder looked like. So he told him that he couldn't park in front of the building. Mr. Fallow said it was all right, he was just going to leave off some manuscripts. Doc was polite but firm. He said it was not all right. He directed Fallow to the visitors' lot." Mongoose looked up at Arthur. "Have you heard this story?"

"No."

"Two weeks later Doc got his paycheck and it was literally three times what it had been. Naturally, he phoned payroll to see if there had been some mistake. They referred him to the chairman's office. Mr. Fallow came on the line. 'Are you the young man who told me I could not park in front of my own building?' he asked. Doc tried to hedge, but Mr. Fallow cut him off. 'Your increase in salary is an expression of my gratitude,' he said. 'I was in error and you pointed it out.' "

"So why do they call him Doc?" Arthur asked.

"Before he sent Fallow to the visitors' lot, he was going to night school. He wanted to be an oncologist and live in Scarsdale. Now he just lives in Scarsdale."

Arthur nodded. "I have heard the salaries are great," he said. "My father had a friend who went to work here, and afterward built a swimming pool. He had it lined with Carrara marble."

"But it wouldn't be wise to come here for the money alone," said Mongoose. This time it was he who brought a hand to his mouth.

"No, of course not," said Arthur.

"How is your father?" asked Mongoose. "I haven't seen him in months."

"Oh, he's all right, I guess. It's been two years since my mother's accident."

"He's holding up?"

"I really don't know," said Arthur, trying hard to keep the anxiety out of his voice. "I suppose he's doing as well as can be expected."

TWO

Arthur was twenty-four years old on the day he first walked through the big bulletproof doors at World Headquarters, and Arthur was desperate. He had started his career with an economic nose dive. He got married early, she got pregnant early and she didn't work. "I'm downwardly mobile," he used to say, and he laughed when he said it, but it didn't sound hilarious. Every month when it came time to pay the bills he would get a call at the newspaper where he worked. It would be Faith, and she would be in tears.

Arthur was always the soul of reason. That weekend he would go to visit his father.

Icarus Prentice was drinking heavily, but even through a fifth of Gilbey's gin he sensed his son's discomfort. He made the writing of the check a lengthy ceremony. First he had to find his glasses, then a pen that worked. He didn't actually ask Arthur how to spell his name, but he did once want to know if his son still used a middle initial.

After the transaction there was some painful small talk.

"The Hammersmiths had me to dinner last week," Icarus said. "They asked for you."

"I never understood why they liked me."

"You talk with them."

"But I talk with everybody."

"I know that. But the Hammersmiths don't know that."

"So how are they?"

"Oh, they're splendid. He's in a wheelchair now."

"How is she?"

"Her legs are fine, if that's what you mean. She never was much to talk to. She'd seen a shrunken head on somebody's mantle in Ardsley. She thought I should write about it."

"Will you?"

"No, of course not. People are so proud of themselves when they come up with some idiotic suggestion for a story."

"I'm sure she meant to be helpful," said Arthur.

"I'm sure she did," said Icarus. "But she's such a tomato."

"She doesn't look like a tomato to me," said Arthur.

"Well, she was a tomato," said Icarus. "He first saw her in a Broadway chorus line. She's still a tomato. An aging tomato."

"Speaking of a different sort of tomato," said Arthur, "I was just talking with Faith about the ones you gave us last time I came over."

"She liked them?"

"She loved them. They're nothing like what they sell at the Grand Union."

Icarus always showed at least a flicker of interest when his son mentioned Faith. Arthur had been living at home when he first started to date the woman he would marry. The third time he took her out, they stayed out until 1 A.M. When Arthur came home, his father was sitting up in his favorite armchair with a Marlboro in one hand and a glass of gin in the other.

"Did you enjoy yourself?" the older man asked, as his son backed quietly into the house, fastening the front door behind him. "Oh, hi, Daddy," said Arthur. "Yes, I did."

"Good," said Icarus. He got up, went to the sink in the pantry and poured out the rest of his drink. Then he stubbed out his cigarette. "If you're hungry," he said, "there's leftover London broil in the refrigerator." Then he started to climb the stairs to his bedroom, but stopped about halfway up, turned and looked down at Arthur. "Are they real?" he asked.

"Are what real?" asked Arthur.

"Her bra," asked the older man. "Is it padded?"

"Oh come on, Daddy," said Arthur. "I think I love this girl. I'm not even sure if she likes me. I can't talk about her as if she were a lab specimen."

"Touchy, touchy," said Icarus tartly. "No need to spring to the parapets. I asked a simple question."

"Okay," said Arthur. "She's real."

Icarus nodded his head slowly, as if considering a problem of international significance. Then he started back up the stairs. "Remember to turn off the outside lights," he said.

But now, since the marriage, Icarus himself had become pious about Faith, and for some reason this made him pious about everything else as well.

"We're both intelligent men," Icarus said once as they walked toward the fenced rectangle of garden to pick some of the famous vegetables. "But when we spend time together we talk as if we were living in a short story written for *The Ladies' Home Journal*."

Arthur assumed that this new formality also had to do with money. Every dollar got between them. They both thought $100 was a lot of money.

Faith didn't think $100 was much money. She wanted to know what took so long.

"We couldn't find a pen," Arthur would say.

"What about the big one the Literary Guild gave him?"

"It doesn't work. We tried it. It's a cigarette lighter."

If Faith had been a subscriber to *The American Reader*, she would have known that $100 is more than a Masai warrior earns in a lifetime; she would have known that Teddy Roosevelt went West with $23.50 in his pocket; she would have known that John D. Rockefeller gave his grandchildren $100 each Memorial Day and collected $150 back on Labor Day. But Faith was not a subscriber.

She thought Arthur was covering for his father when he took so long to get the money. She assumed that I. S. Prentice was rich. He was a snob, but he wasn't rich. Faith didn't make the distinction. "A hundred dollars isn't any skin off his back," she'd say.

But Arthur thought it probably was. One hundred dollars was certainly a lot of skin for Arthur. He was a reporter at *The High Cliff Bugler*. The *Bugler* was to journalism what McDonald's is to steak houses. He had started out making $6,000. In four years he had worked his way up to $6,800. Public school teachers in the *Bugler*'s catchment area earned $7,100 in their first year. Arthur had made the mistake of confessing his salary to the guidance counselor at a local school he was writing about, and the teacher had been astounded. He actually whistled.

"The Daily Bungler's not much of a paper," the teacher said. "But reporters work hard. Nobody can afford to put in a full week for so little money. It's bad for the economy," he said, wagging his head with incredulity. "You should be ashamed of yourself."

Arthur was deeply ashamed. On weekends he read the want ads with obscene interest. "Executive Training: Come to work now at a large equal opportunity employer. Ensure your future." It turned out that the equal opportunity was being provided by Friendly's, and that "Executive Trainees" had to spend at least one year making ice cream sodas.

The search for a new job did not entirely dispel Arthur's fear that he would lose the one he had. When he first went to work at the *Bugler* in 1970, Arthur was told that he was being brought in to substitute for Louise Petman, who had taken a leave to travel through Spain with her husband. "Louise is a good writer," the managing editor explained. "But there's a lot of deadwood around here. Unless you become part of the deadwood, you've nothing to fear."

Roughly half the city room's occupants were fired during Arthur's first year there. He came early, stayed late and brought his lunch in a bag. When the managing editor and the city editor were getting ready to fire somebody, they always had a long chat about it at the city desk. Arthur was sitting at one of the four desks, which—pushed to face each other in the center of the room—formed the geographic area known as the city desk. Arthur's first assignment was to write obituaries and items for the religion page. He rarely left the office. As long as he maintained his post, he thought it unlikely that a plan to get rid of him would be concocted.

Arthur went to lunch just once in his first year at the paper. This was with a friend of his father's. A big, stooped man with black hair and enormous white eyebrows, Allen Wyndham was on the board of the High Cliff General Hospital, and had been involved in local politics. He was also a novelist, although he was considerably less successful than I. S. Prentice. That fact did not go unremarked upon by Arthur's father, who liked to say that his old army pal was "more of a literary busybody than an actual writer." The friends ate lunch every two weeks, and Arthur's father picked up a great deal of bookish gossip on these occasions. He liked to refer to Wyndham as "The Fortnightly," as in "I learned from the Fortnightly that Edward Albee is having an operation for piles."

Wyndham had promised Arthur a list of "useful sources." They met at a luncheonette Wyndham picked, which was near the paper. The restaurant had a nautical theme. There were portholes attached to the wall. Nets had been hung from the ceiling. The waitresses wore black dresses made out of some mysterious material resembling plastic.

"The cheeseburgers are surprisingly good," said Wyndham,

when they were both seated in a booth. "I wouldn't recommend anything else."

When the waitress came, Arthur ordered a cheeseburger.

"I see you have a liver plate today," Wyndham said to the waitress. "How is it?"

The waitress shrugged. Her dress crackled.

"All right," said Wyndham. "I'll have the liver. Medium."

Then he turned to Arthur. "How is your father?" I haven't seen him since the last meeting of the academy."

"He's all right. I guess."

"He's drinking?"

"That's right. But then I can't remember a time when he wasn't drinking."

"Is he interested in your job?" Wyndham wanted to know.

"I guess. Interested enough."

"I'm sure he is," said Wyndham. "I get such a kick out of my own sons."

The food arrived. Arthur picked up his cheeseburger. Wyndham catalogued the triumphs of Pete and Parker. Pete was a bone surgeon living in Cambridge, Mass. Parker was a lawyer for the ACLU. When Arthur asked the elder man about sources, Wyndham waved his hand dismissively, his face darkening with annoyance. Arthur decided that the best way to get the conversation over and scuttle back to the office before he was fired was to eat quickly, and then sit around looking awkward until Wyndham noticed.

"Pete just had a piece in the *New England Journal of Medicine.* It's on posture. I sent your father a copy."

Arthur sucked a splotch of ketchup off one thumb.

"He's been doing very well, but then he did well from the time he was a small boy," said Wyndham. "He was class secretary in elementary school. He always got along. Now that wasn't the case with you, was it?"

Arthur had eaten half of his cheeseburger. Wyndham hadn't touched his fork. "Not exactly," said Arthur, "I certainly wasn't class secretary or anything."

Wyndham chuckled. "I remember your father was upset

about you. Didn't they call you girl names? Didn't they say you had cooties?"

"I don't believe cooties exist," said Arthur.

"Yes," said Wyndham, "but didn't people say you had them?"

Arthur shifted uneasily in the booth. "I suppose some people once said I had cooties."

Wyndham nodded. He cut a small piece of liver, put it in his mouth, chewed thoughtfully and swallowed. "I think it was especially difficult for your father. He's always been a man's man."

Arthur nodded. He picked up a French fried potato, stabbed it into the ketchup and put it in his mouth. The inside of the potato tasted exactly like damp napkins. Arthur wondered idly if Wyndham's liver plate was spoiled. A person who ate spoiled liver could get very sick. A person who ate spoiled liver could die.

"I recall one particular afternoon," said Wyndham. "You know how a siren sounds coming up the street toward you? What's that called?"

"The Doppler effect," said Arthur.

"That's how you sounded." said Wyndham. "You were walking home from school, and you were crying. Your father and I were on the terrace having a drink. The sobs sounded like the siren of an ambulance. *Waa, waa, waa*, like that. We could tell you were getting closer. Your father was understandably concerned. He asked you what the matter was. You stopped crying and when you got your wind back, you said, 'The other boys don't like me.' Then your father said, 'You take things too seriously, Arthur.' He said you should relax.

"He told you to be yourself. 'I told you that before,' he said, 'just be yourself.' That set you off again. 'Oh, Daddy,' you said, 'I *was* myself. I was myself and it's the worst thing.' "

THREE

Arthur stayed late on the evening of his lunch with Wyndham. He found writing painfully slow, and besides, he was never in a hurry to get home. He and Faith lived well above their means in a former cow pasture in North Tarrytown, New York. The cows were gone and the pasture had been disfigured with houses in three styles. The development was called Upcounty Estates. It was exactly 2.1 miles from Faith's parents' house. Faith's mother had picked out the four-bedroom High Ranch, and Faith's father had paid $67,000 for it. "I can't stand the idea of my baby doll living in a slum," he said.

Faith's father also retained the title. His tax deductions as a home owner were subtracted from the carrying costs of the house, and Arthur was supposed to cover what was left in monthly payments to his mother-in-law. This made some sense, because Arthur could not otherwise have afforded the house. It didn't make a lot of sense, however, because he couldn't afford $425 a month either. Sometimes Faith's parents would forgive a payment, and then there were the checks from Arthur's father. So Faith and Arthur lived from gift to gift, clinging to the underside of a class they had both spent their college years claiming to despise.

The house was furnished almost entirely with pieces that Faith's parents or Arthur's parents had been thinking of throwing away. The furniture from Arthur's parents' house was broken, the furniture from Faith's parents' house was in bad taste. The one exception to this rule was a La-Z-Boy lounge chair that Faith's father had given up. This was broken.

The young couple tried to save money by going to Faith's parents' house for dinner two or even three times a week. Irene Hauser was an excellent cook. She had short black hair that she wore in a flip. Even at forty-five, she was cover-girl pretty. Mother and daughter gloried in each other's looks. They went clothes shopping together and frequently traded dresses and shoes. Faith liked to tell about the time she and her mother had gone to Florida on a vacation and a Mustang convertible full of surfers had mistaken them for sisters.

Irene had grown up well below the Mason-Dixon Line, and like a great many Southern women, she seemed still to carry the scars of the War Between the States. There was nothing fair about that war, and so Irene didn't expect anything else in life to be fair either. The North had had a terrible, undeserved edge in heavy industry. The Union armies outnumbered their Confederate foe two to one. The Yankees were engineers, not soldiers. Grant was not a brilliant general. Grant was just too stupid to give up. The boys in butternut outclassed and outfought the federals at every turn. And it was their unjust defeat that made life so hard in Georgia. It was because of The War Between the States that Irene's father was an Electrolux salesman, that Irene's mother was an alcoholic and that the farm next door, and upwind, raised pigs.

The great lesson of Irene's life seemed to have been taught her by Pickett's Charge. It was a frontal attack that had killed all those gallant boys at Gettysburg. If only Bobby Lee had come around from behind. Irene herself would never make such a mistake.

As a girl she had appeared almost to be content. When she came into the fullness of her beauty, she ditched the Southern boy who had squired her through high school, painted her face and booked a roomette for Pennsylvania Station. In New York City she enrolled in Katharine Gibbs, got a job and within a year she had selected her Yankee. Robert Hauser was the son of German immigrants. He was a handsome man with blond hair and a good jaw. He had flown fighter bombers in the Pacific. His degree was in engineering. Whenever Irene caught sight of him she smiled.

She ran the family on a need-to-know basis. Her husband gave her his paychecks, and she forged his signature on the deposit slip. Monday through Friday she packed him a sandwich and cookies or a piece of pie. He got $15 a week for gas and incidentals. It wasn't that Robert could not have been convinced to go along with most of what his wife did, it was just that Irene seemed to think it more ladylike to lie than to argue. Robert Hauser, for instance, insisted that his only daughter never miss a day of school. He had never missed a day of school. So when Faith was sick, Irene would dress her up and leave her at the bus stop, where the little girl—often flushed with fever—could wave to her father when he drove off to work. Once he'd gone, Irene would bring Faith back home, undress her and put her to bed.

"I know some women who enjoy nothing better than complaining about their men," Irene would tell Arthur. "But I love my Robert, and I don't recall the last time we disagreed about anything."

Her conversation never got beyond the brightest civility.

She talked about the weather and when the weather was unpleasant she didn't talk about that. "You get more flies with honey than you do with vinegar," she liked to say.

"You get the most flies of all with shit," Arthur used to think, but he never said anything of the sort.

Robert Hauser was as straightforward as his wife was devious. He was a paradigm of the self-made conservative middle class. He'd done well at the phone company, but he still tuned his own cars, shoveled and caulked his own driveway.

He bought a Corvair in 1966, shortly after it had been featured in *Unsafe at Any Speed*.

"It's good transportation, at an excellent price," he used to say, "and I suppose I have Mr. Nader to thank."

Faith made Arthur change the preshave lotion he used with his Norelco because her father used the same lotion. She took a major in art history from Ohio University. Robert Hauser felt that art was a fraud perpetuated by "faggots and eggheads" who couldn't otherwise support themselves.

He smiled apologetically when he said "faggots and eggheads," as if to indicate that he had been to college and he knew better.

He loved to tell the story about the time the phone company bought a Picasso and hung it upside down in the main lobby of corporate headquarters. "Even the curator didn't notice for a month," he would say, laughing mirthlessly. "I liked it better upside down."

Before he drove the family anywhere, he would wash the windows of his wife's enormous Oldsmobile with Windex and paper towels.

"He doesn't want to mistake a mote of dust for an oncoming vehicle," Faith would tell Arthur when the two were going to dinner with her parents and waiting for the process to be complete. "He thinks that mortality is something you can plan around," she said.

Robert Hauser was stern with his long-haired son-in-law, but kind to him as well. He never made the sort of searing and witty observation for which Arthur's own father was famous. But what Arthur liked most about his father-in-law was the way he treated Irene. Robert Hauser was chivalry in the extreme. He seemed actually not to see the flaws in his beloved. This had never been true of Arthur's own father. Icarus could spot the stains on an alter cloth at fifty feet. And he was not closed-mouthed about his observations.

Because both Faith and Arthur were only children, both sets of parents wanted them for dinner. Before the marriage, Arthur's parents won the competition. After the marriage they lost.

Faith and Icarus had flirted shamelessly during the courtship. After the marriage Faith stopped flirting. It took about a week before Icarus began to consider her one of the family. Then he started to snipe. His new daughter-in-law was surprised. Then she was indignant. She began to associate her predicament with that of her mother-in-law, not because they were similar personalities, but because they took hits from the same literary battlewagon.

Before her first shelling, Faith told Arthur that Icarus was a lot like Winston Churchill. After the marriage Faith told Arthur that Icarus was a lot like Count Dracula.

Arthur shrugged. "Winston certainly drew blood on occasion," he said.

"But I'm not Adolf Hitler," said Faith. Arthur saw less and less of Icarus and his mother.

The food at Faith's parents' house was simple but quite good. Except on holidays, the family ate at the kitchen table. Irene would chatter aimlessly about cooking, cleaning and the wonders of spring. Robert liked to talk about the problems of minorities, only he didn't call them minorities.

Dinner at Arthur's parents' house was formal by comparison. Icarus had once picked a fight with Arthur's mother because she brought the milk to the table in its cardboard container and not in the porcelain pitcher kept for that purpose. The conversation at Arthur's parents' house had always been diverting. The conversation at Faith's parents' house was not. But then Arthur's own manic family had given him a keen appreciation of the value of tranquility. It was pleasant to be around people who couldn't tell a story to save their lives.

The gulf between Arthur and his parents widened after Nathan's birth. Faith's parents were devoted to Nathan. Robert Hauser would get down on his knees and bark like a dog in order to amuse his grandson. Arthur's father could be quite enthusiastic about the idea of grandchildren, but he was easily annoyed by the actual child. He often acted as if Nathan were an unruly pet, and was completely nonplused by the banalities of modern child rearing.

"Why is my grandson wearing a bustle?" he once asked, when he noticed the shape of Nathan's Pampers under a tight pair of pajamas.

So when Arthur's mother died in a car crash, shortly after her grandson's first birthday, it didn't seem unnatural for Arthur and his young bride to stay away from the grieving widower. Besides, I. S. Prentice didn't act the way a grieving widower was supposed to act. Arthur never saw him cry. He alternately boasted about his sexual conquests and griped about being alone. He also continued to complain about Arthur's mother, as if she were still somehow responsible for the little indignities of daily living.

This did not endear him to his new daughter-in-law. Left to his own devices, he lived almost entirely on soft-boiled eggs and Stouffer's frozen dinners. When the crystal was dirty, he drank his gin from a teacup.

Arthur was uncomfortable about his father's isolation and would campaign with Faith to get her to invite Icarus to dinner. But when he won a round, the elder Prentice would arrive late and often drunk. Solitude had not made Icarus any less irascible. Quite the contrary. Faith had a litany of complaints. "He didn't eat. He didn't play with his grandson. He asked again if I dyed my hair."

"But you do dye your hair."

"Why do you defend him?"

"Because he's my father."

"I wouldn't defend my father if he acted like that. I certainly wouldn't have him to dinner in my house."

"But he helped buy this house. Remember, he lent us almost eight thousand dollars for the down payment."

"That was your mother's money. That money came out of her trust. Besides, my father bought the house. And my father likes this house. You know what your father said about it?"

"No."

"I didn't want to tell you this, because I didn't want to hurt your feelings."

"What did he say?"

"Well, when we closed, he had to speak with my mother. You know, to find out who to write the check to. And he told her he'd just invested eight thousand dollars in a house he wouldn't spend the night in."

Arthur shrugged. "It isn't his sort of house."

"That's right. And we're not his sort of people."

The residence in question came with a full acre of lawn. Arthur spent Saturday of every weekend cutting this with the blood-red nineteen-inch Toro that Faith had given him for his birthday.

Icarus showed up once quite unexpectedly after Arthur and Faith settled in the development. He brought two trees he had dug out of the woods around his house. One was a cedar, the other an oak. This was in July. Arthur's father was wearing a pair of the wheat jeans that Arthur had worn at Choate, and a black Fruit of the Loom undershirt with a pocket. His thick brown hair was cut short. He still had a full head of it, without a trace of gray. I. S. Prentice looked boyish. He always looked boyish. But he looked like a very sick boy. His face was swollen. He smelled sweetly of gin and trembled whenever he lit a cigarette.

"I know it's none of my business," said Arthur. "But you should quit smoking."

"You're right," said Icarus. "It is none of your business. Besides, I don't want to live forever."

"I'm not talking about forever," said Arthur, pausing and leaning on the shovel.

"What exactly are you talking about then?"

"The day after tomorrow."

"And aren't we the optimist?"

Arthur wiped the sweat off of his chin with the back of his hand. He reached down and picked up his father's package of Marlboros, knocked one out and lighted it.

"I thought smoking was bad for you?" said Icarus.

"Not if you're smoking other people's cigarettes," Arthur said, smiling and fiddling with his father's butane lighter.

Icarus was sitting Indian fashion beside the half-completed hole. He took the throwaway lighter from Arthur, ignited his son's cigarette and then lit one for himself.

They planted the cedar at one corner of the house, and the oak was set out in the middle of a side lawn. The cedar prospered, but the oak had lost its taproot.

Oaks keep their leaves for a long time. Even a dead oak will keep its leaves for a year. This tree kept its leaves. It didn't grow any new leaves, but it kept the old ones. So Arthur was always careful to mow around the small tree in the middle of the side lawn. He was afraid that if he acknowledged the death of the oak, his father would die. He was afraid that if he pulled up the dead tree, he would kill his father. But he didn't like to see it, either, sitting out there with a few papery leaves. It seemed an apt symbol for his domestic life.

Things weren't quite so bad at work, although Arthur's career was not a triumph either. The *Bugler*'s reporters and editors were kept in a basement of the newspaper building. The advertising salesmen were on the top. The salesmen earned as much as reporters if they didn't sell any advertising. If they did sell advertising, they got commissions and earned more.

Arthur was still young by *Bugler* standards, so his employers were indulgent when not actually enthusiastic. He handed in the notes he wrote for the religion page a day early, and always got at least one back with "See me" scrawled across the top in the writing of Hugh Melvin, the city editor.

The obituaries went right into the paper. The one time Arthur very nearly was fired, it was over an obituary. The call from the Mountain Laurel Funeral Home had come in twenty minutes before that section closed.

The deceased was a forty-nine-year-old Orangeburg policeman. There was no cause of death, but then local funeral homes often neglected to give the cause of death. It was widely known, for instance, that people who died at Memorial Sloan-Kettering Hospital in New York City died of cancer, but the word *cancer* never appeared in an obituary.

This particular Orangeburg policeman spent his off-hours driving a limousine for a local builder who had recently been indicted. What made matters awkward was that the policeman had shot himself. What made them worse was that he lived next door to a woman who free-lanced for the local radio station.

WQSL had a big scoop, with quotes from the district attorney and with the lawyer for the builder noisily refusing to comment. It would have been bad enough for the newspaper to have missed the story entirely, but to have the obituary instead was considered an egregious error.

Melvin had Arthur out for coffee and "a talk."

"I asked if he died on duty," Arthur said. "They said he died in his home. I asked, 'In his bed?' They said, 'In his garage.' I asked, 'Heart attack?' They said, 'That's confidential.' "

"People always lie about suicide," the city editor explained at the end of their session. "Remember that. The family lies. The police lie. Even the medical examiner will lie if he has to. I'd guess we miss about half the suicides, and those are the obvious ones. A lot of people kill themselves in their cars. They go out and drive into a wall. We have no way of knowing what they were thinking."

"My mother drove into a concrete abutment," said Arthur.

"That's right," said Melvin without inflection. "I remember the story."

There was an awkward silence. Melvin mopped the corner of his mouth with a paper napkin. He looked for an instant as if he were going to elaborate, but finally he just sighed and pulled his chair out from the table.

"Keep your eyes opened," he said, as they walked out of the restaurant. "And don't be so damned trusting."

Arthur was deeply remorseful, and stayed in the office until 8 P.M. for three weeks after the incident.

Faith thought he took the whole episode far too seriously. "So what if they had fired you?" she asked. "You'd get a different job and make more money."

She hated his staying late, but then she wasn't particularly demonstrative when he did come home. Ever since they had settled in the suburbs, Faith had been acting like one of those women who think that financial liquidity and sexual potency are different names for the same male characteristic. Since Arthur lacked the former, she didn't see why she should have to bother with the latter.

When he worked nights—and the newspaper often required that he work nights—he'd undress in the kitchen and carry his clothing over his head as he ascended the stairs, so as not to wake his sleeping beauty.

On weekends he'd catch her staring off wistfully into the distance.

"What are you thinking about?" he would ask.

"I'm thinking we need a sofa for the living room," she would say.

"But we never go in there," said Arthur. "We can't afford to heat this house, much less furnish it."

Then Faith would look sad, and this would break his heart. "Why are you always so uptight about money?" she'd ask him in a little girl's voice.

"I'm not uptight about money," he'd say, with a catch. "I just don't have any."

Faith was a substantial woman, five feet seven inches to Arthur's five feet eight. And dramatically well built. She had been captain of the cheering squad at Sleepy Hollow High School. She had shoulder-length blonde hair, blue eyes, small feet and a generous front. She played the viola. Sometimes Arthur wanted a sofa more than anything.

He had been away at boarding school during most of their courtship and had written at least one and sometimes two love letters a day. His devotion was so pronounced that the editors of the Choate yearbook put Faith in the biographical sketch that accompanied his senior picture. "It's not yet certain whether Arthur has Faith," they wrote, "but he wants her more than Aquinas ever did."

FOUR

Most everything of importance that takes place in Westchester County starts at a cocktail party. It was over mulled cider at the Scarborough mansion of banker Frank A. Vanderlip, Jr., that President Woodrow Wilson was first persuaded to give serious thought to a federal income tax. It was over white wine in a kitchen in Croton, New York, that Theodore H. Gass told his superior at IBM, Arthur C. Corning, that he had partially completed the design of a personal computer which he felt could be priced for the general public.

So it was with a mug of beer in one hand and pretzels in the other that Arthur first heard that they were hiring at the world's most widely circulated magazine. This was at the

Hammersmiths' annual May Day cocktail party, held about a month before Arthur's first visit to Paradise. Mongoose told him about the possible opening. Mongoose's given name was Winthrop Quest. He and Arthur's mother had become friends when both performed in an amateur production of *A Doll's House*. Winthrop was a good-looking man, but Arthur's mother said that it was his willingness to grow a beard that made him so important a member of the Indian Dance Players. "He saves the company a fortune in spirit gum and false whiskers," she said. Facial hair was rare in grown-ups in New York State in the 1960s and early 1970s. In young men beards were a commonplace, but in older men they indicated a grotesquely disfigured chin or a pronounced tendency to bohemianism.

Winthrop was a snake charmer. He wasn't a professional snake charmer, he worked full-time as an editor at *The American Reader*, but his great love was for rare and poisonous snakes. When Arthur first met him, he volunteered the information that he had been bitten three times and had nearly died once. He also told Arthur that he could sometimes play a tune on his primitive wooden flute, which would entrance and completely disarm Agamemnon, his seven-foot king cobra.

Mongoose gave the idea of working for The Magazine a touch of much-needed unconventionality. Arthur hoped to model himself after the older man. He'd go to his comfortable editorial office five days a week, make a huge salary and in the meantime he'd raise snakes, or act, or learn to play chess.

Besides, Mongoose made it sound so interesting. The older man was fascinated by every aspect of his employer. He told Arthur that George Fallow first worked on the idea for The Magazine while recovering from shrapnel wounds received at Verdun. Apparently Fallow hadn't graduated from college, and he'd always wanted to improve on his education. In the hospital there was a magazine rack. After a month or so Fallow had read everything on the rack, and he'd read some issues of some magazines more than once. So he started to take notes. He found that he could get all the essential information out of a magazine on about a dozen of the three-by-five-inch index cards the nurses used to write down the temperature and blood pressure of the patients. He found that when he went back to read the index cards, they were so boring and colorless that he didn't enjoy reviewing them and didn't remember what he reviewed. That's when he realized that information wasn't enough. He rewrote the cards so they were interesting to read, but still contained all the essential information in substantially fewer words.

"That's when he got the idea for a magazine," said Mongoose, "and 'Information Plus' is still written on the title page."

It was at this point that Faith came up to the two men. She had a glass of white wine in one hand and a cigarette in the other. Her pale face was flushed with excitement. She was wearing a blue denim skirt and a white turtleneck with vertical ribbing. Her long blonde hair was parted in the middle. Her earrings were gold loops. Arthur told Faith that he and Mongoose had been talking about a job at The Magazine.

"Which magazine?" Faith wanted to know.

"The biggest one," said Arthur.

"Oh, you mean *TV Guide?*"

"No," said Arthur. "The other one. The one with words in it. *The American Reader.*

"I like the job I have," he told Mongoose, "but you can't grow old at the *Bugler*. Not enough money. The only way you can afford to stay in local journalism these days is if you live with your mother."

"But you must be good at it?" said Mongoose.

"I'm all right, I guess," said Arthur.

"Well, if you ever had any trouble, you could always ask your father for help. Have him cover a town board meeting for you once or twice," he said. "I bet that would put your editor on his ear."

Arthur nodded mechanically.

"A person with your advantages can't go too far wrong," he said.

Arthur brought his hand to his mouth.

"*Time* ran a survey of publishing a year ago," said Mongoose, looking at Faith and then at Arthur. "It showed that we offered the most financially satisfying positions in all of American journalism."

"We get *Time*," said Faith. "But I didn't see the piece."

"Oh, it was there," said Mongoose. "In the issue that had runaway husbands on the cover. In any case, I suggested that Arthur come down and see the place. You're more than welcome to join him."

"No," said Faith. "I think this is something you two should work out together. I had an English teacher who said that *The American Reader* is written for seventh graders."

"Certainly we strive for clarity," said Mongoose with some asperity, "but the seventh grader who reads us is precocious."

"It's not just clarity," said Faith. "My mother's family lives in Georgia, and they all read it. I look at it when I go down to visit. Last time I looked at it I saw an article on manners. Can you believe that? I mean, here we just lost the war, senior citizens are eating dog food and that magazine runs an article on how to hold your fork, and why your children probably shouldn't call your friends by their first names. Talk about moving deck chairs on the *Titanic*."

"That particular article—I think it was titled 'Please Pass the Manners, Please'—did very well on the Reader Poll," said Mongoose stiffly. "In fact we had a letter of praise from a reader who also happens to be a professor at MIT. Not that we respond mindlessly to what the readers want. Mr. Fallow has his own very particular concept of right and wrong, and he doesn't betray it."

Faith took a long pull on her glass of wine, and began to look around the room for somebody else to talk to.

Mongoose noticed, and increased the volume of his voice. "I don't suppose you know this, Faith," he said, "but we also sell merchandise through the mail. Do you like records?" he asked.

Faith allowed as how she liked records.

"I believe we sell more recorded music than any other single company. We just recently had a country and western offering titled 'Tumbling Tumbleweeds' that sold a couple of million pieces. We have an enormous list, and this can be used to isolate a market before we even manufacture a product. It's a little like shooting fish in a barrel. The mail-order business is extraordinarily profitable, but Fallow has a veto. The case that comes immediately to mind is that of the digital clocks. A year or so ago the marketing department picked a target section of our readership, and sent out an artist's representation of the clock in a mailing. They didn't actually have a single clock."

Faith had taken Arthur's arm in her left hand and was pointing across the room with her right. "That's Joe Winters," she said. "I don't want to talk with him."

"All right," said Arthur. "You don't have to."

"Am I boring you?" asked Mongoose.

"No, no," said Faith, wagging her head and smiling brightly.

"In any case," said Mongoose, "the response to the mailing was heartening, so they ordered a few thousand pieces and sold them in that geographic region. This is what's called a wet test. The people in charge of the mailing went back to the computer bank and worked up the figures for the entire list."

Faith yawned noisily, but Mongoose continued. "Our full list, you know, has the names and addresses of more than fifty million people in this country. It's much larger than the active list, because it also includes lapsed subscribers." Mongoose took a drink of beer.

Faith was craning her neck to see somebody who had just come in. She nudged Arthur. "Isn't that Holly Wolfson?" she asked.

Torn between his desire to seem polite and his need to please Faith, Arthur simply shrugged at the question.

"No," said Faith, "you must look."

Arthur stood on his toes to see the door. "I think so," he said, settling back down. "It's her hair."

Faith put her mouth to Arthur's ear. "She just had a mastectomy," she whispered noisily. "A radical."

Now Mongoose was annoyed. "If you'd rather not hear the story," he said.

"No, no," said Arthur. "Please continue."

"All right," said Mongoose, somewhat mollified. "The clocks were selling for thirty-nine dollars, and they were being made in Taiwan and cost us about twelve dollars each. The cost of three mailings plus house advertising would have been something like two dollars per clock sold. So the profit per unit could have been substantial. The figures showed that they might have sold five hundred thousand pieces. Of course the marketing people expected Fallow to be enthusiastic. They anticipated a profit of well over ten million dollars."

"How many million dollars?" asked Faith.

"Ten," said Mongoose. "Fallow looked at the workup, and told them not to go ahead."

"Told them what?" asked Faith.

"The men behind the project sent a delegation to The Founder's office. He still said no. So Albert Palumbardo, he's head of circulation, he finally got up the courage to ask why. Fallow said that it had always been the policy of the company to provide merchandise for which there was a real and not just an imaginary need."

"I still don't get it," said Arthur.

Mongoose took a pull on his beer. "He told Palumbardo that most of the people who subscribe to *The American Reader* already have a clock."

A "satisfying position in American journalism" was what Faith wanted for her husband, so she did a one-eighty and approved of his visit to Mongoose in Paradise. After the tour, Arthur updated his resumé, and sent it off with a letter to a Peter Wheelwright—a name Mongoose gave him. Wheelwright said yes. He didn't say yes to a job, but he did say yes to lunch.

★　　★　　★

The Friday of the week before the lunch, the phone rang during dinner. Arthur got it. It was his father's housekeeper. Mrs. Carpenter was a widow in her midforties. She was slender with brown hair and green eyes. She had gone to work for Arthur's father shortly after Arthur's mother's death. She made the beds and prepared the meals. Privately Icarus referred to Mrs. Carpenter as his "faux wife." What she did and did not do for her employer was the subject of bitter discussion between Arthur and Faith.

"I'm setting up an appointment for your father with a doctor," Mrs. Carpenter said without preamble. "He was out raking the leaves and he fell down. He got right up again, and he ate a big dinner. I think he's fine. But I've set up the appointment with that cardiologist Dr. Sneeling recommended."

"Good," said Arthur. "It can't hurt."

"That's right," said Mrs. Carpenter. "It can't hurt. I just thought you'd want to know. And I wondered if you could drive him there. The office is in Tarrytown. I would do it myself, but I suspect he'd like it better if you took him. The appointment is for tomorrow, so you wouldn't have to miss work. It's for one P.M."

"Let me ask," said Arthur. "Hang on." He put his hand over the mouthpiece.

Faith was cutting up Nathan's cube steak. She wasn't having cube steak herself. She was having broccoli with a dietary butter substitute.

"My father has to go to the doctor on Saturday," said Arthur. "Mrs. Carpenter wants to know if I can drive him."

Faith looked exasperated. "Saturday," she said. "Doesn't Saturday ring any bells?"

"No," said Arthur. "Should it?"

"It's only my mother's birthday."

"My father's sick," said Arthur.

"Your father's been sick for years," said Faith. "Sometimes it seems like he's been sick since the day we got married."

35

"But he's sicker," said Arthur. "Or he may be sicker."

'It's up to you," said Faith. "But he would never miss a party to drive *you* to the hospital."

When Arthur put the phone back to his ear, his father was on the other end.

"I overheard the first part of the conversation," he said. "So I picked up. I'm afraid Mrs. Carpenter has gotten a little overwrought. I can easily drive myself to the doctor."

"Are you sure?"

"I fell down raking leaves and bumped my head, and now Mrs. Carpenter's got the wind up. She's always been a little bit of a professional crapehanger. I feel just fine. Do you have other plans?

"It is Faith's mother's birthday," said Arthur.

"Then that settles it," said Icarus stiffly. "I'll drive myself."

FIVE

Tuesday was to be the first official visit to World Headquarters. Monday morning early, Arthur called the newspaper and asked for the city editor.

"Hello, Melvin," he said, holding his nose closed with the thumb and forefinger of his right hand. "This is Arthur."

"Hello," said Melvin. "How are you?"

"Not so good," said Arthur, his nose still clamped shut. "I'd come in," he said, "but I have a fever."

"No, no," said Melvin. "I can hear how stuffed up you are."

When Arthur put the phone down he felt dreadful. Lying was worse than a stuffy nose. But Faith had insisted. "Dress like a hippie," she said, "and they'll pay you with beads and seashells."

So he and Faith went shopping. The largest single purchase was a pair of lace-up shoes that looked like the wing tips that Arthur used to whoop and jeer at when Paul Sheldon wore them junior year in boarding school. "Want to be a banker, do you?" Arthur would say. "Sellout," they used to call him, "Paul Sellout." Now it developed that genuine wing tips were expensive, but thanks to the oppressive poverty of the Third World, there were imitations available, and these are what the young couple settled on. Careful examination revealed that they were made of a material more closely resembling card-board than leather.

"I once had a pair of shoes like this," said Arthur. "If you scrape the toes a big piece of paint comes off. The pulp inside is white."

"They look fine," said Faith. "Just be careful where you put your toes."

On the morning of the big day, Arthur phoned Melvin again.

"Still sick?" asked the city editor.

"Right," said Arthur through his clamped nose.

After this he brushed his teeth until his gums bled. He borrowed Faith's lady roll-on. He had scraped the "I brake for Nukes" sticker off the rear bumper of his blue Ford Econoline.

Mongoose had told him to arrive at 9 A.M. He parked the van at 8:43, so he spent five minutes trying to cut the hair out of his nose with the scissors from the Swiss Army knife he kept in the glove compartment. He hadn't clipped his nose hair since the day he got married. It was a piece of luck that he didn't wound himself badly. He was able to stop the bleeding with a wad of paper towels he found caught under the passenger seat. For months afterward, he would remember the terrible clacking sound his shoes made as he crossed the parking lot. The big brick building did look remarkably like a cake. It also seemed to be examining him through its glass eyes.

Doc was at the front door. He didn't appear to recognize Arthur. He didn't smile either. The receptionist did smile.

She was black. Since this was the early 1970s, all the most conservative organizations had black receptionists. She directed Arthur to the waiting room. A dowdy woman in a green dress came and met him. He supposed that she was a secretary. She brought him to Peter Wheelwright's office.

Wheelright was a large, genial man with the bearing and manner of a Choate master on Parents' Day. He was both dignified and self-effacing. He was wearing a neatly pressed blue work shirt and a black knit tie. The shirt had been washed so many times that the white stitching contrasted sharply with the faded blue cotton.

"I hope you didn't have any trouble finding us," he said, coming from behind his desk and putting an arm over Arthur's shoulders.

Arthur tried to say no, but his voice would not work. Wheelwright didn't seem to notice.

"I was just looking at your bona fides," Wheelwright said, pointing to a manila folder on his desk. "Very interesting. With your sort of background, I wonder why you didn't consider medical school, or a career in the law?"

All the men Arthur met that morning were expensively and yet casually dressed. They seemed to be preserved in amber, caught and held in the yellow light that poured through the building's many windows. They were diffident. After being flattered by Peter Wheelwright, Arthur was led to the opulent office of an executive editor named Allen Parker. Parker told Arthur that The Magazine was "a sort of engine for charity. The Fallows have no children," he explained, "and no debts. So all the profits that aren't plowed back into the company are given away to good causes."

"I didn't know about that," said Arthur.

Parker smiled. "As for the articles," he said, "you may not agree with every word—I don't agree with every word—but every piece we print is thoroughly vetted. We don't allow inaccuracies. It's a little-known fact that this magazine has the sharpest and least-forgiving research department in the industry. Every story in *The American Reader* is true."

Arthur nodded. He hadn't known. He couldn't have explained why, but he was quite taken by the embarrassment expressed by these handsome and well-paid men. There was something touching about their discomfort.

Arthur remembered the one time that *The American Reader* had come up when he was at boarding school. He was on the wrestling team. Sparring partners were chosen for the equality of their skills, so an athlete could easily spend a good deal of time with another athlete he didn't like at all, just because he couldn't quite beat him up and he couldn't quite get beaten either. That's how it was with Arthur and Russell March. The only thing they ever found to agree on was that Cassius Clay shouldn't have had his title taken away. "If he's broken the law," said March, "let them prosecute. He's still the champ." Russell was already planning a lucrative career in the law. "What about you?" he asked Arthur during a break.

"I'm majoring in English."

"What are you going to do with that," he asked, "be an editor at *The American Reader*?" He didn't sneer. He didn't have to.

"What they do should be against the law," he said.

Arthur wanted to know why.

"They plagiarize."

"I thought they were a reprint magazine."

"That's right. They take stuff other people have written, the stuff other people have published, and make it their own."

"But that's not what a plagiarist does."

"Sure it is, a plagiarist is a literary thief, I think that originally the word was used for kidnappers," said March, wiping the sweat off his mouth with the back of one hand. "You want to be on top this time?"

"No," said Arthur. "I've got to work on my escapes."

There was no question that The Magazine was considered banal. In some cases it was glancingly associated with evil. The fat, ignorant witch who sits guard beside Mia Farrow's bed after she's been raped by the devil in the movie *Rosemary's Baby* is seen studying *The American Reader* through glasses as thick as the bottoms of Coke bottles.

Still, as Arthur moved from one handshake to the next he began to experience a deep sense of professional longing. He despised the stereotypes that were articulated so brilliantly in The Magazine, but he'd also been taught to admire good taste, and the men he was meeting that day had great taste. Their accents were grand, their use of language precise. He wanted to be one of these men. He wanted a touch of silver in his sideburns. He wanted to escape from his deep sense of failure. He wanted more than anything to make Faith happy. Maybe if she were rich she'd be happy. Maybe if she were happy he wouldn't be angry with her anymore.

The only difficulty was explaining how employment at the newspaper could prepare anybody for a job at this magazine.

Arthur got around this by saying that he loved words. Both the newspaper and The Magazine used words. They both used the alphabet too, of course, but he couldn't very well say he loved the alphabet. Besides, he, Arthur, had been talking about words his whole life. You had to have some explanation for majoring in English. "I'm no good with numbers" wasn't close enough to the truth. "My father's a writer" was too close. So Arthur told Allen Parker that he loved words. He even treated Wheelwright to the opening lines of Yeats's "The Song of the Happy Shepherd": "Words alone are certain good . . ."

People expected the son of Icarus South Prentice to be literary. So he was literary. But he tried to be current as well. He didn't talk much with Wheelright, or with Allen Parker. He sat quietly in their armchairs and exercised his smile and nod muscles. He didn't know for sure, but it seemed likely that the less he said, the better off he'd be. Both men were quite charming. Longevity was the word that came to mind, and not just longevity at the job, longevity longevity. Was this Camelot he'd stumbled into, Shangri-la?

Courtney Fairchild had a son who was considering Antioch. Would Arthur recommend his alma mater?

"No. I wouldn't think so."

"It's expensive," said Fairchild. "Especially when one considers that the students spend a third of their time holding jobs off campus."

"It is expensive," said Arthur. He remembered that right above the toilet paper dispenser in one of the stalls in the administration building, somebody had written, "Antioch diplomas: take one. Flush $25,000 down the toilet." He didn't tell Fairchild this of course.

"I spent a lot of time in the library," he explained.

"That's one thing I miss about Williams," said Fairchild, running his fingers through thick brown hair. "I miss the libraries, I miss the gym, I miss the sense of order. That's one of the great features of a traditional college, the sense of order."

"Not at Antioch," said Arthur. "At Antioch there was no order. We actually had something called an unlearning center. The first thing you were supposed to unlearn was manners. They used to say that the buildings in Manhattan were supported by a circle of cockroaches holding hands. If you put those roaches through Antioch, and you sent them back to Manhattan, they wouldn't holds hands anymore."

"Well, if you pine for convention," said Fairchild, "this is a good place to come to work."

Arthur did long for the past, but he wasn't at all sure that it was the same past that was longed for by the people who subscribed to *The American Reader*. He had looked at the latest issue of The Magazine before coming to lunch. The lead article was titled "The Day My Son the Hippie Cut His Hair."

"How bad were the courses?" Fairchild asked.

"I actually took one titled 'Shakespeare and Imperialism,' " said Arthur. "I could have taken 'Women in Shakespeare.' I was already taking 'Great Women of the Civil War.' If you want to know what it's going to be like after the revolution, just go to Antioch. It's enough to make anyone a reactionary. I have seen the future and its phones are broken. There was a girl in my dormitory who got fifteen physical science credits for having a baby."

"No!" said Fairchild.

"Yes," said Arthur. "And fifteen credits were all you needed to graduate. She named the baby Lenin."

Fairchild nodded thoughtfully. "You must be famished," he

said. "I'll bring you to the washroom and then we can head up to the guest house for lunch."

The "washroom" had a lounge outside of it. There were four stalls, and the walls were papered. Arthur couldn't pee. He stood in his stall for an appropriate length of time, and then flushed the toilet. The sink had the same style of soap dispenser they'd had at Choate. The soap was also the same, and when Arthur turned the handle, the smell brought him right back to his freshman year.

Arthur and Fairchild met Allen Parker in the main foyer. Parker was talking with Doc. Parker was smiling. Doc was not smiling. Parker and Fairchild and Arthur went out the front door. The oak looked magnificent in full sunlight. Black steel cables glinted in the branches. There was a man in a green uniform on the lawn under the tree. He was fiddling with a huge old Locke mower.

Arthur and six editors ate lunch in an antique farmhouse, which was just up the drive from the main building. One of the editors was a jolly sort named Cunningham who told jokes. Another was the woman he'd seen asleep in the library armchair on his first visit. She still looked great, but now he could see that she might be an executive. There were wrinkles around her blue eyes. She spoke just once during the lunch. Parker asked her to recite her favorite poem, and she did so, charmingly. It was W. B. Yeats's "To a Friend Whose Work Has Come to Nothing." Arthur knew the poem by heart. He came in with her for the last two verses. She didn't seem to mind. She smiled. During the lunch somebody called her Mrs. West, and Arthur envied Mr. West. Arthur noticed that despite her narrow waist, she displayed a healthy appetite.

He didn't talk much at the beginning of the lunch. Every so often he'd answer a question about Antioch: "No, I don't think pot is good for you." "Yes, most of the faculty advisors slept with their students."

He was astonished at how much attention everybody paid.

"We're all listeners," Mongoose had told him. "They're going to want you to make a speech. Don't be embarrassed."

"How can I not be embarrassed?"

"Don't be. Not if you want this job. You're not the kind of guest they usually have at the farmhouse. Usually they have the secretary of state. Try and act like an emissary, a diplomat from a different generation. A warring generation. You've got to speak up. You've got to lay down your sword and shield."

Now Arthur was trying. The vodka tonic had helped. The wine seemed to help. He wanted the job, but it was more than that. He admired these people. He needed them to admire him back. By the time he'd finished his glass of wine, he'd moved from the particular to the abstract.

He'd been asked by an editor named Horster what his impression was of campus radicals. "I suppose this is a cliché," he said, paraphrasing his father-in-law, "but I don't think we should take apart the conventional world before we have something to put in its place. Life in America may not be great, but life in America is probably better than life has ever been at any other place or time.

"Not just for the white middle class," he said, as a waitress in a blue dress uniform cleared away his empty plate. "For everybody. For poor people. For criminals. Especially for criminals." Arthur noticed that his little presentation was greeted with a perfect, expectant silence.

The waitress reappeared with raspberries. Then she came back and poured coffee. Horster took a small silver box from his jacket pocket, removed two tiny white tablets and dropped them into his coffee. "I wish you would elaborate," he said, stirring.

"Take that old hymn: 'Once to every man and nation/comes the moment to decide/In the strife of Truth and Falsehood/for the good or evil side.' "

Everybody nodded. They all seemed quite interested. Arthur took a sip of coffee. "But you know it's been attacked. In some churches it's been taken out of the service."

Fairchild nodded. "Why do you suppose that is?" he asked.

"They think it's sexist," said Arthur. "They even suggest that it's racist. It's not an attack on women. It's not an attack on blacks. It's an attack on evil. And when you can't attack evil, the whole society is in trouble. Don't you think the whole society is in trouble?" he asked, looking at Fairchild.

"Yes," said Fairchild slowly, "but why do you suppose we're in this fix? If it is a fix," he said, wiping his mouth with his linen napkin.

"I blame Freud," said Arthur. "No, that's not fair. I blame our understanding of Freud. His work has been used as the foundation for the belief that evil is sickness and that sickness is sufficient justification for all wickedness. Life should be painless." Arthur paused, but nobody broke in. Nobody was eating either. They were all just sitting there watching his lips.

"That's nonsense," Arthur continued, in his best secretary of state imitation. "Life has never been painless. People regularly get over what was done to them in early childhood. Look at Dickens. Now, if he'd responded to the hardships of his childhood the way you would expect, he never could have written a postcard. But he didn't, and his heroes don't either. They're like their creator. They overcome mean beginnings."

Arthur took a spoonful of berries. He chewed. They were still listening. They were listening to him chewing. He didn't know whether to be flattered or ashamed.

"But mean beginnings haven't been your problem," said Fairchild. Somebody coughed.

Arthur shook his head and swallowed. "No," he said. "My problem is the opposite."

After the lunch, Arthur went up to visit Mongoose. He found the older man in his office, playing an electric keyboard that stood off to one side of his desk and listening to himself through earphones.

Arthur knocked loudly on the open door. Mongoose took the phones off and looked sheepish. "I suppose this seems extracurricular," he said, getting up and walking around to the chair behind his desk. "Actually, I am working on a book supplement about Mozart. The forms of his music are so powerful, so familiar, that they seem to have risen right out of the universal unconscious."

Arthur smiled and nodded.

"So how did it go?"

Arthur shrugged. "No idea," he said.

Mongoose nodded. "That sounds about right," he said. He rocked back in his chair. "But do you want the job?" he asked.

"Sure."

"You want to do this for yourself?" asked Mongoose.

"No," said Arthur. "Not really, but I don't know what that has to do with anything."

"I know what you mean," said Mongoose. "Of course I love Joan, but marriage is like that. Did Cunningham tell his elephant joke?"

"No. He told jokes, but not that one."

"All right," said Mongoose. "An ant falls in love with an elephant. He's never seen anything so beautiful. They have a wild night. The ant wakes up in the morning, and the elephant's dead. 'Just my luck,' says the ant. 'One night of passion and I'm going to spend the rest of my life digging a grave.' "

Arthur laughed. "Good joke," he said, "but in all fairness, I think I was digging a grave before I ever fell in love."

Mongoose smiled. "Then let me show you this," he said.

Under the brass paperweight there was a laminated placard. Mongoose moved the cobra to one side and turned the place mat upside down so that Arthur could read it. "It's a verse from the Gospel," he explained. "We make them available to longtime subscribers. I don't want you to think I'm a Christer, but I've always been fond of this particular quotation."

Arthur read: "Luke 6. Verse 37. 'Judge not, and ye shall not be judged; condemn not, and ye shall not be condemned; forgive, and ye shall be forgiven.' "

SIX

Nathan was in the middle of his terrible threes, and a horror on the evening after the big day in Paradise. He was upstairs in bed, but still crying, when Arthur began his report. He and Faith were in the kitchen, which was the place in the house farthest from Nathan's bedroom. Arthur could hear his son in the distance.

"Daddy, I'll be a good boy if I could just have a glass of strawberry milk. I'm lonely, Daddy. Daddy, I promise I'll be a good boy if I could just have one glass of strawberry milk."

"He's already had one glass of strawberry milk," said Arthur. "And two glasses of water. I feel like a bad father, but we have to let him cry."

"I wouldn't have gone up the last time," said Faith. "Now

he's had too much to drink. He's almost certain to wet his
bed. Speaking of bad fathers, yours called."

"Am I supposed to call him back?"

"He didn't say. But I wouldn't."

"Why not?"

"Just let him wait. He acts so superior to you, Arthur. The
only way to make him take you seriously is to be a little less
obedient."

Faith was wearing a pair of rust-colored corduroys and a
thin white nylon shell. Her feet were bare. Dinner had been
pot roast. Faith's mother had cooked a double portion, and
Faith had served it to her husband and son. She'd eaten one
bite while cutting up Nathan's portion. Her meal was a plate
of lettuce with vinegar. Under her prominent left breast there
was a big gravy stain.

"You look good," Arthur said.

"I feel terrible," said Faith, lighting up a cigarette. "We
were almost arrested at the A & P. Nathan threw a sixteen-
ounce can of corn niblets at an old lady. When I asked him
to apologize, he took another can and threw it at me."

"You still look good."

"You're just horny."

"I thought women liked to be told they look good."

"Not by their husbands, silly," she said, and exhaled some
cigarette smoke through her nose.

The phone rang. It was Arthur's father. "I went to see the
doctor," he said.

"And what did he say?"

"Oh, nothing surprising."

"So you're not sick?"

"No, I am sick."

"Well, what did he say?"

"He said I have to dry out. He said that if I don't, I'll have
a heart attack."

"What are you going to do?" Arthur asked.

"I'll stop drinking, of course," said Icarus Prentice. "What
choice do I have?"

"Good," said Arthur.

"I just thought you'd want to know."

"I did want to know," said Arthur. "Thanks for calling."

"Oh, you're welcome," said Icarus.

"I was concerned," said Arthur.

"I know," said Icarus, and Arthur thought he could hear ice hitting against the side of a glass. "I'm sorry if I upset you."

"That's all right."

"No," said Icarus. "It's unconscionable. I went to see the doctor on Saturday. It's Tuesday, so you've been on pins and needles for four days."

"It wasn't that bad," said Arthur. "I suppose I might have called you."

"That's right," said Icarus, and his voice was suddenly full of menace. "You might have called me."

Arthur took in a deep breath. "I've had a lot on my mind," he said.

"I'm sure," said Icarus, and then Arthur could hear him taking a drink. "How was the birthday party?" he said, and clicked off.

"What was that?" asked Faith when Arthur got back to the table.

"My father," said Arthur.

"You look like somebody just walked over your grave."

"I don't know," said Arthur, and he shrugged. "Maybe somebody did."

"It's your father, isn't it?" said Faith. "What did he say?"

"He said he should stop drinking," said Arthur.

"Well, he should," said Faith. "And he should also leave us alone. I wish you never had to talk with him," she said.

Arthur shrugged. "I don't think that would be so good," he said. "Besides, we need the money."

"Speaking of money," said Faith. "How was your day in Paradise?"

"They're snobs."

"What do you mean?"

Arthur began to run water in the sink. "I'm the one

applying for a job. I'm the one with the fake shoes. I've got the BA from a college that practically went out of business, and they're apologizing. I was charmed, but I'm not at all sure that they were." He put the last dish into the drainer.

Faith asked if Arthur would like a piece of cheesecake.

"Sure," said Arthur, "Let's both have one."

"I couldn't eat a piece of cheesecake," said Faith. "I'm fat, remember?"

"Okay," said Arthur. "I don't really need one either."

"You never gain weight," said Faith angrily. "You're not fat."

"Yes, but I'm not hungry either."

"A cup of coffee?" asked Faith.

"Yeah, a cup of coffee would be nice," said Arthur. "I'll get it." He went to the stove and lit the burner under the Corning Ware kettle that had been among the wedding gifts. Faith's Uncle James worked for Corning. The kettle was a second. Corning employees got seconds free.

After taking down two mugs and putting a couple of teaspoons of instant coffee in each, Arthur walked back to the table and stood behind his wife's chair. He began to knead her shoulders. He could still hear his son sobbing quietly in the distance.

Faith got up, walked to the other side of the table and sat again. Arthur went to the stove and poured water into the mugs.

"You know, it's not really Paradise," he said, giving Faith her cup of coffee and sitting down across the table from her.

"Maybe it is," said Faith.

"No, I mean the place," said Arthur. "The buildings are not really in Paradise."

"Yes they are," said Faith. "My cousin ordered the atlas that shows the world just as the world was when Christ was born, and he sent his check to Paradise, New York."

"The Magazine used to be in Paradise in the late 1920s and early 1930s," said Arthur. "Then it moved to another town right near Paradise, but they liked the sound of Paradise as a mailing address. They get so much mail that they have their own post office. So Paradise is still their mailing address. But Paradise is not where they are. Paradise is a working-class town one exit farther south on the parkway."

He took a long pull of his coffee. He hadn't let the water get hot enough. "But they are certainly from another world. I met a dozen editors today, and nobody was working. Mongoose says it's a jungle in which there has always been enough to eat, and so the animals have never had to eat each other."

"It sounds more like a dairy farm."

"There was one woman in some minor department, I think it was the copydesk. She looked harried. Everybody else was reading magazines."

"What sort of magazines?"

"*Time, Newsweek,* the *Ladies' Home Journal.*"

"Mongoose reads the *Ladies' Home Journal?*"

"Mongoose was reading *Mechanics Illustrated.* I guess there's not an awful lot to do. Mr. and Mrs. Fallow put the first issue of that magazine together in the Reading Room of the New York Public Library, and there were only two of them. Now there are hundreds of people working on it."

"So why don't they fire somebody?"

"Fallow could never do that."

"Did you see him?"

"No, but they talk about him the way monks must have talked about God during the Middle Ages. There's no question that he exists, and that he's all-powerful. The only question is whether he's all-powerful and good, or just all-powerful. If employee benefits are a sign of virtue, then he's definitely good. There's a month's vacation, and Fridays are half days in August. And there's profit sharing. There's medical, of course, and life insurance. They have another program where they send all the editors out once a year for a week. One of them went backpacking in the Rockies. One of them went to Mardi Gras. They're supposed to get a feel for the readers. Business people don't get the week of travel, but associate editors do. That's what I'd be, an associate editor. The week doesn't count as part of the regular month's vacation, and the company pays for everything."

"Can wives go?"

"I don't know. I don't think so. But wives can eat at the cafeteria. The food is marked way down. Somebody said lunch costs twenty-five cents. Drinks are free."

"Drinks?"

"Beverages, Coke, apple juice, tea, like that. No gin."

"I wondered."

"But they say the food is quite good, and you can eat a big lunch for a quarter. I saw the cafeteria. It's got a mural of the British surrendering at Yorktown, and there are upholstered sofas along the walls. I didn't eat there. They give you a ticket when you pay for your food, and they have drawings every month. Ten people win one hundred dollars. That's one hundred dollars after taxes."

"That would be nice. If you won once a month, you could stop visiting your father."

Arthur pretended not to have heard this. "If you don't want to drive to work, you can take one of the company buses. Tickets cost fifteen cents. And this is just the built-in stuff. If Fallow likes something a young editor has done, he'll send the editor and his wife to Colonial Williamsburg for a long weekend."

Faith lit another cigarette. "I went to Williamsburg once with my parents," she said.

"Did you like it?"

"I told you about it. My father drove. The trip started about a month before the trip started. He knew I wanted to go, so he held it over me. Responsibility and opportunity go hand in hand. You know what a pain in the ass he is."

"Yeah," said Arthur. "I guess I do. In any case, if we went to Williamsburg, your father wouldn't have to come."

"But you like the place?" said Faith.

"That's right," said Arthur. "What I especially liked is that the editors are the most-loved. The editorial offices are in the old building, which is the grandest part of the complex. Most benefits are just for editorial."

Faith lit another cigarette. "Sounds like heaven," she said without enthusiasm.

"I don't know. It's like heaven, but it's also odd. There's a sense of menace concealed. At lunch the top editor has a garage door opener, and when he wants something, like salad or more coffee, he pushes on it and a waitress appears. She has those shoes that are supposed to keep you from getting varicose veins."

Faith looked impatient. "You always see concealed menace. What about money? Did you ask them about money?"

"God, no," said Arthur. "I thought you wanted me to get this job."

SEVEN

When he was eight years old, Arthur had collected pictures of naked women. He got these out of magazines that were discarded in the bushes beside the road near his parents' house. The road was a quiet one, with places to park, and the parkers used to open their windows and throw out their empties and their obscene magazines. He went through the magazines, selected his favorite nudes and snipped them out.

He hid his collection in a dictionary for second graders that his mother had given him.

Arthur's father usually worked in the basement, but on the summer of his tenth year, Arthur went on a canoe trip down the Allagash for a month, and Icarus moved his typewriter and ashtray to his son's room.

When Arthur came back from camp, his father moved his office back downstairs. But the pictures were gone. So Arthur went to the basement. His father was typing and smoking cigarettes.

"Did you use my dictionary?" Arthur asked.

"Yes."

"Did you take anything out of it?" he asked.

"You mean the pictures," said his father.

Arthur didn't say anything. He looked at his hands.

"It seems to me," said Icarus Prentice, "that an infatuation with image involves a certain amount of self-love. It's narcissistic." He stopped for a moment and lit a fresh cigarette.

"I don't suppose you have any way of knowing this, but that was Salinger's problem. He fell in love with his image in the glass. He even shaved his head once, as a sort of attempt to disfigure his loved one."

Arthur still didn't say anything. He was tired of hearing stories about how corrupt Salinger was. The only thing he knew for sure about Salinger was that people seemed to think he wrote better stories than I.S. Prentice wrote.

"If it's pornography you're interested in," his father said, "You should read *Ulysses*. The Molly Bloom soliloquy is the best pornography in the English language. There's a copy in the guest bedroom."

There wasn't much more advice until Arthur got old enough to be involved with flesh-and-blood women. Icarus fought routinely with Arthur's mother, and would sit up afterward and read. When Arthur came home from a date, his father was often waiting up. He'd be stationed in his favorite armchair with a cigarette and a drink.

Icarus drank early and often, but like many alcoholics, he seemed not to be greatly affected by the quantities of hooch he put away. He cut the lawn, he drove to the post office, he cracked jokes. He may have remarked on the smell of fresh-cut grass more than your standard suburban householder, but Arthur was not convinced that this enthusiasm had anything to do with demon rum.

There was, however, a limit, and sometimes—after a rancorous dinner with his beloved wife—this limit was reached. Instead of making a clown of him, excessive booze made Icarus Prentice more dignified. He had an English accent of mysterious origin, which was accentuated by the application of Gilbey's gin. After a fifth of lubricant, he sounded like somebody who should work for the BBC, and began to speak in the most sweeping generalities. The future of Western civilization, the war between the sexes, that sort of thing. The nighttime Icarus was precisely the sort of man that the daytime Icarus would have considered a bore.

Arthur knew this, and treated his drunken father with much less respect. He actually talked back, because while the old man's tongue was still poisonous, he was not nearly so quick on his feet.

Arthur valued these conversations, and this was not just because they gave him an opportunity to be saucy. Late at night and very drunk, Icarus would talk with Arthur about Arthur. He would talk with Arthur about how much he loved his son.

"I know it's the tiresome trait of old men to reduce life to simple categories," he said one night, apropos of nothing, "but it does seem to me that my passage into adulthood would have been easier had I known from the beginning that heterosexual love is a species of mortal combat."

Arthur got himself a glass of ginger ale and sat across from his father on the couch. "I brought Lisa Bender to the movies," he said, smiling. "There was some rough and tumble in the popcorn line, but otherwise the evening seemed relatively safe."

"She has a harelip," said Icarus with considerable hauteur.

"She does not have a harelip," said Arthur.

"All right," said Icarus, "she doesn't have a harelip. But you don't love her."

"No," said Arthur. "I don't."

"If you did love her," said Icarus, "you'd be in trouble."

"And why's that?"

"Because there are two kinds of women."

"Really," said Arthur slyly. "I haven't known a lot of women, but it already seems to me that there are more than two kinds. For instance, there are tall ones and short ones. And there's the kind with the harelip. And there are ones with different colored hair."

Icarus cleared his throat and rolled his shoulders, as if he were addressing the graduating class at Harvard. "No," he said. "There are only two kinds. First there are the lovers. These are the women who adore everything about a man. They can't do enough for you. Afterward they make you breakfast. Mrs. Hammersmith is like that. She thinks the sun shines out of her husband's asshole."

"Are they mostly tomatoes?" asked Arthur.

"No," said Icarus. "It has nothing to do with whether they're tomatoes."

"And the other kind?" said Arthur.

"The ball snatcher," said Icarus.

"Which sort of woman would you recommend?" asked Arthur.

"I've always insisted on being the lover," said Icarus.

"So you'd recommend the ball snatcher?" said Arthur.

Icarus nodded. "You don't agree?" he asked.

"I don't agree or disagree," said Arthur. "But I do know you're sitting in your favorite armchair. I also know what trouble the ball snatcher has gone to to have it reupholstered for you."

Icarus took a long pull on his drink. "I forget how young you are," he said.

EIGHT

Two weeks after the first visit to the offices of *The American Reader*, Arthur called in sick again and went back to World Headquarters. They wanted to ask him some more questions, or that's what Mongoose said.

They didn't ask him any questions. Instead he was led quietly from one empty office to the other. He was just beginning to be bored, even annoyed, when he found himself being led toward the throne. "This is it," he thought, his heart racing, his eyes tearing with anticipation.

Fallow was a tall, slender man with close-cropped hair. His office looked like it might be a display in a Madison Avenue antique shop, or a set from Masterpiece Theatre. He sat behind a wooden desk that had been painted black with flowers on it. His skin was gray and he had a great many liver spots. His two long, delicate hands were displayed on the desk's green blotter. The telephone had an amplified earpiece. He rose to greet Arthur, and after shaking his hand, indicated a small armchair with gold feet.

"Have you ever see a chair like that, Mr. Prentice?" asked Fallow.

Arthur looked down at the chair and said he hadn't.

"That's right," said Fallow, "although you may have seen imitations. You probably don't know that the one you're sitting in was used in the staff office of Napoleon during his campaign in Egypt and abandoned there."

There wasn't an easy answer to this. "I know that Nelson defeated Napoleon's fleet in 1798 at the Battle of the Nile," Arthur offered.

"That's right, August 1, 1798, to be exact, but the chair wouldn't have been captured until much later."

Arthur nodded.

"Are you something of a military historian, Mr. Prentice?"

"No," Arthur stammered, "although I have liked the military histories I've read."

"And what military books have you read?" asked Fallow. The only books Arthur could think of right then were *U Boats at War* and *Midshipman Hornblower*, but he didn't think either would make an adequate impression. "I suppose the usual," he said.

"You're familiar with Francis Parkman's work on the French and Indian War?"

It happened that Arthur *was* familiar with Francis Parkman's work on the French and Indian War. This had to do with the fact that Icarus Prentice had a set of Parkman and was always quoting from it, often incorrectly. Arthur had found that if he read Parkman, he was sometimes able to correct his father at the dinner table.

So he nodded to Fallow, but then thought a nod might be misunderstood. "Yes, I like Parkman. When I think of the French and Indian War, though, the first book that comes to mind is *Drums Along the Mohawk.*" It occurred to Arthur that this might have been an error on the level of *U-Boats at War*, but it was too late, so he let the line fall.

"Drums along the what?" asked Fallow, "I have no recollection of that book," he said, and he wagged his head slowly. "I wonder if you could send me a copy?" Arthur nodded. The part he had liked best was the scene where the Indians shoot the beautiful Tory woman and scalp her. He also remembered that the book had been on his summer reading list in the eighth grade, and that was doubtless not going to make the right impression. Arthur wondered if he could come up with a book with a similar title. Fallow had probably read *The Last of the Mohicans. The Tin Drum* didn't seem apt. Arthur thought maybe he'd just forget the request. The Founder was famous for his memory, but he was also eighty-four years old. Besides, many things are lost in the mail.

Fallow asked Arthur what his father did.

"He's a writer."

"A writer," said Fallow, and he wagged his head again. "It must have been a hard life."

Most people knew of I. S. Prentice, certainly most people in publishing knew of I. S. Prentice. Arthur couldn't figure out if this was a canny attempt to draw him out, or if the old man had simply lost touch. So he nodded and tried to put a look on his face that could have passed for a smile in case his legs was being pulled.

"Would you say that your parents did a good job of raising you?" asked Fallow.

This was a tough one. It was the vogue to blame one's parents for what went wrong in adult life. But Arthur realized that if he said they did a rotten job it might do a fatal injury to his own prospects for employment.

"On balance, I'd have to say they did a good job."

Fallow nodded. The Founder rose from behind his desk and waved a hand at the Chagall painting on the wall. Arthur happened to know that it was worth a couple of million dollars. "Do you like Chagall?" Fallow asked.

"Adore him," said Arthur. Faith had been an art history major in college. Arthur had written her Chagall paper. "I love words," he told her.

"My wife is also a great admirer of his work," said Arthur. "We went into Manhattan a week ago just to have a look at the one with the cow in it: 'I and the Village.' There are a million reproductions, of course, but we wanted to see the original."

"And you weren't disappointed?"

"Not at all."

"Well," said Fallow, clearing his throat. "Anyone with the wit to agree with his wife about painting would doubtless be a useful addition to our staff."

NINE

Mongoose called three days later with an optimistic update. "I wouldn't burn my bridges yet," he said, "but they all liked you. Horster in particular liked you a lot."

"He's the one with black hair?"

"That's right. He's the deputy editor-in-chief. He's the anti-smoking editor. Did you know that we don't carry cigarette ads?"

"No," said Arthur. "I didn't know that."

"That's right," said Mongoose. "We came out with the first big piece on cigarettes even before the surgeon general's report. In any case, Horster took me to lunch today just to talk about you."

There followed a couple of weeks of radio silence. Arthur

called Mongoose before the family went on vacation to give him the phone number of the cottage he and Faith had rented on Lake Winnipesaukee. During Arthur's vacation, President Nixon resigned.

It was a week after the end of vacation and six weeks after the second interview that Mongoose phoned with the bad news. Arthur got a letter from Wheelwright two days later. This expressed "sincere regrets" at having to inform him that "the decision has gone against hiring you at this time."

Arthur's heart was broken. Mongoose kept calling.

"Now this is all privileged information," he said, "but you should know that there is a sex discrimination suit being brought against The Magazine, and this makes the management sensitive about what it will look like if they continue to hire young men for the better jobs. Now I've committed an indiscretion in telling you this, and I trust that you won't mention it to anybody on the outside."

"No," said Arthur, "of course I won't, although you make it sound unlikely that I'll ever get a job."

"No," said Mongoose. "They liked you. But it's just not a good time for them to act. The Nixon resignation was taken by some people here as a personal loss. The editor-in-chief was involved in CREEP. He was supposed to have shown up on a golf course somewhere with a brown paper sack with one hundred thousand dollars in it."

"I remember the story."

"In any case, Nixon was considered an ally. He's been here. There's some feeling that his leaving may change the climate in ways that will not be favorable to our organization."

"You're private industry. You're not even sold on the stock market."

"We do our business through the mail, and the postal service is heavily subsidized. But it's not any particular fear that's got them upset, it's just a general feeling of dislocation. I don't think they'll hire anybody for a year or so, but you should position yourself so that when they do hire somebody it will be you. You have to select yourself," he said.

"But I applied for the job!" said Arthur.

"I know, but you still have to demonstrate your interest."

"Don't they have to hire me first?"

"No, you have to show it first. It's almost a tradition. Dean Nichols is now the editor-in-chief. He's been with The Magazine forty years. I believe you met him?"

"I think so. Is he the one with the watercolors of Paris street scenes?"

"No. Courtney Fairchild has the Raoul Dufys. Dean has white hair."

"I remember. He's the one with the pre-Columbian bull on his desk."

"No, that's Allen Parker. Maybe you didn't meet him. He could have been out of the country. In any case, Nichols got hired by sitting on the front steps of the building. The Dean had just gotten out of Harvard, and he'd applied for a job and there wasn't one, so he came to World Headquarters every morning at 8 A.M. and sat on the front steps of the building. He'd stay there until letting-out time, and then he'd go home. Fallow was on a business trip for the first three days. On the morning of Nichols's fourth day, Fallow saw him and asked the receptionist who he was. Remember Rosemary Watts, the head librarian?"

"Yes, she has a silver lorgnette."

"That's right. Well, she'd just gotten out of Radcliffe. She was the receptionist then, and she told Fallow that Nichols was a college graduate who wanted a job. Fallow wanted to know if Nichols had applied, and Rosemary told him that he had, but that the magazine wasn't hiring.

"The next day Nichols was there again at 8 A.M., and he was still there when Fallow went home at lunch to have a tuna sandwich with his wife, The Co-founder. Fallow hasn't eaten red meat since the war. The first war. When Fallow got home, he phoned the office and got Paul Rutherford, who was his managing editor at the time. 'There's a man sitting out on the steps of the building,' he said. 'Could you please ask him to leave?' Rutherford could, and when Nichols wouldn't leave, the police were called, and they escorted him off the property. But the next morning he was there again.

" 'Can we have him arrested?' Fallow wanted to know.

" 'Sure,' said Rutherford.

" 'On what grounds?'

" 'Trespassing.'

" 'How long can they hold him?'

" 'I don't know, an afternoon.'

" 'And he'll be back tomorrow?'

" 'Probably.'

" 'All right, then hire him.' "

Arthur wanted to know if he should go and sit on the steps of the building. Mongoose thought not. "But you shouldn't give up either." So every month or so Arthur would send a love letter to Paradise.

"Dear Mr. Peter Wheelwright," he wrote. "I couldn't help but admire your article in the July issue on teachers. I read 'An Apple for Maria' with genuine pleasure. Working at a local newspaper, I'm all too aware of the fact that teachers are overworked and underpaid. Teachers are indeed the caretakers of our nation's future. They put their reputations on the line five days a week, and they must be treated with respect. They are not treated with respect. I recently encountered one teacher who told me that his salary was so low that he felt it was bad for the economy. 'I love my job,' he said, 'but people tell me I should be ashamed of myself.' Hardworking teachers shouldn't be ashamed of themselves. They should be made to feel proud. I am confident that articles like 'An Apple for Maria' will help to make this true. Sincerely, Arthur South Prentice.

"P.S. I thought the joke about Brezhnev and the devil was hilarious. Too true, but still hilarious."

He signed the P.S. with his initials: ASP.

The first two letters came back with "Ciao" scrawled on them in red grease pencil. Then one was returned with "Cheers" written across the top. Arthur had written an extremely gloomy and moralistic letter in praise of an article about the drought and consequent famine in the Sudan, so he was mystified. Wheelwright couldn't have been cheered by the letter. Was he cheered by the famine?

"Of course not," said Faith. "He didn't read your letter, that's all. Who has time to read letters anymore?"

"So should I keep writing?"

"Certainly. You're making him feel guilty. Every letter he gets and doesn't read makes him feel a little more beholden to you. Keep it up. But don't worry too much about individual words."

So Arthur did keep it up, and while Wheelwright's responses were never encyclopedic, they did get a little bit longer. One particularly rich piece of flattery came back with "I'm pleased to know we have such perspicacious readers out there" crayoned over it. Arthur wasn't on the doorstep, but he was in the In tray.

In the meantime he continued to descend into the basement that housed the editorial offices of *The High Cliff Bugler*. His journalism improved. He had moved out of obituaries in his second year. Since then he had passed through the Orangetown town board to the county. He'd seen a town supervisor indicted. He'd visited a murder scene. Now he wrote features, mostly about poor people and lost pets. He liked his job. But his heart was in Paradise.

TEN

Arthur's son Nathan—now entering the terrible fours—was in the bath with a dinosaur in each hand, and Arthur was on his knees beside the tub. Arthur's one dinosaur was fighting Nathan's two dinosaurs and losing. Eight months had passed since the last visit to Paradise.

The phone rang downstairs. Faith got it. It was Mongoose. Faith took over at the tub. As Arthur went to the phone he could hear her saying to Nathan, "That's not fair. If you're going to have two dinosaurs, then I have to have two dinosaurs too."

"The important thing is to get in the door," Mongoose said a little uncertainly. "I know this isn't a position you would ordinarily seek, but . . ."

"The one person I saw who looked unhappy was on the copydesk," Arthur told Faith when he got off the phone. "She was an old woman, and she looked harried. Besides, I have no talent for detail. You know that."

"What did Mongoose say?"

"He said they don't expect me to be any good. All they want is for me to show a willingness."

"So be willing."

"But there's a test. How am I going to pass a test? I think I should skip this round." Faith didn't agree. "Not when you're trying to support a wife and a son on one hundred twenty-five dollars a week. You shouldn't skip any rounds. Remember, you can wear the shoes."

"I'm supposed to take the test at home. I probably won't see anybody but the receptionist. She's not going to look at my shoes."

"You take the test at home?" Faith asked. "Like the tests we took at college after pass/fail was instituted?"

"I don't know what the test is like, but I do know that I take it at home."

"Well, you're not just going to take it," she said, "you're going to pass it. Trust me."

So Arthur phoned Wheelwright, and was told that the package would be at the front desk and could be picked up any time after 3 P.M. Wheelwright was gruff but friendly. "Enjoy," he said. "It would be good to have a man on the desk. Ciao for now."

The test was an article about the mango, laid out and illustrated as if it had been in The Magazine, only this version was peppered with errors in spelling and grammar. There was quite a lot Arthur hadn't known about the mango. He hadn't known that it was referred to in some circles as the king of fruits. He hadn't known that Buddha often ate mangos, and that Christ may have tasted one. Genghis Khan's army practically lived on them. There was no mention of the one thing Arthur did know about mangos, chiefly that filaments like the bones of a panfish grew out of its center area. He remembered getting these caught in his teeth. He was supposed to correct the document and return it the next day.

It looked as though he was in for a hellish night with the dictionary and with *English Grammar for New Citizens*, a book he'd bought at a church sale after Hugh Melvin and Arthur had a little discussion about his grasp of the essentials. "Your father won the National Book Award," the city editor had said, "and you don't know the difference between a semicolon and a rat's colon."

"Not only am I going to fail the test," said Arthur, "I'm going to fail it on the one night this year that they broadcast my favorite movie on the tube."

"First you'll watch your son," said Faith. "I'm going for a drive, and when I get back we'll take the test together. We can finish it before dinner. We're having grilled hot dogs. Then we'll both watch *Spartacus*. You can start the fire while I'm gone."

As soon as the boy and his father got out onto the cement patio, Nathan wanted to know if they could play catch. "No," said Arthur. "I have to make a fire."

Nathan didn't say anything else until the charcoal had been doused with lighter fluid and was blazing furiously. "Now can we play catch?" he asked.

Arthur brushed the dirt off a section of the patio and sat down. Nathan sat beside him. Arthur put his arm around his son's small shoulders and pulled him into an embrace. "Why don't we just talk," he said.

"What can we talk about?" asked Nathan, leaning against his father's shoulder.

"We can talk about anything you want," said Arthur. "We can talk about your friends at school, or we can talk about how much we like hot dogs, or we can talk about God."

"Let's talk about God," said Nathan.

"All right," said Arthur, "but I don't know much about God."

"Do you know if God is up in the sky?" asked Nathan. He'd picked up a stick and was hitting it against the edge of the patio.

"If you believe in God," said Arthur, "then I think you have to have the sense that he's all around you."

"You mean in the air?"

"The air, the trees, the grass, even in the fire. Especially the fire."

"My teacher said he was up in a cloud."

"Well, don't argue with your teacher about God. That much I know. But I don't think anybody thinks he's up in a cloud anymore, although when I was in Italy I saw a lot of pictures of him as a stern old man with a beard walking around in the sky."

"Like Santa Claus?"

"That's right, a lot like Santa Claus. But Santa Claus only gives things, and they always thought that God could take away."

"What does God take away?"

"If you believe in him, I suppose you believe he can take away your health. Your luck. Like that." Arthur got up to go into the kitchen and get the hot dogs.

It was at that moment that they heard the horn of the Econoline. Then Faith came around the corner of the house, waving an old and faded issue of *The American Reader*. She was exhilarated, and approached her family with the gay and sexy style with which she used to wave the pom-poms when she led the cheering squad at Sleepy Hollow High School.

"Here it is," she said, and there it was on page 125 of the November 1962 issue: "The Magnificent Mango: A Fruit for a God."

"The library carries it all the way back to 1922," she said, as she kissed Arthur on the cheek. "You're going to be a rich man." He noticed that she smelled of a perfume she hadn't worn since high school.

"They'll catch me for sure," Arthur said. "I always get caught. Remember that time I had to spend an afternoon writing the words to that hymn because Gary Swan tipped over Nicole Banner's chair in music class?"

"Sure I remember."

"I had to write out that hymn one hundred times. 'Once to every man and nation comes . . .' " he began.

"Blah blah blah blah blah," said Faith. She had on a tight green skirt Arthur remembered her wearing when she was in high school. It had a zipper on the side. The zipper used to snag. Her sweater was the color of buttercups.

"If I cheat, God will know," said Arthur.

"That's right, but they won't," said Faith, tucking her hair behind her right ear. "They may be rich as God, but they don't have his powers of perception. All you have to do is make some mistakes."

That's how they decided to leave the second *g* in agree. The word appeared twice, and Arthur failed to correct the misspelling both times. This was a genuine error, but the pattern of ignorance it revealed was not significant.

Then they watched *Spartacus* on television. After the movie, Arthur gave his wife a peck on the cheek and went to his room. He'd marched in there after a fight one night a year or so ago, and never marched back out. At first he'd felt sorry for himself, but in time he'd found that sleeping alone alone was better than sleeping alone together. At least he was no longer responsible for his wife's insomnia.

His room was called the sewing room because it had Faith's grandmother's sewing machine. It also had Arthur's typewriter and one gerbil named Fosco. There had been two gerbils, but Count Fosco had killed Sir Percival Glyde. Fosco lived in an orange plastic cube. This was the starter version of a system of cages called the Habitrail, the habit without the trail. Fosco was restless and he used to gnaw on the inside corners of his prison. "I'd let you out," Arthur told the gerbil, "but it's a bad world. The neighbors have cats." There were two sounds in the sewing room late at night, Arthur's regular breathing and the clash of gerbil incisors.

That night Faith came to Arthur. This was her first nocturnal visit to the sewing room in more than a year. Arthur thought she looked great. But then Arthur always thought Faith looked great.

"I couldn't sleep," she said.

"Me either. Let's not do it."

"Let's not do what?"

"The test. Let's not cheat on the test."

"Are you kidding?"

"No, I thought that was why you couldn't sleep."

"I just couldn't sleep. I kept thinking you look a little like Kirk Douglas."

"Thanks, but I don't look anything like Kirk Douglas."

"You do in the eyes."

"You mean when he gets crucified?"

"No, I mean when he's winning."

She sat on the side of his bed. "We should get you a new mattress," she said.

Arthur didn't say anything. He kissed her.

"Would you cover the gerbil?" she said.

"I don't think he minds," said Arthur.

"I know," said Faith. "But I do."

ELEVEN

Some time after they got married Arthur had discovered that if he nibbled Faith's ears, sex wouldn't be a disappointment for her. So whenever he did get her into bed, he tried to nibble her ears. Then she asked him not to.

"It makes me feel so helpless," she said. She was polite, but she was also insistent.

Even before Nathan was born, they'd stopped having sex with any regularity. If there was an advantage to this state of affairs it was that no more sex meant no more children. Arthur remembered seeing a sign at an Earth Day Celebration that had said "Unbridled growth is the philosophy of a cancer cell." When in low spirits he felt that his nuclear family was a malignancy. At least it wasn't spreading.

Nathan was still sleeping in a basket in the matrimonial bedroom when Arthur began to go outside the marriage. He'd leave the newspaper office for some afternoon assignment ten minutes early and find himself heading toward the parking lot of a bankrupt Grand Union. He'd park the van near an abandoned dumpster and try in quiet desperation to comfort himself, to give his rage and sorrow some means of expression. In the van, in the parking lot, he made love.

The perennial awkwardness of postcoital conversation was avoided because when Arthur made love in the afternoon, he didn't involve anybody else. Like the broccoli plant, Arthur was self-fertilizing. Unlike the broccoli plant, he was mortified by this state of affairs. First it was a clear sign of unpopularity, but also it seemed to be some sort of crime.

This pattern had started in early adolescence, faded out when he began to date and then come back with a vengeance. His married life was as barren and solitary as had been his early teens.

Arthur's first experience of physical love had taken place while he was alone with Ian Fleming's *Dr. No*, a book which had been recommended highly by his father. The incident took place quite unexpectedly when he read how the lady spy was shot "slowly, lovingly" to death by one of Dr. No's hired assassins.

The leap of imagination required to inhabit such scenes was not as great as it might have been for other boys, because Arthur found it much easier to conceive of gunplay than of the possibility that a live woman or girl might actually let him put a hand on her hard little belly.

By the time he was eleven, Arthur had started to stay up after his parents had gone to bed in order to be able to watch a certain sort of movie on TV. These films were aired at midnight or 2:30 A.M. The characters were in elaborate costume. Sometimes they wore buckskin. Often they wore togas. A toga was a good sign, because a toga meant Rome, and Rome meant decadence. In the 1950s decadence meant violent death.

This was the sort of film with one hero and two heroines. The drama usually ended with a marriage. Since both women were in love with the same man, and since bigamy is a greater threat to the status quo than homicide, one of the women had to die. Usually it was the one with the black hair. The blonde survived to take the wedding vows.

This was before serial murders had attracted widespread public attention, but there were serials, TV serials, that produced quite a number of dead women. The dramatic equation involved a leading man or men who could not get married. This meant that when a woman was introduced for purposes of romance, she also had to be disposed of at the end of the episode. If she was really in love, the writers found that the most convincing way to dispose of her was with a gun, a knife or even a pitchfork. "Bonanza" was a great show for this. The Cartwright boys were always falling in love. Unfortunately "Bonanza" was shown at prime time, so Arthur's father would often join his son at the set. He'd comment on the bad dialogue, which made it difficult for Arthur to suspend his disbelief. And a suspension of disbelief is necessary for even the most perverted forms of love.

Arthur also discovered a number of works of fiction in which one of the ladies died a sexual death. Lady de Winter gets her head chopped off at the end of *The Three Musketeers*, which is not sexual, but the good little Constance Bonacieux gets poisoned and dies sighing in the arms of D'Artagnan. And deWinter drives a blade into her own yielding body in the middle of the book, in a successful attempt to corrupt the young man who is left as her jailor.

Shakespeare provided a certain amount of excitement. Juliet, of course, sheaths a blade in her breast: "O happy dagger! [Snatching Romeo's dagger] This is thy sheath [Stabs herself]; there rust, and let me die" [Falls on Romeo's body and dies].

Reading *Hamlet*, he started near the end, where the Queen says, "A hit, a very palpable hit."

When bad TV and great literature both failed him, Arthur

turned to his parents' collection of art books. Botticelli painted women being chased by dogs.

He couldn't watch the movies anymore when he got married, and it got so that he knew the scenes in books so well that they no longer worked. So he began to make up fantasies for himself out of whole cloth. He'd think them and rethink them. He'd actually write them out. He'd tell Faith he was working on a novel, but what he was working on was a sort of limited-edition pornography.

He'd feed Nathan, read him a story and then put him to bed. He'd bring Faith her tea and a snack. Sometimes he'd try and kiss Faith. She always rebuffed him, and afterward she wouldn't enjoy her TV as much as she did on nights when he didn't raise the ugly issue of carnality. So when he was strong, he'd leave her alone. He'd pretend not to notice how good she looked in her nightgown. He'd bring her treats and exchange news. Then he'd go off and sit by himself in the sewing room with his typewriter. Sometimes he could actually smell the dust from his father's attic.

After these violent waking dreams, Arthur was much less apt to fight with Faith. Fighting with Faith in the real world seemed infinitely worse to him than committing mayhem in his imagination.

The women he wrote about were always high-breasted and haughty. They were often armed themselves, but not always. Lisa wasn't armed.

She was a big girl. She'd have on a tight blue denim shirt and a white turtleneck with vertical ribbing. She wore a large old-fashioned watch on her right hand. A man's watch.

Lisa was about Arthur's age and had straight black hair that fell to her waist. She lived in a white clapboard house with a set of slate steps that ran down to the street. The mailbox was on the street. The fantasy always started with Lisa down by the mailbox. She'd stand by the side of the road and take some of her long black hair, pull it back behind her right ear.

Then she'd shuffle the envelopes. There would be a newsletter from her congressman, a flier from the local chiropractor and an electric bill. Nothing personal. She'd come up the stairs and open the front door. Arthur would be sitting on the third step of the stairway that led from the entrance-foyer to the second floor. In his right hand he held a small chrome pistol, an automatic with a silencer and a nine-shot clip.

There was always a church pew set up as a bench in the foyer, and Lisa would toss the mail on it and close the front door. Then she'd turn and see the intruder. "Arthur," she'd say, "you're not still angry, are you?" Arthur would smile and bring the pistol up so that she could see it.

"Oh, honey, you're not going to use that," she would say, her voice deepening with fear. "Can't we please talk? You know I didn't mean it." It was never clear in Arthur's imagination what Lisa had done and not meant. Again Arthur wouldn't say anything. In life Arthur was always talking. In his imagination he almost never said a word.

Lisa's bra size was 38D, just like Faith's, and like Faith she had creamy skin and a narrow waist. But she didn't resemble Faith. Faith had round eyes. This girl had slanted, almond-shaped eyes. And although she seemed to know Arthur, the Arthur she knew was from another life. Lisa didn't look like Arthur's mother either.

Lisa looked like Lisa, and she was as real to Arthur as anybody else in his life, but she didn't seem to know any of his other acquaintances. When she saw the gun she'd begin to breathe heavily, and her breasts would rise and fall. She'd put her arms out at her sides, her palms forward. She wore dark, almost-black lipstick and a touch of eyeliner.

The gun would cough, and a gout of red blood would appear just above the waistband of the skirt. Lisa's eyes would roll back for a minute, and she'd look bewildered and mildly surprised. She'd stagger forward, catch the bannister and steady himself. Her pupils would dilate. Her breath would come hard.

"But Arthur," Lisa would whisper, as if she could still make it all okay, "I love you."

Cough, cough, cough.

Then Arthur would drive off to his assignment. He always felt like hell.

TWELVE

The *American Reader* is a corporation as well as a publication, but it's also a state of mind. In fact, there's a remarkable resemblance between World Headquarters and the city-states that dotted the Tuscan hills in fourteenth-century Italy. The buildings are of brick instead of stone, but the high ground has been taken. There are flags, turrets and a cupola with bells. The carillon plays at regular hours. Sometimes the chimes play snatches of show tunes, but often they play the sort of music that would not have been out of place before the invention of the internal combustion engine.

The land is terraced and tightly cultivated. Within the walls the customs, language and orthodoxy are markedly different than they are in the world at large. Arthur's search for employment can be seen in the context of this orthodoxy. It suggests a low-key version of a variety of story that the magazine ran regularly. The trademarked logo was "My Personal Cliffhanger."

Originally these true stories involved the narrator in a moral quandary. One of the pieces that had run in the 1930s told of a mother who discovered that her son had driven the car when two other boys held up a package store. He was not caught, and the mother herself didn't learn of the crime until he had graduated from college and was applying to law school. She felt that he should be punished, but she knew that a police record would "put an end to his career before it had rightly begun." She had to decide whether or not to turn him in.

Another piece that ran in the 1940s was about a man who left a high-paying job in Manhattan to become a carpenter in Bristol, New Hampshire. His twelve-year old daughter was furious with him. He'd limited her options as well as his own. But he stood by his decision and "hoped that some day she too would learn to appreciate the way the early-morning mist looked on Newfound Lake."

In the case of the mother of the felon, the characters retained their anonymity, but in most Cliffhangers the first paragraph had a proper name, a date and sometimes even the weather. This was to assure the reader of the veracity of what followed. A true story, after all, was supposed to be inherently more interesting than one somebody made up.

The Cliffhangers were only moderately successful until the 1950s, when the young Dean Nichols brought in the first grizzly bear. Nichols had made a minor hit with a series on the health benefits of chastity, but this was his big break. *Ursus Horribilis* had run into a young couple on a trail in Yellowstone National Park, knocked the girl to the ground, taken her head in his mouth and bitten down. Her date rushed into the fray. The bear knocked him down, tore all his hair off his head, bit him through the shoulder, then lost interest and wandered away. The victims were discovered by a platoon of Girl Scouts★ (★See "Skirt and Compass," *The Ameri-*

can Reader, May 1948). Both had to be stitched back together like human bean bags, but both survived. The boy got a wig, the girl got a fiberglass jaw and they got married. On their honeymoon they went camping in—you guessed it—Yellowstone National Park.

The other editors cried foul. Where's the decision? they wanted to know. Fallow let the piece go. "It did happen," he said. The readers loved it.

There followed a great onrush of all types and varieties of mayhem. People were eaten and then disgorged by great white sharks, they fell into tubs of boiling lard, they were crushed by railroad engines and trapped under boulders. One man actually went through a grist mill, and lived to tell the story to 100 million readers. Babies fell into swimming pools, grandmothers were bitten by rattlesnakes, newlyweds were trapped in avalanches.

At first there was an attempt to pay lip service to the older, ethical form. There was a pregnant moment written large, when the victim faced death and the eternal verities and decided to go on. "Sammy could see his boot with the foot still in it resting on the track fifteen feet away. The loss of blood was beginning to make him dizzy. He thought he'd just put his head down and rest for a moment. The nearest telephone was two football fields away, and there was no other hope of rescue. But then he remembered Sammy Jr. He thought of the scene at the garden gate that morning. 'I'm going fishing without you today, but I promise I'll take you fishing soon.'

" 'Cross your heart and hope to die?'

" 'Stick a needle in my eye.'

"This was a promise Samuel Trampano intended to keep. He took the lace from the boot that was still attached to his body, tied it around the stump of the other leg and began the dreadful crawl toward the telephone he'd seen near the station platform."

The "Personal Cliffhanger" series began to run very month, and for some reason it was easier to find the catastrophe than it was to find the eternal verities. The moments of reckoning

got shorter and shorter, and finally they disappeared altogether. In one story a skier found himself heading down the
expert slope at Mount Brody and realized that his right ski
was going to go on one side of the Douglas fir up ahead and
his left ski was going to pass on the other. Since this particular
hero didn't regain consciousness for three months, it seemed
unlikely that he had gotten a glimpse of the meaning of life.
So life itself became the meaning of life. That essential upbeat
twist was provided in the little interview at the end of the
piece in which the survivor thanked his or her lucky stars.

And they spoke by the hundreds, from their wheelchairs,
through reconstructed jaws, over the whir of complicated life-
support systems. They were glad, actually glad that what had
happened to them had happened to them. Without the man-
eating shark, without the industrial meat grinder, they never
would have known what was important in life. If they hadn't
been crippled, they never would have learned how to appreciate the little things.

If Arthur's attempt to get a job had been suggested as a
subject for one of the early Cliffhangers, it would have been
turned down. He was faced with a moral quandary, and he
caved in. But if it had been proposed as one of the modern
articles, it would have flown. He did not triumph, but he did
survive.

The drama seemed actually to bore Icarus.

"You'll have to get a better haircut" was all he said.

When Arthur got the job despite his long hair, his father
arranged a celebratory lunch. I. S. Prentice hadn't entertained
often since his wife died, so Arthur was touched by the gesture. Winthrop (a.k.a. Mongoose) and Joan Quest were the
guests of honor. Icarus grilled the lamb himself, and served it
out on the terrace with a dish of his famous tomatoes cut up
and presented with oil and basil. There was just one break in
the gaiety. Arthur had gone into the house to refill a pitcher

of iced tea. Coming back outside, he found his father speaking earnestly to Joan Quest.

"Well, I think *I* understand," said Icarus. "Intelligence doesn't have anything to do with it. They're an equal opportunity employer and he's just exactly what they need: a hippie in a tract house."

THIRTEEN

Faith shook her head sadly. "I'm bushed," she said when they got home and Arthur tried to put his arms around her waist.

Arthur scowled. "Sometimes I'm so lonely," he said.

"You're always lonely after you see your old man," said Faith.

"I'm always lonely," said Arthur. "After I see my father, I realize it."

"I don't think so," said Faith. "You're fine when you don't see him."

"But I can't just write off my father," said Arthur, and he tried again to put his arms around his wife.

"Come on, honey," said Faith, escaping from his embrace. "No big deal. It's not like you were happy when we did do it."

"Sure I was."

"All we ever did afterwards was fight," she said, turning to look him full in the eye. He found the shape of her face very beautiful. He also thought she had a point. It sometimes seemed they'd had roughly the same postcoital fight from about a year after they first did it until Nathan came along and they stopped having sex altogether. It was as if the fight had been scripted by a not terribly serious television writer. They were actors without the authority to ad-lib.

The first time he could remember the fight it had taken place in a nine-dollar motel room just outside of Chillicothe, Ohio. Arthur and Faith had been together several times at this point, but they had always been outdoors. Even in the winter, parental vigilance had forced them into the snows. This was their first attempt at intercourse in a heated room.

Faith insisted that they keep the TV on. "With these walls, you know." The sex was a disappointment. It wasn't a disappointment for him, but it was a disappointment for her. Probably it had been a disappointment for her before, but they'd always been too uncomfortable for her to notice. Now that they were inside, she noticed.

Afterward she said they should get married.

"Just because the sex is bad doesn't mean it's the real thing," he said.

She looked up sternly.

"A joke," he said. "Of course we should get married. You want to get married? Really want it? We'll do it this afternoon."

Faith was sitting at the motel room desk. She was doing something to her face with a pencil. Her blouse was draped over the back of the chair. Arthur was lying on the bed. He was fully dressed. He had his loafers on.

"Why can't you take anything seriously?" she asked.

"I thought that was what you liked about me."

Faith sighed deeply, as if she were dealing with a very slow child. "But some things *are* serious," she said. "If you loved me, you'd know when to stop joking." Then, quite suddenly, she would burst into tears. He'd try to comfort her, but she wouldn't let him. She'd stop crying, make herself up again and announce through trembling lips that they shouldn't see each other anymore.

Arthur was always surprised by the suddenness of this outburst. "I was just kidding," he would say. "Besides, you told me that you never wanted to get married. You told me that the only reason people our age ever got married was to please their parents."

Faith shrugged. "You really are a simpleton," she said.

"Look," said Arthur, "if you want to get married, let's get married."

"I wouldn't marry you if you got down on your knees and begged," Faith would say.

"Okay. I didn't bring it up. Whatever you want."

"I want to be left alone. I don't think we should see each other so much."

"Okay, let's not see each other so much," he'd say. "But I'll miss you."

"Fine," she'd say. "Miss me." Then Arthur would drive Faith back to Ohio University, which was near the border of West Virginia. After a silent parting, he would take the old red Karmann Ghia he'd inherited from his father, and flog it back across the belly of the state to Antioch. Antioch was in Yellow Springs, in the western part of Ohio, near the Indiana border.

When Arthur got back to his campus, he would always get drunk. Or stoned. He would tell anybody who would listen how glad he was that he had broken up with his girlfriend. He would tell perfect strangers that he had had it with women. Just before he lost consciousness, he would go out and find a telephone. "I love you," he would say, "I'm sorry, and I love you."

"I love you too," she would say.

They did once break up for several months. They had had the fight on a Sunday morning in February. Faith phoned her mother that afternoon. She was crying.

Her mother had a plan. "I was going to go to Florida with your father," she said. "He didn't want to take the time off. So I'll go with you instead. You can leave from the Columbus airport this evening and meet me in Miami."

By the time Arthur made his drunken call that night, Faith was on a plane. Faith's roommate told him that she was in Florida. Arthur didn't believe her. He thought Faith was probably just refusing to come to the phone. He got drunk for the next three nights, and made the call each time. On the fourth day he was too sick to try again.

He wrote a letter to her at the end of that week, and one the next week. They were loving letters, but he was careful not to propose marriage. He wanted her back, but he didn't want her to come back against her will.

"She wants to get married," he explained to his father during a phone call.

"So marry her," said Icarus.

"There's no joy in it," said Arthur. "She says she wants it, but when we talk about it she acts as if we were planning a double suicide."

Icarus chuckled. "Smart girl," he said.

"So what should I do?" asked Arthur.

"Marry her," said Icarus. "It's in man's nature to chase women, and it's also in man's nature to be caught by them. You know that."

"But I don't want to spoil her life," said Arthur.

Icarus sighed. "You think too much," he said.

The third letter came back unopened. Faith had written "Return to sender, address unknown" across the envelope in her rounded, childish hand.

This time Arthur asked his mother for advice. "Leave her alone," his mother said. "You're right, she's pretty. But you don't want a wife who thinks in song lyrics. Girls who think in song lyrics are always disappointed."

"Even if it's a sad song?"

"Even a sad song."

After a couple of months, Arthur began to have new girl-friends. He didn't sleep with them. But he did like some of these girls. At least one of them liked him back. By the time he had taken his summer break and returned to school in September, he seemed almost whole. There was only one slip.

This had to do with Arthur's friend, Gary. Arthur and Gary Woodruff shared an admiration for the works of Thomas Wolfe. On this particular afternoon, they drove out into the countryside and found a pile of rocks near a stream. They sat down beside the stream and praised Thomas Wolfe. They both thought *Look Homeward, Angel* was more like poetry than prose. They smoked a lot of cigarettes and killed a half gallon of Almaden Mountain White. Gary had his Pentax with him. He always had his Pentax. He also had a big, black doorman's umbrella. When they were drunk, Gary said that he wanted Arthur to take off all his clothes and sit on the pile of rocks holding the umbrella. Gary said that he would like to take a picture of Arthur sitting under the umbrella in the falling light. Arthur refused. Gary said he'd thought Arthur cared about art. Arthur said he did care about art, but that it was too cold to take all his clothes off. And so the picnic ended badly.

That night Arthur phoned Faith's number, but the girl who picked up said Faith Hauser didn't live in the dormitory any-more. "I'm not sure about this," she said, "but I think she moved out to get married."

Then Arthur got arrested. This was about two months after the incident with the umbrella. He and some fifty other students went to Cincinnati and blocked an induction center. "March on Cincinnati, end the war in Vietnam." That was the slogan. Arthur spent three days in the Cincinnati City Workhouse.

The act was remembered as one of heroism, but it played as fun. The student protesters were housed in their own cell block, so that there was no real danger. There was plenty of grass to smoke, and indignation is a wonderful thing to share. Novelty and a sense of drama made the other students uncharacteristically friendly.

The scene in the dining hall was the one Arthur enjoyed most.

"We had spaghetti and meatballs," he would say later, when his father's friends asked about his activism. "There were men standing in the aisles with automatic weapons. They were prepared to kill me for my political beliefs. It was all very flattering.

"They gave us tea to drink. We actually had those cups you see them rattling the bars with in movies. There was sugar in the tea. So I asked for another cup. The trustee gave me another cup. But the second cup wasn't tea. The second cup was water.

"That was the best part. They weren't even going to give me a second cup of instant tea. I like that sort of blunt hostility. I'm afraid I'm used to having my hostility mixed with love."

This last comment generated a certain amount of uneasy laughter among Arthur's father's friends. They had wanted to make him a hero.

The demonstration made the television news. When Arthur first got back to his dormitory there was a message from Faith. This was a surprise. He hadn't thought of calling her for some time. He returned her call. It seemed the polite thing to do.

"Are you all right?" she asked.

"Yeah," he said, "I'm fine."

Then there was a pause. Arthur could hear Faith breathing on the other end of the line. Suddenly he could picture the nape of her neck, how pale it was. Then he heard a voice say, "I love you." It must have been his voice. There wasn't anybody else on the line.

"I love you too," she said.

They got married over Christmas.

Faith went on the all-protein diet. But they kept right on

having the fight. It wasn't about why he wouldn't marry her anymore. It was about why he didn't love her as much as she had expected. She was surprised how much he didn't love her. He wasn't surprised. He thought he loved her a lot. His empathy was so near perfect that he often acted as if they were the same person. What did surprise him was how little difference all this tenderness seemed to make.

FOURTEEN

Arthur's first office in Paradise was temporary, but still elegant. It had a window that opened, an armchair and a print of a saint. "Training you will take time. We're closing an issue now and busy," he was told, and then given back copies to read. So he sat in the yellow light, dozed over the platitudes and thanked his lucky stars.

"You know, buddy, just 'cause you left the *Bugler*, that doesn' t mean we'll never work together again," said Melvin when he phoned Arthur at home that evening.

"Apply," said Arthur. "I'm sure they'd love to have you."

"First I want you to put in a good word for me."

"I just got here," said Arthur. "I'm the lowest creature on the totem pole."

"Yeah," said Melvin, but you've got the connections. Your father must have had something to do with why they hired you."

There was a pause, and then Melvin went on. "They didn't hire you for your grammar."

"I took a test," said Arthur.

"I rest my case," said Melvin. "If my father climbed up in the church tower of my hometown with a rifle and shot a few nurses, they'd hire me too."

"I think there's got to be some difference between winning the National Book Award and shooting nurses," said Arthur, but he wasn't exactly certain.

Melvin was very interested in Arthur's salary. "You aren't making fifty thousand dollars yet?" he asked. "Now that's real money. When you make fifty thousand dollars, I'll wash your feet and drink the water. You don't make that now, do you?"

"No," said Arthur.

"What do you make?"

"Why should I tell you what I'm making? I still don't know what you're making."

"You want to know what I make?" asked Melvin.

"No, not particularly," said Arthur, "but I don't see why I should tell you what I earn if you aren't going to tell me what you earn."

"All right," said Melvin, "I'll think about it. If I do tell you, though, you can't tell any of your old buddies at the *Bugler*."

"Cross my heart," said Arthur.

"All right," said Melvin. The next two times he phoned, he didn't bring up the subject of money at all. Then he stopped calling. Arthur was sorry when this happened, but he was also relieved. He didn't relish the idea of telling Melvin that his gross income was $9,000 a year.

If Melvin expressed the style of Arthur's new friends, Gary Woodruff, the umbrella owner, had articulated the feelings of many of the old ones. Gary had an aunt who worked in the mail room at *The American Reader*. So he heard about the job almost immediately and fired off a letter. This was three pages long, and deadly serious.

"Dear Eichmann," it began.

FIFTEEN

Faith never had followed *The American Reader*. Having her husband work there didn't change this. But she did keep right up with *Redbook* and the other magazines for the contemporary woman. She frequently reported to Arthur about bachelorettes who were killing bulls in the ring, sitting in boardrooms and otherwise breaking into exciting and previously all-male preserves. Meanwhile, Arthur was having the opposite experience. He was breaking into the sort of dull, unrewarding job that had previously been held exclusively by women.

The department he was breaking into was headed by a Mrs. Josephine Carstairs. Age had whitened her hair, which she wore in a pageboy with bangs, but she had one of those gamin faces that never loses its edge. Her blue eyes were as clear as those of a girl. Her skin had grown a little leathery with use, but the impression was not unpleasant. It was almost as though the head of a beautiful young woman had been carved out of cork.

Arthur had been told by Mongoose that when she was a young woman, Josephine had sold two stories to *The New Yorker*, and might well have continued to write fiction if her marriage hadn't broken up. "It's tragic, but a woman can't support a child with a typewriter unless she's typing somebody else's words," he said.

Arthur spent his second month at The Magazine in Josephine's office. This was supposed to be his training period, but he didn't learn very much about commas, although he did learn a good deal about Carstairs. Arthur encouraged her every digression. She'd spread out the proof she was to check, and he'd spread out his proof, and they'd read silently for a few minutes. Then he'd ask a question. Arthur's first questions were usually work-related, but Josephine almost always used the answer to segue into reminiscence.

Josephine had grown up in Seattle, and had come east for a job as a features reporter on the old *World Telegram and Sun* in New York. "In those days women were expected to write with style, or not at all. There were a few lady reporters, of course, but most women wrote for the society page, or they wrote color. I wrote color."

"What sort of color did you write?"

"I wrote about the squalid housing of the poor, and how the bathrooms weren't clean in the sweatshops. I once wrote a series about an old horse named Trotsky that pulled a hansom cab in Central Park. My editor used to say I always wrote with violins in the background. I suppose he was right, although I resented his having said it at the time."

"What kind of paper was *The World Telegram and Sun?*"

"Oh, it was an awful paper. People are nostalgic about it now that it's gone. Most of them never read it."

It was on the paper that Josephine met Adam Carstairs. "I was charmed. I was a small-town girl, and I thought he was so gay and dramatic. I didn't realize he was drunk. He used to fall down sometimes, even when we were first dating, or he'd drop his briefcase, or forget his apartment keys, but he always made a joke of it. He was really terribly good company. And I guess I was his meat. I was just young and innocent enough not to know what I was getting into. We went to the Plaza for breakfast once, and he had vodka with his orange juice. He'd left his wallet in his other pants. After we'd eaten, he sent me out to the ladies' room. He went to the men's room, and we skipped. He thought this was very funny. A week or so later, we were walking past the hotel, and he had his wallet. I suggest we go in and pay the tab. He was shocked. 'Oh, come on, baby,' he said, 'you don't want them to think you're a rube, do you?'

"I got pregnant. He made a big thing of it at first, sent me flowers and called me the Queen Mother. I began to show. I couldn't get into my best dresses anymore, and I didn't want to stay out all night. He seemed actually to be bewildered by this turn of events. There were a couple of months when he stayed home with me in the evening. We had a tiny little apartment right off Broadway on the Upper West Side. We'd sit there together in the evening, and he'd look out the window like a dog looks out through the bars in a pound. I was reading child-care books, but he wouldn't even read. Then finally, one of his friends gave a party, and he wasn't going to go to it, but he kept talking about it. His friend kept calling up to consult about how many limes he had to get. I remember the limes distinctly."

On the evening of the party Adam had been impossible. So Josie told him to go. "He was out the door like a shot. I guess he thought I would change my mind. Pretty soon he was going out without me two or three nights a week. And by the time Johnny was two, the marriage was over. We split up, and it took Adam another five years to kill himself. Cancer of

95

the colon finally did it, but just about every organ in his body was on the blink. I heard from his creditors for about a year, but finally that stopped as well."

"He never paid child support?"

"My goodness, no. He didn't have the money, but I don't believe he would have paid if he had it. He would have considered something like that improper, almost immoral."

"And when did you come here?"

"Oh, I came here before he died."

"What was it like raising a child alone in the suburbs?"

"They didn't like me. One still doesn't invite a single woman to a dinner party. The men thought I might be available, so they didn't know what to think. The women knew what to think. They detested me. It's different now, but in those days the women were expected to make gardens and babies, the men were expected to make boodles, and that was about it.

"When John was three, we moved from one apartment to another, and our address and familial status came up in some file bank. On Thanksgiving the county sent us a basket. I think the assumption was that any single parent must be black, and therefore impoverished. There are black people named Carstairs, you know."

"Were you impoverished?"

"No, not really."

"Did you give the basket back?"

"I was going to, but when I looked at it I found it so offensive that I couldn't bring myself to try and contact those people. The basket wasn't actually a basket. It was a cardboard box that somebody had cut out to make it look like a basket. But you could still see that it had been designed for Scott Towels. There was a turkey that said right on it 'Property of the U.S. Department of Defense.' I still don't know precisely what that means, but clearly it wasn't Perdue."

"Turkeys that died in battle?"

"Like that. And there were a few tins of pumpkin pie fill-ing, which I imagine they thought that I and the pickaninny would eat right out of the can with a spoon."

"But the job was okay?"

"They didn't really know what to think of me here, but mostly they didn't think much."

"I'm sure that's not true."

"Certainly I'm a paranoid, and I probably exaggerated the situation, but I was definitely not first-string. I always think of Arnold Baker. Do you know him?"

"I know of him."

"He's the book section editor."

"Big man with a lot of white hair?"

"That's right. His hair was black then. He was quite handsome as a young man. Well, we used to park next to each other, but we never spoke. I thought it was rude to see him so often and not to at least exchange pleasantries. But his selections for the book section were so saccharine, so feeble, that I never knew what to say. I didn't think 'What a lot of pap you manage to find' was a good opening. Then he ran a piece of *Cry, the Beloved Country*. So next time I saw him in the parking lot, I told him how much I had admired *Cry, the Beloved Country*.

" 'Oh, that's splendid,' he said, 'I can't tell you how pleased I am to hear that you liked it. I was so afraid that ordinary people wouldn't get it.' "

"What a stupid old shit," said Arthur.

"Now, now," said Josie. "You have to understand that he was raised to be like that. He's considerate if he thinks that he's dealing with an estimable person—the right schools, that sort of thing. Other people don't really count."

"Sort of outdated, isn't it?" said Arthur.

"Yes," said Josie. "But then so is *The American Reader*."

"But we're not a magazine for snobs," said Arthur.

"Not for snobs," said Josie, "by snobs."

Arthur laughed. "Still," he said, "it must have been dreadful."

"If I'd been a writer," said Josie, "I might have enjoyed those years, because most people thought of me as invisible, and I was forced to go places that no other woman went. For instance, I joined the Episcopal church in Paradise. I took my religious training at the same time John took his. He was five and I was almost thirty, but our souls were equally ignorant. The class I attended was composed almost entirely of businessmen and their children. You could hear the wives saying, 'I'm with him all day, and you can jolly well get home early enough on Thursday nights to attend church school.' In many cases the women took the church quite seriously, but the men almost never did. When the men went to church school, it was a form of penance, not to an all-powerful God, but to a fairly powerful woman.

"So the classes were mostly composed of agnostics and their offspring. And once in class, they felt no need to disguise their disdain for the clergyman, who was, after all, a sort of mendicant, a man without real power or wealth. Besides, he believed in a lot of hokum.

"Now," she said, getting up from her desk, "I'm done with this." Josie stood, straightened her skirt and went to the filing cabinet behind Arthur's desk to get a new proof.

Bent over the cabinet, she continued to talk. "I adore John," she said. "And he's probably the only truly worthwhile part of my life, but I can't help but think that things might have turned out quite differently if I hadn't gotten pregnant. I remember beginning to feel odd at just about the time I understood that something was wrong with the marriage. At first I thought I was just allergic to Adam."

"Didn't you use birth control?"

"Yes," said Josie, settling back at her desk, "but they hadn't gotten the bugs out of it back then."

"It doesn't always work these days either," said Arthur. He paused for a minute, looked at Josie and went on. "Nathan wasn't exactly planned. I hadn't even gotten the job at the newspaper yet when Faith got pregnant."

"But you were using birth control?"

"A diaphragm."

"I thought a diaphragm was foolproof."

"Eighty percent of the time it is," said Arthur.

"I really am getting old," said Josephine, taking off her glasses and shaking her head. "This is not the proof I wanted. That's the one great advantage of heading the department. You get to choose the stories you check." She got up from her desk and went back to the filing cabinet.

"Which one did you want?" Arthur asked.

"I wanted the one about how to get a new husband."

Arthur leaned back in his chair. "We aren't suggesting divorce, are we?"

"No, no," said Josie. "It's about how to manipulate the husband you have."

"Break his spirit?" asked Arthur.

"That's right," said Josie, as she searched around in the cabinet.

"You'll tell me if I'm going too far?" she asked, coming back to her desk and smoothing out the new proof.

"Sure," said Arthur. "I'd tell you in a minute."

"Did you talk about an abortion?"

"We never had a chance. It was the craziest damn thing. Faith felt funny, you know, threw up a couple of mornings. So she went to a lab. Not to her regular gynecologist, because we both agreed that he'd tell her mother. We wanted to talk about it together before we made any drastic decision. So she went to a lab in Tarrytown for the blood test. She gave them our home phone number, but they have spaces for two phone numbers. I guess sometimes with the results of a lab test, time is important."

"So she put down the number for her mother's house?"

"That's right. How did you know that?" he said, looking at the older woman's face.

Josie shrugged.

"When the rabbit died," Arthur continued, "they tried our number. We were out. So they called her mother's house. We were there having Mrs. Hauser's pot roast. Faith got on the phone, and she burst into tears. When her mother found out what she was crying about, they broke out a bottle of champagne. I never have liked champagne."

Josephine got up and went back to her filing cabinet. "I really do need new glasses," she said. "You know I got the wrong proof again. There's just one thing I don't understand," she said, coming back to her desk for the last time.

"Yes."

"Why didn't Faith go to work?"

"She did work until she got pregnant. After that she was always going to. Then something would come up, Nathan would get a cold, or her mother would want them all to take a trip. But you know her mother never worked either. I feel guilty enough about the marriage without making her take some terrible job as well."

Josephine looked up, suddenly alert. "Why should you feel guilty?"

SIXTEEN

This was precisely the question that two years of therapy had done nothing to answer. Dr. Green had an office in an apartment building in Tarrytown, and Arthur had gone there once a week.

He did it for Faith. "It's not that I'm unhappy," he explained to his father. "I mean I guess I am unhappy sometimes, but it never bothered me so much before I got married. Now my grief has consequences. I'm ruining Faith's life."

"So you want to cure yourself?" said Icarus.

"I guess," said Arthur.

Icarus lit a cigarette. "It won't work," he said. "But if you really want to give it a try, I suppose I can pay."

When Arthur wasn't talking about how Barbara Stanwyck

died in *The Maverick Queen*, Dr. Green would show him Po-
laroids of the house he was building on Cape Cod.

"We're going to have a lot of wooden floors," Green said,
"and they'd look best if I had them stained and then kept
them waxed and polished. But I don't have time to polish
floors, and I can't afford to hire somebody else to do it either.
Besides, the newer polyurethanes look almost as good."

During his sessions, Arthur sat up on the edge of a not-
very-comfortable sofa. Dr. Green had an enormous leather
chair with a headrest. Sometimes, when Arthur was going on
about masturbation and remorse, Dr. Green would drift off
to sleep. He would compose his face so as to look judicious,
close his eyes as if to concentrate. It took Arthur more than
a year to convince himself that this was really happening. But
once, during a long and impassioned lamentation, he altered
the tone of his voice so significantly that he startled Green
back into consciousness. The doctor sat up suddenly, looked
around, saw Arthur, relaxed his face and settled back into his
chair. A couple of sessions later, the doctor started to lay
himself out for another little nap, and Arthur screwed up his
courage and asked Green if he was tired.

"Tired?" the psychiatrist asked. "Why do you think I'm
tired?"

"Because you keep falling asleep," said Arthur.

"Why do you think I keep falling asleep?" asked Green.

"I guess you're bored," said Arthur.

"No, that's not what I meant," snapped Green. "I want to
know why you *think* I keep falling asleep."

"Because you are startled when I wake you up," said
Arthur.

"Do you often think people are falling asleep when you talk
to them?" asked Green.

"No," said Arthur. "Sometimes I think my father's drunk
when I'm trying to talk to him, and he'll fall asleep when he's
reading and I'm in the room. But I never remember his falling
asleep when I was talking to him."

"I wonder if you think I'm falling asleep because you can't think I'm drunk," said Dr. Green.

"I don't think so," said Arthur.

"Okay," said Green. "Go on then, and we'll get back to this later. Weren't you talking about onanism?" But when Arthur told Faith, she was outraged. "We pay him fifty dollars an hour, and he's taking naps," she said.

"We don't pay him," said Arthur.

"I know," said Faith. "But it's still real money. Bring it up with your father. Have him pay us directly. Tell him that the very best thing for your mental health would be to stop paying Dr. Green."

"I can't really blame the psychiatrist," Arthur said when he spoke with his father. "I'm not the kind of case you can write books about. And I'm late in the day."

"Well, how much of a problem is it?" Icarus Prentice asked. "I mean how early in the session does he nod out?"

"It's not that bad," said Arthur. "I was exaggerating. Once I figured out that it was happening, I learned that when his head started to bob, all I had to do was ask about the house he's having built in Truro. The contractor is way over budget, and they think they're going to have to spend this summer in a motel. None of the plumbing is in. This is inconvenient, because Green has invited family from the Midwest for a week in August. The plane tickets have already been purchased."

"Is that what you talk about?" asked Icarus Prentice.

"Well, it's kind of flattering to have your psychiatrist ask for your opinion," said Arthur.

"What does he ask you about?"

"If they do come, he wants to know if he has to pay for part of their motel costs. If they don't come, he wants to know if he has to pay for the cheap plane tickets they bought and can't get a refund on."

"What did you tell him?"

"I didn't have to tell him anything. All I had to do was nod. He talked for a while about how beautiful that part of the coastline is, and how many people without relatives in the area come there. So he thought he would encourage his sister and brother-in-law to come and stay in a motel, but he would leave the final decision up to them. That way he figured that if they canceled, he could go on about how disappointed he was and they'd be too embarrassed to ask him to pay for the tickets they didn't use. And if they did come, he figured he wouldn't pay for their motel. Then at the end of the week, he'd bring the whole bunch out to dinner at this place that serves fresh lobster."

"And what did you say?"

"I said it sounded reasonable."

"So you didn't really give him advice?"

"Actually, I did. He was also considering the possibility of suing the contractor for the delay and getting enough money to pay for his own motel as well as that of his sister's family."

"Are you kidding?"

"No, it was something he was considering. So I asked if he had anybody in the family who was a good lawyer, who would take the case for free. He said no. So I said he shouldn't try and sue the contractor. If he lost, he'd have to pay all the motel bills and the lawyer's fees. I said that he should let the contractor finish the house, and then if he still felt that he'd been treated badly, he could refuse to pay the last bills."

"That sounds reasonable."

"I thought so."

"But is it worth fifty dollars an hour for you to give legal advice to your psychiatrist?"

"That's what I'm not sure about."

"I'll tell you what," said Icarus. "If you don't think it's worth spending money on Green, just stop going. But if you ever feel the need to go back, you should tell me."

"Okay," said Arthur. "That seems fair."

"I can't believe you did that," said Faith, when Arthur told her what had happened. "You gave up your therapy and the money as well. What's your father going to do with the extra cash?"

"That's his business."

"Fine," said Faith. "I can see just how much you've gained in two years of psychotherapy. I thought the whole idea of this process was for you to learn to stand up for yourself."

Green wasn't any happier about Arthur's decision than Faith had been. Arthur had agreed with Green that they should devote several sessions to a discussion of what it meant to cut off their relationship. But whenever Arthur tried to bring it up, the doctor would say that it was his professional opinion that Arthur shouldn't stop therapy. Arthur would disagree. Then they'd talk about masturbation. After several months of this, Arthur told Green that he wouldn't be coming anymore. "I have to act on what I believe," Arthur said.

"I think you should act on what you believe," said Green. "I'm not at all sure you're right about what you think you believe."

"I've been telling you this for months now," Arthur said finally, "and I don't care if you believe me, this is the last session."

"But I don't think you find therapy unpleasant," said Green. "I think you're stopping it to save your father's money."

"That's exactly what I'm trying to do," said Arthur.

Green moved around in his chair, steepled his fingers and began to speak. "There comes a time in every child's development when he realizes that he's an individual with specific needs. Sometimes children don't make this break. They go all through life as extensions of people around them, and any discovery of individual identity becomes a fearsome revelation." He paused now and rubbed his nose with the back of one hand. "You're one of those children. Sometimes you think you're Faith. Sometimes you think you're your father. Sometimes you think you're your mother. That's why you're always trying to kill your mother in your imagination."

"That's not my mother I'm trying to kill," said Arthur. "That's Sophia Loren or Barbara Stanwyck."

"Honestly now," said Green. "What did Barbara Stanwyck ever do to you?"

"It's not what she did to me," said Arthur. "It's that I'd like to imagine her dying in my arms."

"Why not just lying in your arms?" said Green. "Why does she have to die?"

"I don't think I could convince her to just lie there," said Arthur, and he wondered what sort of chances Green would have getting a date with Barbara Stanwyck. "I don't know why I have these violent fantasies. That's why I came to you. I want to figure out why I'm so angry. I want to figure out why I can't make my wife happy. I think the two are connected."

"That may be why you think you came to me," said Green. "But it's not why you actually came."

"Why did I actually come then?" asked Arthur.

Green shrugged charmingly. "You came because your wife wanted you to come. Now you're quitting for your father. You think that you should save your father's money because you think you're part of him. You work for a magazine because he is a writer. And it's not just your parents you're confused about. You're also confused about me. And you hardly know me. I have been flattered by your interest in the Truro house, but it also seemed odd to me that you should be so fascinated with something that had nothing to do with you. I suppose it's conceivable that at some point Joyce and I might have invited you and your family up for a long weekend. But actually it's unlikely. I worried about that. I talked with Joyce about it. I didn't bring it up here yet, because I thought that it would come out naturally in the course of our work. Now that you've decided to suspend treatment—against my better judgment—I think that it's something you should try to be more aware of."

"But I do care about other people," said Arthur. "I'm interested in them. I care about Faith. I care about my father's finances. Isn't caring about others more than you care about yourself the definition of empathy?"

"No," said Green. "It's the definition of arrested develop-

ment. And I don't know how anyone's going to get you un-
stuck if you stop seeing a professional. Your father's a very
successful man. He must have enough money to continue
helping you."

"How much money my father has is no concern of yours,"
said Arthur.

"You're right about that," said Green. "But you've hired
me to make your mental health my concern. I'm certain that
if I phone your father and present him with the situation, he'll
be happy to continue to pay."

"You will not phone my father," said Arthur.

"What are you afraid of?" asked Green.

"It's not that I'm afraid, it's just that I don't want to waste
my father's money."

"And you consider yourself to be a waste of money?"

"In this case."

Green stood up. Arthur couldn't remember him ever standing up before during a session. "That's one of the saddest
things I've ever heard," said Green. "You really have no
idea."

"I have no idea about what?"

"You have no idea about who you are. And your problem
is compounded by the fact that your father is famous. A great
many people associate with you because of their interest in
your father. I wouldn't be candid if I didn't admit that part
of my interest in you relates to your father. And I don't think
there need be anything wrong with this. You can take advantage of the fact that other people confuse you with your father
as long as you know what's going on. But you're as confused
as they are. You don't know where you begin and he ends.
You don't know where anybody else begins and you end, but
the confusion is most pernicious in the case of your father.
Now we have ten minutes left in this session, and we should
use this time to try and map out what we hope to achieve in
the next few months. I think we can expect to make enormous
progress."

"If we didn't make progress in the last two years, why should we make it in the next few months?" said Arthur. His voice was now trembling with anger.

"This attempt to break off therapy indicates a new seriousness on your part," said Green. "We can take advantage of that and move ahead."

"No," said Arthur. "This attempt to break off therapy indicates an attempt to break off therapy." Arthur got out of his chair and took his jacket off the coat rack. "It doesn't happen often," he said, "and I apologize to Dr. Freud, but sometimes things are exactly what they appear to be. If there are ten minutes left in this session, I want you to accept them as a gift. If you think that all generosity is an expression of illness, then you may see this last gesture as a cry of desperation. But you might remember that you have been charging me a lot of money, and that you have often been tired and distracted." Then he walked out. He didn't slam the door, but he did close it. The patient for the next session was waiting in the hallway on a folding chair.

"You can go in now," said Arthur. "He needs you."

This wasn't exactly the end of the incident. Despite his apparently successful differentiation from his own mother, the late Mrs. Green, Arthur's psychiatrist did not call Icarus Prentice. Faith, however, showed a high degree of successful self-actualization in her insistence that Arthur get $50 a week from his father.

"He gave the money to you before, and he can go on giving it. We still need it. We need it more now."

So, having had a fight with his psychiatrist on a Thursday, Arthur spent a Saturday visiting his father. Icarus was delighted to see the van come down the hill to his house.

"You can drive to the Boxers' stable with me," he said. "With your help, and your van, we can make quite a haul." The Boxers had horses, and the haul Icarus Prentice was planning on was horseshit. Horseshit was the secret of Icarus Prentice's tomatoes."

"I'm writing an article for the local paper about tomatoes," said Icarus. "Help me with the shit and I'll mention your name. I'll make you famous."

"Good," said Arthur. "I'd like to be famous for shit."

They got four garbage pails full, and the whole time Arthur was shoveling manure, he was phrasing his request for money. But he still hadn't said word one when they'd unloaded the garbage pails at the end of the vegetable garden and then rinsed them out with a hose. Afterward they both showered. Arthur dressed in some of his old clothes, and they made a simple lunch of cheese, fruit and crackers. And gin. Arthur had most of the fruit and crackers, Icarus had most of the gin. Then Arthur and his father talked about the new Roth novel. "Gorgeous," said Icarus Prentice.

"That's right," said Arthur, "but I also thought it was incredibly depressing." They talked about the new Updike novel. "Talk about depressing," said Arthur.

"That's right," said Prentice, "but he seems to have been able to describe exactly what it would be like to live in the second circle of hell."

Arthur never did bring up the money. When he got home, Faith met him at the door.

"Did you ask him?" she wanted to know.

Arthur lied. "Yes," he said.

"And what did the old man say?"

"He said no."

"Bastard," said Faith.

SEVENTEEN

For miners it's the rumble of the cave-in. Police dread the crack of a pistol, and the men who walk the tightrope wake up at night in a cold sweat with the memory of that slight scuffing that means the slipper has lost the wire. At *The American Reader* the noise they all feared, as Captain Hook feared the ticking clock, was the rush of blood a man hears in his own ears right before sleep. Editors of *The American Reader* were not supposed to sleep at their posts. It wasn't just the work you didn't do while sleeping. Losing consciousness was considered the demonstration of a bad attitude; it showed a certain biological lack of seriousness.

When Arthur was moved out of Josephine's office and into his own, the ladies chipped in and bought a miniature chest in yellow plastic with white drawers. "For paper clips," Josie explained. There was a ceremony, a selection of prints and the ordering of filing cabinets. When the hubbub died down, he found himself in solitary splendor, with only his work and the passage of time to contemplate.

The round clock above his doorway was just like the clocks they'd used in study halls when he was in school. In the main study hall at The Choate School there had been a sign under the clock that read: TIME WILL PASS, WILL YOU? Arthur had wondered then. He wondered now.

On his first morning alone, the fledgling copy editor got the opening pages of "Does Monogamy Promote Longevity? Seven Scientists Respond," and all of a piece titled "Henry Ford: Genius Americanus." On his second day he got the closing of "Blueberries: Feast on a Bush." Bear berries are the largest of the cultivated highbush variety, and grow to about seven-eighths of an inch in diameter. A copydesk editor was expected to read sections of this obvious prose two or three times over at a sitting. On his third day Arthur got all eight pages of a hefty essay titled "Say 'No!' to Government Waste," and all four pages of "Monterey, California: Food-Stamp Capital of the World." This story began:

"Mimi Hassler leaves the front door of her well-kept ranch house fifteen minutes early on Thursday mornings. In her right hand the slim young attorney carries a smart leather attaché case. In her left hand is a large green garbage bag.

" 'Wednesday is food-stamp day,' she explains. 'They all go to Gourmet Grocers at the corner of Morningside and Broad, and come down my street eating, drinking and discarding the empties as they walk. By the time I've cleaned out my flower bed, the garbage bag is half-filled with empty Dr Pepper cans and Hostess wrappers.'

"But the problem goes well beyond litter, according to Marshall Longman, president of the Monterey Citizens Watchdog Committee. He claims that this subculture is composed of the graduates of a local drug-addiction program. 'We are paying for those cupcakes,' he said. 'They get sober and then they go on welfare. And most of them are more than capable of doing a good day's work. This is a classic case of a program that was designed to help the legitimately indigent, and has spawned a new and pernicious culture.'

"According to the Monterey County Department of Social Services, there were four thousand names on the dole in 1975. Longman has estimated that a third of these people are the young, healthy and well-educated children of the upper middle class.

" 'One of the regulars at the Gourmet Grocery is a doctor of law," according to Longman.

" 'Our problem is location,' he continued, 'The sand on our beach is white and fine. We've got a great climate year-round. The cannery buildings provide shelter when it does rain.'

" 'If the country ran a food-stamp-abuse contest,' said former California governor Ronald Reagan, 'Monterey would win hands down.' "

This was a final proof, so the short item used to fill out the last page was already set in type. It was about a dry cleaning establishment in Columbus, Ohio, so pestered with requests for tailoring jobs that it had changed its name to The Lilies of the Field. When asked about the name, the proprietor would reply tartly, "We do not reap, neither do we sew." Arthur took out his red pencil and wrote: "Ed: should we use this filler, since it refers to a Bible quotation that exactly contradicts the theme of our Monterey story?"

The activity woke him up for a minute, but almost immediately he found himself moving back toward a snooze. He opened his window. Fresh air is supposed to be invigorating. He tried to keep himself alert by resting his chin on a sharpened pencil while he read. He imagined the point of the pencil driving up through his skin and spearing his tongue. It didn't happen. His unconscious kept outsmarting him. His head would bob to his chest, and he'd find that he'd moved the pencil. He went to the bathroom every time he thought of it, which was three or four times an hour.

He was visited one afternoon during his first week alone by

an advertising salesman named Jeff Lloyd. Jeff was about Arthur's age. His clothes weren't quite as good as those commonly worn by the editors, but his eyes were bright.

"You're Prentice, right?" he said, standing uncertainly in the doorway.

"That's right," said Arthur.

"You liked grammar?" asked Lloyd, settling himself in Arthur's armchair.

"Not particularly," said Arthur.

"But that's what you do here, right?" said Lloyd. "Grammar, spelling."

"Yeah, that's what I do."

"I couldn't do that," said Lloyd. "I don't like little things. Details. They don't interest me."

Arthur shrugged.

"I went to Sleepy Hollow with your wife," said Lloyd. "Or at least I think I did. Is your wife a big, good-looking girl?"

"Yes," said Arthur. "That's my wife."

"I used to go to the football games, but I didn't go to see the game. Football bores me. I went to watch your wife cheer. I hope you don't mind my saying this, but that girl was built. It's really sort of a compliment."

"I guess," said Arthur.

"You like your office?" asked Lloyd.

"Yes," said Arthur, looking around as if he hadn't noticed.

"I didn't get an office like this until I'd been here five years," said Lloyd. "They had me out there beating the pavement, and when I was in the building, I had to share space. But I'm not one of the people who resents the advantages editorial employees have always had. You know Palumbardo?"

"I don't know him," said Arthur. "I've heard of him."

"Well, old Repeat gets steamed," said Lloyd.

"Repeat?" asked Arthur.

"That's what we call Palumbardo," said Lloyd. "It's a nickname he picked up when he worked out West. I don't know what it means, but it's easier to spell than Palumbardo. Anyway, Repeat has a case. If it weren't for him, you know, you wouldn't sell so many magazines. That one guy came up with a good quarter of the circulation."

Lloyd explained that the U.S. circulation had been about twelve million when Palumbardo introduced the sweepstakes. "Like all mail-order houses," Lloyd said, "our number-one problem is that people don't open the mail. The sweepstakes cured that. We sent out an outsized envelope—people always open the first outsized envelope they get—and in it we say that the addressee may already have won a million dollars. All they have to do to collect is to send in this card we've enclosed.

"Nowadays we have to state explicitly that ordering one of our products doesn't improve their chances," he said. "But it doesn't matter, because most people don't believe us anyway. They think that if they buy something they have a better chance to win. It costs, what, four dollars and thirty-five cents to subscribe to The Magazine for a year, and they figure that it's worth betting that much to get a million."

Lloyd picked up the miniature plastic dresser on Arthur's desk and began to fiddle with the drawers. "Every piece of mail we sent them has the word *sweepstakes* on it. They think it might be a note telling them where to pick up their million. So they open the envelope. And once you've got them opening the mail, it's only a matter of time before they'll buy something else."

"Palumbardo thought that up?" asked Arthur.

"That's right. Just about everybody in mail order does it now, but we were the first. That one change took the circulation in this country from just over twelve million to just under eighteen. We've had a couple of cease and desist orders brought against us, but we persevere."

Arthur smiled.

"That's our brilliance," said Lloyd. "What we send through the mail is what sets us apart. I had them put me on the master list. I can't win because I'm a company employee, but the stuff is amazing. We've got these people in the palms of our hands. For a lot of them, *The American Reader* is their only regular correspondent."

"I've never seen that stuff," said Arthur.

"Here," said Lloyd. "Give me your name. I'll put you on the list. Understand that you can't win."

"I understand," said Arthur. He took a piece of paper and wrote out his name and home address. Lloyd folded the paper carefully and put it in his jacket pocket.

"What gets old Repeat," said Lloyd, "is that Fallow doesn't really seem to like him much. The old man's one contribution to the whole thing was to insist that they run a little sweepstakes in the cafeteria. He didn't like the fact that employees weren't eligible for the big sweepstakes. He still hasn't taken Palumbardo on a rafting trip. All the founder's favorites are sent to Outward Bound."

Lloyd shook the miniature plastic dresser, and then put it back on Arthur's desk. "Say hello to Faith for me, will you? Tell her I used to sit in the first row of bleachers. I had a hat that said Harley-Davidson on it."

"You had a motorcycle?" Arthur asked.

"No," said Lloyd. "Just the hat."

For Arthur the problem of staying awake was aggravated by the fact that he had never taken typographical errors seriously. Practically every page of *The High Cliff Bugler* had had a mistake or two. On one admittedly unusual day the name of the President of the United States had been spelled three different ways: Richard Milne Nixon, Richard Milhous Nickerson and Richard Mixon. There was an "Ides of March snowstorm" on March third. Even the day and date—printed on every page—were sometimes incorrect for 54,000 regular subscribers.

The vast majority of mistakes went unremarked upon, but one reader sent a letter that was passed around the city desk. "Dear Editor," it began. "I have been married for 35 years. My wife is an excellent cook, but I am not supposed to take her cooking for granted. So every Wednesday she puts on her hat and I take her to dinner. We clean our plates, but we also notice how much the food costs, and how much less we enjoy it than the food we eat at home. When I got back from work last Tuesday, Louise was wearing one of her go-to-dinner dresses. I said it was Tuesday, but she showed me THE BUGLER, which said that it was Wednesday. We went out to dinner. Then on Wednesday it was Wednesday again in THE BUGLER. I took her out again. Since I am not a rich man, and since the bird my wife eats like is the emu, I think you should pay for one of these evenings. . . ."

Given this sort of background, it was difficult for Arthur to keep himself awake in the afternoon with the fear of an extra comma appearing on page 167 of the February edition of *The American Reader*. A private office was a good thing under the circumstances, but one of the many unwritten laws at World Headquarters was that office doors had to be kept open at all times. A mild man in most matters, Mr. Fallow was strict about this. As a young executive he would some-times march through the halls on an afternoon banging open office doors. Now Doc patrolled with a clipboard.

Arthur was told of one young man, now managing editor of *Professional Boxing Magazine*, who had learned to line the spine of *The New York Times* with pencils, and prop his feet up on his desk just so. Thus, with his heart beating forty times a minute and his oxygen consumption below that of an Indian yogi, he was able to give the impression of someone who was scouring the paper for jokes, or the rarer sentimental or jingoistic article suitable for reprint. Then he made the mistake of giving Mr. Fallow's secretary something to type, and she'd returned it while he was deep into rapid eye movements.

But the saddest of all the sleep legends was that of Little Emily Carter. She had been at the company for twenty years, starting as a receptionist and working her way up the logjam of the editorial masthead to the position of associate editor. She was a spinster. Her bulletin board had a picture of her niece. In her wallet she carried a photo of a collie mix named Washington Irving Carter. She owned a small house near the library in Paradise. Her contentment was marred, however, by the knowledge that she was earning less than half of what was earned by young men with her title.

Finally, after an alumni reunion at Vassar, during which an old roommate named Leslie Kateland made fun of the outdated style of Emily's skirt, she sent a memo to Dean Nichols. Emily wouldn't have given credence to a concept as radical as that of equal pay for equal work, but she could lament convincingly.

Nichols found something endearing about an eighty-seven-pound woman, even if she was fifty-three years old. He brought the matter up with his wife. Pamela Nichols—a Holyoke girl—was unsympathetic. "Where's she going to go, *Time* magazine? Send her a note. Mention the trouble you've been having with the Spanish edition. You can recognize the excellence of her contribution if you want, but don't give her more money. She'll be flattered that you responded at all."

It was about a week after Nichols got Emily's memo that his periodontist canceled an afternoon session and he decided to take the free time to walk down to Miss Carter's office. He thought a 35 percent increase was enough for starters. If she pointed out that this still didn't give her parity with men at the same level of expertise, he had a little speech prepared about the realities of the job market. But he expected that Emily would be extremely thankful, as indeed she would have been.

It happened that Miss Carter had been out to lunch that day with another member of the Paradise Historical Society, and while she hadn't had anything to drink, she had finished her chicken salad and eaten two pieces of the seven-grain bread that was baked on the premises. This was quite a heavy intake for a woman of her size. She returned to her desk and opened the *Ladies' Home Journal*. She had finished the editor's note before she drifted off into a pleasant dream in which Vassar and *The American Reader* were combined into a single institution. Emily was appointed proctor of the dormitory in which Leslie Kateland lived. She was just giving Mrs. Kateland two demerits for an untidy bed when the Dean came into her office. Emily was cocked back in her swivel chair with her mouth wide open. The fillings in the back of her mouth were silver. Those closer to the front were gold. Nichols sat on the edge of the desk and took a piece of typewriter paper from the neat pile that Emily kept there. He uncapped the Waterman fountain pen he'd gotten for Father's Day and wrote:

Dear Miss Carter,

We do appreciate your contributions, but I'm afraid that pressing financial needs in other quarters make it necessary for me to turn down your request for a raise at this time.

But keep up the good work. And get some rest.

With love,
Dean Nichols

EIGHTEEN

Arthur was at his post on the copydesk when the phone rang. It was 1 P.M. He was just back from a lunch with the ladies at the cafeteria. He'd had the Waldorf salad. His mouth tasted of mayonnaise.

"Is this Arthur Prentice?" the voice wanted to know.

"Yes."

"This is Dr. Sneeling. I'm afraid I've got some disturbing news," he said in a rush. "But it's not nearly as bad as it could have been. He's already much better."

"Who's much better?" said Arthur, and he felt suddenly as if he'd been hit over the head by a phantom two-by-four. There was a distant ringing in his ears, and the light in his office went from yellow to white.

"You shouldn't be alarmed. He's at Phelps. In intensive care."

"This is my father you're talking about?"

"That's right. The staff at Phelps is really excellent. They know who your father is. He'll get the best care. And of course your father's a strong man, but I'm afraid his constitution has been weakened a great deal over the last few years. The trouble is that we're going to have to detox him right away."

"What does that mean?"

"His situation indicates the need for an immediate withdrawal of alcohol."

"That sounds like a good idea," Arthur said, and he picked up a pen and began drawing X's on the page of his opened desk calendar.

"I think it is, but in another less dramatic case, we might have given some alcohol in IV and dealt with the heart condition first. Then we would start the detox. I'm afraid your father now has something of an allergic reaction to alcohol, so we're going to have to withdraw it right away. This will mean an additional strain on his system," Sneeling said, and then paused.

"Yes," said Arthur.

"You agree?" said Sneeling.

"I don't know," said Arthur. "You're his doctor."

"But you agree that we should detox him right away?"

"I haven't thought about it," Arthur said. Now he had stopped drawing X's, and found that he had written "M A L" in block letters.

"I expect he will be fine," said Sneeling, "but I wanted you to be apprised of the risks."

"Thanks," said Arthur. He had written "P R A," also in block letters.

"We'll just have to see how he responds."

"When did this all happen?" asked Arthur, "C T I C E," he wrote.

"We don't know exactly when it began. He called us this morning. Very noble and all. Just said he was under the weather. But there was something about his voice that worried me. So I sent an ambulance. And he had had a heart attack."

"But he's all right?" Arthur asked, drawing a circle around the word: MALPRACTICE.

"He's all right for now. It's a good hospital," the doctor said. "The problem will be in the next few days. Your father is going to have to detox, and he may hallucinate. If that happens, he may get violent. A member of the family should be there. Your father's housekeeper is with him now, but I think she'd like to go home."

"Is he conscious?" Arthur asked, ripping the page out of his calendar and crumping it into a ball.

"Well, yes and no. He's awake, but he's not making perfect sense either. The problem is that somebody has to be there with him in intensive care. Mrs. Carpenter is exhausted. I wondered if you could come in this afternoon and take over for a while. All you have to do really is sit there."

Josephine was sympathetic, and Arthur was at the hospital in twenty-five minutes. He stopped in the gift shop, but he couldn't think of anything his father would like. He wouldn't want a stuffed dog that played "Those Were the Days" when you wound it up. He wouldn't want a chocolate rose. He might want a package of Marlboros, but Arthur didn't think that a package of Marlboros was appropriate for a man in the intensive-care unit.

Arthur took the elevator with a fat man with a mop and bucket. The man appeared to be in his late fifties. He had quite a large stomach, the features of which were clearly visible through the fabric of his T-shirt. This shirt had been distributed to commemorate a tour by the Rolling Stones.

By the time Arthur had relieved Mrs. Carpenter it was almost 2 P.M. He sat on a metal stool beside his father's hospital bed. Icarus had a translucent plastic tube running out of each nostril, and his arms were fastened to the rails of the bed with thick leather straps. He seemed to be sleeping. He seemed to be having horrible dreams.

At 3 P.M. Icarus woke up. He called Arthur over to the side of the bed and whispered. "I don't want electric shock," he said. "I don't mind the pain, but it could cause a serious imbalance."

Arthur nodded and went back to his stool. Icarus fell into a more restful sleep.

When Arthur took over on the following afternoon, Icarus asked him for a cigarette and a drink. Arthur refused. This made the old man furious, and when an attendant came into the room to check on another patient, Icarus signaled to him as if he were a waiter and ordered a double martini.

"I'd ask my son," he explained in a croaking voice, "but he's a teetotaler. We used to call him Ariadne the most pure."

The attendant looked away.

"Joke," said Icarus. "Just a joke."

The attendant made some adjustments on a piece of machinery attached to another patient.

"The allusion is to mythology," Icarus said.

The attendant seemed not to hear. He checked the adjustment once more and left the room.

Icarus settled back into his bed. "I've raised a prig," he muttered quietly. "God forgive me for it, but I've raised a joyless prig."

On the third day Icarus was subdued. He didn't speak to Arthur at all. Arthur thought maybe he'd lost his voice, but when the nurse came around with the medications, Icarus was quite pleasant, even charming. Had Miss Shapiro ever been to Lincoln Center? Yes, of course the sound was much better in Carnegie Hall.

Icarus didn't say anything to anyone on the fourth day, until Arthur was getting ready to leave. The he signaled for his son to come over to the side of the bed.

"Happy," he said. "This must make you very happy."

Arthur shrugged. "I'm glad you're getting better," he said. "If that's what you mean."

I. S. Prentice nodded and smiled. "That's what I meant," he said. "That's exactly what I meant."

Arthur was getting ready to leave his office in Paradise on the afternoon of the fifth day when the phone rang. It was Doctor Sneeling.

"He's checked himself out," said Sneeling. "He's gone home."

"How is he?" Arthur asked.

"Well, he's not completely recovered yet," said Sneeling. "I would have liked to keep him in for longer, but I can't keep him against his will. He hates the hospital, you know."

Arthur did know. "But how will he be from now on?" asked Arthur. "Will he recover completely?"

"He's got the constitution of a horse," said Sneeling. "His life-style would have killed a weaker man years ago. And I don't think any real damage has been done to the heart. So he could have what amounts to a full recovery."

"Well, that's great news," said Arthur.

"It is," said Sneeling. "But that's only if he stops drinking. If he starts drinking again, he might die tomorrow."

Arthur took in a deep breath. "Does he know that, for sure?" he asked. "Have you made him understand that?"

There was a long pause, and then the doctor made a sound that might, under other circumstances, have passed for a chuckle. "Your father is an extremely intelligent man," he said. "And I've explained his situation in terms that anybody could understand. I told him that if he takes another drink now, it will be the same as playing with a loaded gun. But then I've been saying as much to him for years."

NINETEEN

When *The American Reader* ran an article, it almost always ran a joke as well. Pieces were cut so that there was room for a laugh between indignations. Once in a while the jokes were good enough to bring home. "This guy falls off a cliff," Arthur told Faith one evening, "and just over the edge he finds a root to grab onto. The root holds, but now he's hanging over a two-hundred-foot drop with no way to climb back up. He shouts, 'Help! Help! Is there anybody up there?' A deep booming voice comes back from the top of the cliff.

" 'This is God,' said the voice. 'I can save you, but you have to believe.'

" 'I believe, I believe,' says the guy.

" 'All right,' booms the voice. 'Then let go.'

"There was a long pause, and then the guy calls out again: 'Anybody else up there?' "

Faith laughed. "So you like it? You're getting along?"

"No, not really."

"Look, I know you have a low self-image, but I do expect you to be able to get along at *The American Reader*. I mean, water seeks its own level, but how low can you go?"

"It's not what you think," said Arthur. "Most of the people who work for The Magazine are exactly the sort who would not be caught dead with *The American Reader*."

The cynical explanation was that Fallow resented the upper classes, and got back at them by hiring their children, giving them comfortable offices, fat salaries and nothing to do.

"The names might have come off the roll of English dead at Waterloo," Arthur told Faith. "They shave before dinner, lather with badger tail and are clubbable to a man."

James Horster III was the exception that proved the rule. First he was some sort of fundamentalist. He kept his black hair oiled and combed in an understated version of the D.A. or Duck's Ass, a style that had been popular in the 1950s among those considering a career at the local Texaco. Horster didn't wear a crucifix, but he did own a purple cardigan sweater which had buttons that looked like miniature conch shells. He drove a lima bean–green Toyota with crushed velvet seats. His wife, Lavinia, bred miniature poodles.

It depended on one's political perspective whether or not Horster's supposed connection with the CIA made him a more or less pleasing prospect.

The sweater was hanging over the back of the visitor's chair when Horster sent his secretary to fetch Arthur from his post on the copydesk and bring him in for an interview. Horster was on the phone when Arthur came in. He squinted up through his cigarette smoke, pointed at the sweater and indicated with a wag of his head that Arthur should move it and take its place.

Arthur picked up the sweater with two fingers, moved it to the office coffee table and sat down. He looked at his hands.

Horster was cocked back into an enormous tufted leather desk chair. He was wearing a button-down wash and wear shirt. He was fat enough around the waist so that the middle button had come unfastened. He was being very jolly on the phone. "Tight as a box," he said. "I showed it to Mr. Fallow and he definitely wants it for February. Good solid stuff. Poetry, that's what it is. No, no, I mean it. There's nothing wasted. Of course we'll have to cut it in half, but it's going to be a painful process. And we'll see if we can't fatten that check a little." Every so often he'd creak back in his giant chair and roll his eyes at Arthur in order to indicate that he didn't mean a word he said.

Arthur sat. Finally, after a good eight minutes, Horster got off the phone. Then he called in his secretary. "Would you send Stanton J. Williams tear sheets of the last three pieces we ran on the dangers of cigarette smoke?" he said. "The address is in the Rolodex."

When she left, Horster lit up a fresh cigarette and fixed Arthur with two watery eyes.

"So do you miss newspaper work?"

"I miss some things."

"Did you know that I started out at a newspaper?"

"No, I didn't."

"Ever heard of *The Kansas City Star*? They used to call it the 'Star of the Midwest.' I worked on the rim. Do they still have rims on newspapers?"

"Sure, a place for the guys who handle layout and write the heads. They had one at the *Bugler*."

"But you weren't on it?"

"No, I wasn't."

"Pity, pity. I learned more in my time on the rim than I did in all the years I spent in college and graduate school. Do you know our director of circulation, Albert Palumbardo?"

"No, I don't. I mean I've heard of him, but I've never met him."

"He started out there too. He was in advertising. It was on

126

the rim that I learned about the economy of language. I wrote headlines."

"So you had to write to character length?"

"That's right. Sometimes you'd have room for eighteen characters on a big story. Many people don't read the story at all. What they read is the headline, so that headline had better be right. No room for the sort of self-expression your generation is always clamoring about. I've always thought that training has served me in good stead. It's hard to tell any story in eighteen characters, but it's a damn rare one that can't be told in two pages."

Arthur nodded. It hurt, but he nodded. *"War and Peace,"* he thought. *"Gatsby. Crime and Punishment."*

"I guess I've never told you this before," said Horster, "but I'm a great admirer of your father's work. Now there's a man who doesn't waste words. My favorite story is the one about the housewife who poisons her husband. You know the one I'm talking about?"

"You mean 'Botulism and Botticelli'?"

"Now that's my idea of the perfect portrait of the modern American woman." said Horster. "He's got her down to a tee. I can close my eyes and see that woman coming in to shore on a shell. I read somewhere that your mother had been a beauty queen, just like the character in the story."

"No, she wasn't a beauty queen."

"But she won some award?"

"Yes, but it was for poetry, although she was an attractive woman."

"A blonde?"

"No, she was not a blonde either. Her hair was red actually, a sort of Titian." Arthur stopped and cleared his throat. "But you know she's been dead for a couple of years now?"

Horster got up. "I heard," he said, walking over to the pedestal that held his unabridged Webster's II. "Titian, Titian, here it is. Venetian painter, no, that's not it. A reddish yellow color Titian used for women's hair. Blonde is what we'd call it, right?"

"Her hair went more to red, but in some lights I suppose you could call her a blonde."

"Anybody in your family ever get sick after a big meal?" asked Horster, and he rocked back in his chair and chuckled. "You know, I'm rusty, but I could still write that headline in less than eighteen characters. "PEN MAN POISONED. They'd have to give me a subhead and I've got that too: 'Famed Author Dies in True-Life Reenactment of His Own Story.' "

"Can I have a cigarette?" asked Arthur.

"Certainly," said Horster, and he shook a Kool out of the package on his desk, and then passed Arthur a blue plastic lighter.

"My parents got along famously," said Arthur, after he had the cigarette going.

"I know, that's just the point I was trying to make," said Horster. He grinned and lit himself a cigarette. "I know that you didn't apply for the copydesk at first," he said. "You wanted to be an associate editor, didn't you?"

"Yes," said Arthur.

"But you don't hate the job you have now?"

"No, it's good for me to learn how important the little things are."

"Well, I want you to know that we haven't forgotten that you want to be an associate editor. I don't think that every associate editor we have now is exactly tops, and they should be. What do you know about Mongoose, for instance?"

"I like him. He's smart."

"I know he's smart. And don't take this the wrong way, but I sometimes wonder if he doesn't allow himself to be too easily distracted. This can happen."

"I suppose," said Arthur.

"What about the copydesk? Are the people there earning their keep?"

"I think so."

"Good, that's what I would have supposed. Although that's also a fat department. A good one, but a fat one." He wagged his head. "No, Arthur, we can't relax. We've got to keep this place moving. It's so comfortable here that people are inclined to forget that we're trying to operate a business."

Arthur nodded.

"It's hard to tell what will happen over time," Horster continued, "but I suspect that when we do hire a new associate editor, you'll be the one. Anybody suggests that we get somebody new from the outside and they're going to have to answer to me."

"I appreciate your support," said Arthur.

"But you do think you'd be satisfied with an editor's responsibilities?" asked Horster. "You don't secretly want to be a writer?"

"No," said Arthur. "I enjoyed working at the newspaper, but I think I'm going to like magazine work better."

"Good, good," said Horster, "because editors don't write. There are no hard-and-fast rules here, of course, but if there were, that would be one of them. Take George Mayfair. He came four or five years after I did. He had been a writer for *Time* before we hired him. He started out on a story, and Fallow sent him a kill fee with a note suggesting that he cease and desist. So Mayfair went in to see the old man, and Fallow asked him what he thought of the benefits, which were generous even then. Mayfair said he liked them. So Fallow asked him if he had had an opportunity to use the dental insurance. Mayfair said he hadn't, but that he was pleased to know that it was there. So Fallow is supposed to have said, 'I am sure, George, that you would have written me a beautiful story, but there are thousands of people out there eager to write for me, and I don't have to pay for their teeth.' "

After this interview, Arthur went immediately to see Mrs. Carstairs. Josephine could almost always make him feel better. She was wearing a silk blouse clasped at the neck with a small gold pin. She had on her bifocals, and Arthur wondered where her breasts were under the puff of her blouse. Josephine was reading, but when she heard Arthur's footsteps she looked up.

He came in the door and leaned against the far wall. "I just got called in by Horster," he said.

"That's good," she said. "Horster is Mrs. Fallow's favorite editor. I guess she's made uncomfortable by all those pretty boys on the masthead. They used to go to Sotheby's together to buy furniture."

"He gives me the creeps."

Josephine nodded. "It's been said that he's one of the only men in the world who can be obsequious and overbearing in the same instant. Did you notice the gills?"

"Gills, are you kidding? No, I didn't notice the gills."

"Well, next time you see him, watch closely when he turns his head to the side, and you'll see the top one. There are three parallel lines on each side of his neck. Only one of them shows above the collar of a dress shirt, but when we have the company picnic you can see them all. They're vestigial gill slits. They were open when he was born. His parents had them sewed shut. If Darwin had had Horster he could have saved boat fare to the Galápagos."

"Great, I'm going to have a fish for a mentor."

"He wouldn't be a bad mentor to have. Fallow once said that Horster was one of the only people on his staff he really trusted."

"But he's so oily."

"That's not the impression he gives to Fallow. To Fallow he looks like loyalty with an education. You know he's a lawyer? And he has a doctorate in political science from Ohio University, and a masters in journalism from Columbia?"

"No, I didn't know, although I'm sure he would have told me in time. But I wouldn't think that higher education would necessarily make somebody a good editor for a general-interest magazine."

"There are people here who are brilliant editors, and Fallow likes them for that. There are also people here who Fallow just likes, and so he lets them be editors. I guess the most famous case of that is Paul Winston. He was working at the Arthur Murray Dance Studio in Yonkers when Mr. and Mrs.

Fallow decided they wanted to learn to do the lindy. They liked him, hired him and he worked here for decades."

"In what capacity? Dance editor."

"No, he was book editor. In fact he had Arnold Baker's job."

"Was he any good?"

"I suppose he was all right. And Horster's all right too. It's just that editing isn't his primary talent. He's better at pleasing Fallow than he is at cutting magazine articles."

"How does he please Fallow?"

"Well, he's a kind of caricature of Fallow, a sort of fun-house mirror. He's extremely religious, much more devout than even The Founder himself, but then The Founder is much more devout than most of his editors. Horster is also much more sentimental than Fallow, although Fallow is much more sentimental than any of the others."

"But Horster doesn't seem likable."

"To Fallow he's likable. Wouldn't you like someone who exhibited and then defended all your least defensible characteristics?"

"No, I certainly would not."

"I guess I wouldn't either. But then neither of us is ever going to found a publishing dynasty."

It was trash day, and on the way home from work that evening, Arthur stopped to examine a rocking chair, which had been put out at the curb by a neighbor. The chair was really and truly broken, but the pile of discards also included three metal army-surplus cartridge cases. Arthur put two of them in the back of the van. When he got home there was a note from Faith saying that she and her mother had taken Nathan shopping and would not return until 6 P.M.

Arthur kicked off his shoes and hung his suit jacket on a kitchen chair. He took a flashlight down from the top shelf of the broom closet. He put the cartridge cases and the light down beside the washing machine. He found the iron ring imbedded in the linoleum floor and lifted a section of flooring.

This was the trap door to the crawl space. Setting it to one side, Arthur then lowered himself through the hole.

Standing up straight, his shoulders came just to the level of the laundry-room floor. He took the cartridge boxes and put them on the cement floor at his feet. Then he got the flashlight, turned it on and put the end in his mouth. Crouching and holding the light in his mouth, Arthur moved to one wall of the crawl space and opened a green plastic garbage bag. This contained all of Arthur's worldly goods, or at least all the worldly goods that Faith didn't know about. There were two notebook journals—the ones he kept when he and Faith had broken up. They mentioned his admiration for other women. There was also a hunting knife with a chamois foot for a handle.

Arthur had brought the knife home to Upcounty Estates after one of his hundred-dollar visits to his father's house. "What do you want that for?" Faith had asked.

"I don't know," said Arthur. "To cut things. My father brought it back from Germany for me when I was ten or eleven. My mother said that if I didn't want it, she was going to throw it away."

"Well, I'm with your mother on this one," said Faith. "I won't have that thing around the house. You can put it right out with the trash."

Arthur put the cartridge cases beside the garbage bag, and then, almost on a whim, he put $5 in the bottom of each case. This left him just $7 to last the week. It was Tuesday.

TWENTY

"**A**ctually, he's an interesting character. You know, he lost his right foot in a streetcar accident in Munich when he was a young man. He says we should all stock up on crackers and canned water. He says nuclear war is survivable."

Faith wasn't impressed. "What do you expect him to say? He spent his whole life inventing a bomb, now he wants to see it used."

"I got to write the author's note. Going to have some of my own words in the magazine. Want to hear it?"

"Sure."

" 'Known as the father of the hydrogen bomb, nuclear physicist Edward Teller was born in Budapest in 1908. He came to this country in 1935 and worked on the Manhattan

Project.' I got to write it because everybody's in Monaco for an international conference, and Josie thought the piece needed an author's note."

"The boy at the dike."

"That's right."

"Anyway," said Faith, "I'm glad you got a chance to write something." And Arthur guessed that she was glad.

But a week later he came home scowling. The table was set with a hamburger at Arthur's place and a hamburger at Nathan's place and a plate of lettuce with vinegar for Faith.

Arthur took off his jacket, loosened his tie and sat down. Then he cut his piece of meat across the middle and put half of it on top of the lettuce on Faith's plate.

"Why'd you do that?" Faith wanted to know.

"I think you should eat some meat."

"What if I don't want to eat some meat?" asked Faith, and she took her plate to the garbage and put the hamburger in the pail. Then she went to the sink and washed off the lettuce leaves.

"This is absurd," said Arthur.

Nathan wanted to know what absurd was. Faith wanted to know why Arthur was in such a bad mood.

"I think you should eat something."

"I'll eat a frozen yogurt after dinner."

"I think you should eat some meat," said Arthur.

"There's protein in frozen yogurt," said Faith.

"There are fifteen grams of protein in a four-ounce yogurt," said Arthur. "An adult woman is supposed to get at least fifty grams a day."

"Did they kill your author's note?"

"I was talking about hamburgers."

"But they did kill it. The one about Teller."

"That's right."

"Well, good. They shouldn't be giving that old devil a platform."

"They didn't kill the article. They just killed the author's note."

Faith shrugged. "Listen, I think you should be looking for work," she said.

"Why do I have to eat my hamburger," asked Nathan, "if Mummy isn't eating hers?"

"Because Mummy is a Mummy, and you are a little boy," said Arthur.

The discussion was not resumed until that weekend. The "Mary Tyler Moore" and "Bob Newhart" shows had both been canceled for a special about a serial murderer. Faith didn't want to watch it.

"They say he's good-looking," she said, "but he's not."

Arthur tried to rub Faith's shoulder, and she shrugged him off. "I'll get you your frozen yogurt," he said, "but I do worry sometimes about your diet."

"I'm fat," said Faith.

"You are not fat," said Arthur. "How much do you weigh?"

"Almost one-eleven."

"That doesn't make you fat."

"But I feel fat. I feel monstrous."

"You're not. Sometimes I think you're actually malnourished."

"You want me to eat? Get me that frozen yogurt."

"Sure," said Arthur. "Do you want anything else?"

"Just a cup of tea," said Faith. "With Sweet 'N Low and a slice of lemon. And leave the bag in the cup. I like my tea strong. 'When I makes water, I makes water.' "

" 'When I makes tea, I makes tea,' " said Arthur, heading downstairs. He brought a tray back to the bedroom and put it down on the table at Faith's side of the bed. Faith was wearing a baby doll nightgown like the one worn by Doris Day in *Pillow Talk*, only the material on Faith's nightgown was frankly translucent. Through it Arthur could see her large white lace bra and a pair of dark blue bikini underpants. She was propped up in bed with three pillows. She leaned forward, took the tea from the tray and began to make loud sipping noises.

Arthur pulled over the chair from her dressing table and sat beside the bed. "Aren't you going to eat your yogurt?"

"I like it soft," said Faith. She tested the yogurt's surface with a spoon. "I still don't get what you like about working there," she said.

"You wanted me to work there."

"I thought you were going to get fabulously rich." She picked up the dish of frozen yogurt and began to run her spoon around the edge.

"I passed the editor-in-chief's tea trolley in the hall today. It smelled great. There were three silver chafing dishes and two silver pots. I saw a jar of orange marmalade from Fortnum and Mason. Dean Nichols has tea every afternoon when he's in the office. The night security guards polish the service."

Faith took a deep breath. "It sounds incredibly affected to me," she said.

"If you do something like that with style and you do it for fifteen years, then it's not an affectation anymore," said Arthur. "It passes for the real thing. And it's of a piece with the rest of his life. He hunts over a black Labrador named Lord Byron. When Nichols comes into the office on Saturday—which he does whenever his grandchildren are in town—he brings Byron. There are teeth marks on his desk from when Byron was a puppy."

"How much does he earn, this guy?" asked Faith. She had finished the yogurt. Now she lit a cigarette and put the burnt match into the empty plastic yogurt container.

"I thought you weren't going to smoke in the bedroom."

"But you know I love to have just one cigarette after dinner."

"Then maybe you should have dinner downstairs."

Faith inhaled deeply and blew the smoke out through her nose. "Do you really want to spend the night fighting about one cigarette?" she asked.

Arthur didn't say anything.

"Come here," said Faith. Arthur came over to the bed,

and she kissed him on the cheek. "You're so sweet when you get upset about my health," she said.

"You know I'd do anything for you," said Arthur.

"Anything?" asked Faith, smiling.

"Anything," said Arthur.

"You wouldn't go downstairs and get me an ashtray?"

Arthur smiled wanly.

"And a frozen Milky Way," she said.

"That's what I mean about your eating habits," he said.

"Well, maybe after the Milky Way, I'll have some cottage cheese," said Faith.

Arthur shrugged and went downstairs.

Faith cut up the Milky Way and began to suck on part of it while she smoked.

"How much does Nichols make anyway?" she asked.

"I guess about a million. That's what Mongoose said. He is chairman of the board, you know, as well as editor-in-chief."

"And what does he do, besides drinking tea and hunting?"

"He reads. He reads The Magazine right through every month. Everybody, even Fallow, recognizes that this must be a painful process for a man of his discernment."

"Don't people hate him?"

"No, they like him. It was because of him that Lisha once got a check for seven hundred fifty dollars for working over a weekend on a particularly difficult proof."

"Who's Lisha?"

"She's on the copydesk. She answers my phone sometimes."

"But that check must have been from Fallow?"

"Nichols plays Moses to Fallow's God. When Mrs. Fairchild was hurt in a car crash, Nichols gave Courtney a check for ten thousand dollars with a note that said, 'I know this can't make up for a mother's love, but please take a week off and then spend it on the best nanny that money can buy.' Fallow signed the check, but Nichols delivered it. And wrote the note."

Faith got out of bed and went into the bathroom. Arthur

could hear her peeing. Then she came back and got into bed. Arthur started to leave the room.

"No," said Faith. "You can stay tonight."

Arthur stripped to his Jockey underpants and got into bed behind her. Then he turned out the light. He lay on his side and put one arm around Faith's waist. He could feel the top part of his left arm up against the bottom of her bra.

The phone rang. Arthur picked up. It was Icarus. "Is this a bad time?" he asked.

"No," said Arthur.

"You weren't asleep?"

"No."

Faith sat up and lit another cigarette, putting the match into the ashtray Arthur had fetched.

"How's Faith?"

"She's fine. She's right here."

"And Nathan?"

"He's fine," said Arthur. "He's asleep. What about you?"

"Glad to be out of the hospital."

"I bet," said Arthur.

"I was wondering if you and Faith and Nathan would like to come over for dinner on Friday. I could grill some lamb."

"Great. Should we bring anything?"

"No, just come."

"Who was that?" asked Faith when Arthur got off the phone.

"My father. He wants us next Friday for dinner."

Faith got out of bed and pulled off her nightgown. "I'm so hot," she said. "I always get hot at this time of night."

"Is it all right?" Arthur asked. "About the dinner."

"You don't really want to go, do you?"

"I said we would."

Faith stiffened. "So you'll change your mind."

"What if I don't?"

"It's all right with me," said Faith crisply. "He didn't kill *my* mother."

Arthur got out of bed, picked up his clothes and went back

to the sewing room. It was an act of defiance, but he knew even then that the gesture was pathetic. He wasn't going to be eating grilled lamb anytime soon.

The alarm went off at 6 A.M. Arthur took the first shower. After he got out of the shower, he'd leave the water running for a couple of minutes. Faith hated to find the stall dirty.

He'd dress in the sewing room, go downstairs and make coffee for himself and tea for Faith. He'd bring Faith her tea in bed. Wake Nathan. Dress Nathan. Make Nathan a bowl of Cheerios. Put Nathan in front of the TV. Drink a second cup of coffee. Go back upstairs. Kiss Faith good-bye and drive to work.

But the next morning Faith wanted to talk. So she put on her bathrobe and brought her tea downstairs while Nathan was making a green plastic soldier swim through his cereal.

"I've got a plan," she said. "You want to stay at The Magazine?"

"At least for now."

"And I say we can't afford it, right?"

"Right."

"So you'll stay at The Magazine and we'll economize."

"That sounds all right," said Arthur, clearing away Nathan's cereal bowl. "Now go upstairs and get whatever it is you want for show and tell," he told the boy.

"But that means we're both going to have to give something up," said Faith. "Here's the new budget plan: I won't shop as much with my mother. We'll eat less red meat. We'll stop delivery of the daily *New York Times*. We can cut out the movies."

"Fine," said Arthur.

Faith paused to light a cigarette and wave out the match. "There's one more thing that I think you should at least consider," she said.

"What's that?"

"You're not going to like this."

"Try me."

"I think you should have a vasectomy."

Arthur was tying his necktie. "Isn't that a little drastic?" he asked.

"That's what men always say. A hysterectomy is a good idea, a small operation. A vasectomy, that's a big deal."

"I'm not suggesting you have a hysterectomy."

"But you'd like to be able to screw whenever the impulse arises."

Arthur sighed. "I'd like to be able to screw sometimes."

"Look, it's a very small operation. Just a couple of tiny pin pricks. Your insurance will pay for it. We'll save money on the gynecologist, and we won't have to worry about having children we can't afford."

"That's ridiculous," said Arthur. "Is this part of some campaign on PBS? Are they going to give you a free book bag?"

"A lot of people have had vasectomies."

"A lot of people sleep with their wives."

Faith pouted. "Why do you always have to bring that up?" she asked. "Besides, maybe if you had a vasectomy, we'd sleep together more."

"Maybe," said Arthur. "But that's a chance I'd just as soon not take."

TWENTY-ONE

The *American Reader* prided itself on monitoring a great many publications. The bulk of the articles digested came from a handful of prominent magazines, but once in a long while a joke or a short piece expressing the proper sentiments would turn up in a regional newspaper or a small monthly. None of the associate or senior editors wanted to cover these unlikely sources, but copy editors and secretaries were glad to. If an article was found in the *Beekeeper's Bible* or *The Northwest Oregon Express*, a great noise was made about it.

Arthur went to The Magazine's library. Rosemary Watts signed him up for a subscription to a Methodist newsletter printed in London, Ohio, and titled *We See His Face*. He would also cover the Sunday *Sacramento Bee*. Then he started staying late at work.

Every article in every magazine or newspaper was supposed to be rated by the first reader. Ratings were Usable, Possible and Not Usable. Articles rated were summarized and then judged by the first reader. The publications then went to a second reader, who was supposed to reread and rate all the key articles. The titles of the articles with their often contradictory evaluations were recorded in a black book that executive editors could look at when putting together an issue.

It wasn't always easy to distinguish between an article that was obvious or sentimental and an article that was just right. Mongoose, for instance, had been the first reader on "The Day My Son the Hippie Cut His Hair." He marked it Not Usable and followed up the rating with a hair-raising three-paragraph attack on the character and intelligence of the writer.

Unless there was a closing, the ladies of the copydesk all left the building when official hours were over at 4 P.M. The offices of The Magazine were always quiet, but after 4 P.M. they were quiet in the extreme. Arthur loved to stay late and read. The *Bee* wasn't a bad newspaper, although he found himself lingering over the line drawings of the women in the advertisements for panties and brassieres. Sometimes he'd pencil in arrows sticking out of their backs.

His elders and betters would nod cordially from the hall as they headed for the parking lot. There was a good chance of a visit from Cunningham. Cunningham was a senior staff editor, a large, athletic man with the distinction of having been the first to wear a striped shirt with a plain white collar. He was known to be a great favorite of The Founder.

He told jokes. Outside of this his responsibilities fell mostly into the area of what a less refined organization might have called public relations. He handled inquiries from the press. Also, he was a sort of charity scout. Of course, he was involved with established charities: the United Way, the March of Dimes. Fallow insisted on some charities. The Founder was particularly interested in Japanese culture. But Cunningham was always on the lookout for worthy causes. He visited remedial reading programs, soup kitchens and leper colonies. If he was impressed with the program, he'd bring a representative back to Paradise for lunch with Fallow. These lunches often resulted in generous bequests.

Cunningham also dealt with would-be writers. The Magazine got a vast quantity of material over the transom. One two-page department titled "Have I Got One for You" carried between nine and twelve brief, semihumorous anecdotes from true life. These were culled every month from an average of fifteen thousand pieces submitted. Contributors got $250 for an item.

"So you've got fifteen thousand people who think they have a story to tell," Mongoose used to joke. "Nine of them do."

Cunningham oversaw the army of outside readers who went through this sea of paperwork and cut it down to something that could conceivably be read in Paradise. He also ran workshops for writers. He was a bighearted man and felt that all writers were equal in God's eyes. Unfortunately, God wouldn't publish them and Cunningham couldn't.

It was said that he had active files for more than three hundred would-be writers, and that he got an average of six articles into The Magazine every year. He usually wrote one of these himself.

"You know, I started out on the copydesk," he told Arthur one afternoon. "I had a great job writing radio scripts, then my wife got pregnant. So I came here and the only position they had was on the copydesk. And I can't punctuate my way out of a paper bag. So they gave me the test. But I had a week to do it in. I brought it to the library. Now, don't tell anyone this," he said, leaning in, so that Arthur could smell his after-shave, "but I cheated. I found the article that had been the model for the test. All I had to do was make the two texts identical."

"That's amazing," said Arthur.

"That's right," said Cunningham, grinning. He straightened and headed out the door, stopping to look back at Arthur one more time on the way out. "I left a couple of mistakes," Cunningham said. "I didn't want them to think I was perfect."

The next afternoon he was in again, this time with a joke. "What's the definition of a damn shame?" he asked.

"I don't know," said Arthur warily.

"Bus full of lawyers going off a cliff with three seats empty," he said.

Arthur laughed guardedly.

"The difference between a rooster and a lawyer?"

Arthur didn't know.

"A rooster clucks defiance."

Arthur didn't get it.

"What rhymes with clucks? Two words that rhyme with defiance?"

Arthur laughed.

Cunningham studied his face. "You mustn't worry," he said. "We didn't hire you for your grammar."

TWENTY-TWO

"It doesn't help that you're in an all-female enclave," Mongoose said, when Arthur complained about his salary. The friends had eaten together at the cafeteria and were walking around the building. It was a gorgeous day. The daffodils were in bloom.

"I love Josie," said Arthur. "I just don't like being mistaken for one of the girls. You know how my father was about that."

"Being a woman is a handicap," admitted Mongoose. "They used to have two phantom women on the masthead when Fallow and his wife put out the whole magazine. Just names they put there so that nobody would know the whole thing was put together by two people. And if phantom women can seem real, then real women can become phantoms."

"What about Mrs. West?" said Arthur. "She's still in her forties, and she's already an executive editor."

"Ruth's an exception," said Mongoose.

"Is she very smart?"

"She's smart enough," said Mongoose, "but I don't think her intelligence is the secret of her success."

"So why is she such a success?"

Mongoose looked up and down the slate path to make sure there was nobody within earshot. "Because she cries out," he said.

Arthur blanched. "What?"

"Forget I said that. Just give yourself some time. You'll see what I mean. She made a sort of an end run. But there's the possibility of an end run for you as well."

Then Mongoose explained again about end runs. End runs were made on weekends and in the evenings; end runs were made at parties. A top editor would almost never eat lunch with a copy editor, but it was conceivable that he might invite one to his house to help clean out the garage. If this happened, it was possible that they would go out to dinner afterward. If the steak was adequately prepared, and if the proofreader held his whiskey well, he might then find himself being sucked inexplicably up the masthead.

But it was some time before Arthur got called into the huddle. He'd learned by the experience of painful rejection that his professional exchanges with Wheelwright were to be kept brief, so he was surprised when the executive editor took the proof Arthur delivered, put it down on his desk and asked about Fran Tarkenton.

"He's half the team," said Arthur.

"Do you have plans for Super Bowl Sunday?" asked Wheelwright.

"No, not really," said Arthur. "We'll watch the game."

"If you don't already have specific plans," said Wheelwright, "Martha and I would be delighted if you came by. It's not going to be a big party. Dean Nichols will be in Paris, but most of the executive editors will be there. There will also be some seniors, and a couple of associates. You'd be the only editor from the copydesk, but I can't imagine that the other people on copydesk would really enjoy our little gathering. Actually, there will also be some people from the business side. This will be the first year we've ever included anybody from business. Of course, it's also the first year we've ever had any one from copydesk. It's an informal gathering. People who are in the mood can bring a salad or a dessert."

Arthur said that Faith loved to bake.

"That's splendid," said Wheelwright. "And by all means bring your little boy."

"Absolutely not," Faith said when Arthur brought up the invitation that evening.

"He's more monkey than boy these days, and I'm sure Wheelwright didn't mean it about the kids. Besides, if Nathan stays home you can wear your white slacks."

Sunday afternoon found Arthur in his tight white slacks, a pair of his father-in-law's casual shoes and a plaid shirt that also belonged to his father-in-law. He draped the van's oil-stained seats with beach towels so as to keep their clothes clean. Faith had baked a cake. This was wrapped in aluminum foil and on a plate in a nest of newspapers behind the van's only two seats. Faith had on one of her mother's new dresses. This was of the style worn on TV by the girls on a wagon train. It was calico and fell to the ground, presumably so that the fat, bearded extras who drove most of the wagons wouldn't be incited to riot by a flash of ankle. This prudishness contrasted starkly with the top of the dress, which had a bodice that laced up to a spot directly between her breasts. The lace was fastened with a bow, which gave the impression that if you grabbed the string and tugged, the wearer would be naked to the waist. Faith and her mother were of approximately the same size, except in the bodice. In order to get into the dress, Faith had had to replace the original lace with one from an old hockey skate.

"Can you breathe in that?" asked Arthur, as they pulled out of Faith's mother's driveway. They'd left Nathan to spend the night.

"Sure I can breathe," said Faith, lighting a cigarette. "You don't like the dress? Is that because I borrowed it from my mother?"

"No, it's because it's so, well, it's so suggestive."

"Sexy you mean."

"That's right, sexy."

"I thought you wanted me to be sexy."

"All right, but be careful."

"Careful of what?"

"Nothing. Careful of nothing."

"Speaking of careful," said Faith. "I'm going to have to be careful with my cigarettes. My mother was out, so I gave her half my pack. I know that when you go to a party and have a drink you like to smoke all my cigarettes. You can't do that tonight. Either don't smoke, or bum from somebody else."

The Wheelwrights lived in Bedford. Bedford, New York, has a different look than North Tarrytown, New York. The fences in Bedford are white picket. The fences in North Tarrytown are chain link. If you see a Mercedes at the shopping center in North Tarrytown, it's probably being driven by a drug pusher. In Bedford almost everybody who doesn't drive a Jaguar drives a Mercedes. If Arthur's house had been put on the market, the ad wouldn't have mentioned the town. It might have said, "Home of Washington Irving," or "Riverside village," but it would never have said North Tarrytown, any more than it would have said, "Rich ethnic melting pot" or "Cuban groceries abound."

If the Wheelwright house had been put on the market, *Bedford* would have been the first word, as in "Bedford An-

tique. Lovingly restored, with stables, orchard and pool."
Like most older houses, the Wheelwright place stood near the
road, but it stood alone, and was flanked on the left by an
apple orchard, which was girded by a stone wall. All forty-
three of the Upcounty Estates would have fit in the Wheelwright apple orchard.

"This is Adam," Peter Wheelwright explained, when he
met Faith and Arthur at the door. Adam was a slender young
man with blond hair that fell to his shoulders. He wore a
white button-down shirt with no tie and a red vest.

"Adam wants a motorcycle," Wheelwright explained, "so
he's going to tend bar for his old parents all this year."

"Not just a motorcycle," said Adam sheepishly. "I want a
Harley."

"Whatever it is you want," said Peter, "we'll save money
on bartenders and you'll learn everything there is to know
about the effects of alcohol on small-motor coordination. Besides," he continued, looking at Arthur, "Adam is a great
bartender. What's your pleasure?"

"What are you having?" Arthur asked.

"A silver bullet," said Wheelwright.

"I'll have the same," said Arthur.

"Make that two," said Faith.

"Straight up or on the rocks?" asked Adam.

"Straight up," said Arthur, and Faith nodded.

When his martini arrived, Arthur thought it smelled so
much like turpentine that it was a mistake, or a prank, but he
didn't say anything. It tasted a lot like turpentine too, but
sipping at it gave him something to do. Then an attractive
woman with gray in her hair came up behind them and put
her arm around Faith. "You're Faith Prentice," she said, "and
I'm Martha Wheelwright. We need you in the kitchen."

The pregame show wouldn't begin for another half hour,
so Arthur began looking around for somebody he could bum
a cigarette from. Wheelwright smoked a pipe, but Arthur had
seen Arnold Baker when he first came in. Baker smoked
Marlboros. Arthur found Baker in a back room. The book

editor was sitting on a small sofa that had a black background with green flowers on it. He was wearing corduroys, English walking shoes and a flannel shirt. There was a golden retriever in front of the sofa with its head in Baker's hands. Arthur kneeled beside the retriever. "I love big dogs," he said. "I was raised with Labs."

Baker nodded, said nothing and continued to scratch behind the dog's ears.

Arthur stuck out his hand. "My name is Arthur Prentice," he said.

"Oh," said Baker. "You're the new man on the copydesk. How do you like it?"

"It's fine," said Arthur.

"You're a better man than I am," said Baker. "I wouldn't last a week with those ladies."

"I don't really have much of a choice," said Arthur, and he finished his turpentine in a gulp. "Can I refresh your drink?" he asked.

"Good idea," said Baker. "I'll come with you." He got out of the sofa, and they went to the bar together.

Arthur held out his glass.

"A twist?" asked Adam.

"No," said Arthur, "a martini."

Adam smiled. He picked up a frosted glass pitcher and used it to refill Arthur's glass. By the time this exchange was completed, Baker had already fixed himself a generous Scotch and soda.

"Wheelwright's a conspicuous cheapskate," Baker told Arthur as they walked away. "But he does buy decent Scotch. It may also be that he lets the company buy it." Baker put his Scotch down, and took out his package of Marlboros.

"Could, I, ah, have a cigarette?" asked Arthur.

"Sure," said Baker, "if you want one. They're not good for you, you know."

"I know," said Arthur, "but I like the way they make me feel."

"What do you think of The Magazine?" Baker asked when both cigarettes were burning.

"I like the jokes."

"What about the political coverage? Do you like that? What about the article we ran last month about food stamps?"

"I had a friend at Antioch who was on food stamps," said Arthur. "His father was a surgeon. So there definitely are abuses."

"Sure there are abuses," said Baker. "I'm not saying there aren't. I just don't like all this harking back to the good old days when people used to starve to death."

"I don't think a lot of people are starving to death in this country today," said Arthur.

"What's a lot of people?" asked Baker. "Are two people a lot of people? If two people starve to death, is that too much?"

Arthur shrugged. "I'm trying to be old," he thought. "He's trying to be young. We're both assholes," he thought.

Arnold pulled on his cigarette. "I understand," he said. "You can't talk. But I'll tell you what I think of our articles about foot stamps. I think they suck."

Arthur took a drink. "I wouldn't go that far."

"Well, that's exactly how far I'd go," said Baker, "and I'll tell you something else. I'm not alone. Not by a long shot. We ran a straw poll in 1972 and McGovern won handily. There are something like three hundred fifty people in the editorial offices of the magazine proper. One hundred and ninety of them voted for McGovern."

"That's incredible," said Arthur.

Baker shrugged. "The ballots were anonymous," he said. "What's incredible is the level of pusillinamity. When I try and get something decent into the magazine, like a piece by John McPhee, nobody supports me. Now your father must know McPhee."

"No," said Arthur. "He doesn't. Besides, *The American Reader* has had plenty of distinguished writers."

"Like who?"

"Like Cummings."

"Cummings never wrote for us."

"But you approached him?"

"That's right."

"And he described The Magazine as the world's best seller?"

"That's also right. But he didn't mean it as a compliment. He also described a standard article: 'Eight to eighty, anyone can do it, makes you feel better.' Something like that. Funny, but not exactly friendly."

Baker took a drag on his cigarette. He looked bored. His charm was that he always appeared to be bored. "It's frustrating," he said, "but we get our licks in. I had a memo from Fallow about how much he admired one of our book sections, and I kept it. Then along comes *Cry, the Beloved Country*. Great book, but not for us, right? I did the cut and sent it along with Fallow's memo. So we ran it. Fallow didn't notice, and nobody else made a peep. The readers hated it, of course, but what the fuck do they know?"

Mongoose came up behind Arthur at this point and put a hand on his shoulder. "I'm delighted that Monsieur Wheelwright had the good sense to include you," he said.

"Thanks," said Arthur. "You look different."

"The beard and eyes?"

"That's right," said Arthur.

"It's for a play," said Mongoose. "I have to have a black beard and blue eyes. So I dyed my beard and the blue in my eyes is the blue in my contacts."

Mongoose turned to Baker. "How long has it been since we've run a book section on India?" he asked.

"I don't know," said Baker. "Five years."

"I bring it up because I'm reading that marvelous book they brought out to accompany the public television series on India."

"I've heard about the series, but I was in New Mexico during the first episode," said Baker.

"Well, it's quite good, and the book is illuminating in its own right. Of course, there's a lot on snakes."

"I'm not surprised," said Baker, and he looked at Arthur. "Do you know about him and snakes?"

Arthur nodded.

"In any case," said Mongoose, "the statistics are fascinating. Do you know that fifty percent of the people in India who die of snakebite are actually killed by fright?"

"No," said Baker, getting out a cigarette for himself and offering one to Arthur, who accepted eagerly. "I didn't know."

"It's true," said Mongoose. "Most snakes in India, like most snakes in the United States, are not poisonous. There's a lot of ignorance about snakes in India, and when people get bitten by a common house snake they often die."

"I didn't think people could actually die of fright anymore," said Arthur.

"Technically, it's not fright. It's heart failure, or sometimes even a stroke. It's brought on my fright."

Baker nodded. He looked as if he were about to fall asleep.

Mongoose pressed on. "I mentioned the book because I thought we might use it in The Magazine."

Baker shook his head. "India," he said. "The people who long for the raj don't read our magazine, Mongoose. You should know that by now."

At this point the lights in the living room blinked. "I guess that means the game is starting," said Baker. "Let's hurry and get a seat." He shrugged and smiled in a way that indicated he didn't want to hurry, didn't want to see the game and would be glad to stand. But they all moved into the room with the television. The pregame show was just starting. Faith was standing by the fireplace talking with a tall man of about thirty-five. They were both laughing. The man was wearing a beige fisherman's knit sweater and wide-wale corduroy trousers. He had thinning blond hair and a blond mustache. Faith had one hand on his shoulder.

"This is my husband," she said when Arthur joined them at the mantle. "He's on the copydesk."

"My name is Joseph Bart," said the man in the fisherman's

knit sweater, and he and Arthur shook hands. "Mrs. Carstairs still head up the copydesk?"

"That's right," said Arthur.

"Are you fond of her?" asked Bart.

"Yes," said Arthur, "I am."

"But you don't really like working on the copydesk?"

"It's okay."

"What does he tell you?" asked Bart, and he looked at Faith.

"He says he likes it," said Faith.

"You must be easy to please," said Bart, looking at Arthur.

"I suppose," said Arthur.

"And what about you?" asked Bart, looking at Faith. "Are you easy to please?"

Faith blushed and took a long pull on her cigarette. "That's for me to know," she said. "And for you to find out."

"Would you like another drink?" Bart asked, looking at Faith's almost empty glass. "Yes," said Faith, "that would be nice." Arthur still had half of his martini, so he let them go to the bar together. Then, as if on a whim, he finished his drink and headed off after them. When he got there, they were gone. Arthur had Adam Wheelwright pour him another martini, and then went to look for more of Arnold Baker's Marlboros. He didn't find Baker, but he did find a large woman with implausible blonde hair who was smoking a Kool and telling a joke to Allen Parker. "So when he comes downstairs," she said, "they're all sitting around with silly smiles on their faces, and one of them says, 'While you were making love to that hag, we were down here eating hot buttered corn.' "

"Sarah Morse, this is Arthur Prentice," said Parker, putting an arm on the younger man's shoulder. "Arthur is on the copydesk. Sarah edits two of our humor sections."

"Now that you've met," said Parker, "I think I'd better find my wife, so if you'll excuse me," and he backed away.

"They never let us use the best ones," Mrs. Morse told Arthur, putting a hand on his forearm. "You know the one about the agent named Abromowitz and the man who can sing through his asshole?"

Arthur took a sip of his drink. By the time Mrs. Morse had gotten into the description of the Abromowitz rug, Arthur had begun to wonder if Allen Parker was the one who smoked, and if Sarah Morse had bummed one of Parker's cigarettes.

Mrs. Morse still hadn't produced a cigarette when she got to the punch line. "I'm just clearing my throat," she said. Arthur laughed.

There followed two more jokes, including one about a man who mistakes his penis for a necktie. Then Sarah reached into her purse and produced a red leather cigarette case. She held this unopened for one more joke. Finally, Arthur got a Kool.

Asking Mrs. Morse for directions to the bathroom seemed like a bad idea, so Arthur just nodded, gave his warmest smile and went upstairs. In the hallway he opened one door and saw his wife and Bart looking at a painting of lips on a cloud that hung over the upholstered headboard in the master bedroom. He closed the door without saying anything.

He went down the hall until he found a door with W C nailed to it in brass letters. Inside there was a framed page from a French newspaper to read while pissing. The newspaper seemed to announce Lindbergh's arrival in Paris, but Arthur wasn't sure. When he was done, he went downstairs to the room with the TV set. After this his memories got vague. He had some recollection of a conversation with a man who always put gasoline in the toilets of his house on Block Island when he closed it up for the winter. He remembered eating some honey-roasted peanuts. (This recollection he knew to be accurate, because the next day he kept finding little bits of the peanut skins between his teeth.) He thought that Martha Wheelwright asked him to help her make some of her famous Irish coffee.

He and Faith drove home shortly after 9 P.M. He tried to stay at about twenty-five miles an hour. Faith kept telling him to speed up, because if a policeman saw them he'd know that the driver was drunk. "The police like a cautious driver," said Arthur, "and besides, this driver *is* drunk."

When they did finally get home, Faith phoned her mother and asked how Nathan was. Nathan was fine. His grandmother had cooked him fried chicken, and he had eaten two servings. Faith and Arthur retired to the master bedroom. They both lay down on the bedspread, fully dressed. Arthur remembered wondering if he should move to his own sleeping quarters. He had just decided that he definitely should move when he lost consciousness.

He awoke at 4 A.M. and went downstairs to use the half bath off the kitchen. He had to take a potted philodendron out of the toilet. Then he poured himself a glass of orange juice from a carton in the refrigerator and drank it with three aspirin and a vitamin C. He put another round of pills in his hand, refilled the glass with orange juice and brought it upstairs for Faith. He found her sitting up in bed trying to unfasten her bodice.

"Do you know how many calories there are in a glass of orange juice?" she asked when he offered her the drink.

"No."

"It's what they give diabetics when they're having an insulin reaction. It's almost straight sugar. Pour it out and I'll have water."

Arthur did as he was told, and then tried to help Faith with the dress. She lay back on the pillow and let him work at it.

"This is a double bow," he said. "I don't remember your tying a double bow."

"I tied it at the party," said Faith. "It started to come undone during the first quarter."

"Where did you watch the game?" asked Arthur. "I don't remember seeing you."

"I watched it upstairs. They had another TV on upstairs in the master bedroom."

"Were you alone?"

"No, of course not. Why do you ask?"

"The dress. The guy in the sweater."

"Oh, come on," said Faith, moving her head slowly from side to side. "I'm too tired and too sick to deal with this. If you want to go to your room and fret, you're welcome to. But why not be a sport and help me out of my dress?"

So Arthur worked on the knot. When he saw he had it, he took his left hand and began to stroke the side of Faith's right breast. No comment. So he brought his head down and kissed his wife on the throat.

Faith sighed deeply. "All right," she said, "but make it quick and don't be surprised if I throw up."

When Arthur got his next paycheck it was different, so he got his pocket calculator out of his briefcase and figured out that his salary had been increased to $15,000 a year. This, for a man who couldn't spell and was working as a proofreader, was a baffling occurrence.

He phoned Faith. "Great," she said. "Maybe we'll go out on a limb this month and pay the electric bill."

"Well, it is a raise," said Arthur.

"That's right," said Faith. "One more step in the march of dimes."

Arthur didn't want to ask Josephine about his raise because he was afraid she didn't know about it. He hadn't yet told her that he'd been to Wheelwright's to see the football game. For some reason he thought the two events might be connected. He decided to see Horster. When he went to Horster's office, the door was closed, but Horster's secretary said she'd have her boss give Arthur a call on the copydesk. It wasn't until the afternoon of the next day that he was invited back to his mentor's office.

This time Horster had a manuscript spread on his desk, and he didn't look up when Arthur came into the room. He pointed to the visitor's chair and continued to read through the manuscript, marking it with a red felt-tip pen. After several minutes he got to the last page and looked up.

"Could you bring this across the hall to Miss Sullivan," he said curtly. "Tell her to have it retyped and submitted to the Dean. Then come back."

Arthur did as he was told. When he came back into the office, Horster was on the telephone. Arthur stood uneasily behind the armchair.

"Have them out right now," Horster said into the phone. "Dr. Ruger will work you into his schedule as a favor to the family. Your mother can drive you there and pick you up afterward. Then you can stay in bed. If you wait until you get back to Cambridge, it's going to interfere with your studies. I know Kathy's a great nurse, but I don't think oral surgery is something you need to share. All right, then, think about it. You know where I stand."

Horster hung up, and turned to Arthur. "Sit down," he said. "What can I do for you?" he said. "I'm in a rush. I've got to get to Greenwich Toyota before they close at five P.M. I have many hours of work to do before I leave."

Arthur tried for small talk. "Getting a new car?"

Horster scowled. "No," he said. "It's just a checkup. I got tired of being a patriot two years ago and traded in my last Ford. I've driven Japanese cars ever since. You have a problem with that?"

"No," said Arthur. He took a deep breath and exhaled. "I just want to know what I'm doing right," he said. "I got a raise, so I want to know how I got it, and what to do to make sure I get another one."

"You didn't do anything," said Horster.

"So why did it happen?" asked Arthur.

"Long story," said Horster. "But nobody can live on nine thousand dollars a year in this part of the country. How did you manage?"

"Just barely," said Arthur.

"Well, as soon as we knew we were safe, we gave you a raise. And now that discovery is over, we're safe."

"Discovery?"

"Yes," said Horster. "You didn't hear this from me, but

some of the women on staff here have brought a class-action suit against the company for sex discrimination. One of their arguments is that young men who are hired to work for us are too well paid. So we had to make certain that you weren't well paid at all. But now discovery is over. They've looked at our books. They think you make nine thousand dollars a year. So now it's all right for you to make fifteen thousand dollars."

"Is that the only reason I got a raise?" asked Arthur.

"No, of course not," said Horster. "We like you. But then we've always liked you."

Arthur phoned his father that evening with the news. Icarus seemed pleased. "Are you approaching financial independence?" he asked.

"Yes," said Arthur. And then paused. "Is that a trick question?"

"No," said Icarus. "I don't know what I'd do if I weren't supporting somebody."

Arthur laughed uneasily.

"I'm sorry about the cookout," he told his father. "Nathan was sick. I think Faith takes these illnesses too seriously. But I can't argue with her about the health of her only child."

Icarus didn't say anything.

"Daddy," said Arthur. "Are you there? Daddy." The line was dead.

Three weeks later, Arthur spotted a stranger in the halls at *The American Reader*. He was about Arthur's age. He had a mustache. He was wearing a suit and carrying a notebook.

The following afternoon the deputy editor-in-chief appeared in the doorway of Arthur's office. The young mustache was with him.

"This is Gilbert Collingwood," said Horster. "He's from Time-Life Books. He's just beginning to find his way around, but I've told him that he should ask you if he has any questions."

"I'll be glad to help," said Arthur.

"Good," said Horster.

Gilbert and Arthur shook hands.

Collingwood's hair was butter yellow, his eyes were green and he grinned under his mustache with the comic ferocity of the fox in a children's book. His smile was disarming, but Arthur couldn't quite kick the feeling that this was somebody who should not be left alone with any chickens. "You didn't go to Loomis, did you?" asked Horster.

"No," said Arthur. "I went to Choate."

"That is too bad," said Horster. "I thought it was Loomis. Gilbert went to Loomis. In any case, I hope you two can put old school rivalries aside and help each other. The copydesk has a tradition of being helpful to the rest of the staff. Gilbert is our newest and youngest associate editor."

When Arthur got home that evening, he stopped at the mailbox. There was one big brown envelope with a glassine window. He ripped it open. "You, *ARTHUR SOUTH PRENTICE, OF 17 ICHABOD LANE, NORTH TARRYTOWN, NEW YORK*, may already have won eleven million dollars."

Faith and Nathan were both upstairs. Arthur took off his shoes, loosened his tie and climbed the stairs. Nathan gave him a hug. Faith was on her hands and knees in the shower stall.

"I had to throw out the soap," she said.

"Why's that?" asked Arthur.

"It was covered with hair," she said. "I wish you wouldn't use the best soap. If you have to use it, can't you clean it off afterwards?"

"I'm sorry," said Arthur.

Faith stuck her head out of the shower. She was wearing a pair of his wheat jeans and an old blue work shirt. The shirt had ridden up on her back, and Arthur could see a patch of white skin. Faith's hair was wrapped in a red bandanna. She was holding a sponge in one hand and a canister of Ajax in the other. He was mildly insulted, but he still wanted to get into the shower stall with her and kiss that patch of skin.

"What's the matter?" she asked when she saw the look on his face.

"They hired somebody else to be an associate editor," he said. Faith ducked back into the shower. "Did they say anything to you?" she asked, scrubbing furiously.

"No," said Arthur. "Horster came in with the guy this afternoon and introduced him."

"I thought Horster was the one who promised you that job," Faith said, scrubbing away at the back of the shower.

"You're right, he did."

"You let it happen," said Faith.

"Nobody asked me," said Arthur. "I was presented with a fait accompli. What was I supposed to do when Horster showed up and told me—hit him?"

"No," said Faith. "You couldn't have hit him then, but it's obvious that he's not afraid of you. If they were afraid of you, they wouldn't have done it."

"Nobody's afraid of me," said Arthur. "Nobody ever has been. And furthermore, I don't want anybody to be afraid of me."

Faith stuck her head out of the shower stall again and waved the sponge at him. "That's your problem in a nutshell," she said.

TWENTY-THREE

Equality before the law is the only possible basis for an enlightened society. It must not be forgotten, however, that both justice and equality are man-made concepts. Equals are as rare in nature as a two-headed baby or a four-leaf clover. If man begins to expect equality as a law of nature, then all natural advantages will be considered unnatural, and become a burden to those who possess them. It may be necessary to tax great wealth and to rein in the powerful, but we must not legislate against talent, beauty and intelligence. When and if this begins to happen, the species will cease to evolve. Life

UNDER IDEAL CIRCUMSTANCES WILL BE JUST, BUT IT MUST NEVER
BE FAIR."—LORD BIRKENBRECK (1929)

That was the lead item in the May 1976 "Wisdom You Can
Use." It made Arthur think of Ruth West. She had jet-black
hair and enormous blue eyes. She was also said to have a
wicked backhand, as well as a clay court on which to exercise
it. Mr. West had died of a heart attack sometime in the late
sixties, leaving his widow several million dollars and a house
in Pound Ridge. Ruth had gone on to become The Magazine's
youngest executive editor.

It was the unbroken policy of The Magazine that an executive editor always kept every proof for twenty-four hours.
Sometimes the exec did a good deal of work on the proof
during this period of time; sometimes he or she did nothing.
But the time period remained constant. It was the line that
separated those who put out The Magazine from those who
took responsibility for it.

The first time Arthur brought Ruth a proof, she was wearing tartan slacks and a red silk blouse that buttoned up the
back and pearls.

"What have you got there?" she asked.

" 'A Beagle Named Napoleon.' "

"Is this final?"

"Yes. It's scheduled to close tomorrow."

"Do you like the story?"

"Yes. Mongoose wrote it. It's very tight."

She took the proof from Arthur, initialed it and gave it
back. The entire transaction took less than a minute, but
Arthur kept thinking about it afterward. Faith said that Arthur
hated women, but Arthur wasn't sure she was right. It was
true that he couldn't breathe properly when he was in the
room with a beautiful woman, but he wasn't entirely convinced that this was an expression of hatred.

In his short lifetime Arthur had made a study of beautiful
women, and it seemed to him that there were two types. Type

A spent their lives not noticing how beautiful they were. They avoided mirrors. Sometimes they abased themselves by falling in love with a brute, but more often they were distracted with feverish activity. Unemployed A's had causes: they were vegetarians, feminists or Maoists. If a Type A had a job, she was apt to do very well and become a bank president, a foreign correspondent or a justice of the Supreme Court. The lack of male pride often made these women better at what they did than their masculine competitors. The one fact they could never acknowledge was the fact of their own beauty.

The second type of beautiful woman—Type B—never really acknowledged anything else. Faith was a Type B. She was many other things, but she was a beautiful woman before she was anything else. She'd been an honors student in high school, a talented musician and painter, but she hadn't been raised to paint or play, she'd been raised to marry. And the failure of that marriage seemed to have put an end to all her prospects.

Ruth was a type A. She had an antique looking glass behind the desk in her office and a full-length mirror screwed to the inside of her closet door. She almost never looked at either one. Her beauty seemed not to be much on her mind. But then she didn't have to think about it, because everybody else did. Many of the women on the staff resented her. The men treated her like a cross between a box of chocolates and a land mine.

The second time Arthur brought Ruth a proof she was wearing a loose cardigan sweater over a black silk evening gown. She still had the string of pearls. She got up from behind her desk. Arthur noticed how narrow her waist was in the gown, and how prominent her front.

"I like your dress," he said.

"Here," said Ruth, getting up, "let me give you the full effect." She took off her sweater, dropped it on her desk and turned around slowly. "You have to imagine the shoes," she said. "They're in the closet. Simple heels. Black."

"Looks great," said Arthur. "Where are you going?"

"Oh, it's a bore," said Ruth. "Three of us are flying to Washington this evening to eat dinner with some right-thinking senator or other. I think it's Sam Nunn. It's a command performance."

"And then you spend the night?" Arthur asked.

"No, nothing that simple. We fly down in the company plane. The wine will be standard Madeira. The dinner will be wooden steak with butter sauce. We have to fly back tonight. I won't get into bed until one A.M."

"Sounds interesting to me," said Arthur. "I haven't been out of the state since I graduated from college."

"Well, it's not interesting," said Ruth. "But if you like wooden steak, I can try to get you on the list."

As the issue progressed, Arthur saw more and more of Ruth West. If another member of the copydesk brought in a proof, Ruth would accept it, but then she'd ask for Arthur. If he had read the piece, she'd quiz him on it. If he hadn't, she'd send him to his office with it, have him read it over and then report.

One afternoon she called Mrs. Carstairs at four and asked her to send Arthur down with the proofs of "The Immortal Francisco Franco."

"It's going to take a while," she told Josephine, "so make sure that he's done with his other work for the day. And you needn't wait for us. If we decide that there are any changes that have to be made, we can send them to the printer tomorrow."

When Josephine passed on the message, she asked Arthur if he minded. "I could easily send somebody else," she said.

"No," said Arthur. "I'm happy to work late, but I don't quite get it."

"That woman's mind is as much of a mystery to me as it is to you," said Josephine. "But if I had to guess, I'd say that Ruth West has set her cap for you."

"But I'm married."

Josephine was patient. "Arthur, I think you should know that Ruth has been on intimate terms with a great many of her superiors. And they were all married at the time. I suppose that now that she's gotten to be forty-eight, she'd like to know what it feels like to seduce somebody else."

"Is she forty-eight?"

"About that."

"I'm not even sure she likes me."

"She probably likes you a good deal more than most of the men she's been with liked her."

So Josephine sent Arthur down to Mrs. West's office. In the past Ruth had always gotten up when Arthur came in the door, but this time she just glanced at him. She was wearing an aqua warm-up suit and white sneakers. She was also wearing glasses. Arthur had never seen her in glasses before. He sat in the armchair.

"Not there," said Ruth without looking up. "Sit at the table." Ruth worked at an antique partners' desk. She also had a wooden table set against one wall. Arthur moved.

"Read the proof," she said. "Take your time, and mark it up as you go along. I want your comments," she said. "Not just grammatical corrections, editorial comments."

"Okay," Arthur said.

Then he could hear her get up and walk by him. "I'll be back in fifteen minutes," she said.

Ruth was back in ten minutes, but Arthur had already finished with the proof. He didn't like the piece, but he couldn't think what to do about it. Ruth stood at his right side. Arthur could smell her perfume. He passed her the proof and she stood beside him reading it. When she reached the last page, Ruth leaned forward and put the article back down on the table. Her side rubbed against Arthur's shoulder.

"Do you think we can get away with this?" she asked, and pointed to a line in the story that read: "While misguided American intellectuals have romanticized the failed Spanish Republic, it must be remembered that the cause was financed and then betrayed by Stalinist Russia."

"I read *Homage to Catalonia*, and I guess Orwell gives some support to that argument," said Arthur. "But I don't know if you'd want to call Ernest Hemingway misguided. I certainly wouldn't call him an intellectual."

Ruth laughed. Arthur could feel her rib cage against his shoulder.

"Well, at least Franco's dead," she said. "We call this series 'The Great Immortals,' but they're almost all dead. If they're not dead when we start the piece, they usually die before we hit the stands. Bob Hope's the exception. He's been celebrated twice, and he's still walking around."

Arthur laughed.

Ruth smiled. "Would you mind a tip from a friend?" she asked.

Arthur shrugged. "No," he said. "I guess not."

"You cover 'I See His Face' " she asked.

"Yes, I cover it."

"There was a story about a dog and a boy last month?"

"That's right. An awful story," he said.

"Made you laugh, made you cry?"

"That's the one," he said.

"It's a placement," Ruth said. "Stanton Williams wrote it and they put it in that little magazine so that we could pick it up."

"But I don't like it."

Ruth put a hand on his shoulder. "You don't have to like it," she said. "But you do have to mark it Usable."

TWENTY-FOUR

Arthur was drifting in and out of consciousness over an article about how U.S. car manufacturers shouldn't be forced to install airbags. Josephine appeared in his doorway looking pale and shaken.

"Did you see him?" she asked.

"No. Who?"

"Fallow. He just left. He hasn't been on the copydesk for a couple of years now, and suddenly he materialized and asked to see the masthead. I gave it to him, and he took a pencil and crossed off the editor-in-chief. He didn't say a word about why, he just crossed out one line and left. Ten minutes later the Dean came in and asked to see the masthead. For a second I thought I should show him one of the proofs with his name still on it. But I showed him the one with his name crossed out."

"Did he look upset?"

"He looked fine. He seemed quite composed. He read it, then he thanked me and left."

"That was it?"

"Not exactly. After he thanked me, he said 'God Bless.' "

"Did he used to say 'God Bless'? Was that one of the things he said, like Wheelwright always says 'Ciao'?"

"No, he never said it before, or not to my knowledge."

"And he's not coming back?"

"What would he come back to? They're already clearing out his office."

After Josephine left, Arthur went to the supply closet and got himself a pen and a spiral notebook. He didn't need them, but he didn't want his hands to be empty when he walked past the Dean's office. The door was open. Three uniformed men were emptying the Dean's drawers into cardboard file boxes.

When Arthur got back to his office, he phoned Mongoose. It was almost two-thirty and he assumed his friend would be back from lunch.

"I think the Dean's been fired," he said. "Josephine knows about it. The men with the blue shirts with their names on the pockets are in his office now cleaning out his desk."

Arthur could see Josephine's office from his own. It took Mongoose five minutes to get there. By the time Mongoose came out, Allen Parker was waiting in the hall. Allen was still in Josephine's office with the door closed when Ruth West appeared in the hall. She came into Arthur's office, and nodded her head in the direction of Josephine's door.

"Who's in there?"

"Allen Parker."

"How long has he been in there?"

"I don't know. Five minutes."

"Has Horster already been?"

"No."

"When you talk with Josephine later, try and find out if Horster's been in. Then call me and tell me what you find out. Also, I want you to notice who else goes in."

Arthur nodded toward Josephine's office door, which had opened. Parker came out. Ruth went in.

The halls were still buzzing when Arthur left at 4:45 P.M. He got to Golden's Bait and Tackle just before closing and bought himself a clasp knife with a five-inch blade. The man behind the counter was one of those red-faced types with a gut and a brass belt buckle. "What do you want this pig sticker for?" he asked.

"Fishing," said Arthur.

The knife cost $27.49. He carried it home in his jacket pocket. When he changed out of his work clothes, he put it in his briefcase. Faith never looked in his briefcase.

"So, what got him?" asked Faith, when they'd put Nathan to bed.

"I don't know, but I think it was woman trouble. He had a mistress."

"I've heard of other cases in which men in important positions lost everything because they got caught having an affair," she said, "and I've never understood it."

"You don't think there should be punishment? It's right there in the short form, the Ten Commandments. Thou shalt not kill. Thou shalt not commit adultery."

"It's not the punishment that mystifies me. It's the deed."

"You never want to have a lover?"

"That's right."

"I'm flattered."

"You shouldn't be. I can't understand wanting two men. One man is more than enough trouble for me."

"But another one might be different."

"I doubt it. Men are like pebbles at the beach. They look colorful when you see them below the waterline. Bring them home and put them on the dresser and they're all pretty uninteresting and pretty much the same too."

Nathan was asleep when the phone rang. Arthur was reading the proof of an article titled "Plan Your Own Funeral." Faith was reading a piece in the *Ladies' Home Journal* about how to make Christmas decorations out of popcorn and pieces of common household soap.

"He definitely is fired," said Mongoose when Arthur picked up. "Arnold Baker had a theory that he was just moving offices, but Ginny Ransom has a friend in payroll. He's fired."

"I heard it was woman trouble."

"That's right." Mongoose told Arthur that Nichols had been married when he first went to work at *The American Reader*, and had two daughters. There had been two other marriages since then. Mongoose said that "a great many women, including Ruth West, have been his 'great good friends.'"

"His what?"

" 'Great good friends', that's what *Time* calls it."

"This is the man who wrote about the health benefits of monogamy?"

"Same one."

"So how'd he get caught?" Arthur asked. "Wait a minute." Faith was standing in front of him again, scowling and signaling. Arthur put his hand over the phone. "I'm going up to bed," said Faith. "Turn on the dishwasher. And I want tea."

Arthur nodded. Mongoose was still talking. "Remember the lead piece in last month's issue?" he asked.

"I think so. It was a pickup from *Newsweek*. 'Prayers for the Godless'? I proofed the last three pages."

"That's right," said Mongoose. "I believe their title was something like 'Prayers for Agnostics,' and ours was 'You Too Can Pray,' but it clearly recognized the possibility of God's death, and it was put in the issue by the Dean himself."

"So, he slipped."

"That would have been forgivable," said Mongooss, "but it wasn't the Dean who slipped. It was Mary Bradford. Did you ever meet her?"

"I don't think so."

"Mary was working for Sotheby's when we contracted with

them for an assessment of the value of the corporate art collection; she got the job. She's not nearly as attractive as Pamela—she's the Dean's current wife—but then I suppose the pursuit of novelty must always be one of the greater motives for men like Nichols. The one time I met her she was wearing crimson fingernail polish. She looked like she'd just clawed open somebody's throat."

"I never met her," said Arthur.

"Anyway, Nichols set her up in Paris with her own house," said Mongoose, "and a secretarial staff. I believe she had a butler and a driver. Then she placed the piece about prayer."

"I didn't think it was such a bad article," said Arthur, cradling the phone with his shoulder as he poured the loose English Breakfast tea into the egg-shaped tea ball.

"There was a line in the piece about the death of the Supreme Being. Fallow believes in God as he appears in the Revised Standard. He's not the type that thinks you should believe in The Almighty just because it might lower your blood pressure."

"So ultimately the Dean was canned because of his editorial excesses and not his sexual ones?"

"Both. I think somebody—and I don't know who—gathered all the financial details about the Paris office and used the Godless article to draw attention to them."

"Horster?" Arthur asked, taking down the teapot and putting the ball into it.

"What's he got to gain? He's already deputy editor-in-chief. He'll never go higher." The kettle was beginning to steam.

"What do you mean, he won't get higher?" Arthur said, turning it off. "Isn't that what deputies are for, ascending to the top spot when it opens?"

"Not in this case. Not in this organization. That man's just too ghoulish to be the patriarch."

The kettle was still whistling, so Arthur moved it to a cold burner.

"Besides," said Mongoose. "Fallow would never tolerate an executive who didn't go out among the troops at night."

"You mean like Henry the Fifth before Agincourt."

"Exactly. And Horster doesn't talk with anyone."

Arthur put the teapot on a trivet and began, very slowly, to pour in the water from the kettle.

"He talks with me," he said.

TWENTY-FIVE

The office didn't open for business until 8:30 A.M., but Arthur always got in at around 7:45. The day after the ouster, he had time to scan the front page of *The New York Times* before the phone rang. It was Miss Sullivan.

"Is this Arthur Prentice?"

"Yes."

"'Mr. Horster would like to see you as soon as possible.'"

"Okay," said Arthur. "I'll be right there." He spread the paper on his desk so that it would be clear to anyone who looked in the door that he was in the building, and then went down the hall to Horster's office. Horster was on the phone. When he saw Arthur in the doorway he got off. Arthur stood uneasily behind the visitor's chair with his hands on its back.

He didn't know why, but he had the distinct impression that he'd done something wrong.

"Do you know what a rat fink is?" Horster asked.

"Yes," said Arthur. "I think so."

Horster didn't say anything, so Arthur went on. "I guess it used to be the term for somebody employed by management to infiltrate and betray union movements. Now it's a generic term for anyone who betrays his peers to authority."

Horster nodded.

"Do you know any rat finks?"

Arthur shrugged. "I'm not sure."

Horster pushed back his big chair and lit a Kool. "What do you know?" he asked.

"I only know what Josephine told me."

"Yes," said Horster, and he rocked back in his chair, clasping his hands behind his neck. This shirt had lost its middle button. The undershirt revealed was clean and white. "And what did Josephine tell you?"

"She said that Fallow came into her office and crossed Nichols's name off the masthead. Then she said that Nichols came in and asked to see the masthead."

Horster passed a hand over his head. "What time was this all supposed to have taken place?"

"Right around two P.M."

"Did Nichols say anything when she showed him the masthead?"

"Nothing much. He just said thank you and God Bless."

"God Bless. He said God Bless?"

"Yes."

"I love it," said Horster chuckling. He creaked his chair back. "Prayers from the infidel. Sit down, my friend, and have a cigarette."

Arthur took a manuscript off the visitor's chair and sat. He accepted a Kool from Horster, who then passed him the lighter. A pink one this time, also plastic.

"Now that I know what you know, I want to know what you *think* you know," said Horster.

"Well, I heard a colorful story having to do with a European consultant with crimson nail polish. Do you want to hear it?"

Horster wagged his head. "I'm familiar with that version."

"Is it accurate?"

Horster shrugged. "Let me ask you one more question. Are there any theories out there as to who might have caused the scales to fall from The Founder's eyes?"

"There's a lot of speculation."

"What do you think?"

"It might have been part of somebody's career plan. I'd much rather think it just happened. There are catastrophes that just happen. Volcanoes explode. The earth quakes. There's something primitive about searching for a villain."

"And you think this is a catastrophe?"

"I don't know," said Arthur. He inhaled deeply and then blew out the smoke. The first cigarette was always bitter. "Maybe not. But it certainly is a dramatic change. As a foot soldier, I'm a little concerned. When the elephants dance, the mice get trampled."

"If there were a villain in on this catastrophe, as you so aptly put it," said Horster, "who would that villain be? Aside from me, of course," Horster said, smiling sweetly. At this point Miss Sullivan appeared in the doorway. "I've got Mr. Palumbardo here to see you," she said.

"Send him in," said Horster. Albert Palumbardo was a small man, and a little plump, and very eager. He looked to be about forty-five years old. His hair was brown, moderately long and parted in the middle. He wore a terrific suit.

Horster gave him a smile unlike any smile Arthur had ever seen Horster give before. "This is Arthur Prentice," he said. "He's my ear to the tracks. He's also the man who found that article you admired so much. The story about the boy who loses his dog."

"That's right," said Palumbardo. "And it snows."

"A blizzard," Arthur agreed.

"Honored," said Palumbardo, giving Arthur a small, clean

hand to shake. "You know, I believe we're giving you a raise. Your middle name is South?"

Arthur nodded.

"That's right then. Congratulations."

"Thank you," said Arthur, reddening.

"Oh, no," said Palumbardo. "You should thank Mr. Horster. He's the one who recommended you."

Arthur turned back to his mentor.

But Horster shrugged. "Don't bother," he said. "You'll earn it." Then he turned so that he faced both of his guests. "You two don't know each other yet," he said.

"The honor is mine," said Palumbardo with exaggerated defense.

"No, it is not," said Horster, and he looked sternly at Arthur.

"There's some question these days about the excellence of our editorial offerings," he continued, "but nobody denies that we've got the best circulation department in the history of printed matter. This man is one of the chief reasons anybody reads this magazine."

Palumbardo smiled weakly. "Not even the best circulation manager in the world can sell garbage," he said.

Horster chuckled. "Don't believe him, Arthur," he said. "That's false modesty. I've heard him say he could sell moonbeams if he had to."

Palumbardo smiled. "Of course it would depend on the time of month," he said.

"Arthur and I were just talking about the shake-up," said Horster. "Arthur here was expressing his theory that one of the executive editors might have carried the evil rumors to Fallow."

"I guess they have the most to gain," said Arthur.

Palumbardo was looking idly over the papers on Horster's desk. He didn't seem to be terribly interested in the conversation.

"Exactly," said Horster.

"I don't think anyone much suspects Ruth West," Arthur continued. "But I wouldn't put it beyond Allen Parker, or Courtney Fairchild."

"And Wheelwright?" asked Horster.

"He's too civilized," said Arthur.

"And why exactly would you rule out the charming Mrs. West?" asked Horster.

"Not the type. Besides, she's already got pots of money, a house and a good job."

"'And she's a woman," said Horster.

"That's right, she is a woman," said Arthur.

"I suppose," said Horster. "But then so was Clytemnestra."

When Arthur got back to his office, the phone was ringing. This time it was Faith.

"I set up an appointment for Nathan with a psychiatrist," she said. "He's too old to be wetting his bed every night. It's going to cost seventy-five dollars a session. My mother said she'd pick up whatever your insurance doesn't."

"I don't think we should use my health insurance for a psychiatrist. Not if you want me to get ahead here."

"All right, then my mother will pay for all of it."

Arthur sighed. "Okay, if that's what you want, but I don't have much faith in psychiatrists."

"I don't either, but we don't have a lot of options. I can't very well bring him to see the neighborhood priest."

"Whatever you say."

"The appointment is at five P.M., so if you come home early, we won't be here."

"I don't think I'll be coming home early."

"I know, but I just didn't want you to find a darkened house and be surprised. I'll leave you a sandwich."

"Okay, thanks."

Faith paused, and then went on. "At the age Nathan is, the shrinks usually like to see both parents."

"All right. If he asks, I'll go, but don't you bring it up."

"I wasn't going to. I just wanted to warn you."

It happened that Arthur got home very late that evening. First Ruth had called him in for a report on the events of the day.

"Did Horster ever go and see Josephine?" she wanted to know.

"No, I asked her, and she said he hadn't."

"So how does he know what's going on?"

"He and I had a little session."

"About what?"

"About who might have done in Nichols."

"Does he call you in for these sessions often?"

"It depends on what you mean by often."

"All right," said Ruth. "Let's put it this way. I understand he sent Josephine flowers when her son graduated from high school. Did he know to do that, or did you tell him?"

"I told him. Or I told him about the graduation."

"And he called Mongoose at home when he got pneumonia and was out for a week. Did he notice, or did you tell him?"

"I told him."

Ruth ran a hand through her hair.

"The only thing necessary for the triumph of evil is for good men to do nothing," she said.

"I'm friendly," said Arthur.

"I know," said Ruth, "but you shouldn't always be *so* friendly, and you certainly shouldn't be so damn trusting."

Now it was Arthur's turn to shrug. "I try very hard to get along," he said. "I always have. But that's because it doesn't come naturally."

"So what did he get from you today?" Ruth asked.

"I don't know that he got anything," said Arthur. He wanted to know if I knew what a rat fink is."

"And do you?" she asked.

Arthur shrugged.

"Enough," said Ruth. "Let's do some work." So they

worked until after 5 P.M. on a difficult story about a man who had defrauded the federal food-stamp program while owning a penthouse apartment in Chicago and a center-hall colonial in Fort Lauderdale.

"I think we've done all we can," said Ruth. "Let's give it back to Josephine and see what she says tomorrow. It doesn't close until Thursday."

"What an awful story," Arthur said.

"It's true," said Ruth. "These pieces all sound alike to me."

"So why do you put them in your issue? All that is necessary for the triumph of evil . . ."

Ruth blushed. "Horster would nail me if I didn't. He's even more adamant about food stamps than Fallow used to be."

"I've never understood that about Fallow," said Arthur. "Why should a guy so personally generous be so opposed to a program to feed the hungry?"

"It's really a generational thing," said Ruth. "You've got to remember that his father was president of this little college and never got paid more than fifteen hundred dollars in a year. He gave five hundred of it back to the school. Fallow was one of five children. So they must've been cold, and sometimes they were probably even hungry. Fallow loved his father and admires his memory. So he has to think of the willingness to suffer economic hardship as a virtue."

"Well, I understand that. But Fallow's father was a professor of classics."

"Do you think it's easier to starve if you're a professor of classics?"

"Yes, I do," said Arthur, and then laughed. "I would expect Fallow to understand that some of the people who benefit from the food-stamp program are culturally as well as economically deprived."

"He does understand that. He thinks the food-stamp program is corrupt, and corrupting, but he can be reasoned with. When he was overseeing the magazine, I was able to get him to kill one of these pieces now and again. But now younger editors do most of the signing off on the table of contents,

and Horster's made government excess his particular baili-
wick. You could argue with Fallow being Fallow. This is
Horster being Fallow. You can't argue with an imitation."

Arthur shrugged. "I guess," he said, picked up his copy of
the proof and started out of Ruth's office.

"You want a drink?" asked Ruth.

"I'd love one."

"Do you like Irish whiskey?" she asked, yawning and
stretching her arms out behind her in a way that accentuated
her figure. The warm-up suit—which he presumed she had
worn because she played tennis at lunch—had a zippered front.
The zipper had moved down about three inches. He could see
a patch of white throat and, below this, a touch of what might
have been the top of her brassiere.

"Sounds good," said Arthur.

"You should call home first, so they won't hold the meat
loaf and green beans for you."

"I don't have to," said Arthur. "They're all out."

"Have you ever been to Ballantyne's?" Ruth asked.

"No."

"Good, that's where we'll go. You follow me in your car,"
she said. "Ballantyne's is right in town, across from the dry
cleaner."

But when they passed The Village Cleaner, Ruth's black
Honda didn't even slow down. She headed out toward
Connecticut. Fifteen minutes later she signaled, and Arthur
followed her off the road and into a wooded drive. Ruth got
out of her car, went to the mailbox, then got back in and
drove the rest of the way to a sprawling white farmhouse
with a red barn. A loud barking started up inside the house.
Ruth got out of the car and walked to the window of the van.
She was carrying her mail.

"I'm sorry," she said. "In college they used to call me high
pockets. I've never quite gotten over the habit of thrift. I have
Irish whiskey at home. Actually, I think I've got both
Bushmills and Jameson. At Ballantyne's they'd charge us four
dollars a shot. I hope you don't mind?"

"No," said Arthur. "This is a great house."

"Do you like it? I think it's a little gloomy. Look, you'd better stay in the car while I let Eldridge out. He doesn't understand about strangers."

Ruth went to the door and fiddled for a minute with her keys. The barking stopped. Then it started again and a big Doberman raced out to the van snarling and baring its teeth. Arthur rolled his window up halfway.

"Now, now," said Ruth. "Leave Arthur alone. You go do your business and then I'll put you in the run, baby." To Arthur she said, "Roll up your window the rest of the way and ignore him."

Arthur cranked up his window. The dog snuffled at the tires, and then followed his mistress off behind the house. Ruth came back in about five minutes. "We're all right now," she said.

The front door opened onto a big kitchen with a brick fireplace on one wall. The counters were eggshell and the floor was orange tile. Ruth stopped just inside the door and took off her shoes. "The cleaning woman came today," she said, "and I like to keep the floor clean for at least a day or two."

Arthur took off his own shoes. He followed Ruth into the living room. There was a large painting over the fireplace, and Ruth paused to look at it. Arthur came up to her side.

"Art lesson," she said. The oil was of a man in a devil suit and a woman in a white dress. There was a crowd in front of the couple. The men were dressed in tights, the women in long dresses. In the background you could just make out the mouth of the cave.

"That's ancient Venice," Ruth explained. "When they caught adulterers, they'd wash the woman in holy water and put her back in her wedding gown. The man would be dyed scarlet and given the horns and triton of a lesser devil. They'd put the couple in a cave and close up the entrance with stone and mortar."

Arthur nodded. "You seem to know quite a lot about adultery," he said.

Ruth shrugged. "I guess I know something about love," she said. "This is deep background. I mean, I'd be fired if they knew, but I write a column for the *Ladies' Home Journal*."

"Advice to the lovelorn?"

"Like that."

"What do you tell them?"

"I suppose it depends on what their problem is," Ruth said. "But you want a drink?"

"Yes," said Arthur. "Tell me where the liquor is, and I'll get a drink for you too."

"It's in the cabinet over the stove. Use the glasses on the first shelf. The refrigerator has an ice maker."

"Irish whiskey?"

"No, I'll have Scotch."

When Arthur returned, Ruth was seated on a sofa in the living room, sorting through some envelopes. There was a letter from her congressman and a circular from a local chiropractor. Nothing personal. She took the drink, and he settled in an armchair.

"You know what I'd tell them about love?" asked Arthur. "Assuming anyone wanted to know what I thought about love."

"No," said Ruth, putting down the mail. "What would you tell them?"

"I'd tell them not to."

"Oh, come on, you're too young to be so bitter."

"I don't think it has anything to do with age. Love is something wrong. It's like having the twenty-four-hour bug, only it doesn't last for twenty-four hours."

Ruth laughed. "You make it sound very sexy," she said.

Arthur didn't smile.

"You're disappointed?"

"Mostly I'm disappointed for Faith. She's wretched."

"Maybe you should be nicer to her?"

"I'm as nice as I know how to be. I make her tea. I vacuum the living room. I watch the kid. I go to work. And she's miserable. It's almost as if the things I do for her make it worse. It's like I've done some terrible thing to her, just by being myself."

"But you haven't," said Ruth.

"Yes, I have. She used to be happy. You weren't there. I was. Now she's inconsolable. Won't screw, won't eat. And I don't know what to do."

"What about you? Are you happy?"

"Sure, I'm happy sometimes. But I was happy sometimes before I got married. And before I got married, I wasn't ruining anybody else's life."

"Are you sure she was happy before you got married?"

"As sure as I can be. Or at least she wasn't unhappy on my account. She didn't care enough."

"You're a good-looking guy. How do you know she didn't care enough?"

"We're talking Thanksgiving weekend," said Arthur. "It was my senior year at boarding school. I'd been writing Faith a letter every day for a month or so. We were going to spend Saturday afternoon together. We were going to go for a walk in the woods." Arthur took a long pull on his drink. "I came home Wednesday. I called Faith's house immediately. Her mother picked up; she was so sorry, Faith was sick. Faith couldn't possibly go out. She told me it wasn't serious, but Faith was going to spend all weekend in bed.

"About an hour later I got a call from a guy I knew at Sleepy Hollow High School. He told me he'd seen my ex-girlfriend.

"I asked him what he meant.

"He said, 'I mean Faith. I saw her out in the parking lot in Harry Miller's convertible.'

" 'Talking?' I asked.

"And he said, 'No, I mean they weren't talking much. They may have talked some. I mean they must have had to come up for air sometime.' "

"Nice story," said Ruth sarcastically.

"Not a nice story," said Arthur. "A love story."

TWENTY-SIX

The cafeteria at World Headquarters had a tendency to make a carnival of itself. On Saint Patrick's Day the mashed potatoes were green and the biscuits were soda bread. The servers behind the steam tables wore green plastic hats. The soundtrack from the Disney movie *Darby O'Gill and the Little People* was played over the PA. On the Fourth of July the frankfurters and hamburgers bristled with tiny American flags. The PA played the soundtrack from *Yankee Doodle Dandy*. At first these celebrations were the familiar ones, but with the upsurge of nationalism abroad in the 1970s, the company—which had substantial holdings overseas—had been trying to present itself as an international concern. The cafeteria began to serve bangers and mash on Guy Fawkes day.

On the day after Nichols was fired, small brass cannons had been placed at the corners of the steam tables, and the servers had their heads swathed in ketchup-stained diapers.

Arthur actually felt like celebrating. Ruth had been bucking up his ego. Horster kept promising to buck up his salary. The combination was intoxicating. Besides, he always enjoyed Mongoose. The older man had brown hair and eyes again. He and Arthur picked up their trays. Arthur gave him a questioning look. "Bastille Day," said Mongoose. The menu was blue, white and red. It was posted just after the tray station and its offerings included lamb stew sansculotte.

"That's not much of an achievement," said Arthur. "The hard part is getting the culotte on the lamb. Most lamb in this country already comes without the culotte."

"I heard about this," said Mongoose. "I know there was considerable debate about the music. Somebody suggested they play the 'Marseillaise.'"

"I trust he was fired?" said Arthur.

"He wasn't fired, but they decided instead on the soundtrack from *A Man and a Woman*. Arthur had Fraternity salad, a Jacobin bun and a cup of Dannon vanilla yogurt. Mongoose had Equality stew, which looked just like Salisbury steak, and some Fraternity salad and a bowl of Liberty soup. "Now if you had a piece of dessert called Death, you'd be all set," said Arthur. "Equality, Fraternity, Liberty and Death."

"It's a far, far better thing I do than I have ever done," said Mongoose.

They found a table by a window.

"So who do you think turned him in?" Arthur asked when they were sitting.

Mongoose took a forkful of stew, chewed and swallowed. "I'm not sure. How well do you know Ruth West?"

"I know her."

"I thought that she had made you something of a favorite?" Arthur ignored the question. He took the lid off his yogurt.

"I think it was Horster," he said. "He called me into his office to talk about the switch, and his interest was unseemly."

"That doesn't need to mean anything with Horster," said Mongoose. "His interest in chocolate pudding is unseemly."

"But he asked me if I knew what a rat fink was."

"So what's that supposed to mean?" asked Mongoose.

"It's psychology 101," said Arthur. "He says the obvious so that I'll think it's not true."

Mongoose was not so sure. "I don't know," he said. "It's just too pat. Although there are other people who share your suspicions. Arnold Baker, for instance, thinks that Horster played matchmaker with Nichols and Mary, that he encouraged Ms. Bradford in her editorial ambitions, and then turned them both in."

"Do you believe that?" asked Arthur.

"Just because Horster looks like a scoundrel, that doesn't mean he is one." Mongoose sat back and reached into his breast pocket with two fingers. Arthur perked up, but no cigarette appeared. Mongoose took another forkful of stew.

"So I hear you've met Palumbardo," he said.

"Yeah," said Arthur. "I thought he was nice."

Mongoose chuckled. "Well, that's the impression you need to give if you're going to sell snake oil."

"What do you mean?" said Arthur defensively. "He started out in newspapers."

"He started out in sales," said Mongoose. "He was a salesman at the newspaper, and he's a salesman here."

"Is he good?"

"It depends on what you mean by good. If you mean, does he sell things, he's great. If you mean, does he have a shred of decency, that's different. You know they used to call him Repeat?"

"Yeah, I heard that."

"He worked at a big chemical company. They make shampoo. He was just a young guy—right out of NYU—and the company had a meeting to figure out how to sell more shampoo. Some of the chemists wanted to change the formula in a way that might make the hair look better. Some of them wanted to improve the smell. All the plans would have cost money, and none of them guaranteed a big increase in profits. Then Palumbardo chimes in. He has a plan that will almost double the sales of shampoo. He tells them to look at the instructions on the back of a bottle. The instructions tell the consumer to wet the hair, put in a dab of shampoo, lather up and rinse. So Palumbardo says they should add one word. Where it says rinse and then there's a period, they should put in the word *Repeat* and another period."

"Did they do it?"

"Sure they did. Now everybody does. The other companies took a while to catch on, but they figured it out."

Arthur wagged his head. "Shit," he said. "He seemed so nice."

"He is nice," said Mongoose. "And smart. But that doesn't make him decent."

Arthur ate the rest of his yogurt in silence.

"The board will have to meet now," Mongoose continued, "and appoint a new chairman and editor-in-chief."

Arthur nodded. "This is kind of off the track," he said, "but I wondered if either of your children went to the Evergreen Nursery School?"

"Yes, they both did," said Mongoose. "Why do you ask?"

"Nathan's having trouble, and I'm hoping it's the school and not Nathan."

"What's the problem?"

"They say that Nathan is sad all the time. They have a reading period every day, and a different child gets to pick the book for each session, so Nathan gets to pick a book about every week and a half. He always picks *The Story of Babar*."

"So? That's not bad."

"But all he likes is the part where the mother gets killed. That's all he's interested in. He has the teacher read those first five or six pages a dozen times. 'The hunter has killed Barbar's mother! The monkey hides, the birds fly away, Babar cries.' That's the part he likes. He loses interest as soon as the elephant moves into the city and starts to make something of himself."

"Well, at least he's not materialistic," said Mongoose. "All little Adam ever cared about was the kind of car Babar drove. He wanted a car just like it. He was always complaining that De Brunhoff was not explicit enough about the roadster."

On the Friday after the celebration of the storming of the Bastille, Arthur saw three helicopters parked on the lawn behind the antique farmhouse where he'd been taken to lunch on one of his first visits to Paradise. "It's a meeting of the executive board," Josephine explained. Two days later a memo was issued in which Dean Nichols was congratulated on his appointment as director of new projects, and thanked for his "brilliant service to this magazine."

Arnold Baker was "realizing a lifelong dream to live full-time in his house in Maine. We are saddened by this departure, and will miss his rare combination of sophistication and passion," the memo continued. It was not until the final paragraph that Albert Palumbardo was named chairman of the board. Peter Wheelwright would be acting editor-in-chief.

"What's interesting," said Mongoose, "is that the job's been broken up. Dean Nichols was both editor-in-chief and chairman of the board. This is the first time somebody from the business side has been more powerful than the editor. This is also the first time we've had a memo from the board. Memos usually come from Fallow."

"What surprises me," said Arthur, "is that they didn't give the top editorial job to Horster."

Mongoose chuckled. "You are loyal," he said. "But nobody else expected him to get promoted."

"Nobody but me and Horster," said Arthur.

"That's right," said Mongoose. "Nobody but you and Horster."

"What does 'acting' mean?" Arthur asked.

" 'Acting' means nothing," said Mongoose. "It's Wheelwright now till death do us part."

★   ★   ★

Palumbardo's first official act was to employ a consulting firm that would compare benefits and salaries at *The American Reader* with those at other companies in that part of the state.

Arthur visited Ruth's house three times that month, and it was not until the third visit that she made her speech.

"You see, I was smart," she said without preamble. "I did well in college, but I suppose there will always be a question in some people's minds about whether or not I could have made it without the support of certain older men. Which brings us to you. I'm afraid that in your case there's no question. If I don't help, you'll founder. So we're going to spend our evenings going over proofs. You don't mind getting a little help where you need it, do you?"

"No," said Arthur. "Certainly not. But why?"

"A lot of people helped me," Ruth explained. "And the only way I can be free of that is to help somebody else."

Arthur always told Faith where he was going. He'd stop in Bedford Village on the way to Pound Ridge and send Faith a single red rose.

"I'll have your company tonight, your wife will have flowers tomorrow," Ruth said when she told him to do it. "I insist."

TWENTY-SEVEN

The story ran on the front page of *The New York Times*. Lisha was going to buy a new bedroom set. A copy editor named Mary was getting a lime-green Chevette. Josephine wouldn't say. "It's supposed to be retribution," she said, "and I'm not sure how justice represents itself to me, but I'm certain that it doesn't appear as a chest of drawers or a compact car. Maybe a weeping cherry tree."

"If you're really intent on representing justice," said Arthur, "I would think you'd want cold steel, or maybe a lemon tree."

"Lemon trees don't survive outside in this part of the world," said Josephine. "And the ceilings in my house are low."

"Perfect," said Arthur. "Buy a lemon tree and let it die."

The American Reader did not acknowledge that it had discriminated against its female employees. It did agree, however, to give them $1.5 million dollars in back pay and salary increases. It also paid the lawyers who had brought suit on their behalf. Every one of more than two thousand women on the staff got a check. *The New York Times* reported it as the largest settlement to date in a suit brought by women against their employer. The *Times* also reported that Mr. and Mrs. Fallow were dead.

George and Louise Fallow did not go out in public very much anymore in the late 1970s, but their money still did. They gave a new wing to the fine-arts museum, they gave the reptile nursery to the zoo. They even provided free eyeglasses for every child who needed them in the New York City public schools. Their names were chiseled in stone and etched onto brass plates throughout the New York metropolitan region. With so many monuments, it was no wonder that the *Times* thought they must be buried somewhere.

The mistake occasioned a memo to the staff. Signed "The Former Mr. and Mrs. Fallow," it reported that "the clouds are small, but we each have our own, and the harp music is truly otherworldly."

All the talk of cash payments enraged Faith. "What about the wives of underpaid men, where do they fit into this new scheme of things? I feel now like I'm being discriminated against because I married you."

But eleven days after the *Times* story, Peter Wheelwright called Arthur into his office. "A berth has opened up on the magazine's regular editorial staff," he said, "and we wonder if you're still interested."

The next morning Arthur was called in to see Horster. His mentor wasn't on the phone. He wasn't reading anything either. Arthur took the conch sweater off the visitor's chair and sat down.

"I was wondering if—with all his creative obligations—your father had time to teach you any manners."

Arthur looked blank.

"All right," said Horster, "I'll be more explicit. I was wondering when you were going to get around to thanking me."

Mongoose waited until the afternoon to call. "I was telling Joan about the problems you said Nathan was having at Evergreen," he said, "and she said the school isn't what it used to be. Apparently Miss Ringwald is an intuitive instructor, but she's not very good at picking other teachers. I wanted to tell you that because I felt that what I said at lunch might have sounded unsympathetic."

"Thank you," said Arthur, "but I didn't think you were being unsympathetic."

"Good," said Mongoose, "and I'm delighted about your impending promotion. Now that this has finally gone through, Joan said I have to find a new hobby. You've been my main interest for some time now."

"But you've got snakes," said Arthur.

"I know," said Mongoose, "I have been neglecting my aquariums. In any case, congratulations."

"Thank you for all your support," said Arthur. "And apologize to Agamemnon for me."

Two evenings after this, Ruth had Arthur to her house to work over the proof of a story titled "Suicide: The Tragedy Untold."

"So what sort of editor do you think you'll make?" she asked.

"I think I'll be all right," said Arthur.

"*Splendid* was the word I used," said Ruth. "I told them you'd be splendid." And then, "You remembered to send Faith flowers?"

"Sure, and I brought her chocolates on the day I was promoted. You don't have to teach me to be uxorious. That's not what's the matter with our marriage."

"What is the matter?"

"I guess she's mistaken me for her father."

"She hates her father?"

"It's not exactly hate, but she knows he's one guy she shouldn't sleep with."

Ruth shrugged. "Poor baby. And *you* think she's your mother?"

"Not exactly."

"Life is not an exact science. But if she does think you're her father, there's a simple solution."

"What's that?"

"Make them fight."

"Then she'll be even more upset. Besides, we don't have any money."

Before Arthur drove home that evening, Ruth went up into her study and produced a clipping from the *Ladies' Home Journal*. "Try this," she said.

The piece was two pages long with a picture of a robot.

"Too often sex can be a power game," it began. "and as long as each moment is up for grabs, nobody ever gains control. So partners should arrange to surrender control on alternate evenings. One pleasant and imaginative way to do this is to play at robots.

"The husband is a robot one night. He must pretend to have no will of his own and do whatever his wife wishes. The next night the wife is the robot."

Nathan was sleeping over with Faith's parents on the following evening, so Arthur suggested that he and Faith play robots. "I know it's a silly idea," he said over dinner. "But why don't we give it a try? Tonight I'll be your robot. Tomorrow night you can be mine."

Faith agreed that it was a silly idea, but she said that Arthur could be her robot, her sex slave, if that was what he really wanted to be. Arthur said that that was what he wanted.

"All right, sex slave," Faith said after dinner, "clean up the dishes."

"I always clean up the dishes," said Arthur.

"But that's what I want you to do," said Faith. "Remember, you're my sex slave. And after that I want a frozen vanilla yogurt in bed and a frozen Milky Way. Chop chop."

The next evening Nathan was at home, so Arthur had to wait until the end of the week for his chance to make a sex slave out of Faith.

"All right," he said after dinner, and his voice was almost hoarse with desire. "Come here, robot, and sit in my lap."

"I don't want to sit in your lap," said Faith. "I'm tired. Why don't you clean the dishes instead?"

Arthur waited a week to tell his father about the promotion. They hadn't spoken in some time. Arthur had missed the old man a lot, but Faith had been insistent. "Just see how you feel for a bit," she said. "Give it a try, for me."

So Arthur had given it a try, and how he felt was shitty. Whatever you thought of Icarus—and Arthur's feelings were intensely mixed—the world was a whole lot less interesting without him.

But now he had an excuse. He expected to be snapped at. He expected to be punished for his betrayal, but Icarus was not angry. He was cheerful. Encouraged, Arthur complained about Faith.

"Why do we do it?" he asked. "I mean, why did I get married? You warned me. I mean, I knew exactly how you felt about women."

Icarus paused. "How do I feel about women?"

"I don't know. That they're bad. That the good ones are trouble."

Icarus blew air out of his mouth. "You misunderstand," he said. "I've got company, and I'm sure you're busy too. So I'll try and give it to you as briefly as I can. Women are like the world. Being in love brings you into the world. The world's gorgeous, and it's also punishing. To love somebody is to love the world."

"But it's such a fight," said Arthur. "I hate to fight."

Icarus had cupped his hand over the mouthpiece, but Arthur could hear him calling out to his guest, "I think the fire must be ready by now. The spatula is in the drawer to the left of the dishwasher." Arthur wondered idly what kind of woman would grill an old man's hamburgers. Icarus came back on the line.

"I'm sorry," he said. "I have to get off now, but look, you're right, it is a fight. And sometimes you may think you have a choice. You don't have a choice. If you're not in love you're not alive. You're nothing. Less than nothing."

Two weeks after Palumbardo's ascension, a memo was released showing the results of the study the new chairman had sponsored. It congratulated employees on the lavishness of their working conditions. "Even hourly workers," it said, "are paid roughly the same for an 8:30 A.M. to 4:00 P.M. shift as their opposites in other corporations are paid for working from nine to five, or in some cases from 8:30 A.M. to 5:00 P.M."

When interoffice delivered Arthur's first associate editor check, he took the calculator out of his briefcase and worked through a couple of simple computations. He thought immediately of Hugh Melvin. He kicked off his wingtips—now genuine—and looked speculatively at his stockinged feet.

TWENTY-EIGHT

World Headquarters had two flagpoles. One flew the Stars and Stripes and one the company colors. Inside the central tower was a set of chimes. These played at 8:30 A.M., at noon and again at 4 P.M., when the hourly employees went home. There had once been a keyboard for the chimes, according to Cunningham. This was disconnected in the 1950s and replaced with a mechanical device after a drunken guard got at it one Monday morning and banged out "The Ants Go Marching One by One," while the editors and secretaries poured out of the parking lot and through the big double doors.

The escutcheon above the front entrance featured a representation of a gauntleted hand with a lance. The pommel and hilt were traditional, but the shaft was missing and its place taken by a book, pages flapping. Arthur guessed that this could be loosely translated as "The book is mightier than the lance." He couldn't help but think, though, how dismayed a knight might be upon finding that his chief weapon had been replaced with a book, however timely or readable.

It didn't feel significantly different walking through the front door as an associate editor than it had as a member of the copydesk, except that Arthur had a friend. Arthur and Gilbert Collingwood had passed each other in the halls on a number of occasions before the long-awaited promotion, and had smiled cordially, but they had not exchanged words. Associate editors didn't speak with copy editors.

But now that the fences were down, Gilbert seemed very interested. He came to visit at about 10 A.M. on the first day of Arthur's term as associate editor. He had a cup of coffee and a six-pack of Oreos. He put down the Oreos and began to fiddle with the pencils Arthur kept in a mug beside his plastic paper-clip holder.

Arthur was doing the first edit of an article titled "I Am Bob's Throat." It was part of a series that was working its way through Bob's entire body, switching occasionally to Bessie, as in the case of "I Am Bessie's Breast."

"So you're the famous Arthur South Prentice?" said Gilbert.

"Famous?" asked Arthur.

"You have a famous father," said Gilbert.

"Not the same thing," said Arthur.

"I have trouble concentrating this time of day. I need a break." Gilbert removed his jacket, hung it on the back of the visitor's chair. Then he took a swing with an imaginary racket. "In fact I could do with a little squash about now," he said. "Do you play?"

"No," said Arthur.

Gilbert took another practice swing. "I don't play much anymore myself," he said. "I have trouble with my elbow. A calcium deposit. But I won a championship in Connecticut a couple of years back."

Arthur looked impressed.

Gilbert walked behind Arthur's desk and began to run an index finger over the spines of the books. "It was a bust," he said. "All you get is a sweat suit and a giant goblet. There's a sticker on the goblet that says that it's not advisable to drink out of it. They treat it with some sort of poison in order to make it shine. My wife keeps all my trophies in the back of the closet." Gilbert turned and faced Arthur again.

"Are you married?" he asked.

Arthur nodded.

"Here," said Gilbert. "I've got a picture," and he produced a snapshot of a blonde in a bikini, sitting on the wooden transom of an old-fashioned inboard speedboat.

"We don't have any children," Gilbert said. "I'm too much of a child myself for children. Grace doesn't want them either."

"Does she work?"

"I'm afraid so."

"Why don't you want her to work?"

"I'm old-fashioned. I like them barefoot and pregnant, or at least barefoot."

"She has nice feet."

"Yeah, she used to model. In fact she was once voted the best-looking girl in Dallas. The newspaper ran a contest her senior year in high school. Ever been to Dallas?"

Arthur hadn't been to Dallas.

"I grew up in Fort Worth," said Gilbert. "We had an old house with a lot of gardens. My mother's bed of annuals is in a book about the great houses in Texas."

The next day Gilbert wanted to discuss literature. "If you had to pick out two books to take to an uninhabited island," he said without preamble, as he settled into Arthur's armchair, "which would they be?"

"It would depend on the island," said Arthur, and he looked down almost longingly at page 4 of "Bob's Throat." He'd been wondering if he should cut the epiglottis.

★   ★   ★

"He's like a walkie-talkie," Arthur told Ruth when she asked about Gilbert. "The transmit button is taped down, and the receive button doesn't work at all."

"But you're so polite," Ruth said. "Do you ever try and interrupt?"

"Probably not as hard as I should," Arthur admitted, "but I do try. I told him Cunningham's new joke, the one about three men in a plane with two parachutes and a knapsack."

"I don't remember."

"Henry Kissinger's in a plane with the pilot and a bishop and a Boy Scout. The pilot dies of a heart attack and the plane is going to crash. The Scout has a knapsack with two peanut butter and jelly sandwiches and a hard-boiled egg. There are two parachutes. They're trying to figure out who should die, and Kissinger says he has to have the first parachute because he's the smartest man in the world."

"Now I remember."

"Well, I told him the whole thing. He didn't laugh."

"It isn't a very good joke," said Ruth.

"I laughed," said Arthur.

Ruth chuckled. "You always do laugh," she said. "You're one of the few men I've known who actually likes to listen."

Arthur did like to listen to Gilbert Collingwood. Gilbert's life was a series of thrilling clichés. Arthur liked a good cliché as much as the next man, but it had been his consistent experience that they almost never occurred in life. What Arthur couldn't tell was if Gilbert actually had had the thrilling life, which he subsequently transformed into clichés, or if he'd just strung together a lot of clichés from books and movies and was pretending they were his own. If Gilbert was telling the truth, then Gilbert was way ahead. His life didn't just make a better story, it made a better life.

Gilbert's stories all had a certain plausibility, but then there was a symmetry and drama rarely found outside of B movies. He might well have started in advertising. Advertising was supposed to have guys like Gilbert. And Arthur thought it possible that Gilbert had been chosen to fire fifty people from the firm he worked for in South Africa. Advertising firms did have massive layoffs.

"I was sweating bullets. I thought that every guy I spoke to was going to make a scene. But, you know, forty-nine of the people I fired acted like I was doing them a favor. One of them spat in my face. The moment we got back in the black, I tried to look him up. He was the first one I wanted to hire."

"So did you?"

"He already had a job. A good job. Not as good as mine."

"What did you earn when you were firing people?"

"The last year I was in Joeburg I made one hundred fifty thousand dollars. Didn't save a nickel. I was living with a fashion model. I drank more champagne that year than I drank water."

"Must have been hard to give that up."

"Went cold turkey," said Collingwood. "That's the only way to do it. I took a year off. Did no work. I went to California and lay on the beach. Ever been to Monterey?"

"No."

"Gorgeous town. When I needed to eat, I'd do an odd job. But I didn't work hard. I was one of those lilies of the field Christ talks about. In Monterey I broke even at five thousand dollars. In South Africa it cost me a lot more to have nothing."

"Speaking of working," said Arthur, "I'd better get back to my manuscript."

Gilbert shrugged. "Up to you," he said.

After he was done with Bob's throat—the epiglottis stayed—Arthur got an article that was part of a series called "At Large." These pieces profiled people who had been charged with numerous crimes but never convicted.

"The Wallet King of Times Square" came in at thirty-five pages. The subject, a Mr. X, brokered stolen wallets and handbags. Horster had told Arthur he should read an article at least three times before marking it. "You must know the piece better than the author knew it," he said. "And none of your changes can be arbitrary. Paul Rutherford was the first editor Fallow hired, and he used to say, 'If it is not necessary to change, then it is necessary not to change.' "

It was 3:04 P.M. by the time Arthur was done with the third reading. His head was reeling. Gilbert usually came around at about that time of day with a chapter of his autobiography. Arthur gazed dreamily out of his office window. His new view was of the Italian garden. This was a series of white gravel paths and thickly planted rectangular flower beds. A bronze boy stood on a rock in the center of a marble pool. If it was summer, and there wasn't a drought, water spurted out of the top of the boy's head.

Mongoose had told Arthur that the spray used to come from "a more biologically correct aperture," but that when the Fallows brought the statue from a villa outside of Florence, they had had the penis soldered shut and a fresh hole bored in the boy's bronze skull.

Arthur's eyes were just closing when the phone rang. It was Icarus Prentice.

"I'm going to Vermont for a week starting Monday," he said. "I just wanted you to know, in case you tried to phone."

"Thanks," said Arthur. "Where are you going?"

"It's one of those bicycle trips. You ride a certain distance every day, and then stay at an inn."

"Are you going alone?"

"No, I've got a date."

"Good. Give her my love."

"It's my love she wants."

"All right then, give her your love."

Arthur wanted to ask his father if he was drinking, but he didn't dare.

Arthur read about The Wallet King until 3:14 P.M. Then he

got up and headed down the hall. As he approached Gilbert's office, he heard the voice of Dennis Cunningham.

"So now only the bishop and the Boy Scout were left. The bishop said, 'I'll go without the parachute. I've had a rich, full life and I'm ready to meet my Lord.' But the Boy Scout said, 'No, Father, we don't have to argue about this, because the smartest man in the world just jumped out of the plane with two peanut butter and jelly sandwiches and a hard-boiled egg.' " This was the joke Gilbert had already heard, the one he wouldn't even let Arthur tell him. So Arthur paused in the hall, he wanted to see how rude his friend would be.

The sound he heard was loud, all right, but it wasn't rude. Gilbert was laughing. "That's great," said Arthur's friend. "The smartest man in the world, ha ha ha. With my knapsack. Ha ha ha. I can't wait to tell Grace."

TWENTY-NINE

The single great advantage to having James Horster as a mentor was that one didn't have to share. Arthur adored Ruth, but then a lot of people adored her. Cunningham still visited Arthur in the afternoon, and he still told jokes. He also visited Gilbert in the afternoon. He told Gilbert jokes: the same jokes.

Horster had used Arthur to cultivate his image as a mingler, but this was a sham. Aside from those who were so pathetic that his displeasure could have brought them immediate ruin—his secretary, his wife and a half a dozen writers—Horster seemed to be without intimates.

"He and Cunningham are both monsters," said Gilbert. "Horster has no surface, Cunningham is nothing but."

Arthur bridled. "I like Cunningham," he said. "I like his jokes."

"Sure," said Gilbert. "You know where he gets them, don't you?"

"No, where does anybody get a joke?"

"Cunningham gets his out of the files. They're old jokes."

"Why would we keep old jokes on file?"

"To make sure we don't use them again. The rule used to be that a joke could never run twice in *The American Reader*. Now the rule is that a joke can't be used again until ten years have passed. Cunningham fishes all his jokes out of the older-than-ten-years file."

"But wouldn't an old joke sound old?"

"Not necessarily. There are constants in the human experience."

"What about political jokes? What about Henry Kissinger and the parachute? That isn't a fifteen-year-old joke."

"Sure it is. It was about Adlai Stevenson fifteen years ago. Before that they probably told the same joke about Harold Ickes. There have been airplanes for a long time, and Boy Scouts, and bishops."

Gilbert's cynicism kept him lodged at his same spot on the masthead, while Arthur floated mysteriously upward. Two months after Wheelwright made him an associate editor, the shuffle caused by Arnold Baker's departure opened up a senior editor slot, and he was given that. His salary was bumped from $53,000 to $79,000, and he was assured that his bonus would bring it to $85,000.

Faith still wasn't interested in screwing, but she did begin to iron her husband's shirts, even though they were wash and wear. Besides, Arthur wasn't as interested either. "Power is the sex of the seventies," said Gilbert Collingwood.

"Wrong as usual," said Arthur. "But not dead wrong."

The fledgling exec spent a long weekend with a handful of top editors discussing the future of publishing at a place called The Woods of Westchester. He spent another long weekend at a conference center on the coast of North Carolina. This featured representatives of other publications, and the subject was the use of computers in magazines with a circulation of more than one million. Arthur's schedule included three private tennis lessons and an afternoon of deep-sea fishing.

In light of his new earning power, a system was set up whereby he took over the full payments on the house in Upcounty Estates, with the understanding that when he could foot the down payment, the deed would be turned over.

At work he was assigned his own personal secretary. Linda Patterson was young and not unattractive. She had had acne as an adolescent and her cheeks were badly pitted. But her eyes were a rich brown, her hair was blonde. She had a good figure and a warm smile.

She had been some sort of chess champion in high school, and used to spend her lunch hours working out problems on one of those tiny magnetic chess sets that are sold at airports. She almost always wore cowboy boots.

Linda typed Arthur's letters, answered his phone and fetched his morning coffee and the *Times*. This made Arthur a little uncomfortable, and he would sometimes get Linda her tea in the afternoon.

Linda spent a lot of time telling people that her boss was at a meeting. Arthur usually was at a meeting, sometimes with Horster, and sometimes alone as a representative of the deputy editor-in-chief. He carried his big clasp knife with him everywhere. Most of the time he kept it in his briefcase, but sometimes, when alone in his office, he'd take it out and open the blade. Just owning the knife made him feel better. It reminded him of his new understanding of the world he lived in.

Meanwhile, he did less actual work in a day than he had done since college. The frightful job of sitting alone in an office with an article for The Magazine was now well beneath his legitimate area of concern.

"I don't edit anymore," he complained once, during a break in one of Collingwood's autobiographical recitations. "Sometimes I help Ruth with a proof. But I spent more time doing actual line editing when I was on the copydesk."

"You're not supposed to," said Collingwood. "I had a friend at Random House. He said that only the least successful editors actually sit in their offices editing copy. A moderately successful editor is in his office, but he doesn't edit. He talks on the phone. A really successful editor is almost never in the office. You make decisions. That's what they pay you for."

But Arthur had a nagging suspicion that he was being paid for spending time with James Horster. Wednesdays the two families often dined together in the dairy barn that the deputy editor-in-chief had purchased and remodeled. Arthur usually sat next to Lavinia. As the wife of a powerful man, the former Miss Georgia Peach wielded a good deal of power.

She had an almost perfect figure, masses of yellow hair, wide green eyes and pearly white teeth. She was also bonkers.

During high school Arthur had worked one summer at a mental hospital, and had found to his surprise that he rather enjoyed the company of the insane. But that was because when he was with them, he didn't have to pretend that they weren't insane. With Lavinia he did, and this, he found, was extremely hard work.

Lavinia wasn't just crazy, she was crazy and proud of it. If, for instance, she said that she had had chicken dumplings for lunch with Frank Sinatra, one was not supposed to contradict her. One was not even supposed to look politely away. If you did look away, she'd snap at you. "You don't believe me?" she'd say. Lavinia was insane, but she was not stupid.

"You know, this sounds grotesque," Arthur said to Ruth when they were working on a proof together one afternoon, "but being with Lavinia is a little like being with Horster. They're both odd in their own ways, and my job is to pretend that this is not so. It's hard work. The trouble is, their insanity has become an advantage, and my relative sanity is a weakness. I suppose it's because I'm afraid of them. Horster can be wonderful, of course, but any little change in the weather can make him into a first-class shit. I never know when it's coming. But I know that one of the things that excites his wrath is any situation in which my relative sanity is contrasted too sharply with his sense of the world."

Ruth smiled. "What does this remind you of, Mr. Prentice?" she said in a mock Viennese accent.

"I don't know, Dr. West," said Arthur. "I suppose it reminds me of my father."

"Right," she said. "Leave it to Arthur to figure out the obvious. And what about it reminds you of your father?" she said.

"Well, he's crazy. Or at least he's very unconventional."

"And who else does it remind you of?" asked Ruth.

"I don't know?" said Arthur.

"Come, come, Mr. Prentice," said Ruth, slipping back into her fake Viennese accent.

"Faith?" said Arthur.

"Two for two," said Ruth.

"So what am I supposed to do about all this?" said Arthur.

"I don't know," said Ruth. "Knowledge is power."

When Arthur got out of Ruth's office, he went directly to Horster. The purple sweater with conch shells wasn't there. Instead there was a common ski sweater with silver buttons and reindeer. Arthur moved it to the coffee table and took a seat. Horster was on the phone.

"Look, Sal," he said, "you were the one who suggested that we prune back all the flowering crabs. I'm more than willing to pay for any treatment you think might save the trees, but if they die anyway, I'll expect a discount on the replacement. How much was it I paid for them?

"That's what I thought. They were no bargain.

"And that's what you said, but if they die, that doesn't prove that it was clever to buy the most expensive trees, does it?

"No, I won't be home on Saturday, but my wife will. You can talk with her. So we will all keep our fingers crossed, and

I'll speak with you when I get back, which will be a week from Friday."

Horster put down the phone and grinned at Arthur. "The house is supposed to be a joy," he said. "The roof leaks, the basement is damp, the trees die. The septic overflows. I often feel like Job.

" 'Lay not up for yourselves treasures upon earth, where moth and rust doth corrupt, and where thieves break through and steal,' " he said. "Thieves and gardeners," he added. "And plumbers."

"I haven't had the opportunity," said Arthur.

"You will," said Horster, "and you'll live to rue the day." Then he rocked back in his chair, lit a cigarette for himself and passed the pack and lighter to Arthur.

"Where I'm going," he said, "is to the advertising meeting. I'm giving the editorial presentation. My subject is gifted authors, which is why I called you in. In the thirties and forties we used to have the best writers in the world. We took articles from *The New Yorker*. We even ran a little department of pieces from 'Talk of the Town.' Fallow made a point of courting the best writers of his time. In fact, we have a file of the letters he sent to Woolcott Gibbs. Have you seen it?"

Arthur hadn't seen it.

"I'll ask Miss Sullivan to send you a copy. Ross and Fallow had lunch once. It wasn't a success. Two years later *The New Yorker* ran a series attacking us, which was later brought out in book form." He took a long drag on his Kool, let the smoke out through his nose. "A nasty book," he said.

Arthur nodded.

"After the attack they wouldn't allow us to use anything they owned the rights to. But *The American Reader* still had a reputation for getting the best writers sooner or later. That's the great thing about this country, it doesn't matter what your politics are when you're young. Sooner or later you come around to a place where writing for us begins to make sense. Did you know that we had Max Eastman on staff at the end?"

Arthur didn't know.

"He'd been editor of *The Masses*. He'd been tried twice for sedition. He even edited Marx, and we got him to write for us. We probably would have gotten John Reed if he'd survived. *Ten Days Revisited*. Of course Mr. Fallow used to pay well. Our standard fee is twenty-five hundred dollars for a free-lance article. When you work in the insurance and other benefits, the staff writers get closer to twenty thousand dollars per piece. We couldn't do that for your father, but we could easily give him ten thousand dollars for the right article."

"But my father isn't exactly our sort of writer, is he?" said Arthur.

"So much the better," said Horster. "We don't want him to write us a short story. We want a true episode out of his life. How often do you visit with your father?"

"I don't know. Once every couple of weeks."

Horster looked disappointed. "You always gave me the impression that you two were close," he said.

"He's important to me."

"But you never see him?"

"I see him."

"Well, next time you talk to him, bring it up," said Horster with a sigh. "You're his son. I can't imagine somebody giving his son to an organization he wouldn't write one article for." Horster chuckled, as if mildly amused by this idea. "In any case, let's have him to the farmhouse for lunch."

"Okay," said Arthur. "I'll ask him. But I don't see what you could have him write."

"He's a father and husband. Have him put down something about how much his family means to him. Does he have pets?"

"We've always had dogs."

"But we've had so much on dogs. What about cats?"

"We had ring-necked doves for a while. My father doesn't like cats."

"Doves are too clearly symbolic. Cats are a much better idea. He must have some story to tell about a cat. Did his parents own cats?"

"I don't know."

210

"I wonder if a cat ever saved anybody's life in your family. Did you ever read 'Tipper the Rescue Cat'?"

"No."

"Wonderful story. It ran sometime in the late 1940s. We sold a million copies of it in reprint. They built a statue of Tipper in Indianapolis. Have Index dig it out for you. In the meantime, speak with your father. I'm going to hint around about the quality of our writers at this advertisers' meeting. I won't be explicit, but it would be encouraging if you had something to tell me when I got back. You look uncomfortable."

"I'm just surprised, I guess."

At this point Miss Sullivan stuck her head into the office.

"Mr. Palumbardo is here," she said.

Arthur got up.

"No," said Horster, "we need you."

Arthur sat back down. Palumbardo came in and smiled at him. Hands were shaken all around. The chairman was wearing a blue-and-white-striped shirt with a plain white collar. A Cunningham shirt. The tie was power red.

Palumbardo had a manila folder, which he put on Horster's desk and tapped with his index finger. "The way I see it, we can save a couple of million dollars a year," he said.

Horster turned to Arthur. "You know Cunningham?" he asked.

Arthur shrugged.

"Do you like him?"

"Yes, I do."

"But he's not much of a worker?"

"Well, it depends on how you define work," said Arthur. "A company has many needs."

Palumbardo smiled. "We mean work," he said.

"He's not one of our bright young Turks," Horster said, and smiled.

"No," said Arthur. "He's not young."

"I'm afraid," said Horster, frowning now, "that he doesn't value the magazine."

"No," said Arthur. "I wouldn't go that far."

"But he doesn't believe in our articles," said Horster.

"I don't know," said Arthur. "He might. There are people around who believe less."

"Like who?" asked Horster.

"There are a lot of them," said Arthur. "Gilbert Collingwood doesn't believe, really. Neither does Mongoose. But they're both useful members of the staff."

Palumbardo nodded.

Ruth was out of town that next week for a conference on women in publishing, and so when Arthur stayed late, he stayed in his own office.

Cunningham came by at about 5:25 P.M.

He stopped in the hall outside Arthur's opened office door. "Ah, lonely boy," he said.

"Lonely," said Arthur, "but not necessarily blue."

"You often stay late," Cunningham said.

Arthur nodded.

"Can't get your work done during regular hours?" he asked with mock severity.

"That's right," said Arthur.

"You know that Fallow used to insist on having everyone leave at four P.M. It was one of his edicts, like keeping office doors opened and driving American cars. He never had a family of his own, so he wanted to be certain his editors didn't neglect their children."

"Did everyone really go home at four P.M.?"

"Some people did. But then there was what we used to call the parking lot crowd. They would get in their cars at four P.M. and drive around the parking lot until Fallow left. Then they'd come back to the office."

"What if Fallow caught them?" asked Arthur.

"Actually," said Cunningham, "he caught me once."

"How was that?"

Cunningham shrugged. "I was forgiven."

Arthur nodded.

"So this guy falls off a cliff," Cunningham said, "but on the way down he grabs a root. Now he's hanging by one hand over this two-hundred-foot drop. Then he hears a voice. The voice says, 'This is God.' "

"I heard it," said Arthur. "Wasn't it in The Magazine?"

"How long have you been here?" asked Cunningham.

"Three years."

"Shit," said Cunningham. "I must have been in the wrong file."

"Wait a minute," said Arthur. "I know the joke, but I want to know the answer to it. What if it was God? Then what should the guy do?"

"You haven't read the Bible for a while, have you?" asked Cunningham.

"Not since I was confirmed," said Arthur. "No, that's not true. We studied some of it as literature when I was at Choate. But I still don't get the joke. What's the answer?"

"The answer is, you let go," said Cunningham.

"I still don't get it," said Arthur.

"Nothing to get."

THIRTY

Arthur phoned his father that night. This was Wednesday. Icarus Prentice didn't pick up until the seventh ring, and Arthur thought he could tell by the slight slur in his voice that his father was drunk. Maybe he just has his lips too close to the mouthpiece.

"I was wondering if it would be all right with you if Nathan and I came over for a visit Saturday," Arthur asked.

"Certainly it would be all right. I had a date, but I'll cancel it."

"Don't," said Arthur.

"Of course I'll cancel it."

"Are you sure?"

"Of course I'm sure. My date can come tomorrow. I'd love

a visit. Besides, my date was just going to help me in the garden. You can do that."

"Good then," said Arthur.

"Do you need money?"

"No, it's not really about money. I just thought it would be nice to see you," Arthur said, and it was only half a lie. "Faith is going to a plant sale. Nathan's a handful, but we could talk some."

"I'm afraid that there's not a lot to eat. I suppose we could go to Lucy's Family Restaurant."

"Lucy's would be fine. I wouldn't worry. Nathan is happy with cheese and crackers, and I seem to be able to get fat on the fluff in my pockets."

"Fine, I'll look forward to seeing you then. Does Nathan like parrots?"

"I don't know. I suppose."

"Good, then we can show Nathan the parrot. When would you come?"

"Around eleven A.M., I guess."

The next day Gilbert asked Arthur if they could talk off the record.

"Sure," said Arthur.

"All right," said Gilbert. "Off the record then, isn't this place a little weird?"

"I guess it's unique," said Arthur in a successful attempt to choose exactly the wrong word.

"It all looks weird to me now," said Gilbert, "especially since Arnold Baker was fired. I think they're going to clean house. If they can fire Baker, they can certainly fire Cunningham."

"I suppose he could be fired," said Arthur. "His politics have always been off line. He is a kind of liberal, you know. But then politics have never been taken that seriously around here."

"You haven't heard about the incident with the flag?"

"That was years ago."

"Eight years. They sent an American flag sticker out to everybody who subscribed to the domestic edition. They also sent one out with every paycheck, and suggested that employees put it in the windows of their cars. And then they sent Doc out to the parking lot to see who had the sticker on their car and who didn't."

"But Peter Wheelwright didn't put a sticker on his car. He hasn't exactly been penalized."

"How do you know? You didn't see his bonus check for 1968. He could have been killed for all we know. What we're seeing now might be the flight of the phoenix. Besides, I don't like having to pretend I like these terrible articles," said Gilbert. "First we have a piece about how great the government of South Korea is, and that makes me sick. Then we have a piece about how horrible the drifters are in Monterey, California, and that makes me sick too. General Park stands for everything we're against, and Monterey is one of the few truly beautiful places in the world. Park murders people who want to vote. We think that's fine. People in Monterey want to sit around and read, and we think that's criminal."

Arthur shrugged. "You're just frustrated," he said. "Remember, I spent a year on the copydesk. When things start to move, you'll see it's not that bad."

"I just don't like being part of it," said Gilbert. "Some people claim that we have no influence on world affairs. But this is a democracy we live in. A healthy majority of the voters read *The American Reader*. And they take us seriously. They believe every word is true. That's what we tell them, and that's what they believe. So it may well be that we're in a position to precipitate a world depression, or a nuclear holocaust."

"I suppose that was always true," said Arthur.

"But Fallow believed in the articles we ran. Sometimes he was wrong, but he had a moral system. Now The Magazine is run by hypocrites and timeservers. If you have a congruent system of philosophy, and you adhere to it, and you make a terrible mistake, that's tragic. But if all you care about is your income and the title they've given you at a second-rate magazine, and you push civilization into the void, well, that's not even tragic. It's ridiculous."

Arthur got out of his chair. "What makes you say we're second-rate?" he asked sharply.

When Arthur and Nathan arrived at his father's house at 11:20 A.M. that Saturday, the place appeared to be deserted.

Heart attack, Arthur thought. He's had his second heart attack. He's lying on the bathroom floor. He died alone. Arthur rang the doorbell. Then he knocked awkwardly on the frame of the storm door.

"Hello. Daddy. Hello."

A dog began to bark from someplace upstairs. "Let's go home now," said Nathan.

"Grandfather is waiting for us," Arthur said. "I think we'd better go in. He might be sick." The front door was unlocked. Arthur let himself into the living room, pulling Nathan behind him. Leander, the old black Labrador, came unsteadily down the stairs and licked Nathan on the cheek. Nathan shrieked. "Let's go home, Daddy," he said.

"Don't you want to go to a restaurant?"

"I want to go home," said Nathan.

Arthur ignored his son and moved to the bottom of the staircase. He called up the stairs. Still no answer.

They found Icarus Prentice sitting on an aluminum beach chair in the attic. He was watching the old black-and-white television that Arthur had spent so much time with. The straw carpet was still in place. Icarus was wearing chinos, torn at one knee, and a blue Brooks Brothers shirt. The old kind, without the pocket. He was not wearing shoes. Or socks. There was a glass of clear liquid on the floor by the chair. Arthur couldn't tell for sure if it was gin. It might have been some very clean water.

Icarus Prentice looked up from the TV, and for a second

he didn't seem to recognize his son. Then he smiled. "Oh good," he said. "You decided to come."

"Yeah," said Arthur, a little bewildered. "I said I was going to come."

"But you often don't."

"Not when I say I'm going to come."

"Well, in any case, you did," said Icarus.

"Are you sick?" Nathan asked.

"No," said Icarus. "Why would you think I'm sick? Why would he think I'm sick?" he said, looking to Arthur.

"No reason," said Arthur.

"Well, I'm not sick," said Icarus, "but I am embarrassed. I don't like to be caught up here watching the moving pictures like some frustrated housewife."

Arthur shrugged.

Icarus got up from his chair. "Can I interest you in some tea?"

"Tea would be great," said Arthur, and he and his son and his father headed down to the kitchen.

"You know what's so sad about daytime television?" Icarus said, as he put on the kettle. "It's the hope. It's the forced cheerfulness. 'You'll be fully licensed to operate heavy equipment,' that sort of thing. The advertisements tell the women that they are all going to lose fifteen pounds and use the hair dye of professionals. The men are going to get a job driving a truck as big as the *Queen Mary*. And I can see them, legions of them, and they're sitting around in dark rooms across the country, drinking gin and eating barbecued potato chips. They're not going to drive a truck. They're not even going to take out the garbage. It makes me want to slit my throat."

"So why watch?"

"Because I'm alone," said Icarus Prentice. "Because I've already read *Ulysses*. Because I'm sixty-seven years old, and I don't have any hobbies."

"You could go on a trip," said Arthur.

"I don't want to go on a trip."

"But you don't have to sit around watching TV," said Arthur.

"I wasn't watching TV. I was watching a movie with my dog. Leander likes old movies. He's especially fond of Westerns, but anything with a lot of people on horseback appeals to him. Doesn't it, Leander?" Icarus said, his voice deepening with affection for the first time in the conversation. Leander's tail thumped twice against the kitchen floor. "But Leander doesn't like being alone with me any better than I like being alone with me. He's heard all my best stories."

Arthur flashed on his own domestic arrangement. "I wouldn't think that being alone would be that bad," he said.

There was a pause. There was often a pause before the strike. "And what exactly would you know about being alone?" said the elder man in a mumble. When Arthur's father was being poisonous, he would often mumble, so that Arthur would never be entirely certain that his father had said what he had. This meant that if Arthur responded angrily, it might easily seem as if he had started the fight. Arthur didn't like to start fights. So he did what his mother had always done. He made busy, he began to open and close the doors of the kitchen cabinets.

"I know there are tea bags here somewhere," he said, reaching around behind some jars of jelly.

"What could you possibly know about being alone?" Icarus muttered, lighting a cigarette. "Married to a cheerleader, living in a development and working at the world's least-distinguished magazine. I'm sure the only place you're ever alone anymore is the toilet."

"I think Mummy left the tea over here," said Arthur, opening the cabinet behind the stove and producing a box of Best Value tea bags.

Then, just as suddenly as it had begun, the attack was over. There had been one thing about it that could never be adequately explained to a psychiatrist. Sure, Icarus was bitter and unhappy, and certainly his observations were inspired by his own conspicuous need. But when he said something cruel about his son, it was almost always true.

After the tea, Nathan went upstairs to Arthur's old room to look for toys, and Arthur and his father went out to the garden. Arthur helped his father spread salt hay and stake tomatoes, then they all got in the van and went to the diner. Icarus whispered to Lucy when they first sat down, and she brought him a tall glass with clear fluid and ice.

"What's that?" Arthur asked.

"Lemonade."

Icarus cut up his meat loaf special, but he didn't eat more than two bites of it. He didn't eat any bread sticks either. Nathan ate all but one of the bread sticks and none of his grilled cheese. Arthur had his own steak sandwich, half of Nathan's grilled cheese and one bread stick.

Icarus said almost nothing during the meal, but on the way out of the restaurant he put his arm around his grandson's shoulders. "I'm sorry about your father eating your sandwich," he said.

"He always does that," said Nathan.

The parrot was a Mexican Double Yellow Head. He lived in a gilded cage at Croton Liquors. He wouldn't say anything. His eyes were cloudy, and he had very few feathers.

"I'm surprised he won't talk for you," said the woman at the cash register. "He likes children."

Arthur wanted to know what happened to the feathers.

"He pulls them out himself," the woman said. "He's bored with me."

The lady who operated Croton Liquors was about twenty pounds overweight, and was wearing a purple jogging outfit. Her lips were painted bright red, and her eyelids were the dark blue of a three-day-old corpse. She used the hair dye of amateurs.

"You must be Arthur," she said. "Your father is always boasting about you. Then she held him at arm's length. "So handsome," she said. "And this must be the famous grand-child." She gave Nathan a big kiss.

"Yech," said Nathan.

The woman was only slightly taken aback. She gave Nathan a green lollipop from a cardboard box that said something about the Lions Club and multiple sclerosis. "To clear your palate," she said. There was dust on the lollipop's cellophane sheath. It didn't look like she had much call for lollipops.

Back at the house, Icarus put the liquor away. "For company," he explained. Then he and Arthur sat in the dining room, and Nathan went up to Arthur's room to play with the plastic farm animals he'd found that morning in an old tackle box. Arthur and his father talked about Nixon (vile). They talked about Ford (The nation has had some of its most prosperous years under stupid presidents).

They talked about *The American Reader.*

"But you like it?"

"It pays better than the newspaper did."

"And you get along?"

"I suppose you could say that."

"That really is splendid," Icarus said. "I admire your forti-tude. I wouldn't last a minute in a place like that."

It wasn't an unpleasant visit. Or it wouldn't have been un-pleasant if Arthur hadn't wanted to ask his father to lunch at *The American Reader.* He wanted to ask, but he was too fright-ened. The words unspoken collected in his throat, and made it difficult for him to breathe.

The next morning he called Icarus from the office. This time the phone rang eleven times.

"It was a great pleasure to see you both," Icarus said. "I hope I wasn't too harsh about your job."

"No," said Arthur, "although I'm not sure it is the world's least-distinguished magazine."

"Did I say that?"

"I think so."

"Of course it's not the world's least-distinguished magazine. It's very distinguished. You must accept my apologies."

"No apologies necessary. Fathers and sons have to fight sometimes. It seems unavoidable. It's the law of nature."

"Maybe, but I don't remember ever fighting with you."

"Oh, come on, Daddy. I used to make you furious."

"What do you mean by that?" said Icarus, his voice rising in protest.

"Well, you hated the sound of my voice when I was a boy."

"I don't recall anything of the sort."

"Remember, I had a high voice?"

"All children have high voices."

"That's what Mummy said, but it didn't keep you from hating it."

"I didn't hate the sound of your voice."

"You said you did. Remember, you were working, and I was playing with a friend in the yard? We were laughing, and you came out and yelled at us."

"You were giggling."

"That's right. You came storming out of the house and said you hated that sound. You said I sounded precisely like a fat woman."

"I was trying to work."

"Yes, but we weren't in the yard near your office. We must have been fifty yards from you."

"Well then, I'm sorry. I didn't mean anything."

"Look, Daddy, it doesn't matter. But you did mean something. You hated the sound of my voice. I started stealing cigarettes when I was six years old. I thought they would help deepen my voice. I remember I read once that Lauren Bacall got her great voice from going up into the California hills and shouting the Ten Commandments until she damaged her vocal cords. But there was no place I could go off to and scream. Besides which you probably wouldn't have liked it if I ended up sounding like Lauren Bacall either."

"Oh, Arthur," said Icarus.

"It's all right," said Arthur. "It was a long time ago. I'm fine. It doesn't matter. But you shouldn't go around saying we never exchanged words."

"I have no recollection of any of this," said Icarus. "Although I do remember that you hated it when I kissed your mother."

"I don't remember that."

"Well, I do. You'd seen *Swiss Family Robinson*, and you liked it all but the kissing. That's what you said. And we teased you about it, but you got back at us. Because after that, whenever I'd touch your mother, you'd screw up your little face and say, 'Stop that. You're ruining the movie.' "

"How old was I then?"

"I don't know. Seven or eight. Old enough to know better."

"All right, I apologize."

"So do I. In any case, I thought we had a pleasant visit Saturday."

"We did," said Arthur. "Of course we did."

"I wouldn't say you had an idyllic childhood. But I don't think I was responsible for your unhappiness. I thought that I was entirely supportive. I do remember having expressed concern that one time you wanted to be a woman on Halloween. I seem to have said something injudicious."

"I never wanted to be a woman on Halloween. That was my friend Ronald Anderson who dressed up as a receptionist. I was a hoot owl that year."

"Well, anyway, that was the only time I ever remember quarreling with you," said Icarus.

Arthur didn't say anything.

"I don't remember any other fights," said Icarus. "I just didn't think it appropriate for a twelve-year-old boy to dress up in heels and a tight skirt."

"That was Ronald Anderson," said Arthur. "I was a hoot owl."

"Maybe," said Icarus. "I suppose I should know better than anyone what a temperamental instrument human memory can be," he said.

Again Arthur didn't say anything.

"Did Nathan like the parrot?" asked Icarus.

"He asked this morning if he could have a parrot for his

birthday. But I wouldn't take that too seriously. When we went to the circus he wanted to know if he could have an elephant."

"Do you want a parrot for your birthday?"

"I don't think so. I certainly don't want a parrot without feathers."

"I suppose I've gotten used to that, but you're right, it is distressing. Baldness in birds is a problem that rarely gets the attention it deserves."

"About the world's least-distinguished magazine," said Arthur. "I want to ask you a favor."

THIRTY-ONE

That night Arthur dreamt the title: Edgar Allan Polecat. It woke him up, and he lay on his back working on the opening paragraph: "The barometer had been falling all day. That afternoon there was a dusting of snow. So after Abigail served me my chop and greens, I helped clear the table and went out behind the house with the axe to split some kindling. I am not a woodsman in the exalted sense of the word, but I have always felt—as does my neighbor, Lawrence Rockefeller—that there is a mysterious but palpable connection between mental equilibrium and the performance of simple but necessary chores.

"The first cry I heard sounded precisely like that of a big woman in excruciating pain. I put the axe down and headed up the drive at a trot. Route 9A takes a murderous plunge down one side of the valley I live in. I thought a car must have jumped the curb.

"When I reached the top of the drive, I saw the cat halfway up the telephone pole. I would not have thought such a small animal capable of this much desperation, but when he saw me he yowled again.

"I walked back to the house. This must have been the winter of 1958. My son, Arthur, was in the third grade, and had just memorized *The Raven*. It was Arthur who insisted on the adoption. I am not fond of cats, so I was acting without self-interest. How could I have known that this thoroughly disagreeable creature would someday save my life?

"We lived then, as we do now, in a town that is best known for something it keeps trying to forget. But when people think of our town, they think of the prison. When they don't think of the prison, they don't think of our town at all. The prison is famous. The prison has its own electric chair. Back in the days of capital punishment, residents of the town were supposed to be able to tell the moment they executed somebody at the prison, because the extra draw on municipal power would cause the lights to blink. I've heard this denied. Prison officials claim that they have their own generator. But I do remember having to reset the kitchen clock when they killed the Rosenbergs in June of 1953. Maybe it was a coincidence.

"The penitentiary is down by the river. It's situated on a highly desirable lot. There have been a number of proposals to reclaim the space for a luxury high-rise. But the prison itself is not a handsome structure. The walls are cement. The towers are crossing-guard orange and bristle with unsightly machine guns. This is not one of those country club establishments they sent the Watergate conspirators to. The ones they send up the river to our prison are the bad ones, so when there is a breakout the neighbors take it seriously.

"But I suppose you should get to know the cat first. Arthur insisted on the name. 'It's perfect,' he said. 'We found him on a pole. He was making horrible screaming sounds. We can call him Edgar.' "

"The ASPCA has an outlet just down the road from our house, and that's where I wanted to take Edgar. But Arthur was adamant. He'd been going to Bible class that winter in preparation for his First Communion, and had been using what he learned to make me very sorry. Piety is my son's least-becoming quality.

" 'He's not lovable, or useful,' " I said.

" 'The Bible is explicit on that point,' Arthur argued. 'Jesus said that the ones who are not lovable are the ones that we are supposed to love.' "

"That same night Edgar showed his appreciation of our hospitality by leaving what my great aunt Elspeth used to refer to as a 'calling card' at the foot of my bed.

" 'In cat language it's a sign of respect,' Arthur explained. 'He knows you're head of the household.'

"I told Arthur that Edgar didn't know the half of it, but my hand was stayed."

That was as far as the story got. Arthur thought maybe he'd write the piece and submit it under his father's name. Icarus Prentice wasn't going to volunteer to write for the world's least-distinguished magazine. He had agreed to come to lunch, but he had not agreed to write.

It was at about this time that Irene heard about the Bedford house. She had friends in real estate, and one of these friends thought that Irene should at least look.

"The only way to get Robert out of the place we're in would be with a bomb," she said, "but Faith might be interested."

Faith was interested. The house was advertised as a "Bedford antique, lovingly restored." It had been restored, sometime at the end of the eighteenth century, after British regulars burned it to the ground. Its current owners were a couple of young men who worked in the city and used it as a weekend retreat. The floor had a high polish, the trim was painted and there were fresh lilies in the front hall, but the house was still a ruin. No basic work had been done since the 1920s. The floor joists creaked threateningly, and Arthur suspected the winter wind would blow right through the clapboard walls.

Monthly payments would be roughly twice what they were on the house in North Tarrytown. Arthur still hadn't taken title to that house. But the middle-aged woman who showed them the Bedford antique explained that there are three considerations in shopping for real estate: location, location and location. The house was a wreck, but it was in Bedford, Bedford, Bedford. Faith adored it. If Arthur continued in his upward climb at The Magazine, all would be well, but if he ever faltered, he would be blanketed in bills.

He thought idly of running away from home. He had almost $4,000 in his cartridge boxes. He'd learn from Mongoose how to dye his hair. He'd buy contacts to make his brown eyes blue. He'd take a train to Manhattan and visit The Wallet King of Times Square. He'd buy new ID and then fly off to Monterey. He'd lie on the beach and eat Devil Dogs. He'd buy Marlboros by the carton. He wouldn't throw his wrappers on the street, but he might hang around with people who did. It was also possible that nobody in that group littered. *The American Reader* could easily have exaggerated that part of the story.

But first he would at least try to produce an Icarus Prentice story for *The American Reader*. He couldn't write the story to his father's specifications, but he might be able to write it to *American Reader* specifications. And then he might be able to get his father to sign it. Probably he couldn't, but that was a bridge he could cross when he came to it.

Besides, this was a lie with a tradition. Stories written by famous people for *The American Reader* were often not written by famous people. The famous people signed them of course. That's what they were called: signers. Most signers came from politicians, people used to having their opinions, and even their autobiographies, composed by out-of-work English majors.

But there were also celebrity signers. Writing is a tiresome business. Sometimes the celebrities got people on their personal staffs to compose touching anecdotes revelatory of their essential goodness. Sometimes their staffs had other, more pressing business, and then the writers of *The American Reader* did the job.

The other common form of homegrown article was the placement. A placement was an article written for *The American Reader* by the staff of *The American Reader* and then published in another magazine. The piece was then picked up and condensed.

In the 1940s *The New Yorker* attacked this policy in print, writing that "not content with having reinvented the magazine, Mr. Fallow has gone on to give the term *plagiarism* a new meaning as well. Readers holding patents for the wheel, the lever, and other like inventions are well advised to beware."

So if Arthur was going to make up a story about his father, it would be well within the tradition of The Magazine he was inventing it for. Research seemed like a problem, until he talked with Gilbert. Gilbert had spent a month "helping out" in research during his first year at The Magazine.

"That's one department I'm proud of," Arthur had told Gilbert once, apropos of nothing. "Critics might not like the conclusions we come to, but they have to pay attention to the facts."

Collingwood was grinning. "There's a lot you can do with a fact. Remember, for instance, the 'Personal Cliffhanger' about the guy who lost both arms in a brush chipper?"

"Sure, I remember," said Arthur. "It was one of the most popular articles we ever ran. Nichols sponsored it way back in the days before the flood."

"I know the woman who researched that piece," said Collingwood.

"That was the one about the lumberjack?"

"That's right," said Collingwood, helping himself to an Oreo. "The lumberjack wasn't a big reader. They sent him the manuscript, but when Sheila Blythe called him . . ." Gilbert paused. "Do you know Sheila?"

Arthur didn't.

"You should meet her. She's a riot. Especially when she's talking about research. Anyway, when Sheila called the lumberjack a week or so before closing, he hadn't looked at it. So she read it to him over the phone. He loved it. Right up until the part where he finds the meaning in life. I guess the writer had gone a little overboard with the epiphany stuff. He had a long upsweep about how happy this guy was.

"Meanwhile our armless hero is out there in Oregon in some house trailer. He's living alone with a small color TV. He gets two channels. He'd learned to switch between the stations with his toes. What he'd do when the phone rang was he'd knock the receiver onto the floor and then lie beside it so he could hear and speak. When the conversation was done, he'd pick the handset back up with his teeth and hang up. So he's lying on the floor of his house trailer, hearing Sheila read him this story about how happy he is. She finishes the story and she doesn't hear anything. First she thinks the line has gone dead, then she can hear him crying.

"Finally, after what seems like hours, he can talk again. Now he's furious. 'That's a crock,' he says. 'Do you honestly think I'm happy that I lost my arms?'

"Sheila was copesetic, as cool as they come. You have to be to succeed in research. First she waited for him to calm down. Then she said, 'But you're happy sometimes?'

" 'Sure I'm happy sometimes, but I was happy sometimes when I had my arms. Just because I lost both arms doesn't mean I'm crazy. You think my brains are in my wrists?' "

"So what did she do?" Arthur asked.

"She told him he couldn't get his arms back. She told him he could go along with the story as written. Or he could ask for changes. She told him he could lose the story and his arms, or just his arms. She said it was entirely up to him."

"Jesus," said Arthur appreciatively.

"And that's how we ran it, without any concession to what the lumberjack really felt. If you'd just put in one paragraph about how he answered the phone, one picture of that house trailer, there would have been no story."

"So why are we always crowing about our research department?"

"It's as good as they come. But it's a little like the Maginot Line. If you go right at it with a lie, you're cooked. But you can always come around from behind. The guns only point one way."

When Arthur asked around, it seemed that Collingwood was right. Once in a great while the department would kill an article that might otherwise have run, but mostly not. A particularly tough group of researchers in the Paris office had combined forces to stop a couple of pieces that had been planted by the Defense Department. But then these articles were clearly puffs. They touted weapons systems that weren't working.

No valorous clique of researchers had come forth to stop or even blunt the series of optimistic pieces run in the late 1960s under titles like—and including—"Why We Are Winning in Vietnam."

Some researchers made a fuss, but most researchers did not. Most researchers did what they were supposed to do no matter what. Once, in the mid-1970s, The Magazine had gotten permission to run one of Woody Allen's stories. Permission had been granted grudgingly, and then on the condition that *The American Reader* run the article in its entirety, undigested and unchanged. But the piece still went to the research department and a lengthy report was prepared, in the pages of which every one of Allen's hilarious historical reenactments—how the Earl of Sandwich invented the sandwich—was carefully corrected and made dull by at least two authorities. The report was as absurd as the essay it was about.

With this kind of slow-footed opponent, Arthur thought his chances were good. He didn't have a lot of witnesses to suborn. The main character would be a cat. A dead cat.

So he began to retire to the sewing room early, and he and the solitary murdering gerbil would spend time with the typewriter. In the meantime, the lunch with his father and The Magazine went off without a hitch. Practically without a hitch.

When the big morning came, Arthur was relieved of his editorial duties so that he could pick his father up and drive him to World Headquarters. Arthur thought Icarus seemed very distinguished, which probably meant he had been drinking.

"How many drinks do we get with lunch?" the elder Prentice wanted to know.

"I didn't think you were going to drink anymore," said Arthur.

"And I didn't think I was going to be going to lunch at *The American Reader*," said Icarus.

Arthur shrugged.

"How many?" asked Icarus.

"Usually it's one," said Arthur. "And wine with lunch. That's if Fallow doesn't come. If Fallow comes it's just one drink."

Icarus Prentice nodded. "But he probably won't come," he said.

"No," said Arthur. "He probably won't."

When they got to Paradise, Horster met them in front of the building. Doc held the door open for the distinguished guest. The guard seemed to emanate respect, but he was still scowling.

Horster wore a blue blazer under which Arthur glimpsed a shirtfront of blinding whiteness. The deputy editor-in-chief appeared actually to have grown larger around the waist in honor of the event. He was certainly more verbose, and larded his conversation with words whose exact meanings he seemed not to know. He was like Howard Cosell with real hair.

Horster and Arthur gave Icarus a tour of the art collection.

Icarus liked the Van Goghs. "Isn't it odd," he said to Horster, "that an organization with an international reputation for cheerfulness should so relish the works of a suicide?"

Horster chuckled politely. Then Peter Wheelwright and Allen Parker joined them at the marble foot. The bells were ringing their noon ring when the little party stepped out of the front door. The tune was "A Mighty Fortress Is Our God."

"Catchy," said Icarus when the bells stopped.

"That's right," said Horster. "But we don't just play hymns. Now they've got show tunes, and even some of the early work of the Beatles."

"It must be quite a treat to hear 'She Loves You' on a carillon," said Icarus, as they began the walk up to the farmhouse. When Icarus commented on the beauty of the orchard, Horster explained that the trees had been brought in fully mature in 1939.

"I would think the expense of such a move prohibitive," said Icarus.

Horster smiled and wagged his head. "Not then," he said. "Of course, you couldn't do that sort of thing today."

When they got to the dining room, Ruth West was already there. Fallow was not there. Fallow was not coming.

"You shouldn't be offended," Horster explained. "He doesn't really like writers."

Arthur's father grinned. Arthur's father did a lot of grinning that day. He grinned at the paintings in the farmhouse dining room. He grinned at the antiques. He grinned at Ruth West. He even grinned at the cashews when Arthur passed them around. What the editors of *The American Reader* really wanted to talk about, it developed, was Harold Ross and the old *New Yorker*. But Icarus Prentice seemed reluctant to do so.

"I didn't know Ross that well," he explained, and so the conversation shifted gradually to Prentice's own work. One of Arthur's father's best-known stories had been made into a movie, and Allen Parker wanted to know if Prentice thought that the movie had done justice to the original.

"No. Certainly not."

"I'm glad to hear you say that," said Allen, "because I didn't think so either."

"I wrote it as a story," said Prentice. "I didn't write it as a screenplay. The move from one medium to another is always problematical. Making a short story into a movie is a little like trying to represent a baseball game in the markings of an Oriental rug. The process is fascinating, and it can even be illuminating, but the translation is not exact."

Ruth West wanted to know if Icarus Prentice had spent much time with Charlton Heston during the shooting of the movie.

He had.

Then Ruth wanted to know if Heston was as imposing as he seemed to be on the screen.

Icarus Prentice thought so. "I can't abide his politics, but then I don't suppose you can blame one man for the fact that we now look to actors and singers for our wisdom. Of course you know that in the world of my parents an actor never would have been invited to dinner."

All this talk of celebrities reminded Allen Parker of the course he once took from Robert Frost. "It was in the spring of my senior year at Amherst and I'm afraid my mind was mostly out the window. I had to write a paper on Wordsworth, and I remember thinking it excellent. I was a straight-A student, but Frost gave me a D. And he wrote, 'This is a hand job,' across the top of my paper. I was furious."

"I can see that," said Arthur.

"Well," said Allen, turning away from Arthur and addressing Icarus. "He might have had a point."

Ruth West had hunted eggs on the White House lawn. "There's a picture of me in a little blue dress with President Truman," she said, "but I don't remember when it was taken. The only recollection I have of the entire visit is that of a pair of shoes. They were big, and I believe they belonged to the president, but I'm not sure. They could just as easily have belonged to a Secret Service agent. I was looking for eggs."

"What were they like?" Icarus Prentice wanted to know. "We are all familiar with his hats, but even Merle Miller is silent on the subject of his shoes."

"Oh, no," said Ruth with real dismay in her voice. "Now I'm afraid you'll be disappointed in me. I don't remember. They might have been brown, and they might have been black. All I know for sure is that they were big. And they had those little holes in them."

"Big's good," said Arthur's father. "Big's very good."

The conversation was animated, but it was not casual, and by the time the blueberry tarts arrived it had deteriorated into the formality of a press conference.

Allen Parker: "Did you always know you wanted to be a writer?"

Icarus Prentice: "That's a difficult question. It's almost impossible to separate a person's natural inclinations from his or her response to stimulus, but I have a story I tell to interviewers, and it seems to please them, so maybe it will satisfy you as well. My parents had a complete set of the works of Shakespeare. This was kept under lock and key in a glass bookcase in the parlor. By the time I was eleven years old, my father had lost his job and my mother had opened up a gift shop. My father did not stay in the house during the day. He used to go to a local lunch counter and have an onion sandwich and a bottle of Guinness stout. He'd spend the afternoon playing draw poker at the firehouse. My mother did not come home until six. I used to get home from school shortly after lunch. I found the key to the glass bookcase in my father's cuff-link box. So I spent my afternoons reading the plays. I read from *Henry the Sixth,* Part One. 'Hung be the heavens with black, yield day to night!' I read right through to the epilogue of *King Henry the Eighth:* 'Tis ten to one this play can never please/All that are here: some come to take their ease . . .' I'm afraid I can't finish it anymore."

But Peter Wheelwright could. He cleared his throat and said: " 'All the best men are ours; for 'tis ill hap/If they hold when their ladies bid 'em clap.' "

Icarus Prentice clapped, and Peter Wheelwright blushed.

"In any case," continued Prentice. "I know that the plays seem rather tame by today's standards, but growing up as I did, in a different time and in that part of New England, I found the work delicious. Of course it was forbidden, but it was also actually shocking. I was hooked.

"I didn't want to think anymore about my father's petty sorrow, or my mother's equally petty commerce. I dreamt of kings and murders. My imagination and my sense of possibility were both inflamed."

Allen Parker: "So you didn't have the *McGuffey Readers,* or *The Happy Hollisters?*"

"We had some children's books around the house, but they wouldn't have been kept under lock and key, would they? If I'd spent those rainy afternoons with the *McGuffey Readers,* I would almost certainly have become a different man." There was a pause in the conversation.

James Horster: "I wondered how you came up with the idea for 'Botulism and Botticelli.' I admire that story a great deal, and I wanted to know if there was an occurrence in your life that prompted it?"

Icarus Prentice: "There was a case. It was in the press. A husband ate some cold soup and died. So the probability of such an occurrence was presented to me, as it would have been presented to anybody living in Westchester at that time. But as for the story itself, it came from the same place they all come from. It was a gift."

Ruth West: "You've already mentioned Shakespeare, but I wonder if there are any other writers, not commonly read today, who you think have been important to your development?"

Icarus Prentice: "I'm afraid it's folly to place too much emphasis on any one writer. I would never mark out any ten books as essential. Arthur and I, for instance, have very different tastes. We both love Joyce, but Arthur likes Albee. I can't abide his later plays. Arthur also gets involved with magazines that I won't tolerate," Icarus said, smiling sweetly at the assembled editors.

Nobody said a word.

Icarus took a drink from his water glass.

"What magazines?" Parker finally asked.

Icarus smiled. "When he was very young, he used to read *Field & Stream* from cover to cover. Articles like 'How to Bag Your First Buck.' "

Everybody laughed.

Icarus dabbed at his mouth with a linen napkin. "Our appetites remain quite different," he said, pausing to let that one sink in. "Any actively literate adult will find that his tastes alter as he passes through life. I read all the time, of course, and I read very quickly, but I find that my own preferences have changed and changed again. I remember that as a boy I admired *Bleak House* enormously, but I looked at it again last summer, and Esther Summerson struck me as a royal pain in the ass."

Peter Wheelwright: "Wasn't it Oscar Wilde who said that you'd have to have a heart of stone not to laugh when Little Nell died?"

"That's right," said Icarus, "but the single most moving scene in the Edgar Johnson biography of Dickens is when the crowd gathered at the docks in New York to meet the boat that came in with the last installment of *The Old Curiosity Shop*. I don't remember the scene exactly, but I believe it was some roustabout who went out into the harbor with the pilot, and as soon as they got within hailing distance of the boat from England, he climbed out on the bow and began to shout, 'Little Nell, is she dead?' at the top of his lungs."

Allen Parker said, "Those were different times."

"Certainly," said Icarus. "But the books live. I thought at first that you could just cut Miss Summerson out of *Bleak House*, but without her there would be no book at all. Now it may be that it's no longer a contemporary story, but I'm inclined to think that there are young men all over this country reading *Bleak House* today with tears streaming down their cheeks."

Arthur didn't say anything. He was beginning to have hope. How could such polite editors ask a great man of letters to write about his pet cat? As usual, Horster was the hitch. Horster had the garage door opener, and he'd pushed it the last time so that the waitress in the blue dress could come in and refill everyone's coffee cup. When the woman began to make her rounds, Horster darted a meaningful glance at Allen Parker. Parker sighed and cleared his throat.

Allen Parker: "This is a hypothetical question," he said, looking at Icarus Prentice. "But just suppose you were offered a huge sum of money," and he held his hands up, palms facing together, to indicate a space between them that could hold a bundle of cash. "If the rate were extremely attractive, would you ever consider writing for *The American Reader*?"

Prentice was grinning again. He cut himself a piece of tart with the edge of his fork. "Not even a writer of fiction can answer a hypothetical question," he said.

That night Arthur woke again and lay in bed. The gerbil was chewing busily on the edges of his transparent cage. Arthur was thinking of the cat. Arthur knew for a fact that there had been a prison breakout in 1958. The two men had been caught at a shopping center outside of Yonkers forty-eight hours later, but nobody knew for sure what they'd done during the time they were on the loose.

He was awake until 4 A.M., but he worked the story right through to its uplifting conclusion: "As the second dark form receded into the night, I knew that I owed my life, and possibly the lives of my children, to the raucous cry of a cat. 'Truth,' I thought, 'charity, hope, faith.' And everything was as wonderful, wonderful, wonderful as it ever had been."

THIRTY-TWO

"Come in, come in," Horster said when Miss Sullivan arrived at the office door with Arthur the next morning.

"I was just on the phone with your friend and mine, Mr. Wheelwright," said Horster. "He was thanking me for arranging yesterday's lunch. Here, sit down," said Horster pointing to the armchair. Arthur moved the conch sweater and sat.

The deputy editor-in-chief leaned back in his chair contentedly. "I have to tell you that I was surprised at the success we had," he said. "Frankly, I was afraid that your father wouldn't want to come to lunch. I thought he might be too much of an egghead for us. The Adlai Stevenson school, if you know what I mean. But he seemed so down-to-earth. He really was delightful. Do you know if he reads The Magazine regularly?"

"No," said Arthur. And then, apologetically. "He doesn't read a lot of magazines. Mostly he reads novels. He has to read a lot of novels. He's on panels."

"I see, I see," said Horster, trying to hide his disappointment. "Well, in any case, I think now that we should go ahead with my project of getting him to write for us. I'll be entirely frank with you, Arthur. We don't have any place in *The American Reader* for a sort of *New Yorker* story. You know those clever pieces of fiction they run where nothing happens, but you feel a little sad about it anyway? Isn't there a name for that sort of story?"

"Slice-of-life?"

"No, I don't think that's it. Whatever they're called, we don't want one.

"But your father," said Horster, and he wagged his head appreciatively. "Every time he opens his mouth it's a story. We must get him to write an original for us. I think it would be best if you approached him about it first. The trick here is coming up with just the right subject. Of course, your father should write the story to his own high standards, but it's important for us to get him off on the right foot, so to speak."

"I think when my father writes a story," said Arthur, "he likes to come up with the idea himself."

"And that must be the hardest part," said Horster. "Which is why I'm so sure he'll be delighted to get some help. Now we've already closed January, and it's probably too late for February, but if we got the first draft in a month or so, we'd be set for March or April."

"I believe my father usually hands in finished copy," said Arthur.

"Yes, of course," said Horster. "But we still might want to do a little tinkering. Oh, and by the way, I'm afraid your friend Collingwood isn't going to stay with us."

Arthur swallowed.

"He wasn't happy here," said Horster. "Friday will be his

last day officially, but I don't think he's going to come in again."

Arthur didn't say anything.

"You liked Collingwood?" said Horster.

"Yes," said Arthur. "I'm going to miss him."

"So will I," said Horster. "But he was a luxury."

Arthur thought he'd try the two-pronged attack. He'd finish "Edgar Allan Polecat," and then phone his father. If, as he suspected, his father would not write for *The American Reader*, Arthur would submit his own work over his father's name. It wouldn't be the first time their identities had gotten confused.

So he spent his evenings for the next two weeks polishing his manuscript, and he got something that he thought was moving without presenting the slightest challenge to the status quo. Ruth West had told him that the most successful stories in *The American Reader* were "the prose equivalent of a piece of marzipan fruit."

"You mean cloying?"

"I mean a good one should spoil your appetite," she had said.

Having completed his preparations for the dishonorable course, Arthur thought he would give the honorable course one more try. Faith didn't like it when Arthur phoned his father in the evenings ("because it always makes you upset"), so he made the call from the office. It was, after all, a business call.

"So lunch wasn't so bad," said Arthur without preamble.

"No," said Icarus, "lunch was fine."

"Weren't you impressed with the art?"

"Yes," said Icarus, doubtfully. "But I had a terrible sense of déjà vu. That foot they have there in the main foyer?"

"You mean the Michelangelo?"

"That's right. But you know, my sainted mother had that same foot. The same exact one. In plaster of Paris. She used it as a paperweight."

241

"This one is marble," said Arthur.

"Of course," said Icarus. "Certainly it's marble." There was an awkward pause, and then Icarus asked Arthur what he was calling about.

"Just to make sure you had a great time and, well, there is something else."

"What's that?"

"I don't know quite how to bring this up," said Arthur, "but the people here seem to have their hearts set on having you write for The Magazine."

Icarus Prentice cleared his throat. "I'm not surprised," he said. "I had the feeling that there was a subtext to the veal chop. Although I'm not sure they would have dared it on their own."

"They're not on their own," said Arthur. "They have me. I don't know how to get around it."

"It's not my problem, though, is it?" said Icarus Prentice.

"No," said Arthur. "It's my problem, and if you won't do it, I'll understand."

"Would you?"

"Yes," said Arthur. "I would."

There was a long pause, and then Arthur said, "So you won't do it?"

"I didn't say that. Do you have any idea what they want me to write?"

"I think they want you to write about cats. First they wanted you to write about dogs, but then they thought they've had too much about dogs recently. That's when they came up with cats."

Icarus didn't say anything.

"You have written widely," Arthur said. "You and Allen Wyndham put out the regimental newspaper when you were stationed in Georgia."

"That was wartime."

"You just wrote a piece for *Parade* in praise of readers."

"I think readers are terribly important."

"And you interviewed Sophia Loren for *The Saturday Evening Post*."

"I know Sophia Loren is terribly important."

"You even wrote a piece in praise of Suntory Scotch. Didn't you write the Rolex ad?"

"No. I let them take my picture, but I didn't write the copy."

"Oh, I thought you did. Although it didn't sound like you. I mean it wasn't what the reviewers call lambent."

"You're damn straight it wasn't lambent."

"But you could be lambent for *The American Reader*."

"Not on cats I couldn't. Not for *The American Reader* or anybody else."

"So what could you be lambent on?"

"I could be lambent on tomatoes."

"They want cats, Daddy. They have their hearts set on cats."

"But I hate cats. They're sexually ambivalent. I can never tell if a cat is male or female unless I turn it over."

"There must be something about cats you like."

"Wouldn't they like it better if I wrote about how much I loved tomatoes?"

"I don't think so."

"Well, let's give it a try. I just happen to have a spare essay on tomatoes."

"Are you talking about the one you wrote two years ago for that woman at the local newspaper?"

"It wasn't that long ago."

"Sure it was. Nathan was four; he's almost six now. Besides, what if somebody read it in the local paper?"

"Nobody saw it."

"How can you be certain?"

"I'm certain," said Icarus with growing asperity, "because they didn't print it. The woman I wrote it for got a job doing public relations for the United Way before I finished."

"So you never turned it in?"

"No, I wrote it just for her."

"A sort of love note on tomatoes?"

"That's right. How do I love thee, let me count the tomatoes."

Arthur didn't say anything.

"Tell you what. I'll give you the article, and you can see what they think. If they like it, they can have it. If they don't like it, we can decide what to do next."

"Okay, that's fair enough. Why don't I come over on Sunday morning with Nathan and pick it up?"

So Arthur and Nathan visited the homestead again and picked up the manuscript. They also went to Lucy's for lunch, and afterward they saw the parrot.

"I thought you'd quit drinking," Arthur asked his father after the visit to the liquor store.

Arthur was driving and his father was sitting in the front seat beside him. At first he didn't say anything. Then, very slowly, he turned to face his son.

"Well then, you thought wrong," he said flatly.

When Arthur got home that afternoon he read the manuscript. He was worried. The word *tomato* didn't appear in the piece once. Not once.

On Monday he went to The Magazine's library and spent some time with the *Britannica*. Then he put in a call to Miss Sullivan. It was two days before he was summoned to Horster's office, and the deputy editor-in-chief was not alone.

Horster was at his desk. Palumbardo was in the visitor's armchair. Palumbardo got up, smiled at Arthur and then left.

Horster pointed to the armchair. Arthur sat.

"I hope you've got good news," said Horster.

"Well, I guess," said Arthur. "I've got good news, and I've got bad news."

"Give me the good news first."

"My father has written an article for us."

"The bad news?"

"It's very short. And it's about tomatoes."

"Tomatoes?"

"Tomatoes are interesting," said Arthur. "What do you know about them?"

"I have them in salads," said Horster. "Sometimes I'll have a slice of tomato on a hamburger. I know that a tomato is a vegetable."

"Wrong," said Arthur triumphantly. "Botanically the tomatoes themselves are fruit. The plant is a tender perennial, although it's cultivated as an annual. Tomatoes grow naturally in tropical South America, but they weren't introduced in Europe until the sixteenth century. And they weren't eaten in this country until the 1820s. People used to think they were poison. There were even some who felt that the tomato, with its succulence and bright coloring, would excite devilish passions."

"All right," said Horster. "So there's quite a lot about tomatoes I don't know."

"Volumes," said Arthur.

"If your father is that interested in tomatoes, have him write about them and we'll see. But I'm not sanguine about this project."

"I've already got the piece," said Arthur, and he reached into his jacket pocket and pulled out a sheaf of folded yellow foolscap.

Horster took it and looked at the paper. "Is this it?" he asked.

Arthur said it was.

"Is this the paper your father always uses?" he asked.

Arthur said it was.

"That's fascinating!" said Horster. "One of the best writers living in this country today, and he uses the cheapest paper you can buy. Why do you suppose he uses this paper?"

"Like you said," said Arthur. "It's the cheapest paper you can buy."

"Listen," said Horster. "I'm eager to read this, but I'm just not going to have a chance today. I'll read it tonight. We can talk tomorrow."

Two days later Arthur was called back to Horster's office.

Horster was not alone. Joseph Bouton, the head of sales for the Southwest, was also there. Arthur was introduced to Bouton.

Bouton wanted to know if Arthur was any relation to Icarus Prentice, the writer. Arthur said that Icarus Prentice was his father. Bouton said how much he had enjoyed the public television presentation of three Icarus Prentice stories. "If you see your father," he said, "tell him how much I enjoyed those shows. Tell him I'm going to read the actual stories now as soon as I get a chance. My wife's going to buy me the book for Christmas."

Arthur said that he would tell his father how much Joseph Bouton had enjoyed the television shows.

Horster told Bouton he'd see him at lunch, and then Bouton left. Horster opened his desk and withdrew the sheaf of foolscap and put it on the desk top.

"What is this?" he asked, pointing at it as if it were a frog he meant to dissect.

"It's an Icarus Prentice original."

"What's it about?"

"Tomatoes."

"But it doesn't have any tomatoes in it."

"Don't you like the way it's written?"

"Certainly I like the way it's written," said Horster, helping himself to a cigarette. "It's beautiful. But there isn't a tomato in it."

"He wrote it in April. There aren't any tomatoes in April in this climatic region. There are tomatoes in the grocery store, but there aren't any tomatoes outdoors."

"So how do we even know what it's about?"

"I thought we could have a long introduction in italics. We could explain who Icarus Prentice is, and do a brief history of the tomato."

"But even supposing you did this prologue, which might be almost as long as the article itself, how would our readers know that the two pieces were connected?"

"They'd know because of the manure."

Horster stood up and snorted. "Are you trying to kid with me?" he asked.

"No," said Arthur. "Of course not."

"But manure is used for all sort of plants," said Horster, sitting down again. "They might think the piece was about cucumbers, or roses. The manure could also be for cucumbers."

"I suppose that's so."

"I have to tell you, Arthur, I really am curious. Why did your father write this? Did he write this article with *The American Reader* in mind?"

"No. When he wrote it, he was thinking of a girl."

"I still don't get it."

"It's about gardening. It's about preparing the ground. You don't just start out with tomatoes. In many ways this is an *American Reader* message. First you must prepare the ground."

"Your father doesn't expect ten thousand dollars for preparing the ground, does he?"

"I don't think he expects anything. He didn't mention payment."

"All right then, we'll keep it, but I'm not sure we'll be able to use it. In the meantime, work on him about cats. That's what we really want, an article on cats."

Arthur went back to his office and phoned his father.

"They don't like the piece on tomatoes," he said. "I mean, they think it's beautifully written and all, but it doesn't fit into the format here. They still want you to write about cats."

"But I can't write what I don't care about," said Icarus.

"You don't really have to write it. Just sort of type it. It would be easy. I could do it."

"Oh, really? I didn't know you considered yourself a writer."

"I'm not. You don't have to be a writer to write the article I'm talking about."

"Have them run the piece on tomatoes, and then we can talk," said Icarus Prentice.

Arthur sighed. "All right," he said.

Icarus didn't say anything, but he didn't hang up either. Arthur was wondering if he should take the initiative and hang up himself, when his father broke the silence.

"Do you remember Allen Wyndham?" he asked.

"Sure," said Arthur.

"He thinks I should stop drinking."

Arthur took a deep breath. "So do I."

"Do you really?"

"Yes, I really do. In fact," said Arthur, "I've often said as much."

"But it helps me get along. Alcohol makes me pleasant, makes me independent."

"I still want you to stop drinking," said Arthur.

"Even if it means I'll be more demanding?" asked Icarus.

"Come on," said Arthur. "What kind of monster do you think I am? Of course I want you to stop drinking."

"Wyndham wants to take me to an AA meeting tonight. Do you think I should go?"

"Certainly I think you should go."

"But they're a bunch of Christers. They wear bad shoes, they read silly books. I won't be able to stand them."

"Maybe not," said Arthur. "But you could give it a try."

Icarus didn't say anything.

"If you don't give it a try," said Arthur, "you'll probably have another heart attack."

"All right" said Icarus. "You don't need to be melodramatic. I'll give it a try then, but don't expect anything."

"I won't," said Arthur. "But I'd be delighted if you went."

When Arthur got home that evening, Faith and Nathan were at her mother's house for dinner. Faith had left him a tuna salad sandwich and a note. The note told him to call Allen Wyndham. Wyndham was upset. "He won't go," he said. "They expect him. It's all set up, but he told me he won't go. He said he's too tired."

"All right," said Arthur. "Where's the meeting?"

"Over here. In High Cliff."

"When?"

"At eight P.M. That's just an hour from now."

"All right," said Arthur. "I'm leaving right now. I'll go to his house and try to get him. If I can get him I'll bring him to the meeting. Where's the meeting?"

"It's at Saint Matthew's. Why don't we meet at the diner? We can have a cup of coffee. Then you and I can bring him to the parish house together. You remember the diner?"

"The Starlight?"

"Right."

"I should be there in half an hour," said Arthur. "If I can't handle him, if he refuses to come, I'll phone you."

Icarus was too drunk to put up a fight. He wasn't nice about it, but he didn't struggle. "If it isn't little Lisa, the light of the world," he said when he met Arthur at the door. But he didn't close the door in his son's face. He let Arthur in, and he let Arthur put on his socks for him. "Do you see yourself as Florence Nightingale?" he asked as his son put on his shoes and tied them. He meekly put on his own coat and a scarf that had belonged to Arthur's mother. They drove to the diner. Wyndham was waiting for them in a booth. Icarus nodded to his old friend.

"Did lovely Lisa put you up to this?" he asked.

Wyndham looked down at the table uncomfortably. "Arthur and I both thought it would be a good idea," he said.

"And what, exactly, is the idea?" Icarus asked.

"I don't know," said Wyndham, looking into his cup of coffee. "Saving your life."

Icarus chuckled mirthlessly. "The two of you," he said, "you're like a couple of hysterical old women."

"All right," said Arthur. "Supposing we are a couple of old women, why don't you just humor us?"

Icarus put his hands out, palms upward. "You haven't given me a choice," he said.

The waitress appeared. Arthur ordered coffee. Icarus ordered coffee and began to order scrambled eggs with bacon, but both Arthur and Wyndham agreed that there wasn't time for this.

After coffee they all drove to the parish house in Wyndham's Buick. Arthur sat in the backseat. Then Arthur and Wyndham escorted Icarus into the building and down a long cement hallway. Off the hallway there was a doorway, and just outside the door they were met by a fat, bearded man who seemed to know what they were about. He nodded to Wyndham and smiled at Arthur. "Tonight's a closed meeting," he said. "Come back in an hour."

"Are you going to be all right?" Arthur asked, looking at his father.

"He's going to be fine," said the fat man. "Nothing to worry about. We can take it from here," he said, smiling at Arthur.

"You know, he's pretty hard to pin down," said Arthur. "He's a writer."

"Well," said the fat man. "I don't know much about writing, but I know all there is to know about drunks." He pulled Icarus inside the door and closed it gently but firmly, so that Arthur and Allen were outside and their distinguished charge was no longer with them.

They went back to the diner together. All the booths were taken, so they sat at a rickety little table with two chairs. The waitress brought them coffee. They sat there for some time drinking coffee and not saying a word.

Wyndham finally broke the silence. "You think it will work?"

"I don't know," said Arthur. "It's really up to him. If he wants to kill himself, there's not much you or I or anybody else can do about it."

"And you think he wants to kill himself?"

Arthur shrugged. "He's got me convinced," he said.

"I guess you're right," said Wyndham. "Maybe these people can change his mind."

"He's stubborn," said Arthur.

"At least we will have tried," said Wyndham. "And without you I wouldn't have gotten this far."

Arthur shrugged. "Vice versa," he said.

Wyndham called the waitress and ordered another round of coffee.

"Do you think I'm a bore?" he said, without looking up.

"No," said Arthur, "of course not. Why do you ask?"

"You worked over here for years and we only had that one lunch."

"I was busy," said Arthur.

Wyndham smiled. "My sources weren't that useful?"

"No," said Arthur, and he laughed. "They weren't even sources," he said.

"And you didn't like hearing about my sons?"

"No," said Arthur, "I didn't mind that. Honest I didn't."

"I shouldn't have made a joke of your childhood troubles," said Wyndham. "I told my wife about our lunch later, and she said I was a fool. Your father always made up such great stories about you that I got used to not thinking of how that sort of thing might make you feel."

Arthur smiled. "So did I," he said.

"I love your father," said Wyndham. "But being his son probably wasn't easy."

"No," said Arthur.

"You know, I wondered about your father when we were in the army," said Wyndham. "He was always great company, and a good friend, but he seemed so different than the rest of us. It was as if he was hiding something."

"Well he's certainly different," said Arthur. "But I don't know that he hides much. I think he's more exposed than most men."

"I don't know what I'm trying to say," said Wyndham, and then he looked at his watch. "I think it's time we went and got our student," he said, signaling to the waitress for a check. Then he turned back to face Arthur. "Can we be friends now?"

"Sure," said Arthur.

Wyndham held out his hand. "Friends then," he said.

Arthur put out his own hand. "Friends," he said, and they shook.

Icarus was still a little drunk when they picked him up at the parish house, but he also seemed altered in some way. He was furious, of course, but that wasn't all of it.

Arthur drove his father back to the homestead. The old man didn't say a word. He didn't even thank his son for the ride.

But Wyndham phoned late on the evening of the following day. "I think it took," he said gleefully. "You know Larry?"

"The fat man?" asked Arthur.

"That's right. The fat man. He just called me. He said your father came to the meeting tonight. On his own steam. Sober."

"Hot shit."

Arthur was happy. But Horster was not. He wanted to know about the cat story.

"My father's been sick," Arthur explained.

"Well," said Horster. "Be as helpful as you can. But get on him about this. A good editor doesn't just edit stories, he makes them happen."

"And you think I'm a good editor?" asked Arthur, a little surprised.

"Either you're a great editor," said Horster, "or you're fabulously overpaid."

So Arthur spent the evening going over "Edgar Allan Polecat." The next day he brought it to the office and retyped it on foolscap. That afternoon he brought it to his mentor.

Horster had him sit in the visitor's chair and wait while he read it. When he was finished, Horster knocked a Kool out of the package he kept in the breast pocket of his shirt, lit it and passed the pack to Arthur. Arthur took a cigarette for himself, lit it and then passed the pack back.

"This is magnificent," Horster said as he blew smoke out through his nose. "It's got the one thing absolutely necessary for an article in *The American Reader*. Do you know what that is?" he asked.

Arthur didn't.

"Veracity. It's absolutely one hundred percent true."

Arthur nodded.

"People don't know how much talent and energy are required to tell the simple truth," said Horster.

"That's right," said Arthur. "They don't."

"This is a textbook example of what an article for *The American Reader* should be," said Horster, "and yet it's better than that. They say excellence is in the last two percent. This has the fingerprint of greatness. I'm going to show it to Wheelwright this afternoon, but I'm sure we'll buy it. I think we should save it for next November. November's always our biggest issue, and this is a piece we're particularly proud of. I'm sorry you felt the need to put us through the charade about tomatoes before letting your father write this. It doesn't matter now. All is forgiven."

When Arthur walked in from the parking lot the next morning, both flags were at half-staff. Doc was at the front door, and Arthur thought he looked even more glum than was his wont.

"What are the flags for?" Arthur asked. "Did we lose a former president?"

"No," mumbled Doc. "God is dead."

Cunningham came over the intercom at 11 A.M. and asked that everybody in the building observe a minute of silence. Both Mr. and Mrs. Fallow were dead. They had died in bed, on the same night, perhaps within the same hour. "It is hard to find anything to be thankful for in this event," said Cunningham. "But wherever they are, they're together."

The staff at the cafeteria wore black armbands. The next day the portrait of Modigliani's mistress was taken out of the front foyer and replaced with an oil of George Fallow wearing jodhpurs and sitting on a palomino. Helicopters appeared again on the lawn around the farmhouse.

The memo was distributed the following day. It was two pages long. It announced that Peter Wheelwright would head up the book division in Manhattan. Cunningham was taking early retirement. James Horster was appointed editor-in-chief.

Ruth had taken a week in Europe, but she was expected back on the first Monday in September. When Arthur went around and spoke with her secretary, he was told that Mrs. West was on "extended leave." Arthur went back to his office and called the Pound Ridge house. There was no answer.

So Arthur called his father. They talked about the weather. Arthur thought he could hear ice in a glass.

"Have you had any more thoughts about writing for us?" he asked.

"No," said Icarus Prentice. "I have not."

"This is a completely different subject," said Arthur. "And the two subjects have nothing to do with each other. But have you been drinking?"

"No," said Icarus. "I haven't had a drink in five days now."

"But I heard ice in a glass," said Arthur.

Icarus chuckled. "That's ginger ale," he said. "They encourage us to drink a lot of soda pop."

"But you're not drinking?"

"Nothing but ginger ale," said Icarus.

"That's great," said Arthur. "I really mean that. It's great. Don't you feel better?"

Icarus paused. "No," he said. "I feel dreadful."

It took two weeks to double the cost of lunch at the cafeteria. The subsidized bus service was discontinued a week later. Hours were increased so that the regular work day ran from 8:30 A.M. until 5 P.M., with a half hour off for lunch. The day for hourly employees had always run from 8:30 A.M. until 4 P.M. One month after Horster's promotion, Albert Palumbardo was profiled in a national magazine as the "archetypal modern manager." He was quoted as saying that he meant "to bring *The American Reader* into the twentieth century."

"George Fallow was a rich man," he said, "and he ran this as a rich man's company. He had a personal fortune of many millions of dollars. I don't have that luxury." The reporter lacked the wit to point out that the Fallows had had to borrow the money to print their first issue.

Employees whose salaries were found to be way out of line with their counterparts at IBM or American Can were pensioned off. Doc was one of the first to go. He was fifty-eight years old. He had a BS and one year of medical school.

THIRTY-THREE

It wasn't until the second month of Horster's reign that Arthur and Mongoose finally met for lunch. "Now we can celebrate your promotion to senior staff editor," said Mongoose. "Any objection to the Road House?"

Arthur had no objection. Inflated prices at the cafeteria had increased business at the Road House, so Mongoose suggested that they get there before noon in order to be certain of a table. Ordinarily they might have driven together, but Mongoose said that he wanted to leave the office at 11 A.M. and go out to the local pet emporium. "I have to buy some fresh mice for Agamemnon," he explained.

Arthur had settled at a booth, and was reading a description of the battle of White Plains off the paper placemat when Mongoose arrived. The older man's hair was blond again, but long this time, and held up behind his neck with a blue rubber band. His eyes were brown. He was clean-shaven. Mongoose was wearing a pair of beige chinos, a white dress shirt, a blue-and-red-striped necktie and a navy blazer with brass buttons. He came directly to the table and sat, but did not look Arthur in the eye.

"Something the matter?" Arthur asked.

"I'm surprised that Horster could give you up."

"What do you mean?"

"Don't you eat with him usually?" Mongoose asked.

"No, almost never. He just likes to keep me on tap. I often eat alone and in the cafeteria. I'm sorry I had to cancel so many times."

"So why did he let you off today?"

"He's in Paris."

Mongoose nodded, and then he smiled. He wouldn't look Arthur in the eye, but his tone lightened considerably. "I don't suppose I'm in any position to criticize," he said. "I've been buying mice, and I wear my hair like a schoolgirl. I must look a little ridiculous."

"No," said Arthur.

"The pigtail?" said Mongoose.

"You forget I went to Antioch," said Arthur. "The chairman of the philosophy department used to braid his hair."

"I'm in *Billy Budd*," Mongoose explained. "The director is very hot on having us all live the part."

"Are you Billy or Claggart?"

"They haven't decided. We have a young man who's much better looking than I am. By all rights he should be the foretopman, but he's not yet that good an actor. So he and I are learning both parts." At this point Mongoose picked up the ketchup bottle and began to fiddle with its cap. He still did not look Arthur in the eye. "If the young man gets more comfortable on the stage, then he'll be Budd."

"That's a lot of work, learning both parts."

Mongoose shrugged, put the ketchup bottle back down and turned to the waitress, who had just appeared.

"Anything from the bar?" she asked.

Mongoose asked for a Molson. Arthur wanted an Amstel Light.

"I think we can order," said Arthur. Then he nodded at Mongoose. "It's on me," he said. "Or rather it's on the company."

Mongoose did not acknowledge this comment. "I'll have the Bedford Burger," he said. "Burned to a crisp."

Arthur asked for the three-egg omelette with Mexican vegetables.

"What's your take on the office now that Captain Vere is dead?" asked Arthur, taking a sip of his beer. "I hardly knew Fallow, but he really was the sun in the morning and the moon in the evening for us, wasn't he?"

"That's right," said Mongoose. "Existentialism has come to *The American Reader*. And I'm afraid it doesn't bode well for yours truly. I've never been a team player. When they begin to scrutinize the budget, I'm going to turn up as an expendable."

Arthur shook his head. "You're as safe as houses," he said.

"What about your friend Collingwood?" asked Mongoose. "Was he safe?"

"He's left for a better job."

"That's not the way I heard it."

"Well, it is the way I heard it. Gilbert and I were friends. I heard the same thing you did. I was told he'd been fired. I heard it from Horster, but when I spoke with Collingwood, he said it wasn't true. He said he'd wanted to get fired for the severance, but that actually he already had another, better job."

"But Horster didn't like him?"

"I don't know. I guess not, but that's not why Gilbert left. He's gone back into advertising. They even gave him a contract, or that's what he told me. And a Lincoln Town."

"What about Cunningham? And your friend West? Did she leave for a better job?"

"I don't think she's left at all," said Arthur. "She's on a leave. First she went to Rome. Then she took a leave."

"I heard she was fired because she was writing for another magazine."

"How would anyone know that?"

"You know it."

"But I didn't tell anyone."

"You told me."

Now Arthur picked up the glass ashtray, looked at it and put it down. "I trust you," he said.

"But I'm probably not the only one you told," said Mongoose. "And she's certainly not the only one who has been fired because you knew something, or suspected something."

"Who else?"

"Arnold Baker, for one."

"I liked Arnold Baker."

"But you talked about him to Horster."

"Yeah," said Arthur. "But I talk about everyone."

Mongoose didn't say anything. The lunch had arrived. The older man removed the top of the bun from his hamburger and put ketchup on it.

"What do you really think of that guy Horster?" asked Mongoose. "Now that he's got the rod of state, what do you think he's going to do with it?"

"I don't know," said Arthur. "He certainly cares about The Magazine."

"He cares about something," said Mongoose, "but I'm not sure it's *The American Reader*."

"I don't think that's fair," said Arthur. "He just wants a more businesslike operation."

Mongoose picked up his hamburger, looked at it as if planning where to bite, changed his mind and put it back on the plate. "Yeah, I can see that," he said. "Palumbardo and

Horster were cut from the same piece of cheap cloth. The polyester brothers. Repeat and the creep."

Arthur cut a small piece off the end of his omelette. "You have to admit that there has been a lot of activity at The Magazine that has nothing to do with putting out *The American Reader,*" he said, and then put the piece of omelette in his mouth.

"And why ever not?" said Mongoose. "The entire editorial budget was never more than ten percent of cost. They spend more on one mailing than they do on writers and editors for a year. Fallow always wasted money on editorial. When you get a goose who lays golden eggs, you don't scrimp on his corn ration."

"I didn't know the editorial budget was so small," said Arthur.

"It's not small. It is a small percentage of total expenses. Fallow used to try and get it over ten percent, but he couldn't do it," said Mongoose. He looked at his burger but didn't pick it up. He took another pull on his beer.

"Even a chemical business or a electronics firm will invest in research and development. They count on losing money on R and D. But then once in a while somebody discovers something, and it turns out to have been worth the gamble. Fallow kept the editorial budget fat in the hopes that somebody would think something up that might not have occurred to him if he'd been working fourteen hours a day sorting old jokes. And it worked. Somebody with time on his hands thought up the Condensed Book Club. Now we sell almost two million copies of every volume. Somebody who was underemployed came up with the Human Body Series."

"I Am Joe's Man Gland?"

"That's right."

"How long do you suppose it took to think that up?" Arthur said, and laughed.

Mongoose didn't laugh. "It was only the most popular series of articles in the history of magazine publishing."

"All right, all right," said Arthur. "But a huge amount of that money was wasted."

"Certainly it was wasted. Sometimes by good-hearted people who hadn't a clue, and sometimes the money was squandered by corrupt editors and writers who only wanted to make themselves rich. But the system worked."

"You think that's over now?"

"I know it's over. I guess you haven't heard today's news."

"No."

"For a guy who is supposed to be so plugged in, you don't seem to know much. They're shutting down the Japanese edition. They're going to fire the entire staff."

"Why?"

"Because it's not profitable."

"So maybe they should shut it down."

"What about the people who work there? Getting fired in Japan is not the same as getting fired in the U.S. It's a disgrace to be fired in Japan. In Japan it's not unheard of for somebody to commit suicide after being fired. Usually, when somebody is fired in Japan, it means he or she did something unforgivable. And we're firing the entire staff."

"When was this announced?"

"This morning. They're selling off that great piece of real estate General MacArthur gave us. That'll be enough to cover the losses for the last couple of years."

"I guess I missed the memo. I was in a meeting with some guys from advertising."

"You're often in a meeting with some guys from advertising."

"So what's wrong with that? Advertising brings in a lot of money. We need advertising."

"We never took an ad until 1955."

"You really are on the rag today," said Arthur.

"We not only take ads," said Mongoose. "The business people run the magazine. Wheelwright didn't fight Palumbardo, and Horster doesn't want to fight him. The editorial budget is now seven percent and these cretins want to cut it. Horster goes around acting like we're wastrels. Of course the men in business love that."

"I suppose they like it."

Mongoose wagged his head. "Fallow always treated the business department like a poor cousin. We were paid more. We also got more perks. Now that they have the power, you can bet they're going to use it. Making up for the past deprivations."

"If it's all so bad," said Arthur, "why is Horster going along with it? He's an editor."

"Not much of one. He never would have gotten to be editor-in-chief if he hadn't cut some sort of deal with Palumbardo."

Arthur let that one go.

Mongoose held his fork to the light. There was a little bit of dried egg yolk on one tine. He signaled to the waitress, who replaced it.

"Has he been talking about me?" he asked Arthur, still not looking him in the face.

"Well, no, although he thinks you should do more animal stories. You're one of the only editors they have ever allowed to write, and he thinks you should take advantage of it."

"What sort of animal stories?"

"Wasn't the one about the beagle a hit with the readers?"

"Yes, but I actually had a beagle named Napoleon. I didn't make that up. When Nappy died, I swore I'd never get another dog."

"I know," said Arthur. "It was in the story."

"So how can I write another dog story?"

Arthur shrugged. "It's just that Horster thinks you did such a good job with Napoleon."

"So he wants a sequel?"

"I didn't say that."

"But he's critical of me?"

"He's a little critical. I wouldn't take it too seriously. He's critical of everybody," Arthur said, and paused. Then he went ahead. "You probably shouldn't buy mice during business hours."

Mongoose was looking at his burger as if it might bite him. His complexion darkened.

"Listen," he said, and now he was looking Arthur in the eye for the first time. "I'm about three times as smart as you are. I got you this job."

Arthur took another bite of omelette and chewed. He thought he could taste some onion, but the eggs seemed to be entirely without flavor. He swallowed. "I think it's unrealistic," he said, "not to expect to be supervised by anybody."

At this point Mongoose reached into his jacket pocket and produced a package of Marlboro Lights. He shook out one cigarette, tapped the filter against the face of his watch, put the cigarette in his mouth and lit it. "You know what the difference between your career and my career is?" he said, blowing smoke out through his nose.

Arthur shrugged. "I know some differences," he said.

"The difference," said Mongoose, tapping the ash from his cigarette into the glass ashtray, "is that you are willing to eat shit, and I am not."

"I suppose that's one difference," said Arthur. "But you've got to realize that I was brought up that way. It turns out to have advantages. And one of the reasons I don't mind being a manager is that I can help my friends."

Mongoose shook his head. "I hear now you've got your father writing on cats," he said. "Maybe you could get John Updike to write about pigeons."

Arthur shrugged.

"And I bet Horster has been complaining about my lack of output."

"Now you're being sensitive," said Arthur. "He complains about everybody. I'm sure he complains about me to other people."

"I doubt it," said Mongoose.

"Why? Why wouldn't he complain about me?"

Mongoose picked up his napkin and wiped his already clean hands. When he looked back at Arthur the anger was clear on his face. "Because you're his rat fink, that's why. Because you're a manifest asshole. Aren't you the one who filled him in when Nichols made his sudden departure?"

People at other tables were turning to look.

"We talked, if that's what you mean," said Arthur, attempting to keep his voice in the lower register.

"Oh, I see," said Mongoose.

"What was I supposed to do, not talk with him?"

"Nobody else talked with him."

"He's my mentor. So we get along."

"And who would you not get along with?" asked Mongoose.

"There are people I don't get along with."

"But you got along fine with Ruth West. And now you're getting along fine with the man who fired her."

"Nobody fired Ruth."

"Of course you're right," said Mongoose sarcastically, putting out his cigarette, half-smoked, and getting up from the table. "Nobody fired Collingwood either. Nobody fired Baker. Nobody fired Cunningham. Nobody's going to fire me."

Arthur shrugged.

"I've known you since you were a boy. I just can't help thinking how ashamed your father would be."

Arthur was too surprised to react. He was too surprised even to be angry.

"You don't mind eating alone, do you?" Mongoose said. He put both hands on the edge of the table and leaned his face into Arthur's.

"Breaking bread is an ancient ceremony, and I am no longer inclined to break bread in your presence," he said. Arthur could smell the older man's breath against his face. Cherry cough drops? Arthur looked down at his plate. Mongoose stalked out of the restaurant.

Arthur took a bite from his omelette. Then he signaled the waitress for the check.

"Something wrong?" she asked.

"No," said Arthur. "Nothing wrong with the food. Just please bring me a check." He took the butt of Mongoose's cigarette out of the ashtray, straightened the end and lit it.

*　　*　　*

When Arthur got back to the office, he tried Ruth's number. This time she was home.

"Hi, it's Arthur. How are you?"

"Fine."

"How was Rome?"

"Old, very old."

"Are you ever coming to work again?"

"Did he put you up to this?"

"Did who put me up to what?"

"Horster. Your friend James Horster?"

"No, of course not. He hates you."

"Okay then," said Ruth, and there was a touch of disappointment in her voice. "So this is just a social call?"

"I was curious. I wondered where you've been."

"I've been home."

"I miss you. Collingwood's gone now. Cunningham's retired. Mongoose won't talk with me. You're gone. I've never been this isolated."

"You could have called me before now."

"I tried. I tried to call you weeks ago."

"I must have been outside. I put in a lot of bulbs this year."

Arthur noticed that he was winding the cord of the telephone tightly around his hand.

"Are you alone?"

"It's just me and Eldridge."

"What about a drink then?"

"Okay. Actually, why don't you come here for dinner tomorrow? I'll make you spaghetti and meatballs. Does that sound all right?"

"Spaghetti and meatballs sound great," Arthur said, and then he caught himself. He remembered that Faith wanted him to go look at that house again. "What about next week?"

There was a pause on the other end of the line. "But I invited you for tomorrow," Ruth said.

"I know," said Arthur. "And I want to come, but everything's up in the air now. I think we'd better wait until next week."

Ruth didn't say anything.

"I'll call you Monday."

Ruth still didn't say anything.

"Is that all right?"

"Sure," said Ruth, and hung up.

THIRTY-FOUR

The next morning Arthur didn't bother to phone Miss Sullivan. He waited until 9:30, and then walked to Horster's office. The editor-in-chief was on the phone with Greenwich Toyota. "All right then," he said, "you'll tell me the best time to trade in and trade up. I'll trust you." He put down the phone. When he saw Arthur, he looked surprised. "Did I call you?" he asked.

"No, but I need to talk."

Horster nodded. "Come in then and close the door."

"How was Paris?"

"Busy."

"I understand it's a beautiful city."

"That's right. We'll have to send you there. But right now

I'm busy. You didn't come in here to ask about Paris. What's up?"

"It's about that cat article," said Arthur as he moved the sweater out of the visitor's armchair and took a seat.

"You mean the one your father wrote?" asked Horster.

"That's right."

"What's the problem?"

"My father wants to know how much you're going to pay for it."

"I suppose we'll pay the usual. We're reworking the payment schedule, but it'll be more than two thousand dollars."

"Two thousand dollars?"

"That's not bad for fifteen sheets of the world's cheapest paper."

Arthur felt his throat constrict. "You told me you'd pay him ten thousand dollars for the right piece. You had Allen Parker intimate that *The American Reader* would pay any amount of money for an original."

"Yes Arthur, but we're all on a very tight leash now. We have to prove to business that we can do an excellent job, and do it within a reasonable budget. I thought you understood that. Not that you've suffered any hardships since I took over."

"But you said you wanted exceptional writers."

"And I do. That's why we went to all that trouble to get your father to write this one story for us."

"Well, you got him to write for us, but now you have to pay him."

"We will pay him."

"How much?"

"I don't know. We'll pay him whatever the going rate is for a first-time original. I think it's two thousand seven hundred fifty dollars."

"That's not enough. *The New Yorker* pays him more than that nowadays."

"Yes, Arthur, but his son doesn't work for *The New Yorker*."

Arthur got up, walked behind the armchair and grasped the back of the chair with both hands. He took two more deep breaths, but his voice still came out in a croak. "I'm sorry, but it's still not enough," he said.

"I'm sorry too," said Horster, growing stern, "but it'll have to be enough," and he knocked a cigarette out of the package on his desk. He did not offer one to Arthur. Miss Sullivan appeared in the doorway.

"I've got the chairman's office on the phone," she said. "I said that you were in."

"All right," said Horster. "I'll pick up in a minute." Then he turned to Arthur. "We can talk more tomorrow," he said. "I understand why this might be an emotional issue for you. But I am convinced that we can work it out. You do not have a problem. Believe me, a lot of people on staff here are going to have problems in the very near future."

"Hello," he said into the phone. "All right, I'll hold." Then he cupped one hand over the mouthpiece and turned back to Arthur.

"Pass me one sheet," he said, pointing to a pile of yellow paper at the far corner of his desk. Arthur did as he was told. Horster took a Flair pen from the inside pocket of his jacket. He wrote something on the page, folded it in half and passed it to Arthur.

Arthur opened the sheet of paper.

Horster still had his ear to the phone, his hand over the mouthpiece. "What does it say?" he asked.

"One hundred twenty-five thousand dollars."

Horster nodded. "Like that?" he asked.

Arthur shrugged. "Sure. What's not to like?"

"All right," said Horster. "Then we agree. You can't let your father's expectations ruin your career for you. That would be absurd. Besides, it's not as if he were hurting for cash."

THIRTY-FIVE

When Arthur pulled up the drive to the house in Upcounty Estates that evening, there was a big pink bow on the mailbox and another on the kitchen door. Faith met him at the door with a kiss. She seemed to be excited. She was wearing her tight green skirt and the yellow sweater. The cheating outfit.

"Where's Nathan?" he wanted to know.

"He's spending the night with my parents. I made you pot roast. I used my mother's recipe. It'll be just like the meals we used to have when we first got married."

Arthur stopped in the kitchen to take off his jacket. He kissed Faith on the cheek.

She smiled up at him warmly. "I thought we should have dinner alone," she said.

Faith lit the candles, and sat down to a plate of lettuce with vinegar. Arthur sat down at his pot roast and cut a piece.

"Aren't you going to ask me what this is about?" asked Faith.

Arthur put the piece of meat into his mouth and chewed. "What is this about?" he asked obediently.

Faith picked up her knife and fork and held them poised over her plate of lettuce. "It's a way of thanking you for the last couple of months. The new house we're looking at. The flowers. The promotions. The money. Things are going well for once."

"I suppose," said Arthur. "They're going better."

"All right," said Faith. "They're going better. And I have some news."

"What's that?"

"I saw Doctor Morris today."

"You're all right?"

"Yes, I'm fine. Sound as a horse, he said. And we talked about my having something done."

"Having what done?"

"Guess."

Arthur shook his head and went on chewing.

"All right," said Faith. "I'll tell you," and she came over and stood behind Arthur's chair. She put her arms around him and kissed him under the ear. He could feel the pressure of her bosom against his back. "I want to have him remove my IUD."

Arthur put his fork down.

"But when you saw Nathan's shrink, he said you were malnourished."

"And when you saw him, he said you were neurotic."

"Okay, but my neurosis isn't going to hurt the fetus. Your being malnourished might."

Faith sighed. "Do you want me to eat some meat?" she asked.

"Yes," said Arthur. "I'd love it if you ate some meat."

Faith went back into the kitchen and cut herself a piece of pot roast. She brought the plate back to the table.

"You happy?" she asked.

"Yes," said Arthur, cutting himself another forkful of pot roast. "I am happy."

The phone rang. Usually Faith was the one to spring for the phone. This time she did not. Arthur went into the kitchen and got it on the third ring. It was Icarus.

"Is this a bad time?" he asked.

"No," said Arthur.

"I'm sorry to bother you like this."

"Bother away," said Arthur.

"I finally got the Salvation Army to agree to make a pickup. I promised them the love seat. And your mother's old dresser. They are going to come sometime tomorrow morning. So I was moving the dresser downstairs. This is a little bit embarrassing."

"Go on."

"I dropped it. I'm not hurt or anything. But it's caught in the stairwell. If it stays there, I'm going to have to go out the window in order to get into the kitchen. I don't know what I'll do when Leander has to pee."

Arthur didn't say anything.

"I suppose I could construct a sling," said Icarus, "and hoist him in and out from the second story."

"No," said Arthur. "I'll be right over. I'm sure we can move it together."

He hung up and went back into the dining room. Faith smiled and held up her empty plate.

"See," she said. "It's all gone."

"Good," said Arthur. "I mean that's not just good, it's great. She presented her cheek, and he kissed her chastely. Then he sighed. "Look," he said. "I have to go to my father's house. It's an emergency."

"It's always an emergency with him."

"Well," said Arthur, "it often is."

"I thought maybe now that God showed him how to quit drinking, we were going to have fewer emergencies."

"It's a ten-minute drive," said Arthur. "Besides, we don't know for sure if he has quit drinking."

"What's the matter?"

"He dropped a chest of drawers."

"Is he caught under it?"

"No, but it has blocked the staircase."

"So he can stay upstairs."

"But then the dog can't go out."

"So they can both stay downstairs."

"I think I should go."

Faith got up from the table and cleared away Arthur's plate. Arthur followed her into the kitchen. "You have to understand this," he said.

Faith shrugged. "I don't have to understand anything," she said. "You don't get along with your father. You never really have. But when he says jump, you jump."

"And what do I do when you say jump?" asked Arthur.

"You complain," said Faith.

"Maybe," said Arthur. "But I also jump."

"I'm your wife."

"I know," said Arthur. He reached out for her arm, but she pulled it away.

"I'll be right back," he said.

"Please," said Faith. "Don't do me any favors." She ran lightly up the stairs and slammed the bedroom door.

Arthur went into the laundry room, opened the crawl space and retrieved the two cartridge boxes. He guessed that he had almost $5,000. It wasn't a lot, but it was at least $1,000 more than he'd borrowed from his father over the last five years.

He stuffed the money in one of the cases, clamped it shut and put it in the back of the van. He also took his knife out of his briefcase, wrapped it in paper towels and put it under the van's passenger seat. Then he drove to his father's house. Icarus met him at the door. He was dressed in a pair of old chinos and a gray crew-neck sweater that had belonged to Arthur's mother. The dresser was wedged in the stairwell, but it didn't block the passage. Arthur didn't say anything about this.

Together they took out the drawers. Arthur took one end of the chest, his father the other. Arthur went first and backward. Even across the width of the dresser, he could hear his father's labored breathing. Icarus had to stop three times. After getting the chest out to the drive, they moved the drawers down as well, and slid them back into place.

"What about the sofa?" Arthur asked.

"I can manage," Icarus said.

"I'll help."

"Don't you have to go home?"

"Not right away."

"Won't Faith be concerned if you don't come back right away?"

"No," said Arthur. "She won't."

He got on one end of the love seat. His father got on the other, and they moved it out to the drive.

"You know, the sofa is in terrible shape," said Arthur as they went back toward the house. "But that dresser's not so bad. You could have used that."

"I don't have that many clothes," said Icarus.

"You could use it for manuscripts. You're always complaining about losing manuscripts."

"I suppose," said Icarus, "but I don't think I could stand to have it looking at me. And besides, I'm sure your mother would have been happy to have it go to the poor."

Arthur shrugged. "I suppose," he said.

They were in the kitchen now, and Icarus was putting on the kettle. "Are you anxious to get home?" he asked.

"No, not really," said Arthur.

"Would you like a cup of tea?"

"A cup of tea would be great."

Icarus reached up onto the top of the refrigerator and brought down a package of Marlboros. He opened this and lit one for himself.

"A cup of tea and a cigarette," said Arthur.

"I thought you had quit smoking," said Icarus.

"I have a cigarette once in a while," Arthur said.

Icarus shook out a second Marlboro, and gave Arthur his lighter. Then he sat at the kitchen table. Arthur stood with his back to the counter. He took a pull on the cigarette and knocked the ash into the sink.

"I didn't really need to call you," said Icarus. "As soon as I got off the phone, I found that I could move the dresser so that Leander and I could go up and down the stairs."

"That's all right," said Arthur.

"It's odd, but I feel much more frail now that my veins aren't full of gin."

Arthur nodded.

"You heard what happened to Mongoose?"

"What happened to Mongoose?"

"I thought you would have heard."

"No, I didn't hear. I don't seem to hear anything anymore."

"He's at Phelps. One of the snakes got him. He was at home alone when it happened. The snake bit him and then got between him and the phone. So it took him a long time to call for help."

"Oh shit."

"Oh shit is right."

"Is he going to die?"

"That's not clear. The doctors seem to think he'll live, but they are being mysterious about it. It looks like he may lose the use of his right arm. It's lucky he works at 'Mother Magazine.' At least they'll take care of him."

The kettle began to whistle. "Would you mind if I had a drink?" Arthur asked.

"No, of course not. What do you want?"

"Something a little stronger than tea."

"Like a glass of gin?"

"That's right."

"Well, you know where it is. But I'm afraid I can't join you."

"Please don't join me," said Arthur.

Arthur turned off the kettle and went into the pantry. He couldn't find the gin. He filled an eight-ounce drinking glass almost to the top with Dry Sack, and went back into the kitchen. His father was pouring hot water over a Lipton tea bag.

Arthur drank off a third of the glass of sherry. Then he shook his head. "I've forgotten how sweet that stuff is," he said.

"Yes," said Icarus. "I always thought sherry was beneath contempt. Then I didn't get along so well with gin either."

"I guess I'm shook up about Mongoose," Arthur said. "I don't suppose I should be telling you this now, but he got sore at me the other day. He called me a manifest asshole, whatever that is." Arthur took another pull on his drink. "There's also trouble on the home front," he said.

"What trouble?"

Arthur shrugged.

Icarus coughed into his hand. "You know what I think?"

"Yes, I do know. 'Be firm,' that's what you've always said. 'Assert yourself.' But it's not easy."

"Of course it's not easy. You're right about that. But the other's not easy either. Being too reasonable can be a serious handicap."

Arthur smiled. "I bow to your superior wisdom," he said, but he didn't sound convinced. "Faith would kill me if she knew I was confiding in you."

"What are you fighting about this time?"

"She wants another baby."

"I thought she wanted you castrated?"

"She did, but she's changed her mind."

"So have a baby."

"It's not that simple. The fight's also about money. Speaking of which," said Arthur, "I have something for you." He went down to the van and brought up the cartridge box. He put it on the table. "Payback," he said.

Icarus opened the box of cash. "Have you been dealing drugs?" he asked.

Arthur laughed. "No," he said, "I'm an editor for *The American Reader*. It's what I owe you," he said. "It's what I borrowed."

Icarus looked into the box. "Is this what you're fighting about?" he asked.

"No," said Arthur. "She doesn't even know about it. We're fighting because she wants to have another baby."

"And you don't?"

Arthur shrugged. "I guess not. Nathan isn't having a wonderful life. I mean he's a great kid, but he hasn't been happy. I almost never see him. He lives with his grandparents. They're good to him, but he'll never grow up under them. Faith still hasn't."

Icarus took a sip of tea. "Nathan seems all right to me," he said. "I haven't seen him in some time now."

Arthur pulled out his wallet and showed his father a recent photograph of his son.

"He has Faith's chin," he said.

"Then he'll be handsome," said Icarus.

Arthur put the wallet down on the table. "I suppose he is all right, but he's not happy."

"Is there anything I can do?" Icarus asked.

"Actually," said Arthur, "there is."

"What's that?"

"Remember that article they wanted you to write? The one for *The American Reader*?"

Icarus nodded.

"I wrote it."

"Good," said Icarus, "A piece on the virtues of cats seems perfect for you. Do they like it?"

"Yes, they do," said Arthur. "They love it."

"Well, great. But how can I help?"

Arthur cleared his throat. He wondered if this was going to hurt more than a vasectomy. "They like it because they think you wrote it. I told them you wrote it."

Icarus rocked back in his chair. "You mean you wrote it and used my name?" he said. His voice had an edge.

"That's right."

Icarus shrugged. "Is it heartwarming?" he asked.

"Yes," said Arthur.

Icarus blew smoke out through his nose. "That's what I was afraid of," he said. "And it's made up?"

"That's right."

"And you want me to pretend I wrote it?"

"That's right."

"You want me to pretend it happened?"

"That's right."

Icarus nodded. Icarus sighed. "Okay," he said. "As long as I don't have to read it."

"Is this really all right?" Arthur asked.

"Sure," said Icarus. "It's a fraud, but it's a very old one."

Arthur took another long pull on the glass of sherry. "You're not going to change your mind?"

"No, of course not."

"You can have the money."

"I don't need the money."

"But you can still have it."

Icarus shrugged. "There's something you should know," he said. "I guess I always assumed you understood it. I assumed a lot of things when I was a drunk. But in case I was wrong to assume it, I'm going to tell you."

Arthur helped himself to another cigarette. "Shoot," he said.

"I just wanted you to know that I'm aware of the fact that it's a pain in the ass being the son of Icarus South Prentice. We haven't talked about it much, but it must be a pain in the ass."

"That's right," said Arthur. "We haven't talked about it."

"I suppose people sometimes try to approach me through

you," said Icarus. "They see something in you that's not there."

Arthur nodded. "I like the attention," he said. "So sometimes I'll mention that you're my father, when it doesn't really need to come up. Then they'll treat me with more respect, but finally they find out it's me. Then they're disappointed."

Icarus nodded.

"And a lot of people call me Icarus," said Arthur. "Icarus and Arthur don't even sound alike, but if they're asking me a question about books, they'll forget themselves and call me Icarus. It's worse with writing. Some people think that anything I write is a violation of copyright. I know it's your name, and you've distinguished it. But it's also my name. It's the only one I've got."

Icarus laughed. "I suppose that's right," he said. "It is a violation of copyright." He put his cigarette down in a clay ashtray, and scratched at the end of his nose. "I wonder sometimes if it wouldn't have been easier for you if I'd been a plumber."

Arthur finished his sherry. He puffed on his cigarette, he wiped his mouth with the back of his hand. He waited. His father didn't say anything. Not "What a great plumber you'd be," not "Of course I have hopes for your own writing, son." His father didn't say anything. Not word one.

"But I'm not sure I would have been a good plumber either," Arthur finally said.

Icarus shrugged. He seemed to have lost interest.

Arthur put out his cigarette. "I guess I should go," he said.

Icarus got up. "Let me walk you to the car," he said.

Arthur climbed up behind the wheel of the van, started the engine and watched as his father headed back to the house. Icarus was a graceful man, but there was something awkward about the way he walked away from his son, something awkward and yet familiar. Arthur had noticed this before, but he'd never quite understood it. Now he realized that he'd seen the walk before. It was the way the movie cowboys walked when they thought someone behind them might pull a gun.

By the time Arthur got home that night the house in Upcounty Estates was dark. The ribbon had been taken from the kitchen door. Arthur went inside, took off his shoes and tiptoed up to the sewing room.

When he got up the next morning, he couldn't find his wallet. So he dressed without it. He took all the change out of the Corning Ware sugar bowl. He put this in his suit pocket. It created an unsightly bulge, but he estimated that he now had enough cash to last the day. He could have an apple for lunch. Apples at the cafeteria now cost $1.25. He might find his wallet at work. Faith didn't open her door at all while he was dressing, so he drove off to World Headquarters without seeing her.

He couldn't find his wallet at work. He wanted to call Faith to see if she could find it at home. He thought he'd better not. He thought he might have left the wallet at his father's house. He phoned twice. There was no answer.

He called the hospital about Mongoose. A nurse told him that Mr. Quest's condition was stable, but that he was not yet well enough for visitors. Arthur knew from his years on the newspaper that a person could be paralyzed from the waist down and the hospital might still say that his condition was stable. Stable meant stable. It didn't mean good.

When Arthur got home that evening, the house was dark. There had been a rash of burglaries, so all the doors were locked. He broke a pane out of the kitchen door with his elbow and let himself in. Once in the house he turned on all the lights and the TV set. He spent a half an hour looking for his wallet. He couldn't find it. He took a plate of cheese and crackers up to the sewing room and lay in bed for a while reading *The Godfather*. He often read *The Godfather* when he was upset. He had read it many times. He wanted so badly to be a reasonable man. At about 9 P.M. he went downstairs and turned off the lights and the TV. Then he went up to bed. By nine-thirty he was asleep.

He woke at 4 A.M. from a troubling dream and went to the bathroom. After he'd flushed the toilet he got back into bed. Faith appeared in the doorway. She was wearing a black lace bra and panties that matched. Over this she wore one of his blue work shirts. Unbuttoned.

"I guess you and your father had a toot yesterday," she said.

"I had a toot," said Arthur. "My father had Lipton tea."

Faith went over and sat in Arthur's desk chair.

"You haven't seen my wallet, have you?"

"No, why do you ask?"

"It's lost."

"Well, I haven't seen it."

"All right," said Arthur, and he shrugged. "I must have left it at home."

"This is home," said Faith.

"I mean my father's house. I must have left it at my father's house."

Faith didn't say anything for a minute.

"Do you want to talk now?" she asked.

"I'm a little tired," said Arthur.

Faith got up. "All right," she said angrily, heading for the door.

"Okay," said Arthur. "But let's go downstairs. I don't want to wake Nathan up."

"He's still at my parents' house."

"Let's go downstairs anyway. I can make some coffee."

"You need coffee?" asked Faith.

"I wouldn't mind having some," said Arthur.

He got out of bed and pulled on his underwear, his suit pants and a T-shirt that said he supported public television. When he got downstairs, Faith was already seated at the kitchen table. Now she was wearing his brown terry cloth bathrobe over the bra and panties. The robe was not tied. As she moved, he kept catching glimpses of her underwear.

Arthur went to the sink and filled the kettle. Then he remembered that he hadn't watered the jade plant in the dining room. He brought the kettle into the dining room and started to water the plant. The water wasn't being absorbed by the soil in the way he expected it to be, so he stuck a finger into the pot. There was a full serving of pot roast right under the first layer of dirt. Arthur went back into the kitchen, refilled the kettle and put it on. Then he sat down across from Faith. "There's pot roast in the jade plant," he said.

"I know," said Faith. "Who do you think put it there?"

"I don't know."

"Guess."

"You did."

"That's right. Compost is good for jade plants."

"But that means you didn't eat your meat."

"No, it doesn't. That was your pot roast I put in the plant. Remember, you didn't finish your dinner? I finished mine."

Arthur nodded. "That's right," he said, "I didn't finish my dinner."

"So what about babies?" asked Faith.

"I still don't want a baby," he said.

"Why not?"

"I wish I had a time machine," he said. "That way the old you could argue with the new you, and I could keep out of it. As it is, I always find myself defending some position you took six months or a year ago."

"Very funny," said Faith.

"No, it's not funny, it's serious," he said with real pain in his voice. "You wanted to have me castrated. Now you want to have another child."

"You should be pleased," said Faith. "I had doubts about our future. Now you're doing well at work. You send me flowers."

"But you wanted me castrated?"

"I wish you wouldn't exaggerate like that. I didn't want you castrated. I wanted you to have a vasectomy. They're not the same thing. Thousands of men have had vasectomies."

"I know," said Arthur. "Didn't Mrs. Gandhi give each and every one of them a transistor radio?"

"Something like that."

"Probably a lot of men have been castrated too, but that doesn't make me want to line up."

Faith lit a cigarette. Her robe fell open, revealing her large breasts and the pale skin of her belly. "I don't understand why you're picking a fight about this now. I'm not telling you to have a vasectomy now."

"Yes, but consistency is important."

"It's the bugbear of little minds, if that's what you mean."

"All right, but just for this little mind, I do think we should take a look at the immediate past. It wasn't that long ago that you didn't want more children, and now, suddenly, you do."

Faith shrugged. "I suppose that's right."

"What if you change your mind back? We're not going to be able to disappear the baby. We can send it to your parents' house a lot, but he, or she, will still be our baby."

"I won't change my mind. I want another child, and a year from now I will still want another child."

Arthur pulled out his chair and stood up. "My father was always a child," he said, "still is a child. It's very charming, even admirable, but it doesn't make for happy offspring. You and I are doing the same thing. We're children, and it isn't making for a happy Nathan. He never gets to be a child. It's already too crowded in the nursery."

Faith began to cry. Arthur gave her a tissue. She wiped her eyes. "It's for you," she said. "It's to bring us together. We don't have anything in common anymore. You keep going over to that woman's house."

"That woman helps me," said Arthur. "She also insists I send you flowers. We have our work in common."

"I bet that's not all you have in common."

"Yes it is," he spat back, really angry now. "What did you and I ever have in common, except that we liked to screw? We used to like to screw."

Faith bristled. "Look," she said, "if you want to have a big fight we can have one, but it's on your head."

"I don't want to have a fight of any size," said Arthur, and he went to the window and pretended to look out into the night. "I just don't want to have another child right now. You almost never see Nathan. And Nathan's interesting. A baby is going to be less interesting. You already say you can never do what you want. Have two children and it's going to get worse."

Faith didn't respond. Arthur walked over to her and put a hand on one of her arms. "What about your health? Did you ask Morris about your diet? Did you ask him if fifteen grams of protein a day is enough?"

"He's a gynecologist. He doesn't know about nutrition."

"I thought they did know about nutrition."

"Maybe some do," said Faith, smiling wanly. "Dr. Morris doesn't. His favorite food is Hostess Sno Balls."

"Then we need a better gynecologist."

"I love Dr. Morris."

"All right then, but I don't want you getting pregnant until you've seen a doctor who does know something about nutrition."

"Be realistic," said Faith. "Money does make things easier."

"That's not why you want to have more children, because you can afford them."

"It's better than having them because you can't afford them."

"I suppose, but not much better."

"Well, things are different now. Besides, we have four bedrooms."

"We bought the big house, or rather your father bought the big house, because in developments the larger houses are more apt to appreciate in value. It was an economic decision. It was an attempt to protect your father's investment. Your father did not buy a big house so that we could fill it up with expensive babies. Also, I thought you wanted to move."

"To a neighborhood with better schools."

"And a higher overhead."

"Babies don't cost that much. He can use Nathan's old crib, and I still have a lot of stretchies."

"But you don't eat enough to get pregnant."

"I don't know what they told you in medical school, Dr. Prentice," Faith said with loathing, "but a woman doesn't get pregnant because she eats meat."

Arthur took a cigarette from Faith's pack and lit it. He inhaled deeply and blew the smoke out through his nose.

"But you used to love to eat," he said. "Remember that place in Irvington with the rafters? You'd have the king burger, and leave nothing on your plate?"

"That wasn't healthy."

"Healthier?"

"I was fat."

"You were not. I could take my two hands and put them around your waist, and my fingers would almost meet. Do you remember that?"

"Yes," Faith said, reluctantly. "I remember." And then, almost cheerfully, "I think they've closed the Horn & Hound anyway."

"No, they haven't. They were shut for a week. Remodeling or something. They're open now."

"They did have great hamburgers," she said.

"That's right," Arthur said. "Let's go tomorrow. I mean tonight. Let's go when I get back from work." Then he remembered that he'd lost his wallet. But he didn't say anything.

"It could be a celebration," said Faith, brightening considerably.

"A celebration of what?"

"We could celebrate first, and then afterwards we could do the thing we're celebrating."

"You're putting a lot of strings on this hamburger."

"So why are you so dead against it? You're doing great at work."

"Not anymore."

"What do you mean by that?"

"I had a fight with Horster."

"Oh," said Faith, suddenly very alert. "There's something you're not telling me."

"No," said Arthur, "there's nothing I'm not telling you. But Horster and I did have a disagreement."

"You got along with that shit for years, and now they make him editor-in-chief and you fight with him. I can't believe this is happening," she said, her voice rising.

"It's not happening, sweetie. It already happened."

"So. You'll go in tomorrow and apologize," she said coldly.

"That's what I thought I was going to do, but now I'm not so sure."

"Why not?"

"Because I don't like this whole thing. I don't like doing what I have to do to succeed there, but I also don't like what I get for succeeding. I should quit and go back to the newspaper."

"You can't do that."

"Sure I can. Melvin would hire me in a minute. In fact, I talked with him just last week. He's managing editor now. They'd love to have me."

"And we could go on welfare."

"No," said Arthur, "we could live here. We couldn't move, but we could live here."

"You are incredible," Faith said, and she was beginning to get red in the face. She stood and walked over to the sink. She washed her hands, dried them on a paper towel and then lit another cigarette. The one she had been smoking was still burning in the ashtray on the kitchen table.

"Listen," she said. "This is not your life to screw up." There were tears running down her cheeks. "This is not just your life. We've been living off my parents for years, and you owe them. You can't fuck up for the hell of it." She began to hit at the counter with both her fists. "Shit!" she said.

"Shit, shit, shit." Arthur was surprised at the violence of her grief.

"Get out of this house," Faith said, turning and pushing him toward the door. "Get out of my house."

"No," said Arthur. And then, with growing uncertainty, "I won't." And then, "I love you."

"You do not," said Faith, sobbing now. "That's the biggest fucking lie of your life. You say you love women, but you don't love women," Faith screamed. Her face now was crimson with rage. "You hate women. That's the one thing you learned from your father. You could have learned how to be a great writer, but you didn't. You can't even spell 'cat.' You work for the fucking *American Reader*. The only thing you learned from your father was how to hate women. You hate everything about me." She began to push Arthur toward the door. "Out of my house," she said, and she was still again, but now she was crying quietly, determinedly. "I want you out of my house."

"I won't leave," said Arthur.

"Yes, you fucking well will leave," she said, pushing hard against his chest. He stood still, and she began to scratch at his arms and face.

Arthur backed out of the kitchen, through the fire door and into the garage. He opened the garage door. Then he climbed into the van and pulled out into the drive. He got out of the van and took a pair of shoes off the metal shelf in the garage. They were the fake wingtips he'd bought for his first trip to Paradise. He put them on, closed the garage door and got back into the driver's seat.

He didn't exactly know where to go. He drove back by World Headquarters. He thought of going in, but he didn't want anyone to see his red eyes. So he went to an all-night diner, but when he got there, he remembered that all his change was in his suit jacket. He sat at a back booth and pretended to be interested in a copy of the business section of a newspaper that somebody had left there. There was an article on the advantages of owning a Deepfreeze. He read this right through. The waitress came and wiped his table. "Can I help you?" she asked.

"Do you accept credit?" he asked.

The waitress laughed hoarsely and went back to the counter. "Hey Joe," she said, calling into the kitchen. "We got a comedian out here."

Arthur walked stiffly out of the diner. He climbed into the van and headed back to the road his father lived on. The house was dark.

He went up the drive. He stopped the van and sat still in it. No lights came on. He would go in and look for his wallet. Maybe his father would be sitting up in the darkened dining room. Or maybe he would be asleep, in which case Arthur thought he would get his wallet and leave without being discovered.

The front door was open. Arthur went into the kitchen. He turned on the overhead light. He thought his wallet might have been on the kitchen table. He didn't see a wallet. Maybe his wallet was in the dining room.

Arthur recognized the gun first. It was the single barrel 20-gauge shotgun his father had given him for his fifteenth birthday. Arthur remembered his father telling him over and over again that he must never point a gun at anything he did not intend to kill. Now the gun was pointed at Arthur's head. The man pointing it was his father. His father was naked.

"Oh, hi Daddy," said Arthur.

There was no reply.

"It's me," said Arthur.

"I know that now," said Icarus, still training the gun at his son's head.

"So put the gun away," said Arthur.

Icarus continued to point the gun at him.

"Stand still," he said.

"Fuck you," said Arthur.

Icarus lowered the gun. "You know that if I'd still been drinking I probably would have shot you," he said.

"Yes," said Arthur. "I know that. Am I supposed to be impressed?"

"I might have shot you anyway," said Icarus.

"That's right," said Arthur. "You could have killed me, and then you could have had everyone feel sorry for you. FAMOUS AUTHOR KILLS SON IN TRAGIC MISHAP, that sort of thing. You could have come out for gun control. You would have been great on the evening news."

"Well, it is lucky that you kept the kitchen light on," said Icarus. "If the light hadn't been on, I would have been inclined to pull the trigger."

"You know what?" said Arthur. "Any father can kill any son. It's nothing special. You can kill me. I can kill Nathan. That's just the way the world was made. In fact, there's substantial evidence that you did kill me, without benefit of firearms."

"Jesus," said Icarus, breaking the gun and removing the shell. "Aren't you full of it tonight? You been reading Hesse again? Or is it Erich Fromm this time?" He put the shotgun back into the coat closet and put the shell up on a high shelf.

"What if I haven't been reading anything?" said Arthur. "What if I haven't even been thinking of something I read?"

"You aren't drunk, are you?"

"No," said Arthur. "But I'm not the one who gets drunk, remember?"

"All right," said Icarus, holding his balls with one hand while he extended the other. "Truce?"

"Sure," said Arthur, sticking out his own hand. "Why not?"

"As long as you're here," said Icarus, "why don't you have a cigarette? I'm going to go back upstairs and get a robe. I'll meet you in the kitchen."

Arthur went into the kitchen. He found his wallet in the fruit bowl on the kitchen table. He got a package of Marlboros down from the top of the refrigerator and lit one. Then his father came in.

"I found my wallet," said Arthur. "I must have left it here by accident."

Icarus nodded. "I noticed it," he said. "I would have called you, but it's so beaten up, I thought the painter must have left it."

Arthur didn't say anything.

"Are you still fighting with Faith? Is that why you're so testy?" said Icarus. He had a robe on, and it was fastened at the waist, but his balls were still clearly visible.

"No," said Arthur. "I was testy because you were pointing a gun at my head. But yes, I am fighting with Faith. She wants another baby."

"And you don't?" asked Icarus, lighting himself a cigarette.

"I don't want her to destroy herself. Besides, Nathan is sad."

"You were sad when you were a little boy."

"I know."

"I think you turned out fine."

"That's nice of you, but I'm not sure I'd agree."

"Nobody intelligent ever thinks they turn out fine. People who think they turn out fine don't."

"I think it would have been better if Mummy had lived."

"Talk about non sequiturs," said Icarus, and then sadly, "Arthur, it is time that you learned the basic rules of logic. Your ignorance has a way of making you perfectly incomprehensible."

Arthur shrugged. "I just think it would have been better."

"You mean better for me, or better for you?"

"Better for both of us, I suppose. But I was thinking of myself."

"How so?"

"I'm afraid of Faith. I'm afraid that if I'm not perfect for her, we're going to fight a lot. This sounds crazy, but I'm afraid that if we fight a lot, she'll die."

"Faith strikes me as a robust young woman," said Icarus. "I don't know how you two fight, but it probably won't kill her."

"It killed my mother," said Arthur.

"No, it did not," said Icarus. "Your mother went driving

in an ice storm. She wasn't killed by me. I don't make ice storms. Sometimes I invent them, but I didn't invent this one."

"I didn't know there was an ice storm."

"Why should you know?"

"There wasn't any ice that morning."

"It melted."

"Why didn't you tell me?"

"I didn't think it was important."

"I want to ask you one more question."

"Okay."

"You promise you won't get angry?"

"No, I don't promise."

"Were you and Mummy fighting when she went out that night? Hadn't she just found out that you had a thing going with Mrs. Rice?"

"No."

"But you did have a thing with Mrs. Rice?"

Icarus sighed, as if dealing with a very slow child. "Yes, as you so cleverly put it, Mrs. Rice and I did have a thing, but we're not talking television here, Arthur, or an episode from *The American Reader*. Your mother had known about Ellen for years. She didn't discover my infidelity on the night she died. She and Ellen used to go to antique shows together."

"And talk about the size of your cock."

Icarus shrugged. "I'd like to think so, but what they probably talked about was end tables."

Arthur didn't say anything.

Icarus broke the silence. "So you thought I drove your mother to suicide?"

Arthur shrugged.

"I was never sure," Arthur said, almost in a whisper. "I just suspected."

"Was it that sleeping beauty of a psychiatrist who first gave you that idea?" asked Icarus.

"No."

"Didn't he talk about the mortal combat between fathers and sons?"

"No," said Arthur. "I believe it was Sophocles who first gave me that idea. Green and I talked about violent sex and his house on Cape Cod. Remember, he wanted to know if he should sue the contractor?"

Icarus wasn't listening. "I just wish you'd had some sort of education," he said. "If you knew anything, you might not be susceptible to all this quackery."

Arthur shrugged.

"One more thing," said Icarus.

"Sure."

"Where ever did you find those preposterous shoes?"

Dawn was breaking when Arthur got back to Upcounty Estates. He took the hidden key from under the doormat. He let himself in. Then he walked to the bottom of the stairs in his stocking feet. Then he stripped, and climbed the stairs holding his clothes over his head as if he were a soldier fording a shallow river. He could see that there was a light on in the master bedroom.

"It's me," he said. "It's not a rapist. You don't have to call 911."

Faith came out into the hall. She was in her nightgown. Her face was streaked with tears. "You can stay here until you go to work today," she said. "But that's it. This is my house, and I want you out of it tomorrow. I want you out of it for good." She went back into the bedroom and slammed the door.

Arthur retreated to the sewing room and lay on his back on the bed. In two hours he would have to get up and go to work. He turned onto his stomach. He couldn't sleep. He was horny.

Lisa wore her tight blue denim shirt and a white turtleneck with vertical ribbing. She had that big old-fashioned watch on her right hand. A man's watch. She was down at the mailbox. There was a newsletter from her congressman, a flier from the local chiropractor and an electric bill. Nothing personal. She came up the stairs and opened the front door. The man was sitting on the third step of the stairway that led from the entrance-foyer to the second floor. In his right hand he held a small chrome pistol, an automatic with a silencer and a nine-shot clip.

There was a church pew set up as a bench in the foyer, and Lisa tossed the mail on it and closed the front door. Then she turned and saw the intruder. "You're not still angry, are you?" she asked, breathlessly. The man smiled, and brought the pistol up so that she could see it.

"You know I didn't mean it," she said.

It still wasn't exactly clear what she had done but not meant.

Drifting off to sleep, Arthur looked at the clock radio across the room. It was 6:25 A.M. He had to wake up in forty-five minutes. It was still difficult to get comfortable. His side hurt where it had been hit by the imaginary bullets.

He didn't have his epiphany until he was preparing for work. He had just spread on the shaving cream, and was looking at his face in the mirror when it came to him. "Look in a mirror," he thought, "and you see your father's face." So he looked. Then he got it.

"It's not some strange woman I want to kill," he said aloud. "It's not Sophia Loren. It's not my mother. It's not Faith. It's me. It's the woman in me.

"And I'm doing it for you," he said to the mirror. "Because you couldn't do it to yourself. Which was probably a great thing," he said, "although nobody knew it at the time."

THIRTY-SIX

There was a squad of neatly dressed Asian demonstrators out at the end of the corporate driveway with placards. The messages were in Japanese. Arthur wondered idly if the protestors had flown all the way from Tokyo.

Inside, he was surprised to find that Horster had not phoned. Arthur had a fresh copy of *Woman's Day* to read, in which the first reader had recommended what seemed to be a promising article on a pretty little girl with cancer. So he hung his jacket up behind the door, went downstairs for a cup of coffee and began to read. The piece was a disappointment, and he marked it Not Usable. His comment: "Little girl contracts rare form of cancer and dies. Nobody learns anything. Or feels better." He skimmed the rest of the issue, and had a costly, solitary lunch at the cafeteria. Now at least he had a wallet. The phone rang at 1 P.M. Arthur got it on the second ring. It was Faith. Of course he could come home. She wanted him to come home. "More than anything."

"I love you," she said.

"Okay," he said.

"And I'm doing what I can about money," she said. "My mother and I are making these little crates as gifts, with cheeses in them, crackers and jam."

"Oh."

"We're going to sell them."

Arthur nodded into the phone.

"We'll be working on them late tonight. I thought I'd bring one to your father tomorrow."

"That would be nice," said Arthur.

"Each little crate will cost about twenty-five dollars," she said.

"I'm sure he has twenty-five dollars for one of your little crates," said Arthur.

Horster came in at five. He was wearing the sweater with the conch shells. He was beaming.

He pulled up the armchair and sat in it. "I just heard that you're thinking of moving to Bedford," he said. "Congratulations."

"Thank you," said Arthur.

"It's the Tate house I believe?"

"That's right," said Arthur.

"Did you know that Lavinia and I looked at it before we decided to remodel the barn?"

"I hadn't known," said Arthur.

"It's a wonderful little house."

"Thank you," said Arthur.

Horster shook a Kool out of his package and offered it to his protégé. Arthur took it. Horster shook out another cigarette, put it in his mouth and lit them both.

"I think I've ironed out our little problem," he said. "I spoke with Palumbardo. We have a big hole in the March issue. We lost our story on corruption in the building unions. So we can make 'Edgar' the lead piece. We pay more for lead pieces. So your father will get ten thousand dollars."

Arthur nodded. He didn't believe Horster for a minute. He thought his father would probably get the $10,000, but he didn't think this was because of any union story. What was it about this sort of man that made it impossible for him to back off?

"We're all clear then, right?" said Horster, running his finger along the edge of Arthur's desk.

Arthur smiled.

Horster smiled back. He started to leave, but paused briefly at the door. "Ten thousand dollars is a lot of money for fifteen pages of the world's cheapest paper," he said.

Arthur sat still for a minute. He stood, sat back down, picked up the phone and dialed Ruth West.

"You remember that spaghetti dinner you offered me?" he asked.

"Sure, you want it?"

"Tonight, is that possible?"

"Anything is possible."

"That would be great. If you'd still have me, that would be great."

Then he called Faith. She wasn't home, so he phoned her mother.

"Oh, Arthur," said Irene, with a great deal of apparent warmth. "She'll just die when I tell her you called. You missed her by two minutes. We ran out of ribbon. We're getting it wholesale, so she had to go to Peekskill. But she should be back by six."

"I'll be gone by then," said Arthur. "Tell her I'll be at Ruth West's house if she needs me."

"Well, that's all right then," said Irene. "She meant to be home for you, but we've been so busy. Wait until you see these packages. They're much more attractive than the ones they're trying to sell at Altman's. Faith is going to bring one to your father."

"I know," said Arthur. "That's great."

When he drove out of World Headquarters late that afternoon, the Japanese editors were still in place. They seemed very composed. Some of the posters had been translated. Arthur read one of them. "American Reader Unfair to Japanese Workers!!!" it said in thick magic marker. Arthur didn't think this tactic was going to win a lot of sympathy.

The demonstrators were not marching. They were not even chanting. They were standing there, politely, holding up signs. They had placed themselves just beyond the edge of The Magazine's property. This put them on the land belonging to the local high school. There was a football game going on behind them. Arthur could hear the beating of drums.

He thought it odd that the Japanese had become the corporate conscience of America. They were a constant and galling reminder of the fact that it could work, it could all work splendidly. They made reliable cars, cheaper televisions, faster computers. And while Japanese technology was up-to-the-minute, the Japanese ethical system was simple, outdated, paternalistic. Thinking Americans had discarded all that nonsense decades ago. The new America had existentialists on the assembly line and barbarians in the boardroom.

It was ironic that they should be the victims of the corporation's new cost-cutting program. Fallow had always been so interested in Japan.

When he stopped at the traffic light just before Pound Ridge, Arthur checked under the driver's seat to make sure he had his big knife. It was there, wadded up in a piece of paper towel. Then he drove into the village and stopped at the liquor store. A bell rang when he crossed the threshold, and a little man in a white dress shirt and a gray cardigan sweater came out of a back room.

"I want a bottle of good champagne," Arthur said.

The man led Arthur to the back of the store and picked a bottle off a long wooden rack.

"This is Moët & Chandon," he said. "It's a fine bottle of champagne. Very dry. Twenty-eight dollars."

"What's the best champagne you carry?" Arthur asked.

"Then you want Dom Pérignon," said the liquor store man, and he went into another room and returned with a cardboard box.

"How much is that?" asked Arthur.

"Seventy-six dollars," said the man. "It'll be a little more if you add the tax."

"Then I'll have the other one," said Arthur.

After the liquor store, he went to the florist and arranged to have half a dozen roses sent to Faith. He asked for another half a dozen and waited impatiently while the girl behind the counter wrapped them.

"Put Bufferin in the vase with them," she said.

Arthur nodded.

He had used up his cash at the liquor store, so he paid for the flowers with a check.

"You aren't any relation to I. S. Prentice?" asked the girl.

"Yes," said Arthur, "he's my father."

"Oh my God," said the girl, "is that right?"

Arthur nodded.

"I loved *Couples*. I heard it was literature, and I don't usually like literature, you know, but I thought it was such a great book."

Arthur nodded.

"Let me ask you this," said the girl, "was that woman your mother? I mean the first woman, was she your mother?"

"I don't think so," said Arthur. "You see, John Updike wrote *Couples*."

"Are you sure of that?" the girl asked, looking perplexed. "The book about adultery?"

"Yes," said Arthur, "I'm sure. My father wrote about adultery, but Updike wrote *Couples*."

Now the girl was shaking her head. "I don't know much about books," she said. "But I read *Couples*, and I'm pretty sure you're wrong."

Arthur picked up the flowers. "Maybe I am," he said. "Maybe my father wrote *Couples* and never got around to telling me," he said, backing out of the store.

When he pulled up in front of the house in Pound Ridge, there was no other car in the drive. He took the knife out from under the seat and stripped off its nest of paper towel. He opened the large blade, snapped it shut and put the knife in the right pocket of his suit jacket. The bulge was hardly noticeable. He sat in the van for a minute to make sure that Eldridge wasn't loose. Then he got out and rang the doorbell. There was no answer. He peered in at a window. The house had been stripped of most of its furniture. He looked at his watch. It was 6:08 P.M. Ruth had asked him to come at six.

He walked slowly back to the van and got in. Then he heard the sound of tires on the gravel drive. It was the Honda. Ruth had Eldridge in the back, so Arthur stayed in the van and waved idiotically through the window while she got out. She was wearing blue jeans, a red flannel shirt and cowboy boots. And a cowboy hat. A red bandanna was tied loosely at her throat. She looked great. She also looked to be about eighteen years old. Ruth put Eldridge in the run and came back to the van.

Arthur climbed out clutching his bottle of moderately priced champagne in one hand and the flowers in the other. Ruth went back to the Honda and got a grocery-store bag.

"I'm sorry I wasn't here when you arrived," she said. "I had to get this." She reached into her brown paper sack and withdrew a large white onion. "And this," she said, pulling out a quart bottle of Dr Pepper.

"Well," said Arthur. "You got me," and he pulled the Moët & Chandon out of its bag. Then he blushed. "And I brought you flowers," he said.

"I guess we're going to have some party," said Ruth.

"That's right," said Arthur. He walked up to the front door with Ruth and stood to one side while she worked the key. He noticed how tight her rear was in the jeans. He also noticed how small she was. This came at him with the force of revelation. Even with boots, she was a good three inches shorter than he.

When she got the door opened, he saw that a large piece of white paper had been put on the kitchen floor. The kitchen table and chairs were gone.

Ruth put the hat on the counter, took the roses from Arthur and put them down beside the hat. Then she reached up and took a large pot from the rack that hung over the place where the kitchen table used to be. "We can sit on boxes in the dining room."

She put the pot down and leaned back with her elbows on the counter behind her. She leveled her gaze at him, and he noticed how dark her eyes were. Her hair was up on her head in a chignon. "I don't need the money," she said, "but I liked having a job. Horster never could have fired me without your help."

"You don't think I turned you in?"

"You were the only one who knew about the column."

"But I didn't say anything."

Ruth sighed. "You've gotten to be a very convincing liar," she said, smiling pertly. "But I don't believe you."

Arthur brought his right hand to his mouth. "So why did you say I could come over?" he asked.

"First," said Ruth, "you've got it backward. You invited yourself. Second, for the experience. I've led a sheltered life. I thought it would be fun to get to know a whore."

Arthur started toward the door, but Ruth put a small cold hand on his shoulder. When he turned again to face her, she hit him in the stomach. Her fist was very small, and the blow didn't really hurt. It was a surprise, though, and it knocked the wind out of him so that he had to sit on the floor. He was a little embarrassed.

She stood over him.

He looked up at her and smiled.

"My wife tried to beat me up when she was kicking me out of the house," he said. "Now you're hitting me. She didn't hurt me either, but I don't like the pattern."

"A pattern?" asked Ruth.

"Sometimes it seems I've spent my entire life as a sort of punching bag for women."

Ruth was standing above him, still scowling, but no longer furious. "It must be something you do," she said, "because I've never hit a man before."

"I suppose you're right," said Arthur, getting up. "But I don't think I deserve it. Or at least not in your case. I didn't tell Horster anything about you."

"Nothing?"

"Not one word."

"Why should I believe you?"

Arthur sighed. "You don't have to believe me," he said. "But it's the truth."

Ruth didn't look convinced.

Arthur shrugged. "Horster's my mentor," he said. "But I'm not Horster. I didn't fire you. I didn't even know you'd been fired."

"But you are his confidant," said Ruth. Then she walked back to the sink and began to pour water into the pot. "He must have had a reason to fire me."

"Sure he had a reason," said Arthur. "He doesn't like you. And he doesn't think he can control you. Two reasons."

"Maybe you're right," said Ruth. "In which case I owe you an apology."

"I'll take spaghetti and meatballs instead," said Arthur, rubbing thoughtfully at his stomach. "You could fight professionally," he said.

"Thanks," said Ruth, looking at the knuckles of her right

hand. "You've got a hard stomach. You do a lot of sit-ups?"

"No," said Arthur. "I just worry."

"What about?"

"That my father will die. That my wife will die. That the one woman who likes me will sell her house and move away. Where are you going?"

"California. Isn't that where Americans go when life isn't working out?" Ruth turned on a front burner and put the pot on the stove. "I know this will sound odd to you, but I like having an empty house. I had an estate sale. I thought I'd miss all my stuff, but I don't. I feel better not having it."

"What about Eldridge?"

"He's going to live in the country. I have a cousin with a farm in New Jersey. He's got two sons who have always loved the dog."

She reached up again and took a cutting board down from the same rack that had held the pot. Then she looked around. "Now I'm embarrassed," she said. "I don't have a single knife left in this kitchen. How am I going to make the sauce?"

"I've got a knife," said Arthur. He took out his big clasp knife, opened the blade and passed it to Ruth, handle first.

"Some knife," she said.

"I know," said Arthur. "But it's sharp. It'll cut your onion."

Ruth put the onion on the board and turned to face Arthur. "What do you get when you cross a donkey and an onion?" she asked.

"I don't know."

"A piece of ass that will make you cry."

Ruth sliced off the end of the onion, then she held her face up. "This always makes me cry," she said. "Here," said Arthur. "Let me do it." He went to the counter and took away the onion and the knife. He cut one slice. "Is this the right thickness?" he asked.

"That's fine," said Ruth. She was taking down a frying pan.

"So when are you leaving?"

"Day after tomorrow," said Ruth, opening a jar of Ragú and pouring it into the pan.

"So if I hadn't decided to come here tonight, I wouldn't have seen you again?"

"That's right," said Ruth.

"You would have stood me up?"

"I don't know if that's accurate," said Ruth. "I wouldn't have seen you again, but it didn't sound like you would have noticed." And then, changing the subject, "Look, when you've cut about half of it, drop the slices into the sauce."

"Are you going to change your name?" asked Arthur.

"No," said Ruth. "Why should I?"

"I don't know," said Arthur. He stopped slicing and began to put rings of onion into the sauce, which was bubbling on the heat. "I just thought that a name change was part of the package. I guess I'd like to change my name."

"Well, I don't want to change mine," said Ruth. "But what do you think of the rest of it?"

"I think it's courageous," said Arthur. "I'm envious."

Ruth came over to his side, got up on tiptoes and kissed him on the cheek. "I'd invite you," she said lightly, almost mockingly. Then she went back to the stove and put salt and olive oil in the pot of water. "But I know for a fact that you're in Horster's plans. I heard that he's been bringing your name up at board meetings. You'll be the youngest deputy editor-in-chief they've ever had. Besides, I can't ask you to escort an old lady to the coast. You've got a wife to think of and a house."

"I know," said Arthur. "But you could ask."

"I would," said Ruth, "but if there's one thing I've learned in all my long and painful years of living, it's that a woman should never ask a man to give up his career."

"But you could ask," Arthur said.

Ruth didn't ask, although they did share a pleasant dinner. After eating, Arthur helped to clean up, and then went home. Ruth walked him to the door, but they didn't kiss. Their lips had never even touched.

★   ★   ★

Faith wasn't at the house when Arthur got there a little after
9 P.M. He still had the bottle of champagne. He and Ruth had
had Dr Pepper with the spaghetti.

The kitchen table had a note on it and a chicken salad sandwich in Saran Wrap. The note under it had three hearts drawn
at the end. He didn't read the note. Just crumpled it up. Then
he unwrapped the sandwich, smelled it. He walked into the
garage and put the sandwich and the note into the garbage
pail. Then he went upstairs and went to bed. He must have
been exhausted because he slept right through his alarm. He
didn't wake up until 9 A.M. Nobody else was home. Faith
must have driven Nathan to school. Arthur didn't reach
World Headquarters until 9:30 A.M. He read manuscripts until
just before noon, at which point he stepped outside the front
door, just to see what sort of day it was. It was a fine day.
A green Toyota sedan pulled up in front of the oak and
parked. Horster got out. He looked mildly apologetic. "Gut-
ters and leaders," he said.

Arthur looked confused. "What about them?" he asked, not
willing to reveal his ignorance.

"The house," said Horster. "They were doing some work
on the house. I had to be on-site. My wife is far too reasonable
to talk with workmen." Horster turned and looked at his car.
"I think I'll just leave it here," he said.

"It's fine with me," said Arthur. "A Toyota's a nice-
looking car."

"Thanks," said Horster. He grinned and passed in through
the door. Just then the bells began to ring. Arthur couldn't
name the tune, but it was a cheery one. It might have been a
show tune. It might have been a hymn. There were cheerful
hymns. "Relax," he thought. "Just relax. Be yourself."

Horster came into his office shortly after 2 P.M. The dead part
of the afternoon. He had the layout for "Edgar Allan Polecat."

"I thought you'd like to see this," he said. "We paid two thousand dollars for the illustration."

He put the pages on Arthur's desk and sat in the visitor's armchair. He smiled at Arthur. Arthur smiled back.

"We had to make one tiny improvement in the text," said Horster.

"Oh."

"*Raucous* is a bad word. I'm sure your father didn't mean to use that word. The raucous cry of a cat doesn't sound right. Crows have a raucous cry. Cats don't. I think what he meant was *piercing*."

Linda appeared in the doorway. "It's your wife," she said.

"Tell her I'll call her back," said Arthur. He turned back to Horster. "Raucous," he said. "Raucous or no story."

Horster shrugged. "Whatever you want," he said. He didn't seem to be annoyed. "But you should really ask your father," he added. "I'm sure he'd agree with me."

"You ask him," said Arthur. "You want to know where he stands on this, you ask him." Linda was still in the doorway. She looked embarrassed.

"I think you should speak to her now, Mr. Prentice."

"Okay," said Arthur. "What line?"

"She's on line twenty-nine."

Horster stood. "See you later," he said, and winked.

When Arthur picked up, Faith was in tears. "What's the matter, honey. Calm down. What's the matter?"

"It's your father," said Faith.

"What about my father?"

"I brought him one of my packages," said Faith, between sobs.

"All right, all right," said Arthur. "What did he say this time?"

"He didn't say anything," sobbed Faith. "He's dead."

THIRTY-SEVEN

The funeral service was held at All Saints' Episcopal Church in Tarrytown, New York. Mrs. Carpenter and her employer had been regular communicants for years. She made the arrangements. She also engaged a caterer so that there would be something to eat and drink at the house afterward.

Having acted as the great man's personal secretary, she was in a position to know who should and should not be invited. The gathering included several prominent writers. Arthur insisted on a healthy contingent from the staff of *The American Reader*. And one from Alcoholics Anonymous.

Faith had trouble settling on the right dress, and by the time they arrived at the church, most of the pews were filled. Faith found a seat in the rear. Arthur moved up to the first row. All the seats were taken, so he stood uneasily in the aisle.

The priest was one of those gorgeous young men who swelled the orders in the late 1960s and might well have revitalized traditional religion had they not moved so quickly into high-paying corporate jobs. He spoke briefly, charmingly, quoting both Christ and Elisabeth Kübler-Ross. Then he stepped away from the pulpit and gestured toward it with one arm. "I knew Icarus South Prentice on Sundays," he said. "You people knew him the rest of the week. So please, speak. Let us remember. Let us share."

Allen Wyndham was the first to take the stand. He had a fist full of notes, and spoke for half an hour. He quoted extensively from his own novels. The work was not stylish. But Arthur wasn't annoyed. Style was still at the center of Arthur's inherited faith, but Wyndham was a good man. He had adored Icarus. This too was important.

Horster and Palumbardo arrived late. They stood together at the back of the church. When Wyndham spoke of the "costs of greatness," both men wept.

Arthur's was not the second speech, nor was it the last. It came somewhere in the middle. He took a turn because such a long time had passed after the last speaker. But when he got to the pulpit, he saw that an elderly and distinguished painter—complete with cane and young wife—had been heading purposefully up the far aisle. Still, once he'd been seen, Arthur thought he might as well go on, get it over with. Besides, the artist was just opposite an empty section of bench. Arthur paused and raked the pews to make certain that the family physician was absent as promised. "I'd love to attend the service," he had told Arthur, "but I'm locked into a time-share in Cancún."

"When I phoned Dr. Sneeling, he meant to console," Arthur told the audience. "He said that anybody who had achieved what my father had would be proud to die.

"I was polite," said Arthur. "But I didn't want to be. What

I wanted to say was, 'All right, Doctor, we'll put your name on all the books.'

"I think the doctor might have gone for that," said Arthur. "Then he could die the day before yesterday. My father could live another thirty years."

Arthur and five other people he hardly knew carried the coffin to a car, and the car went to the graveyard. The hole was surrounded with indoor/outdoor carpeting in bright green, and Arthur could easily imagine how furious this would have made his father. After the burial Arthur moved uneasily through the assembled mourners, inviting people back to the house. Faith and Mrs. Carpenter had already gone there to prepare for the guests. He sprinkled invitations throughout the crowd, then positioned himself in what he thought was an obvious spot so that he could give directions.

His first taker was a dignified old guy with liver spots. The man said he knew Icarus from his days in the theater. Arthur didn't remember that his father had ever been involved in the theater, but he didn't argue. He just gave directions. Then he was approached by an extraordinarily handsome young male. He might have been a man, but he might still have been a boy. Arthur didn't recall that they had ever met.

"You're coming to the house?" he asked.

"I don't think so," said the boy/man. He seemed shy. He was dressed in a not particularly becoming suit and a pair of desert boots.

"I don't want to pressure you, but you're more than welcome. There will be plenty of food."

"I wanted to speak," the boy/man said. "But I didn't think you'd like it."

Arthur shrugged. "I don't know why not," he said innocently. "I mean it's a bad day, but it's not anything anybody said." He smiled and shrugged again. "Most everybody did speak."

The boy/man looked uncomfortable. "Your father was so good at expressing himself," he said. "I'm such a bumbler."

Arthur smiled. "Well, you wouldn't have been the only

bumbler who spoke," he said. And then, "I wasn't exactly Winston Churchill."

The boy/man raised his eyebrows. "I thought you were more than adequate," he said in a voice that was completely without conviction.

"How did you know Daddy?" Arthur asked.

"Oh, I used to help around the house. And we traveled together sometimes."

"I don't remember that."

"Mostly it was after your mother died."

"I still don't remember," Arthur said, bringing a hand to his mouth.

"I guess he didn't always keep you posted, although I distinctly recall him telling you about one bicycle trip we took," the boy/man said. "It was in Vermont," he said, smiling wanly. The two looked at each other for a long minute. Then the boy/man shrugged. "Whatever," he said, and walked off.

The next person in line was Mrs. Allen Wyndham. "You look upset," she said.

"No," said Arthur, "I'm fine."

"You could be upset," said Mrs. Wyndham. "It's allowed."

"No," said Arthur, still struggling to get his breathing under control. "I'm fine."

"Then you have to be honest with me," said Mrs. Wyndham.

"I'll try."

"Did he go on too long?"

"No, no," said Arthur, shaking his head. "I thought he was brilliant. Really I did."

"Sure, sure," said Mrs. Wyndham, and she rolled her eyes. "It's kind of you to say so. Who was that young man you were just speaking with?"

"I don't really know," said Arthur. "Some friend of my father's."

Mrs. Wyndham shook her graying curls. "You're not going to believe this," she said, "but he looks just exactly the way your father used to look forty years ago."

Arthur smiled. "I like to think my father had a better suit," he said.

"No," said Mrs. Wyndham. "If anything, the suit was worse. He looked terrific, but it wasn't much of a suit."

Then Horster was at Arthur's side. He took his employee's left arm in his own right hand. "I remember when my father died," he said.

"How was it?"

"Nothing. When he died, it was nothing. Then a year later, I was sorting through some books and it hit me."

"Did you cry?"

Horster shook his head. "But I knew that something precious had ended." He cleared his throat. "You won't allow yourself to see it now, but it is also a beginning."

"I hope so," said Arthur. "But I can't get him out of my mind. It may be a beginning for me. But I don't see how it can be a beginning for him. He's what we're here for."

"Cheerful, cheerful," said Horster, smiling.

Arthur shrugged. "I can't always be," he said. "I can't always be cheerful."

"Laugh and the world laughs with you," said Horster. "Cry and you cry alone."

Arthur stayed at the graveyard until everybody had gone. Then he walked back to the hole. An awkward aluminum scaffolding had been used to lower the casket into the ground. Now two men were squatted beside this smoking cigarettes. They were both wearing jeans. One was a big man in a red sweater. He had blond hair and a blond beard. The other was clean-shaven. He wore a blue sweatshirt with "Property of the Denver Broncos" in white letters across the chest.

The one with the red sweater looked up as Arthur approached. He stood. Then his companion stood. The one in the red sweater spoke first. "Family?" he asked.

Arthur nodded.

He dropped his cigarette onto the ground beside the hole and stubbed it out with the toe of his work boot. "Close family?" he asked.

Arthur nodded again.

The gravedigger shrugged. "And you don't feel nothing?" he asked softly.

"That's right," said Arthur, surprised.

Now the man in the blue sweatshirt was shaking his head. "Nobody does," he said. "When they're that close you never feel it." He coughed into his right hand, and then cleared his throat. "You never get over it either."

Back at the house Arthur found himself having a long and awkward conversation with a writer whose work he greatly admired. The man seemed very relaxed, genial for a person of such talent. He had often been on panels with Arthur's father. "Of course I adore X," Icarus used to say, "but I've read so much about the size and configuration of his cock that when I have to look at him for any period of time, he begins to appear to me as a sort of a hard-on with a hairpiece."

X had recently been attacked in the cover story of a small but respected magazine. They'd called him a literary dinosaur. Arthur never would have mentioned the piece, but X brought it up. "Sometimes I do feel a little bit like a living fossil," he said.

"They're just sniping," said Arthur. "I've always admired your wig, I mean your work. And so does everybody I know."

Life after the death went on in its accustomed trajectories. The legal problems that had threatened the article about union corruption melted away as expected. "Edgar Allan Polecat" was scheduled for the following Easter. "It's such a great story, we don't want to go off prematurely," Horster explained. "We should wait and make it a rebirth."

In the confusion of such a sudden and unexpected loss, Arthur had not spoken again with Ruth. She didn't come to the funeral. He didn't go to the airport. He got one postcard a month after she left. The picture was of a girl in a bikini. "Dear Arthur," Ruth wrote. "So, so sorry. Wish you were here." The return address was Monterey.

After the funeral Arthur and Faith treated each other with a sort of casual kindness, as if they just happened to be lodgers in the same boardinghouse, as if they had never really met. They approached one another with the exaggerated civility of strangers who have been thrown into intimacy by some tragedy, a blizzard or a flood.

Oddly, Arthur found that he no longer had a need for sexual fantasies. He had made up his mind a thousand times to stop his violent imaginary cycle, but he had never been able to do so. Now, suddenly, the habit fell away. It was almost as if it had belonged to somebody else.

He was still lonely, and despite his newfound prominence at work, still frustrated. But the rage was gone. He missed love and he missed a feeling of power, but he no longer saw any connection between the two.

Arthur's corporate star continued to rise. As for babies, the question never came up. He and Faith didn't argue about it. They didn't have to. She didn't have her IUD removed, but it wouldn't have mattered if she had. They never slept together. Nor did they quarrel.

Arthur had inherited some cash, and he was making enough money to carry a substantial mortgage, but the Tate house was going to cost $300,000, so they still wanted Robert Hauser to make a contribution and cosign the loan. He seemed at first to be willing enough. The contract was signed, and all went according to plan until a week before closing. Then Robert took a day from work and accompanied Faith, her mother and a local engineer on what was supposed to have been a routine inspection. But Robert went into the basement and discovered that most of the plumbing was cast-iron.

The closing was postponed, and there followed two weeks of evening hell.

Arthur would sit at the kitchen table with a mug of instant coffee and listen to one half of the escalation.

"But, Daddy," Faith would say, sweetly, "I'm not saying you're a bad father. You've always given me everything I wanted. Well, everything I really wanted. And I want this house."

Then Robert would begin to fire his what-ifs.

Arthur couldn't hear his father-in-law's presentation, but he watched Faith's neck redden as she tried to bang each serve back over the net.

"The foundation's fine now. But if a pipe should break and if the joists were damaged by water, then we'd just have to hire a carpenter.

"We could use bottled water. You forget that I went to Girl Scout camp.

"I love that house. I don't ever plan to move, but if we had to, I don't think we'd have any trouble selling. Bedford is Bedford after all."

Then, for a good five minutes, Faith wouldn't be able to get a word in edgewise. Her whole body would stiffen as she listened. "So what?" she'd finally say, her voice cracking. "It's got four acres. We can be bears if we have to. We can use the woods."

There would be another pause to listen, and then she'd make her last speech. "If you don't want to sign the loan, you don't have to." Another pause and then, "Why do you care so much where my shit goes?" and finally, "I wouldn't let you buy that house if you got down on your knees and begged."

Then she'd put down the phone, rush up to the master bedroom and slam the door. The first few times this happened, Arthur tried to bring her something—tea, or frozen yogurt—but she was inconsolable, and far too angry to eat.

The contract was voided, the initial check returned by the seller, but Arthur still expected a happy ending. And a reconciliation almost certainly would have been effected had not a pair of matched Wall Street lawyers come off the street one Saturday morning with a cash offering of $325,000.

So Arthur used the relatively small inheritance he had gotten from his father for the down payment and bought the house he did live in. "I don't care where I am," Faith said when they signed the papers. "As long as I don't owe that bastard a thing."

So that winter, they saw no fathers. It was a cold year, and Arthur understood for the first time why people would move to Florida or California. He spent three days in Fort Lauderdale at a conference on "Truth in Journalism." He gave the keynote speech, in which he stated again the belief that he had been presented with when he first interviewed for the job. "You may not agree with our opinions," he told a somewhat skeptical audience, "but I challenge you to question our facts."

Mongoose didn't come to work until several months after the funeral, and when he did appear he seemed fine everywhere except the eyes. They looked defeated, frightened. He and Arthur ate lunch, and he was extremely polite, even deferential. It was almost as if Mongoose had been bitten by Arthur instead of his own pet snake.

Arthur still spent a lot of time with Horster. The editor-in-chief was one of those men who liked to say "I read omnivorously." Arthur had known his boss for long enough to have figured out that "omnivorously" meant one best-selling book a year. The year after Arthur's father died, Horster read a book on computers. Palumbardo had recommended it. Afterward, Horster lectured at some length on the "relative inefficiencies of a human staff."

"I can see his position," Faith said, when Arthur reported the editor's enthusiasm. "I mean not being human himself."

"You know they have computers that can do all the proofreading for you," Horster told Arthur. "They don't have babies, they don't need raises, they don't retire. You just plug them in and they'll proof the entire magazine. And do it in about ten minutes."

"That software is still a long way from perfect," Arthur said. "I understand that computers are getting more and more powerful, but a lot of that power can't be applied yet."

Horster didn't agree. "All a computer does," he said, "is answer yes or no. The circuit's opened or the circuit's closed. It's as simple as that. So why should we pay a half a dozen ladies on the copydesk to sit around and vacillate when we can buy a machine that knows how to make up its mind?"

It was fall again and was almost a year after the funeral when "Edgar Allan Polecat" began its final trip through the editorial mills. Sheila Blythe was the researcher, but she never asked any difficult questions. Mostly she wanted to talk about how much she admired the late Prentice. "As a poet, you know," she said by way of explanation. Arthur couldn't tell if she'd actually read any of the novels. In any case, she seemed to have no trouble accepting the falsehoods with which she had been presented.

The week before Halloween, the story passed its last hurdle. Horster sent Arthur a copy of the proof with "Congrats!" crayoned across the title page. When Arthur got home that evening, the house was empty. He thought he had a vague memory of being told that Nathan was with his in-laws and Faith was at an evening aerobics class. Arthur now had his own key to this house. He let himself in and disabled the newly installed burglar alarm. Then he went out and checked the mail. There was an oversized envelope from the offices of *The American Reader*. He walked into the garage, stood by the garbage pails and turned on the overhead light. His thumb caught on some papers in the bottom of the envelope, so that the first thing that came out was a flier for a new book. *Extraordinary Stories from Everyday Life,* it was titled, and the realistic painting on the cover was of a car that had stalled on a grade crossing. The front seat was empty. There was a small boy strapped into the backseat. He had honey-blond hair and wore a red-and-white-striped polo shirt. The train was about twenty feet from the car and the little black lines the artist had drawn indicated that it was going fast.

Arthur crumpled the flier and threw it into the garbage pail. Then he took out the opening letter. "DEAR ARTHUR SOUTH PRENTICE," it began, "YOU HAVE BEEN A

VALUED CUSTOMER FOR 4 YEARS." The 4 was typed in on a dotted line. "We at *The American Reader* would like to acknowledge the *pleasure* we have taken in continuing to address your reading and entertainment needs. Enclosed please find a fully laminated place mat, which has been engraved with an inspirational quotation from Holy Writ.

"Luke 6. Verse 37," the place mat read. "Judge not, and ye shall not be judged; condemn not, and ye shall not be condemned; forgive, and ye shall be forgiven." Arthur put the placard down on a shelf and passed through the fire door and into the kitchen.

He turned on the overhead light, which buzzed ominously. Then he took off his suit jacket and loosened his necktie. The table had a sandwich on it and a vase with a couple of dead roses.

There was a piece of notepaper under the food. "Sweetheart," it read. "There's soda in the refrigerator. Eat, drink and be merry." Then Faith had drawn three small hearts.

Arthur opened the refrigerator. There was a full quart bottle of Dr Pepper. He poured himself a glass.

He sat alone at the kitchen table. Alone in an empty house. The overhead light was still buzzing. "I'll need a new starter," he thought, "or a whole new light." He unwrapped the sandwich. It was chicken salad. He took a bite. He had a drink of soda. Then he began to cry. He sat there at the table and bawled. The outburst only lasted about five minutes, but afterward he was weak as a kitten. He dried his eyes with a paper towel, rinsed his plate and glass, climbed the stairs and went to bed. By the time Faith came home he was fast asleep.

The next day was as clear as a fall day ever gets anymore within fifty miles of New York City. The Japanese protestors were in place. Arthur reached the office before 8 A.M. Linda was already at her desk. She was wearing a red blouse, a black leather skirt and boots.

"You look great," said Arthur.

"Thank you," said Linda.

"You should always wear boots," said Arthur.

"I always have," said Linda.

"Oh," said Arthur, mildly embarrassed. "I guess I never noticed."

Miss Sullivan phoned at 9 A.M. to make sure that Arthur was in. "Mr. Horster wants to meet with you later," she said.

"Fine," said Arthur. "When?"

Miss Sullivan sighed. "I can't be sure," she said. "His schedule for today is brutal. It'll be sometime after lunch."

"Okay," said Arthur. "I'm here."

It wasn't until almost 6 P.M. that Horster showed up in Arthur's office. He had a new layout for "Edgar Allan Polecat." His face was wreathed with smiles. He put the proof on Arthur's new wooden desk.

"So what do you think?" asked Horster.

"They did a nice job," said Arthur.

"A great job," said Horster. "It's too early to be certain, but I think we have another 'Tipper' on our hands."

Arthur nodded.

"If this story doesn't win a prize," said Horster, "I don't know anything about publishing. Wasn't it Edgar Allan Poe who said that there was nothing in the world more beautiful than a dead woman?"

"Something like that," said Arthur.

Horster winked. "Now Poe was a freak," he said. "You and I, we don't have to wait. Our wives are already beautiful."

"Thank you," said Arthur stiffly. "Lavinia is certainly a beautiful woman."

"That's right," said Horster. "But I was talking about Poe.

And what I was going to say is that Poe was mistaken. It's writer. There's nothing more beautiful in the world than a dead writer."

"Why do you suppose that is?" asked Arthur, suddenly interested despite himself.

"I don't know for sure," said Horster. "We worship movie stars when they're young. We love politicians when they're old. Artists have to be dead and buried. This piece is going to be much more powerful than it would have been a year ago," he said. He tapped the layout on Arthur's desk. "We are going to do your father proud."

Arthur could hear the blood in his ears. "Why are you always so sure about what would make my father proud?" he asked.

Horster shrugged. "You don't need to be a mind reader to know how to please an author," he said. "Your father wrote this story. We're going to play it up."

"And you like it, right?" said Arthur. "I mean really like it?"

"Of course," said Horster.

"Then there's something I think you should know."

Horster rolled his eyes merrily. "You certainly have gotten temperamental in your old age," he said. "What should I *really* know?"

"He didn't write that story," said Arthur. "I wrote that story. I made it up. And it's not true. Not one word."

For one excruciatingly long moment, Horster didn't move, nor did he say anything. Then he picked up the layout and walked quickly out of the office. He almost ran. He left his cigarettes on the desk.

A minute later he was back. He came in the door and looked Arthur carefully in the face, looked at him as if he'd never seen him before. "Plagiarist," he said.

Arthur shrugged. "Well, not exactly," he said, suddenly very relaxed. "I mean it depends on how you define the word."

Horster's eyes were black with rage. Arthur could hear him

breathing. Then the editor-in-chief picked up his cigarettes and went away.

Arthur got up himself, moving slowly, as if he'd just woken from a bad night's sleep. By the time he had stepped out of his office, Horster was gone. Josie was walking up the hallway.

"What did you do to him?" she asked. "He looked like he'd seen the boogeyman."

Arthur shrugged uncomfortably. "It wasn't a monster," he said. "It was me."

"What did you tell him?"

"The truth."

Josie bobbed her head. "You should know better," she said with mock severity.

"I do know better," said Arthur. He leaned back against the wall. He felt dizzy.

Josie wanted to know if he was all right.

"Sure I'm all right."

"So why do you look so bad?" Josie asked.

"It's not physical. I mean it's not a heart attack," Arthur said, grinning awkwardly.

"Are you certain?" asked Josie, putting a hand on his shoulder. "You know that a heart attack doesn't hurt in the heart. It hurts in the shoulder, sometimes even the arm."

"I know," said Arthur. "We had an article, 'How to Plan Your Own Heart Attack.'"

Josie laughed despite herself. "No, it was 'How to Plan Your Own Funeral.' The other one was, 'Thank God for My Heart Attack.'"

"Either way," said Arthur. "This isn't one of those. It's not even a Maalox moment."

But Josie led him back into the office and made him sit down. "You're right near the phone. If you don't start to feel better, call security."

"Okay."

"Promise?"

"I promise."

"Look, I have to walk this proof down to the mailroom, but I'll stop here again on the way back to my office."

"Okay," said Arthur. "But I'm already better. Go on now."

Josie did go on. And Arthur did sit still. But he didn't feel better, not in a minute, not in five minutes.

Finally he stood up. Movement seemed to lessen the pressure. He walked to the van. He drove home in a trance.

Faith and Nathan were in the playroom. Nathan was watching cartoons. Faith was beside him on the sofa. She had newspaper spread on the coffee table. She was trying to glue together a broken teacup. When Arthur appeared in the doorway, she looked up from her work.

"Josie called," she said. "She wanted to know how you were."

"I'm all right," said Arthur.

"You don't look so great," said Faith. "Is there anything I can do? Do you want a cup of tea or something?"

"No thanks. I think it's good. I'm remembering now how Daddy felt when he stopped drinking."

"How'd he feel?"

"Like I do now. Like shit."

Faith looked worried. "Sit down," she said.

Arthur shrugged.

"Let me do something."

Arthur grinned. "You want to be my robot?"

Faith didn't say anything.

"Can I be one too?" asked Nathan, turning off the television.

"Yes," said Arthur.

"I know about robots," said Nathan.

Arthur took off his jacket and slung it over one shoulder. Now he stood at the counter that separated the kitchen from the playroom. "Tell me what you know," he said. He was speaking to Nathan, but he was looking at Faith. She was sitting on the sofa with her feet crossed under her behind, Indian fashion. This made her look small, girlish.

"Some of them look like people," Nathan said, "but the ones that work on assembly lines don't. They look like a praying mantis. Some are wrenches, some spray guns for paint."

"That's right," said Arthur.

"And there are other ones the police use to defuse bombs," Nathan said. "That way if the bomb goes off, nobody gets killed. Nobody but the robot gets killed."

"Did you learn all this in school?" Arthur asked.

Nathan nodded. "Mrs. Rush says that by the year 2010 mechanical workers will outnumber people in many areas."

"I'm not sure you'll have to wait until 2010."

"What sort of robots are Mummy and I supposed to be?" asked Nathan.

"Ones that eat hamburgers," said Arthur.

"What do they do?"

"Go to dinner at the Hound & Horn."

As he spoke, Arthur was struck again with his wife's beauty. Her sweater was buttercup yellow. Under this she had a cream-colored skirt. She was wearing glasses, but on her even glasses were becoming. Now she took them off and looked up at her husband.

"What if I don't want to be a robot?" she asked.

"That's okay," said Arthur. "In fact I'd like it better. I don't really want a mechanical device for a wife. But you do have to eat a real dinner. After the day I've had, I'm going to insist."

Faith put down the teacup. "You fought with him," she said. "You told him to go to hell."

Arthur shrugged. "Look at it this way," he said. "If your father knew what I'd done, he'd think I was an asshole. He'd be sick about it."

Faith picked up a piece of paper towel and began to rub the glue off of her hands. "Well, that's something," she said.

"And now that I've got him on the ropes," said Arthur, "I'm going for the kill. I'm moving back into the bedroom."

Faith didn't say anything.

"When I wake up in the middle of the night, I don't want to hear a gerbil. I want to hear my wife."

"Do you think Nathan should be part of this discussion?"

"Yes, I'm certain Nathan should be part of this. Nathan," Arthur said, turning to face his son, "I want to sleep in the same room with your mother."

Nathan looked back at his father and swallowed. "Are we out of money?" he asked.

Arthur sighed. "We can still afford dinner," he said.

Faith got up and crossed the playroom. She took Arthur's right hand in both of hers. He could feel the rough spot on one of her fingers where the glue must have spilled. He could smell her sweet breath. She kissed him ever so gently on the lips. Then she took his right hand, drew it down and pressed it against her belly. "Buy me something to eat," she said.

So Faith went up to the bedroom to put on makeup, and Arthur brought Nathan to the half bath off the kitchen. Standing beside his son, he caught a glimpse of his own haggard face in the mirror. He thought maybe his father had been right all along. "So all I ever had to do was assert myself," he thought. "God helps those who help themselves." Although Faith had seemed awfully acquiescent. It was almost as if she'd anticipated his own change of heart. Which was odd, when he thought of how much he had surprised himself.

It wasn't until they'd all gotten into the van, and Arthur had backed out of the drive, that he saw the pink ribbon on the kitchen door. There was another one on the mailbox. He turned to his wife. "So how the hell is Dr. Morris?" he asked, smiling. "Still eating Hostess Sno Balls?"

ABOUT THE AUTHOR

Benjamin Cheever lives in Westchester County, New York with his wife, the film critic Janet Maslin, and their two children. He edited *The Letters of John Cheever* (1988).

Cheever, Benjamin.
The plagiarist.